A VERY PARTICULAR MURDER

'For God's sake!' the woman cried. 'As if Cambridge isn't big enough for both of us! First, it's Uncle Max, now it's Christopher. When am I going to be allowed to do something because it's what *I* want? And what I want is to be near Tawno all the time, so long as I live.' The dark eyes darkened further. Remarkable, thought Jurnet, unmoved but admiring, against the blonde skin, the ash-gold hair. 'I tell you this, Inspector – not sentimentally, like a silly female who reads too many women's magazines – I tell you because it's true. If Tawno had drunk that poisoned juice, I would have put out my tongue and licked the last drops off the sides of the glass, so as to be dead with him.'

A VERY PARTICULAR MURDER

S T Haymon

ARROW BOOKS

Arrow Books Limited
20 Vauxhall Bridge Road, London SW1V 2SA

An imprint of Random Century Group

London Melbourne Sydney Auckland
Johannesburg and agencies throughout
the world

First published in Great Britain by
Constable and Company Limited 1989

Arrow paperback edition 1991

© S T Haymon 1989

Phototypeset by Input Typesetting Ltd, London
Printed and bound in Great Britain by
Cox & Wyman Ltd, Reading

ISBN 0 09 971600 3

1

Darkness had almost filled the canyon at the foot of the castle mound when, moving at snail's pace, they came, little by little, over the fine bridge which sprang across the chasm separating the Norman keep from the rest of the city. At the rate the line of cars was moving the two had plenty of time to admire the great stone bulk directly ahead, by day brutish but turned by flood-lighting into a fairy palace, spun sugar against the velvet sky.

The Superintendent leaned forward in the passenger's seat of the Rover, pulled down the sun visor with its inset mirror, and made minute adjustments to his already impeccable black tie. The bugger looks pleased with himself, thought Jurnet, piling additional fuel on to the anger already burning inside him like indigestion. Did the little tin god really have to leave it to the last minute to let his underling know that his presence was required at the castle that very night; a night, moreover, when, if the bloke at the hire agency was to be believed, Angleby was into the *dolce vita* like nobody's business, everybody from the masons to the model railway club descending on the racks of dinner jackets like a plague of locusts? For the umpteenth time Jurnet moodily swivelled back into place the made-up bow which had worked its way up his left ear, feeling as he did so the jacket too tight across his shoulders, too short in the sleeves; wondering for how long his braces were going to be able to support the tonnage of trouser tailored, at a guess, to accommodate a woman eight months gone with quads.

Wounded vanity? Not a bit of it – or only a little bit. Jurnet had long accepted his superior officer's effortless elegance as a cross he was doomed to bear. The wound was deeper. All day long, whatever had occupied his surface attention, the detective had felt vibrating through his whole being the slow march of minutes progressing like troops at a state funeral towards that moment in the evening when Miriam had arranged to telephone from Israel. As it was, in six, no, five minutes – Jurnet glanced at his watch to confirm the crass inhumanity of time – whilst he looked like being still marooned on this stone raft in space, the telephone would ring out in his flat, and go on ringing until, incredulous, it petered out, unanswered. From the moment he had opened his eyes that morning Jurnet had anticipated that call, until he had come almost to believe that, lifting the receiver, he would feel desert heat on his face and the brittle air of the development town at the back of beyond where Miriam was engaged in setting up the knitting project which was to be an extension of her thriving business in Angleby. Listening, he felt, he would have to screw up his eyes against a sun which must surely have brought out the delicious freckles on her nose and bleached the red lights in her hair to gold.

He would hear her voice. Most of all, he would hear her voice.

Instead of which, here he was, stuck on the castle bridge till the small hours, in all probability, all to celebrate the three hundredth anniversary of the birth – or was it death? – of that long-haired oddball in baggy breeches who sat in bronze in the Haymarket holding a skull in his hands like he'd just finished his dinner and wasn't sure what to do with the bones: Sir Thaddeus Brigg, scientist, philosopher and almost everything else you cared to think of, proof at least that not everybody born in Angleby was thick as two planks.

It was, as Jurnet for all his carry-on very well knew,

his mates, his own unique species, who were holding up the cavalcade, busy where the bridge debouched on to the wide gravelled space which lapped the castle walls; checking invitations against lists fastened to clipboards; lifting boot lids; opening rear doors for a brisk but comprehensive once-over of the back of the car. The Superintendent, peering upward through the windscreen at the sculpted battlements, commented: 'Room on that roof to land helicopters by the gross. I only hope the Chief was right in deciding six sharpshooters were enough.'

'So long as he hasn't forgotten the paras,' Jurnet growled, letting the frayed hems of his patience hang out without caring who saw them. In his inner ear the phone had already begun to sound its forlorn tocsin. 'Someone on the Council gets this brilliant idea there's money to be made out of one of our ancient eggheads, and we end up lumbered with a major security operation. We don't go to all this trouble for the royals.'

The Superintendent lowered his gaze to his subordinate, and said in tones of rebuke: 'We have some very valuable lives here.'

The subordinate, who harboured the quaint idea that all lives, even the lowliest and most alienated, were of equal value, managed with difficulty not to say so. Instead, with a pretence of sweet reasonableness: 'I wouldn't mind betting, back in their colleges or research institutes or whatever other mousehole they've crawled out of, they go about their business like any other citizens.'

'Very likely,' the other conceded. 'That doesn't absolve the city of its responsibility.' Taking care not to disturb the set of his dinner jacket, the virgin crease of his trousers, the Superintendent twisted round in his seat so as to confront his companions more directly. 'It's the very number of them, don't you see? What you have to realise is that by the time they've all got here Angleby will contain within its boundaries a significant

3

percentage of the people upon whose mental processes in the years to come may depend the very survival of the planet as we know it.'

Or its destruction, thought Jurnet, bloody-minded but again with the sense to keep his mouth shut.

'Think what a single bomb might do, dropped on such an assembly!' The Superintendent, carried away by his vision, sounded almost enthusiastic. 'Alter the history of the world! Or then again, consider the opportunities for hostage-taking! What, relatively speaking, is the worth of another Einstein?' At this gem of wit, Jurnet forced his features into the expression of appreciation clearly expected of him. 'Agreed,' the Superintendent continued, acknowledging the tribute with a gracious nod, 'the Council had no idea what they were starting – the Lord Mayor told me so himself. Who would have thought old Sir Thaddeus was held in such esteem abroad? Of course one knew about his *Religio Aleatoris*, that masterpiece of moral philosophy – '

'Of course!' agreed Jurnet, not bothering to disguise his mockery. *Religio what*? 'All *I* can remember about the geezer is that he once gave evidence in court against two poor old women that got them hanged as witches.'

'He was a man of his time,' the Superintendent observed indulgently. 'But also, it now appears, a man of our own, equally. He seems, quite intuitively, to have discovered the essentials of quantum physics all of three hundred years before anybody else thought of it; though of course he didn't call it that. Now that he has come into his own at last it's not surprising that physicists the world over are eager to come and do honour to his memory.'

'Pity they couldn't do it in their own backyards.'

The Superintendent said coldly: 'You've no local pride, Ben, that's your trouble.'

Fortunately for Jurnet, who loved his native city to the point of idolatry, the car in front moving off at that moment gave him something else to do beside reject

4

the unjust accusation in terms he knew he would immediately be sorry for. Only a grinding of gears betrayed his anger.

His desolation.

The telephone had stopped ringing.

Jurnet inquired, taking care: 'What you haven't told me, sir, is what I'm actually here *for*. I take it we're as thick on the ground indoors as out?'

'Quite the contrary! We want our visitors to enjoy their stay in Angleby. We've gone on the principle that so long as we've made absolutely certain nobody can possibly gain unauthorised entry, there's nothing to stop a happy and relaxed evening being had by all. Naturally, we've shut off the rest of the museum.' The castle, having long outlived its original function as the symbol of a hated despotism, to say nothing of later incarnations as a gaol, a barracks and stabling for Oliver Cromwell's horses, had, with the mellowing of time, evolved into the repository of the city's corporate soul. 'We turned everybody out at three o'clock sharp and went over the place with a fine-tooth comb. That little coxcomb, the curator, wasn't best pleased. Acts as if the place is his personal property, only lets the public in as a favour. By the time we finished, if there was so much as a black beetle left wandering about without a pass, I'd be surprised. I'm only here tonight to keep a benign eye on things, and you, as ever, to support me in that worthy enterprise.'

Jurnet sighed, then got down to cases.

'What about the caterers?'

'Ah! The proverbial weak link, eh? I can only say that Palmers have been most co-operative. As they should be. They've catered enough civic functions' – again a little simper signalled an imminent *bon mot* – 'to know on which side their bread is buttered. No waiters – only waitresses of an age beyond the seductions of perfidious foreigners. And no casual labour in the kitchen. Just the same, we've got a few men back of the swing doors, if only to make sure the food handlers wash their hands when they come back from the loo.'

The Superintendent tenderly found a new position for his superbly clad buttocks.

'The chief thing,' he announced, not batting an eyelid at the gargantuan fib, 'was that I didn't want you to feel left out. Somebody, after all, had to mind the shop – but, from one or two comments you let drop, I couldn't help wondering whether you didn't feel a little peeked. After all, intellectual giants such as Angleby is privileged to entertain tonight aren't likely to pass this way again in a hurry. It's like seeing Halley's comet. You'll be able to tell it to your grandchildren.'

If – Jurnet made the silent qualification – the intellectual giants haven't vaporised us all into interplanetary dust before I've had a chance to beget any. Aloud he said, scarcely damping down the irony: 'Very kind of you, sir. What I'm not sure of, though, is exactly what *is* this knowledge these men possess which makes them such potential targets for the villains.'

'I'm not sure I'm the one to ask,' the Superintendent responded with what was, for him, an astonishing modesty. 'Subatomic particles and all that. You ought to get a book out of the library.'

'If it's all down in black and white for anyone with a library ticket to get hold of, why should anybody bother to hijack them?'

'For what they may come up with next, man! One of the faculty up at the University told me there's a rumour going about that one of the papers to be delivered during the week will be another of those milestones in the history of mankind like Newton and gravity, or the Earth going round the sun instead of vice versa. These chaps, let me tell you, are getting close to the core of things. Don't tell me the thought of probing the ultimate doesn't excite you, Ben, even a little?'

'Brings me out in goose pimples. Only wish it was

Rotary here tonight, or the annual convention of pin-cushion manufacturers.'

The Superintendent frowned his disapproval. 'Not like you to run away from a challenge.'

'Anywhere to run, you wouldn't see me for dust! That's the trouble with these know-alls. Never think of asking first who wants to know.'

2

In the castle vestibule the air was a jangle of voices being jolly in several languages. The men laughing, embracing, slapping each other on the back, did not look the kind to pierce through the last veils of illusion to ultimate reality. It could equally have been a gathering of accountants, wholesale grocers, or manufacturers of National Health dentures. Jurnet could not decide whether this appearance of ordinariness was reassuring or deeply disturbing. What lethal extravagances of cerebration were massing like storm clouds behind those unremarkable brows?

Their womenfolk, so far as the detective could glimpse them among the press which filled the space wall to wall, looked a pleasant enough bunch. The sole beauty in Jurnet's line of vision – a slim blonde whose aura of incense and lilies was belied by eyes of a startling darkness, was escorted by a gangling man wearing clerical grey and a dog collar, and by a blond boy, not quite a man, evidently her son and very like his mother except for eyes that, whilst dark as hers, were bright and demanding. When Jurnet by chance met his roving glance, the boy held the confrontation boldly, did not look away.

There was something vaguely familiar about the clergyman, so that when, a lank strand of sandy hair falling over one eye, the latter made his way towards Jurnet, threading himself between the merry groups with practised meekness, the detective was not unduly surprised. By the time the man had reached his objective, he had got him taped.

'Feldon St Awdry, isn't it?' Jurnet got his blow in first. 'Have I got it right?'

'You have indeed!' The clergyman smiled, disclosing large teeth set rather haphazardly into an expanse of pallid gum. 'Simon Maslin,' shaking hands. 'Our chalice and paten, if you remember – '

'I remember all right! We never recovered them for you.'

'Not your fault, Inspector!' The Revd Simon Maslin returned earnestly. He had more the air of a curate than an incumbent. Impossible to imagine him higher up the ecclesiastical tree than its lowest branches. 'I'm sure you did everything that could be done.' The man actually blushed as he came to the matter in hand. 'I know it's not something to take up a police officer's time with. It's only that I can't find anybody else to ask – '

'What's the trouble?'

Mr Maslin pushed the hair away from his eye with a knobby hand. He had a way of bobbing about that was neither a tic nor a twitch.

'The thing is, we have Professor Flaschner with us–' the clergyman pronounced the name with reverence, clearly convinced that Jurnet would recognise the hallowed syllables. 'In our care, so to speak. He has a heart condition, you know, and I really don't think he should attempt the stairs. I was wondering if there was a lift anywhere' . . . voice trailing away, 'though he keeps telling me not to fuss . . .'

Jurnet looked across to the noble flight which led up

from the vestibule directly to the Great Hall. People – including the Superintendent, in urbane conversation with a Japanese gentleman as well tailored as himself – were already beginning to make their way up; a way Jurnet had looked forward to following. Ever since he was a boy, when the Great Hall with its display of armour had been his favourite place in the whole museum, he had longed, once through the turnstile, to spring up those stairs two at a time, the shortest distance to his destination. But no. The powers that be in their stony unreason had decreed that the stair was to be labelled Way Out, a stair no more to be ascended by mere mortals than Jacob's ladder. Visitors to the museum wishing to reach the Great Hall were obliged, whether they would or no, first to trek through the flora and fauna of Norfolk, its geology, agriculture, industries; past paintings of the Angleby School, mementoes of the county's worthies, as well as the lovingly assembled gleanings of local middens Paleolithic, Bronze Age, and medieval. That night, coming into the building, Jurnet had taken in the situation at a glance, and rejoiced. For once he was going to be allowed to go up the down stair.

'There *is* a lift,' he admitted, abandoning his childish dream. 'I'll show you.'

'No, no! If you would just tell us where – '

'Doubt you'd find it on your own. Anyway, the museum's shut off and you'll need a bit of clout to get through.' On a sudden thought: 'Hang on a minute, will you?'

Leaving the clergyman standing uncertainly, moving his hips and elbows in a manner that suggested he could do with a restringing, Jurnet edged his way neatly to the mahogany counter which stood alongside the vestibule entrance. He noted that with true Norfolk prudence the lady who had charge of the pamphlets and postcards had removed every last one. Evidently, in her book, the new magicians were no more to be trusted than the

9

old. At the back of the counter, however, the folding wheelchairs were stacked as usual.

Mr Maslin looked unhappy when he saw what the detective had brought back.

'Oh dear! I doubt whether the Professor – '

'That's OK. If he doesn't need it, he can push *me*. I warn you, it's quite a walk.'

The crowds were thinning, moving steadily towards the stairs. Ahead, Jurnet could see, intermittently visible, the ashen-gold hair of the woman with the dark eyes. The answer to the question of whether its owner wasn't a bit long in the tooth to wear it the way she did, spread out over her shoulders like a young girl, the detective set aside until he could get a good look at her face.

The woman moved with her son down the length of the vestibule. The detective could see no one with the pair who might be the mythical professor; only, as he and the vicar drew near, Alistair Tring, the curator of the museum, the man whom the Superintendent had earlier characterised as 'that little coxcomb', could be heard complaining shrilly to somebody out of sight: 'Get up, sir! Get up at once!'

'Oh dear!' the Revd Maslin, with a despairing glance at his companion, darted ahead. Jurnet heard his voice raised in an introduction he evidently expected to put all to rights: 'This is Professor Max Flaschner – '

'I don't care if he's bloody God almighty,' retorted the curator, his small beaked face red with passion. 'Nobody sits on the exhibits in *my* museum!'

At the far end of the vestibule Jurnet now saw that the Buddha was still in place. Well, of course. Enormous, of some black basaltic rock dense enough to lend mass a new meaning, it had obviously been too much of a job to move just for one night, the way the smaller bits and pieces which normally cluttered the vestibule had been cleared away. Jurnet both knew and did not know the statue, since, on his juvenile visits to the museum, its impassive, inward gaze had always disconcerted him, made him hurry past without really looking. Seated in the capacious lap was a large man who had been larger, his skin no less than his elderly dress clothes proclaiming that, once, additional flesh had filled out that powerful frame, filled in the grooves in the cheeks, the hollows under the eyes.

Eyes that twinkled with a mischievous humour, however.

'My good sir,' said the large man, in a heavily accented voice that illness had not deprived of its authority, 'you have my permission to put here a small plaque, nothing fancy, to say that here rested the celebrated bum of Professor Max Flaschner, physicist, Nobel Laureate and clown.' Dismissing the small man from his attention as one might dismiss a fly with a well-directed flick of the wrist, the man tilted his face upward and, in a different tone, spoke to the Buddha. 'I thank you for your courtesy, Master.' A pause, then, lower: 'And for your strength.'

'The fellow's drunk!' Alistair Tring pronounced, looking at Jurnet for support. He adjusted his gold-rimmed spectacles and looked again, closer, at the lean Mediterranean features which were such a trial to their possessor. 'You're police, aren't you? I know I've seen you before somewhere. Can't you do something about this buffoon? I told the Lord Mayor what would come of using the castle – but would he listen?' Puffed with the self-satisfaction of having been proved right, the coxcomb looked ready to crow. 'And your lot's not much better! D'you know what they've gone and done upstairs? Only taken the helmet off every suit of armour and left it upside down at its feet like a ruddy piss pot, that's what, on the chance there's a terrorist inside!'

Jurnet said: 'Sounds a reasonable precaution to me.'

'Balls!' The curator's invective resembled his clothes; an advertisement that, anno domini notwithstanding,

11

he was still up front with the trend-setters. 'You've no idea how stupid they look, standing about without their heads, like something out of a song by Gracie Fields.'

'Better them than the visitors, I should have thought.'

'Hm!'

It dawned on Jurnet that it was less a protective love for his artefacts than a consuming jealousy which motivated the curator's attitude towards his unwelcome guests. *Who did they think they were*, the lucky buggers whose exhibits needed no dusting, no labels, no glass cases for children to foul up with snot and time-expired bubble gum?

'I am refreshed,' announced Professor Flaschner, carefully lowering himself from the Buddha's lap to the floor. The boy came forward to take his arm.

'Christopher!' the Professor lovingly cupped a hand along the soft curve of cheek. 'So tall! Tawno will be amazed!' Smiling: 'All the same, when you see him, round your shoulders a little, eh, or he will be jealous.'

Professor Flaschner seated himself in the wheelchair without having to be persuaded. He leaned back, drew a trembling breath. Then: 'Tawno's going to be angry I drove.'

'You *were* naughty.' It was the first time Jurnet had heard the blonde woman speak. Now that he saw her close to he had to admit that, even next to her teenage son, she looked OK with her hair streaming over the simple shift of some grey, silky material which came down to her ankles but left her arms bare. Extremely OK. The voice, however, a little girl's voice, was a whit discomforting. It was a long time since Mrs Maslin had been young enough for a voice like that. She said to the Professor: 'You know we'd already arranged to meet the train.'

'From Cambridge to Angleby is not far. Tawno would have hated to be here for three days without his own car to get about in.'

'He could always borrow ours. Tawno knows that.'

12

'He knows.' The man still had a powerful charm. He reached for Mrs Maslin's hand, bent over it and kissed the slender fingers lightly. 'Thank you for everything. It is lovely for him to be among old friends. But still the rascal would not be happy without his toy.' Again the laboured breath. 'One day soon he will have to grow up, won't he? Forty-seven – it is more than time.' Twisting to look over his shoulder: 'And who is the kind gentleman to whom I am indebted for this fine chariot?'

The Reverend Simon Maslin effected another of his introductions, all elbows and stumbling compliments.

'Detective Inspector Jurnet has been kind enough to say he'll show us to the lift – '

'Us? My dear people, please! When it is time for my cortège I will let you know. Meantime, please, the rest of you, to go the same way as everybody else and keep an eye out for Tawno. If he doesn't see me the moment he comes into the room he will be anxious. An inspector!' This time, with an effort which set a vein in his forehead visibly throbbing, the Professor swung his whole body round, so as to get Jurnet squarely in his sights. 'A detective inspector! It is too much honour!'

'Happy to oblige.'

Claire Maslin and her son looked at Jurnet as if seeing him for the first time. It was as if only the Professor's attention had made the detective real to them.

The boy looked puzzled by what he saw, a reaction to which Jurnet, whom many years in the Force had reluctantly convinced that he did not conform to most people's idea of what a police officer ought to look like, was quite accustomed. Not for nothing, he had to acknowledge, did his mates, even if carefully behind his back, call him by the hated nickname of Valentino.

The woman was less puzzled than puzzling.

Jurnet was not a vain man. On the contrary, his looks were an embarrassment, an involuntary deception he sometimes felt ought to be actionable, if only he knew in what court, and against whom, to institute proceedings. It was simply that he had lived with them long enough to know their effect on women. Most were attracted by them, a few dismayed; but none was indifferent unless her attention was already spoken for elsewhere. Mrs Maslin, having been made aware of the tall, dark man waiting behind the wheelchair, glanced at him briefly, and away again.

At the Revd Mr Maslin she did not look at all.

3

'I will let you into a secret.' The professor chuckled. His voice sounded stronger.

'He was right, that little bluebottle back there. I *am* drunk – not so drunk as I was, my good sir, which is a pity, but drunk enough. All the way from Cambridge I thought to myself, what shall I do if I am stopped by the police and – what do you call it? – breathalysed? What will Tawno say?'

Manoeuvring the wheelchair through the gate at the side of the turnstile and thence along the corridor which curved out of sight towards the first of the museum galleries, Jurnet offered at his most policemanly: 'I should have thought Mr Tawno's opinion one way or the other was the last thing to worry about in the circumstances.'

The other's response was a laugh of surprising strength.

'*Mr* Tawno! Is it possible the name of Tawno Smith is unknown to you?'

The detective, unappeased: 'Perfectly possible.'

'I am delighted to hear it! Do not think I make fun, Mr Jurnet, I am quite serious. How full we are of our own importance!' Quietening: 'Would it help my credit with the gendarmerie to say that today is the first time I have tasted whisky since I was a boy in Vienna and it made me sick? Does it help that I drank very little – did not set out to make myself drunk – did not even realise that was what I was, until I was far along the road, thirty miles or more, when I could just as well continue as go back?'

'It happens,' admitted Jurnet, relenting. 'Only, once you recognised your true state, you should have stopped at the earliest opportunity and handed over your car keys before you – or anyone else – could come to harm.'

'My true state.' Professer Flaschner repeated. He was quiet for a moment, reflecting. 'But then, Tawno wouldn't have got his car, would he?'

Sergeant Bowles was standing at the grille, his expression wistful. In a glass case behind him a heron stuck its bill into a painted river morosely, as if it expected no good to come of it. In this, at least, it was correct. Further back, concealed among plastic reeds, a bittern pointed towards the sky. Suspended on delicate wires from the ceiling, a silent scream of black-headed gulls, wings spread, red legs dangling, hung in a frozen gale.

'Enough to give you the willies!' exclaimed Sergeant Bowles, a large, comfortable man not far from his pension; a widower usually happy to take on any duty that would keep him longer away from his empty home. At the sight of Jurnet and his companion his face brightened. 'Beginning to think there weren't anything left in creation that weren't stuffed. Including myself.' To Jurnet: 'You coming through, sir?'

'Please. We're on our way to the lift.'

'Oh ah.' Sergeant Bowles operated the security catch, and folded the grille back sufficiently to let the wheelchair through. 'I'd better let the boys know to expect you.'

'You better had. Wouldn't want them coming at us with guns blazing.'

'They'd never do that, Mr Jurnet! The sergeant looked shocked. 'Not with all this glass about!'

Jurnet pushed the wheelchair onward, passing at intervals young PCs who – such was the atmosphere of the untenanted rooms, blazing with light but cheerless as catacombs – were exaggeratedly glad to greet the little procession and exaggeratedly sorry to see it go on its way. Pushing the wheelchair into the corridor which led to the lift, Jurnet observed: 'Not such a bad idea at that to stand a few stuffed people about after closing time. Then it wouldn't seem so empty.'

'You are talking to a particle physicist,' Professor Flaschner pointed out. 'Emptiness is a concept quite beyond us. It is the price we pay for seeking to know more of God's business than He willingly divulges. In the cause of knowledge we deny ourselves the sublime benison of solitude.' The man moved his shoulders as if shrugging off an unhappy thought. 'Have you, for example, heard of a neutrino?' Sensing rather than seeing the detective's shake of the head: 'The universe is awash with them, my friend. We swim, we drown in them. They can pass through the entire earth, from one side to the other, and their passing changes nothing. As you push me through these rooms which you call empty, thousands of them are passing through you all the time, piercing you like St Sebastian's arrows, only quite without pain.'

'Cheeky blighters!' exclaimed Jurnet, undisturbed. So long as the scientists invented things which did nothing, hurt nobody, he could go along with their little games. The Professor, however, seemed to find his standing-room-only universe on the sad-side. He slumped further down in the chair. Hoping the old fellow might find another's ignorance restorative, Jurnet said: 'Me, I've just about got used to the Earth not being flat. Still think it's a pity it isn't. Sure you could have fallen off the edge if you weren't careful, but now that we know it's a ball – well, I mean, it's *all* edge, isn't it, in a manner of speaking?'

The ruse worked. The Professor straightened up and burst out laughing. 'Now I know why grown men spend so much time kicking about leather balloons, or smashing at rounded objects with cricket bats, tennis racquets, golf clubs, hockey sticks. They are taking their revenge on that abominable rotundity without edges which is yet all edge, with no beginning and no end!'

He was still laughing when Jurnet wheeled the chair into the lift, a cavernous box worked by a mechanism which should itself have been on show in the museum as a masterpiece of primitive technology. As Jurnet wrestled with the ropes and levers the Professor sat quietly, the humour slowly fading from his face like the dying embers of a fire. He seemed to be making a tremendous effort, summoning up all his powers for the junketing ahead.

Filled with pity, the detective ventured: 'If you don't mind me saying so, you'd be much better off at home, tucked up in bed.'

Professor Flaschner said: 'You have been very kind. I had not thought policemen were so kind. I shall never worry again to be in the hands of the police.'

'So long as you don't drink and drive! I mean it, sir – I'd be happy to see you back to your hotel.'

'That would indeed be emptiness! Like a child sent up to bed while downstairs the grown-ups are dancing to the music. Besides, then I shouldn't see my Tawno.'

4

At the small door which led into the Great Hall underneath the minstrels' gallery, the Professor gave the
order to halt. From behind the door came the sounds
of the party: laughter, the tinkling of glasses. The Professor levered himself out of the wheelchair, took several more of his deep, trembling breaths.

'From here on, my friend, take note, I am no more
an invalid. I suppose there are some seats in there?'

'If not, I'll soon find you one.'

'More kindness! Not, I regret to say, like some of
my confrères, waiting in there to see the broken old
man who has shot his bolt and now talks only
nonsense.'

'Would it be giving the wrong impression in the
wrong quarter if you took my arm, or would you
rather I went ahead and found your Tawno for you?'

'My Tawno!' The mere sound of the strange name
seemed a balm. As if he read the detective's mind, the
Professor said: 'An odd name, is it not? Would you
like to know how my Tawno got his name?' Without
waiting for an answer: 'It is the Romany word for
small. My Tawno is a gipsy – what do you think of
that? A gipsy I found on a bomb site in Dusseldorf late
in 1947. Some gipsy boys, part of the flotsam of war,
were scavenging there. Only I happened to know that,
before the bombing, there had been on that site a factory making chemicals to kill Jews in the gas chambers.
The ground was contaminated, there was danger to the
children, and I ordered them to go away. All ran off
except the smallest, a boy no more than five years old

who came up to me and kicked me in the shin, the little devil!' The Professor broke into a chuckle of proud recollection. 'My Tawno, even in those days! The other boys called him that because he was so little. And Tawno he has remained ever since. Tawno Smith. I gave him the surname myself. Many gipsies are smiths. It is an honourable pursuit among them, and besides–' diverging – 'do you know any German, kind policeman? Do you know what a *Flaschner* is?'

Jurnet shook his head.

'It means a tin-smith. It was a sign that my little gypsy and I were meant for each other.'

Professor Flaschner sighed. A drop of moisture – a tear? – rolled slowly down the deep grooves on either side of the commanding nose. He ought to be in bed, the poor old geezer, Jurnet thought again, as the man took his arm, jauntily.

Jurnet could hardly believe his eyes. He had been aware that for some time past the Council had made the Great Hall available for hire, but it was knowledge which, until that moment, had held no meaning for him. The idea of that great raw space, with its rough-plastered walls and arrow slits, as background to a wedding reception or masonic Ladies' Night, was too absurd to be entertained seriously. Now that he actually saw with his own eyes the round tables with their tablecloths put on catercornerwise, a silver vase with a single rosebud in the centre of each; the gilt chairs, the fussily folded napkins, the show-off of cutlery and glasses, he could have fallen about laughing if only it hadn't seemed to him so sad, the way progress invariably took the guts out of things.

The Professor's entrance created a little stir among those nearest the door. Some German physicists, already seated, stood up and bowed: one or two of those standing about clapped softly, their smiling women making little gestures of respect and admiration. One of the latter, generous of hip and bust, an Italian by the look of her, plucked a rosebud out of one of the little vases and went to fix it in the Professor's buttonhole, aware that the bare, raised arm showed her figure to advantage. Discovering, too late, that the dinner-jacket lapel boasted no buttonhole, she stuck the flower coquettishly behind her ear. Professor Flaschner, without releasing his hold on Jurnet, leaned forward and kissed the jewelled lobe.

Not at all abashed, the woman exclaimed: 'Dear Max – still the *cavaliere! Il cavaliere errante!*' Laughing: '*Supratutto errante!*'

'And you, signora – *supratutto bellissima.*'

'Uncle Max!'

The man who accosted them looked either younger or older than his age: either a young man whose skin had lost its elasticity betimes, or a middle-aged one whose youthful lineaments the years had blurred rather than erased. The swift, suspicious glance he darted at Jurnet made the detective come down on the further side of forty.

'Uncle Max!' the man repeated, seizing the Professor's hand, his arm, in a handshake which was more of an embrace. 'Are you all right? Somebody said they'd seen you in a wheelchair!'

His reception of the salutation friendly but on the cool side, Professor Flaschner responded: 'You mustn't believe everything you hear, Adam. Just as I too do not believe everything. You know how Tawno exaggerates. It's his nature, he can't help it. Which is why I tell him to stop talking nonsense when he tells me that you are driving him round the bend.'

'*Me* driving *him!*' The man's voice rose. Conscious that ears were being pricked up all round, he lowered its tone, but not its intensity. 'Uncle Max!' he begged. 'Can I have a few words? Just a minute or two, in private?'

'No one will hear, so long as you stop shouting.' Taking in the other's meaningful stare directed at Jurnet, who would have moved politely away had not the Professor gripped him firmly: 'This is Mr Jurnet, my very close friend, from whom I have no secrets.' And to Jurnet: 'And this is Mr Adam Pender, who works for Tawno as an assistant.'

'I can certainly tell Tawno's been talking to you!' Adam Pender observed bitterly. 'Not co-worker, you notice, nor colleague, nor member of the team. That's all he allows me – assistant! Somebody who cleans off the blackboard after he's finished writing on it!'

'You have done more?' Professor Flaschner inquired courteously.

The man's face flushed dark red.

'I've done every damn thing I've been given a chance to do. *And* made a good job of it. You ask him if I haven't. It's not my fault Tawno covers up his equations with his arm whenever I'm in the vicinity.'

'My poor Adam,' said the Professor, with every evidence of sympathy. 'It is indeed hard that the Master of the Universe distributes His gifts in such unequal shares. I see you believe that, for justice to be done, you must share with Tawno the Nobel Prize which will undoubtedly come his way sooner or later, unless something unexpected intervenes. But would that be justice? Will not the assessors want to know what, beside cleaning the blackboard, has been your contribution?'

'You saw my article in *Nature!*'

'One that, if I may evoke avuncular privilege, seemed more to ventilate your ignorance than air your knowledge.'

'Naturally you're on Tawno's side! Dr Turnbull sent me a very appreciative note.'

'Dr Turnbull, as you very well know, would say anything – even,' with a smile for Jurnet, 'that the Earth was flat, to do Tawno down.' With no apparent change of subject, Professor Flaschner continued: 'And tell me, Adam, how is *your* wife?'

'*There* you are!' Christopher Maslin came up, looking excited. A handsome lad, Jurnet thought, who would not have looked out of place on the ceiling of his father's church, tooting on a golden trumpet. On second thoughts, perhaps not: the bold eyes were not angelic. Judging from the flush which extended from forehead to chin, he had not said no to the waitresses of a certain age who were going about the room proffering trays loaded with glasses of champagne.

'Tawno's not here yet. Mother was beginning to think you'd got stuck in the lift. You ought by rights to have come in by the other door so that the man in the red coat could have announced you and the Lord Mayor and the Lady Mayoress shaken you by the hand.'

'What an honour to have missed!' Professor Flaschner ruffled the boy's fair hair and smiled down at the glowing countenance. 'And did the man in the red coat announce *you* with due pomp and circumstance?'

Christopher Maslin's face wrinkled with a comic disgust which Jurnet mentally chalked up as a point in the boy's favour. His physical advantages had obviously given him no undue conceit of himself. 'The Reverend and Mrs Maslin and Master Maslin – Master! I ask you!'

'Never mind. One day, when he has to announce Doctor, or Professor, or even – who knows? – Lord Maslin, you will have your revenge.'

The boy's smile was followed instantly by a small frown.

'I told you, Uncle Max! You never believe me. I'm going into the church.'

'In that case, he will announce the Archbishop of Canterbury!'

'You're disappointed in me,' Christopher persisted, not laughing.

'Tawno may be,' was the response. 'You will have

to ask him. You know his high hopes for his godson. For myself, – ' the Professor spoke with great tenderness – 'the way that leads to happiness is the one I would choose for you. Assuming He exists, I am sure one is just as likely to find God in church as inside the atom.'

A little embarrassed, Jurnet suggested: 'Perhaps in the meantime the young man could conduct you to your table – '

'Your table too, my friend!' Professor Flaschner tightened his grip on the detective's arm. 'You have still to meet my Tawno.'

Conscious that the Superintendent, ensconced in a nearby embrasure and apparently absorbed in discussion with a foreign gentleman whose beard was carefully parted in the middle so as not to obscure the order hung round his neck on a crimson ribbon, nevertheless had him piercingly under observation, Jurnet muttered something about having to attend to security.

'So that is why a policeman has come to our party!' the Professor exclaimed. 'To make sure we don't get away.' Holding up his hand to block a disclaimer: 'Don't expect me to believe it is us you are here to protect, and not the citizens of your fair city, put in peril by our invasion. And quite right too! *We* are the dangerous ones.'

Inwardly agreeing, Jurnet nevertheless protested: 'You don't look very dangerous to me.'

'A policeman judging by appearances! That is not at all how it is in the detective stories! Don't be deceived, my friend. Einstein was cuddly like a teddy bear. If you were a child you wanted to take him to bed with you – yet with one little equation he turned the world upside down. My advice to you, Inspector – my advice as a friend. If you do come upon a bomb here tonight, hidden in some dark corner, don't tell a soul. Leave it ticking away and run like hell.'

Professor Flaschner disengaged his arm from the

detective's and took Christopher Maslin's instead. The man's face had lost its grey, the purplish redness which had supplanted it equally foreboding. 'Now I am going to sit down and wait for my Tawno.'

Trailing a waitress with a load of used glasses Jurnet went towards the kitchen. The swing doors, one for In, one for Out, were set in the wall underneath the minstrels' gallery some medieval governor of the castle had hung on to the undressed flints along one side in the forlorn hope of making the place cosy. Sid Hale, a detective inspector with a long face that looked perpetually saddened by the world's follies but never surprised by them, was leaning on the balustrade of this excrescence, gazing down at the throng with an apparently casual interest which missed nothing. *He* hadn't let himself be conned into a monkey suit, Jurnet observed with a mixture of envy and self-hate. As if the thought had winged itself across the space between them, Sid Hale, with no remission of melancholy, favoured his mate with a head-to-toe inspection, then put his bunched fingers to his lips and kissed them, before splaying them out in a gesture intended to be Gallic. Jurnet put two fingers up in reply, unfortunately just at the moment the waitress with the glasses looked over her shoulder to see who was following her.

'Evening,' he said disarmingly, and, intimidated by her glare, going through the wrong door and narrowly avoiding collision with a tray of appetisers on the way out.

Sergeant Jack Ellers, on duty in the kitchen, was conscientiously sampling a salmon vol-au-vent.

'Nothing toxic so far,' the chubby Welshman greeted his colleague. 'Not that it signifies. Once Rosie takes a gander at my waistband when I get home she'll slaughter me anyway.' He swallowed the last delectable morsel and eyed Jurnet up and down. 'I see rompers are in this year.'

'Adding my bit to the gaiety of nations.' Jurnet cast an appreciative eye about the organised chaos of a caterer's kitchen in full operation. Professionalism in any sphere pleased him, even an expertly blown safe affording him a certain aesthetic pleasure in a job well done. 'Everything OK here?'

'Got the Super on your tail, have you?' asked Jack Ellers, interpreting the question correctly. 'Give him my love and tell him the chicken marengo is out of this world. If *you're* eating with the quality, take the saddle of lamb.'

'I'm not good enough for the chicken what's-it?'

'Made out of old boots. My Rosie wouldn't feed it to the cat.' With a sunny smile: 'Just the thing for superintendents.'

5

There was a seating plan pinned to an easel at one end of the hall. Jurnet did not consult it, knowing his name could not possibly appear there. The Superintendent's was another matter. A quick glance round the room at the now seated guests was enough to disclose him at the top table, with a dainty little Chinese woman on one side and the busty Italian, the rose still in place behind her ear, on the other.

Feeling out of it and more than half-inclined to retreat once again to the kitchen and the sight of Jack Ellers' familiar face smiling in welcome, he felt absurdly pleased to find Christopher Maslin at his side, announcing that Uncle Max had sent him to guide the detective to their table.

'Are you sure there's room?'

'Tawno still hasn't come, so there's his place. When he does, Uncle Max says, they can always squeeze in an extra chair.'

'I don't know if I should – '

'Oh *do* come on!' the boy interrupted. He looked more excited than ever. There were, Jurnet saw, bottles of wine on the tables, white and red. What had the kid been knocking back this time?

When he reached the table, Christopher leading the way, almost running, the nature of the boy's intoxication was made clear. Next to Professor Flaschner, on one side, was the empty chair – Tawno Smith's chair, Ben Jurnet's chair for the nonce. On the other, a large, square-shouldered man with a mop of greying hair sat next to a young girl.

The girl was a knock-out, a girl to bring a lump to the throat because of the certainty that such beauty could not last. What a wonderful woman she was going to be when her brilliant promise fulfilled itself! Yet the half-opened bud had a poignancy which had to be lacking in the fully fledged flower. She might become more beautiful: she could never be lovelier.

Her beauty eclipsed the other two women at the table as a spark is eclipsed by flame. Claire Maslin looked suddenly absurd, her little-girl face a travesty. The second woman, seated next to Adam Pender and, thought Jurnet, probably his wife, was of a different kind: a predator. Pender, now that the detective got a good look at him, had a well-nibbled look.

As for the boy Christopher, Jurnet had been partly right about him. He was drunk, but not with wine. Drunk with love. Lucky little bugger, thought Jurnet, remembering the eminently forgettable love objects of his own adolescence.

Professor Flaschner's complexion had changed yet

again, not for the better; the red deepening to purple, a sense of blueness, of cold. But his spirits seemed in fine fettle.

'My friend Efrem,' he exclaimed, clasping an arm round the square shoulders on his right, 'meet my friend Mr Detective Inspector Jurnet. My friend Mr Jurnet,' – smiling at the detective who had slipped as unobtrusively as possible into the vacant seat – 'meet Mr Efrem Ahilar, my friend from Israel.' Across the Professor's shrunken body, the two men nodded to each other, united in an instant conspiracy to keep the old man happy.

'My friend Efrem', the Professor went on, 'is also my twin. Don't look surprised. We have the evidence to prove it, haven't we, Efrem?' The Israeli nodded, rather unwillingly. 'When they numbered us like cattle at Treblinka,' Professor Flaschner continued notwithstanding, 'this twin of mine, whom I had never seen before in my life, stood in front of me in the line. 547160, eh, Efrem? The number is forever tattooed on our forearms and on our hearts. We could show you the forearms, if it did not mean rumpling up the sleeves of our beautiful evening clothes. As to our hearts, you must take our word for it. But how twins, you ask? I will tell you. It was the most wonderful thing, a sign from heaven, revealed only to our two selves, that, despite appearances, the Nazis were doomed. Through some incredible slip in their so far infallible system we were both given the same number! 547160. You notice that I intone those integers as if chanting a litany – as why should I not, since they were as much a promise to us as the rainbow was to Noah. By that one mistake we knew that, against all the odds, the world would survive its descent into the abyss, and we with it.' Painfully taking on a new cargo of breath, the Professor touched Efrem Ahilar's arm. 'Efrem is my conscience.'

The Israeli laughed, the laugh of a man at ease with himself and with the world about him.

'Every time we get together Max beats his breast because, after the war was over, he did not, like me, take himself off to help build the Land of Israel. As if it were somehow more meritorious to plant an orange grove than, as he has done, take man a few steps further towards an understanding of the universe.'

'It *is* more meritorious,' Professor Flaschner insisted. Turning towards the detective, he asked: 'Have you ever been to Israel?'

'No,' Jurnet answered, seeing Miriam brown and beautiful in the desert sun.

'My own travelling days are over.' The blue in the Professor's face had sharpened. 'Today, Efrem has to carry all my messages, be my go-between. The Lord will understand. If you ask him why he is here in England – ask him, you'll see! – he'll say it is to see his granddaughter safely settled in Cambridge. Esther has been in the army, she can shoot every separate pip off the five of diamonds, and still she needs a chaperon! My twin, you see, is shy of saying out loud that he is here to say goodbye to his twin for the last time.'

Efrem Ahilar protested easily, with no apparent regard for the blue, the purple, the grey, in the other's face: 'Come off it, Max! You and I have said more farewells than Dame Nellie Melba. I came because Esther asked me to. Why, with the universities we have in Israel, the girl hankers after a piece of paper with Cambridge written on it, is something you'll have to ask her, but for a granddaughter actually to want a grandfather's company is a request too precious to refuse. She is, if I say it myself, as beautiful as the dancing stars, but mad, poor girl – stark, staring mad!'

Esther Ahilar blushed charmingly. In an English almost without accent she insisted: 'I wanted to come to Cambridge, Uncle Max, because you are there and you never come to Israel to see us.'

'I will come,' said the Professor. 'One day I will come.'

Christopher Maslin interposed, breathless: 'I'm going up to Cambridge myself in October. We could meet—' Overwhelmed by his own audacity and the knowing eyes of the adults, he finished weakly, 'We could play some tennis, or something.'

The girl smiled at the boy kindly, as at a child. She was at least a year older.

'I'm afraid I don't play tennis.'

Adam Pender's wife, her large red mouth moist with red wine, said: 'You could always teach him to shoot the pips off the five of diamonds. Or something.'

Jurnet had missed the first course. When the waitress came to take their orders for the second, the detective, in some obscure act of contrition for not being home when Miriam phoned, asked for the chicken marengo.

'When you bring the food,' commanded the Professor, 'bring with it, my darling, if you please, a very large glass of orange juice for the guest who has still to arrive.'

After a quick look round the table to make sure she had got her numbers right, the waitress announced with satisfaction: 'We haven't any orange juice, sir. And, begging your pardon, you're all here already. One too many, if you must know. Eight a table, that's the rule, and you're one over. That's why you're so bunched up.'

The Professor returned: 'We are bunched up, dear lady, because we are dear friends who like to be close. When the guest who still has to come arrives, we shall be even closer. He does not drink wine and he is always thirsty after a journey. So, my good woman – a large glass of orange juice, if you please.'

The broad smile which accompanied this last must have contained some hidden ingredient of either threat or cajolery, unless there was something to be read in the blue face which could not be gainsaid, for the waitress unpleated her mouth and said apologetically: 'I'm afraid there's only orange squash, sir.'

'See what you can do. I have unbounded confidence in your powers.'

When the woman had gone, Professor Flaschner remarked to the detective: 'I expect, as a policeman, you know all about gipsies and wine.'

'Only that they have a name for holding their liquor badly. Mr Smith is sensible to keep off it.'

'*Mr* Smith!' The Professor dwelt on the syllables as if they held some special meaning. '*Mr* Smith has a sensible head on his shoulders. More than could be said for our revered Sir Thaddeus, eh, Simon?'

Startled to be singled out, the Revd Simon Maslin stilled his jerks and jolts with difficulty.

'Not Sir Thaddeus's fault, Professor! Put it down to those Victorian iconoclasts – '

'What is this about a head?' Efrem Ahilar demanded.

'Only that he lost it, sir. Sir Thaddeus. Literally. Or' – the clergyman's smile hovered tentatively, not trusting its own provenance – 'I suppose one should really put it the other way round and say that it was his head which lost his body. They were doing something dreadful in the crypt – the crypt at St Blaise's, that is, where he's buried – and the whole place simply caved in. Those glorious Gothic arches! Tombs split open, bones everywhere, male and female all mixed up together. When they came to clear up the mess, they found Sir Thaddeus Brigg's head safe and sound in what was left of his resting place. Amazingly lifelike, they said, most of the hair, auburn just as in his pictures, still attached to the skull. But which of the skeletal bones were his no one could say, and nobody seemed to care much. There's a story that a farmer offered to cart the lot away for nothing, so long as he was allowed to grind them up for bone meal, and that the offer was taken up.'

Mrs Pender demanded: 'Do you mean that tomorrow, at the service, there'll only be a head inside the tomb? It really is too ridiculous.'

'They didn't even bury that again – put it in a glass case, if you can believe it, in the medical museum of the Norfolk and Angleby Hospital, where it stayed for the best part of fifty years; until people began to realise what a great man Sir Thaddeus was and they started a society and collected enough money to pay for a fine new tomb back in St Blaise's again.'

'So it *is* just a head?'

'Not just. Even after all that time they found, when they began to look, that there were still some loose bones left lying about in the crypt – unclaimed, as you might say. So they swept them up and put them into the new tomb as well.' The clergyman concluded with a simplicity which hinted at a different person beneath the gauche exterior. 'Whenever I find myself in St Blaise's I say a little prayer for those unknown bones which suddenly found themselves in such exalted company.'

'Kismet!' declared Professor Flaschner. 'The first man to discover the random universe and he gets himself buried with a job lot of skeleton! He and God must have cooked it up between them as a practical demonstration of what they had in mind. Keep quiet in church tomorrow and you'll hear the pair of them laughing!'

6

Dr Spencer Turnbull, President of the International Sir Thaddeus Brigg Society and Chairman of the Sir Thaddeus Brigg Tricentennial, came over to the Professor, temporarily deserting his own place at the high table, next to the Lady Mayoress. Dr Spencer Turnbull was an American whose gnomic commentaries on Heisenberg's Uncertainty Principle had, among his students, earned him the nickname of the Principal Uncertainty. Was he a genius? Was he a quack? In all likelihood even Dr Turnbull himself did not know the answer to those questions, or, if asked outright, might equally well have responded 'neither and both', years passed in the pursuit of quantum physics having permanently damaged his sense of that rough-and-ready working arrangement known to the non-initiates as reality. Only two things Dr Turnbull was positive about. He regretted that he was not an Englishman and therefore could never become a Lord or even a Sir; and he did not like people who slept with his wife.

The waitress, busy serving the main course, looked up from Jurnet's chicken marengo and eyed the newcomer without love, demanding of Professor Flaschner with disbelief: 'This isn't him you're expecting?'

'Certainly not.' The Professor cupped his hands round the full tumbler she had placed at the side of his plate. 'But this *is* the genuine article! Woman, you are an angel!'

The waitress went as pink as Dr Turnbull's bald head and said huffily, to hide her pleasure: 'None of that concentrated stuff! I saw some oranges out there doing nothing, and I said to one of the lads, "Squeeze 'em!" '

'Tawno will prostrate himself in adoration at your lovely feet. Spencer!' – turning to the new arrival – 'You have come to say hello to Tawno and the naughty fellow isn't here yet. As perhaps you know, he has been in London today, delivering the Ponsonby Lecture. I'm afraid they must have kept him. Never mind! Sometime during this three-day, three-ring circus you have so cleverly arranged for us, the two of you will undoubtedly find a few moments to chew over subjects of mutual interest.'

Dr Turnbull's smile, his range of expression being small, wavered only a little.

'Actually, Max, it's you I wanted. You ought to be at the top table. You know we had a place for you there.'

The Professor replied blandly: 'I preferred to be among friends.'

'Ha! Ha! Still the old Max! I heard you hadn't been well – but still the old Max!'

A rasping breath issuing from blue lips, Professor Flaschner pronounced: 'I am, as you see, in blooming health.'

'I can see you have a good colour. To be truthful, I came to beg a little favour. I wondered if the committee could count on you to propose the toast to Sir Thaddeus tonight. I shall be delivering the eulogy in depth in church tomorrow, so a few brief remarks will be fine. Folks seem to be expecting me to make them as well, but–' the doctor giggled – 'they'll be getting tired of the sound of my voice.'

'You are too modest, Spencer, as well as too kind. The answer, however, is no. My health, to be honest, is blooming, but not all that blooming. There is some danger of frost. But I could always, if you like, ask Tawno, when he comes, to stand in for me.'

'*If* Tawno comes,' Dr Turnbull countered sourly.

'He is hardly someone to be relied on. I suppose you know he refused outright to supply the committee with advance information as to the nature of the paper he's giving on Wednesday. You must see that it puts us in a very awkward position.'

'Ignorance, my dear Spencer, as I don't need to tell you, is always an awkward position. Though you have only to look at Tawno's previous work to see what has to be the next step – or dare I say, in the context, the ultimate one?'

Dr Turnbull's shallow eyes bulged a little.

'He's been talking to you!'

The Professor shook his head.

'He doesn't have to. You forget I am a Jew. I do not need to be persuaded that God is One.'

A brown hand reached across the tablecloth, grasped the glass of orange juice; raised it to lips that were full and sensuous.

'That saved my life!' said Tawno Smith.

As if at a signal, the polite symmetry of the table fragmented into a swirl of energy. Cutlery clattered down any old how on to the barely tasted chicken, the saddle of lamb. The little chairs were scraped back, pink napkins tumbling out of laps as the company as one, rose to its feet. There were handshakes, embracings, kissings on the mouth.

Only Jurnet, who even took a mouthful of the chicken, which was not half as bad as Jack Ellers had warned, kept his place. He and the Professor. The Professor opened his arms. Tawno Smith came into them like a child, put his arms round the old man and kissed him lovingly.

'You smashed up the Porsche, eh? Ran it into a wall, turned it over in a ditch. Tell me the truth, you old blackguard!'

'What are you talking about?' the Professor exclaimed, delighted. 'I drove it from Cambridge with a finesse to bring tears to the eyes.' He fished in a trouser pocket and with some difficulty brought out a car key on a ring as well as two door keys, each attached to one of those slabs of metal hotel proprietors use to discourage guests from departing with them still in their possession. 'I signed in for both of us while I was about it. The car's in the car-park, not a scratch on it.'

'In that case, it's me who's the blackguard for ever letting the key out of my possession. I must have been mad. As you are,' – putting all three keys into his jacket pocket – 'for loading yourself down with half a ton of metal instead of leaving it at the reception desk.' In a voice that was gentle, concerned, Tawno Smith asked: 'How are you, Uncle? Are you feeling better?'

'Much better,' the Professor replied, transfigured with happiness. 'Better and about to be best. In a few minutes' time, when I have taken my tablet, you'll see me dance upon the table!'

'Take it now, then. I can't wait!'

Tawno Smith was a slight man of medium height who gave the impression of being neither slight nor medium. Brown, with white teeth and black hair that curled like a faun's, he imposed himself hard-edged upon his surroundings, a presence. Not young, but one who had improved on youth, turning the first rough sketch into a work of art, retaining its flat belly, its lean strength, whilst refining its louche hesitancies into a global self-possession which yet retained elements of the urchin, up to mischief and glorying in it. He moves like a bloody ballet dancer, Jurnet thought, resisting the obvious attractions of the man. If there was one thing he distrusted more than beauty in the male it was winning ways.

Still, it had to be admitted, the bugger had what it took. Whatever the Professor might assert to the contrary, it was unthinkable that neutrinos passing through that snazzily suited torso could emerge unshaken. There was a definite electro-magnetic field. People at the adjoining tables were drawn into it: you could tell by the increased resonance of their voices, an access of vivacity and appetite. And on Tawno Smith's own circle, those at the centre of the force, the effect was astonishing. Claire Maslin and Mrs Pender, having received each their due share of kisses and compliments, smiled at each other with grace and understanding. The Reverend Simon Maslin achieved an ease of discourse which must have knocked him speechless had he thought to take note of it. Young Christopher, addressed as one adult to another, grew visibly in confidence, staring at Esther Ahilar with a bolder eye.

With the girl herself it was exactly the reverse. Beneath Tawno Smith's admiring gaze she reddened, grew childish, reached for her grandfather's hand. Mrs Maslin and Mrs Pender exchanged looks of sentimental reminiscence.

Alistair Tring had appeared on the scene from somewhere or other, miming affability. Even Adam Pender and Dr Turnbull were not immune to the general enchantment, caught up willy-nilly in Tawno Smith's web. Not to be enmeshed was not to be free but to be forsaken.

'Adam!' Tawno Smith exclaimed as, eyes shining, he grasped the other's proffered hand. 'You've finished being angry with me!'

'I have not!' was the rejoinder from an Adam Pender grinning from ear to ear.

Dr Turnbull said: 'I'm counting on you, Tawno, to propose the toast to Sir Thaddeus.'

'In orange juice? The old boy'd turn in his grave! How many bottles was it – ten? twenty? – he and the king knocked back between them the day Charles knighted him? No – that's a job for you, Spencer, a kindred spirit!'

Dr Turnbull, who had a weak bladder and seldom drank anything stronger than Malvern water disguised with a lemon slice and an olive to look like a dry Martini, preened with pleasure at this picture of himself, so cocky and cavalier. 'Do you think so? It's just that I thought, as I'm down to deliver the eulogy tomorrow – '

'Can't have enough of a good thing!'

What a kerfuffle, thought Jurnet, who would have liked to get stuck into his chicken marengo. And now it looked like being his turn to join the circus.

'Tawno, you monster, come here!' called Professor Flaschner. 'I want you to meet my friend Detective Inspector Jurnet.'

The man came at once, bending over the Professor with a veneration that seemed curiously old-fashioned. Hard not to like the fellow, Jurnet thought resentfully, the chicken in its tasty goo congealing on the plate.

'A detective inspector!' When Tawno Smith smiled, tiny points of flame seemed to ignite, dance in his eyes. 'Don't tell me Uncle Max has been getting into trouble with the fuzz!'

'He's security.' The Professor dropped his voice conspiratorially. 'The balloon is timed to go up at ten o'clock.'

'Let's hope it's when Spencer is proposing his toast! I'm delighted to meet you, Detective Inspector Jurnet. You mustn't mind my uncle's sense of humour.' An arm round a bony shoulder, he laid his cheek without embarrassment alongside the cheek of the old man. 'He's really the best fellow in the world. That is,' – with a sudden recollection – 'he is so long as he remembered to bring my paper with him from Cambridge as well as my car.'

'Of course I remembered!' said the Professor. 'It's safe in my wardrobe back at the hotel. Didn't you go there yourself to change?'

'It was so late, I came straight on from the station. Changed in the Gents downstairs, overlooked by a statue of Diana they said they'd had to move out of the vestibule to make room. Quite an eye-opener for the poor girl. By the way, I left my bag there. Remind me to pick it up when we leave.'

All this was said with Tawno Smith's cheek still against the Professor's. Suddenly something, in the texture or the temperature of the skin perhaps, changed the bantering tone to one of anxiety. The younger man straightened up, grasped the Professor's hand.

'Uncle, you haven't taken that pill!'

'Stop fussing!' Professor Flaschner ordered, but he looked terrible. He fumbled in a pocket and brought out a pretty little pillbox made of gold. 'A present from this rascal,' he said to Jurnet, more gasp than utterance.

'Never mind that!' Tawno Smith snatched the box, opened it, 'Here!' pressing a tablet into the Professor's hand. 'You'll need some water – damn! There isn't any. Take it with this – ' Tawno Smith lifted the remainder of the orange juice to the sick man's lips.

The Professor, who had obediently placed the tablet in his mouth, twisted his head from side to side, his lips closed tight. His breathing had become fast and shallow. One hand had splayed itself against his shirt front as if his chest were hurting him. He seemed to be trying to say something.

'I'll try and get you some water to wash it down. Don't try to talk,' Tawno Smith ordered. 'Drink this.'

The Professor let out a harsh cry, an effort which twisted his face into a travesty of mirth. He swallowed the juice and nodded at the other as if to indicate that the pill had gone down.

'Stay still. You'll feel better in a minute, you dear old muggins!'

But Professor Flaschner quite obviously did not feel better, either in a minute, or in two, or three. The hand that had been spread against his chest clenched, reached out blindly and clutched at a corner of the tablecloth. A shudder shook the emaciated frame. The hand on the cloth tightened. In a crackle of glass and a clank of bottles, wine red and white spilled on to the pink linen. Chicken and lamb, turned arsy-versy, mingled their savoury juices. The tumbler teetered on the edge of the table before tipping its remaining juice into the Professor's lap and crashing to the floor between his sprawled legs.

The Professor's eyes were wide, as if with surprise, but the pupils were invisible, or extinguished. The odour of orange juice was heavy on the air.

Tawno Smith shouted: 'Uncle Max!'

7

There was nothing Jurnet needed to do. Two members of the St John Ambulance Brigade, craggy men moving with a precision which was at once matter-of-fact and compassionate, were suddenly present as if summoned by somebody rubbing a lamp – unless it was Sid Hale, from his crow's nest up in the minstrel's gallery, who had identified the need and done something about it.

'Leave it to us, sir,' one of the St John's men said, moving Tawno Smith aside with an absence of emotion which was of itself therapeutic. The two of them moved the Professor from his chair to the floor, disposing the inert body in what the detective recognised as the classic recovery position – face down with head to one side, the arm on that same side right-angled at the elbow, the leg bent. How it brought back the first-aid classes he had been required to attend long ago! – a skill grown rusty since most of the bodies which he encountered nowadays in the way of business were beyond recovery, in this world at any rate.

Judging from the small area of cheek and nose visible, Jurnet did not give much for the Professor's chances. In what, in other circumstances, could have been a richly comic act, full of knockabout humour, the St John's men were taking incredible liberties with their distinguished casualty; tickling him, demanding to the point of tedium, 'Can you hear me? Can you hear me?'

To it all, the Professor responded with a massive inattention. His forehead, what could be seen of it, was beaded with sweat, the greys and blues of his complexion positively iridescent. It was going on too long, thought Jurnet. Too long for the suffering creature – it was becoming a misnomer to call it human – down on the floor, too long for the friends who had to see it suffer, certainly too long for the assembled guests, none of whom, eggheads as they were, seemed up in the etiquette appropriate to such a contretemps. Some stood, some remained seated. Some picked at their dinners absent-mindedly, surprised at last to find their plates bare. Others, more fatalistic, tucked in without shame. The low buzz of conversation which had supplanted the earlier babble had about it an only partly concealed undertone of spleen. As the Preacher was only too right in saying, there was a time to be born and a time to die; and for anyone with a particle of consideration for his fellow beings, the latter (to say nothing of the former, for that matter) was definitely not at a celebratory dinner of the Sir Thaddeus Brigg Tricentennial.

Just the same, once the ambulance had arrived, once the stretcher-bearers had borne the Professor away and the St John's men faded back into the obscurity from which they had emerged, there was a flatness in the air, as if a cabaret act were over and nobody was quite sure what came next on the programme. The waitress, with another to help her, bundled up the sodden tablecloth,

40

spread fresh linen; set out new glasses and bottles of wine. Jurnet noted that she pointedly omitted to bring further supplies of meat knives and forks, the chicken and the lamb gone for a burton, but only spoons and forks for dessert, for sherry trifle or *marquise à l'ananas*, whatever that might be: also, with exquisite tact, two places fewer, Tawno Smith having accompanied his uncle to hospital. Even the excess chairs were whisked away lest their emptiness offend. Enjoy! Enjoy! The lad from the kitchen who cheerily sloshed water over the spilt orange juice, was tartly told off to make a proper job of it.

The toastmaster in the red coat having prayed silence for the president, Dr Spencer Turnbull rose like a good anchorman to tie up the loose ends, bewailing the heart attack which had laid low their 'esteemed – dare I say beloved? Yes, I dare – ' colleague, and to invite the assembly to stand for a minute of silent prayer for his speedy recovery.

Dr Turnbull folded his hands over his lower abdomen and bowed his head to show how it was done. The particle physicists stood obediently, but few, Jurnet noted without surprise, followed their president's example in any other particular. To have done so, the detective supposed, would be equivalent to an acknowledgement that the world was flat after all.

At the Professor's own table, his friends stood about in shocked surprise. Even Simon Maslin who, if anyone, should have known where to find strength, stood blank-faced, twitching. Adam Pender looked dazed; Efrem Ahilar, the Israeli, yellow, older. Somehow the table had rearranged itself. Esther Ahilar and Christopher Maslin were now side by side, seeking out each other by instinct and putting as much space as possible between themselves and the rest.

There was death in the air and they wanted no part of it, being young and consequently immortal.

41

Jurnet was standing in line, his shoulder nudging Diana's marble buttocks, waiting to collect Tawno Smith's travelling bag, when the Superintendent came into the cloakroom wanting to know what in heaven's name was keeping him. The Superintendent was not in the best of moods.

'Heart attack!' he snapped. He sounded let down. 'They phoned from the hospital to say he died twenty minutes after admission.'

'Looked as if it could have happened any time.'

'Did it? I noticed you seemed to be very matey. Look here – what are you queuing for? You didn't bring a coat.'

Jurnet explained about Tawno Smith's bag.

'Thought I'd get it back to his hotel for him. The bloke was so cut up he's probably forgotten all about it.'

'Who is this Smith? What is he to the dead man? *His* name, I understood, was Flaschner.'

'Tawno Smith,' Jurnet elaborated, not disguising his satisfaction at knowing something the Superintendent didn't. 'Famous particle physicist. Kind of unofficial adopted son. Anyway, he went with the ambulance.'

The bag was supple, expensive. Even with Jurnet's ID card in front of his eyes the cloakroom attendant hesitated before handing it over. Outside, in the soft damp of a September night, the Superintendent waited fretfully whilst Jurnet locked it in the boot and came back to the driving seat. The car was scarcely over the bridge and winding downhill towards the castle bailey before his superior officer had launched into a catalogue of the evening's woes and shortcomings.

The woman on one side of him had spoken only Italian, the wisp of Eastern promise on the other nothing at all. He had been able to snatch two mouthfuls, no more, of the best chicken marengo ever to come his way before the commotion at Jurnet's table had put everything at sixes and sevens. The wine, on

42

the other hand, had been an insult to the memory of Sir Thaddeus Brigg. Persons with heart conditions should have the consideration to avoid functions whose smooth running they were liable to disrupt by coming down with attacks at inconvenient moments. Jurnet was surprised that the absence of terrorists was not included in the list of grievances. It was, pronounced the Superintendent in conclusion, a deeply boring evening which would cost the city in policing charges a good deal more than it was worth.

Jurnet said consolingly: 'You never know what may happen tomorrow.'

'Nobody's going to try anything on in church. Bad publicity.'

The car stationary at a traffic light, Jurnet looked up to the top of the mound, to where the great keep, still floodlit, hung suspended in darkness. An eminently suitable place for trying things on.

The Superintendent was off on a different tack.

'Did you know that florists work the night through when they've got a big order on? I've got Dave Batterby over at Bell and Fortune's to make sure nothing goes into tomorrow's tributes to Sir Thaddeus except flowers and whatever they use to tie 'em together. Ideal spot to hide a plug of plastic explosive, inside a wreath.'

'Dave at the flower shop! He must be calling down blessings on your head. When I saw him this afternoon he was already streaming with hay fever like a waterfall.'

The Superintendent, his good humour restored, leaned back in his seat with a satisfied chuckle. 'He was, wasn't he?' Dave Batterby was a sore trial to Angleby CID, its resident yuppie, the man who was going places, even if, as sometimes appeared likeliest, it was only out on his backside.

Still, few of the bugger's fellow-officers, Jurnet reflected, transfixed with a sudden pang of lively hatred,

43

would have been prepared to go to the Superintendent's length to make their dislike explicit.

'I warned him, if he took antihistamine and dozed off I'd have his guts for garters.'

Jurnet, who found Batterby's premonitions of greatness as much a pain in the arse as anybody, refrained from comment but rearranged his itinerary. Instead of – his original intention – driving the Superintendent out to the suburbs, to his house overlooking the golf course, he made for Police Headquarters above the Market Place. There he drew up outside the car-park, where his own car awaited him, hiked Tawno Smith's bag out of the boot, and bade his superior officer a cheery goodnight.

The Superintendent, who knew very well wherein he had offended, slid over to the driving seat without a word. Only when he had fastened his seat belt did he lean out of the window to inquire: 'Ever hear of the geodesic of the space-time continuum, Ben? The company we've been keeping tonight must have put me in mind of it.'

'Can't say I have, sir.'

'As I understand it, it's the easiest distance between two points. Not necessarily the straightest, but the easiest. How is it, Ben,' – releasing the handbrake, engaging gear, moving slowly away from the kerb – 'that you and I *will* insist on taking the hardest way home?'

Jurnet drove to the Virgin, where he delivered Tawno Smith's bag before driving home. Driving slowly towards the emptiness which awaited him, the detective wondered if the grieving gipsy physicist faced the night similarly uncomforted. Once the ambulance men had departed with their casualty, and Smith with them, the others at the Professor's table had left within a matter of minutes. They had left sorrowful, distraught; yet none had spoken of following to the hospital.

Could blonde Mrs Maslin, brunette Mrs Pender,

really have gone tamely home to their marital beds, abandoning their darling in his hour of need? Unless Mrs Turnbull, the president's wife, had put forward a prior claim, on grounds of protocol?

None of his business, Jurnet thought, climbing the stairs to where the silent phone accused him. Everything about the flat accused him: 'this purpose-built apartment', as the estate agent had phrased it, neglecting to specify what that purpose might be, and Jurnet not liking to ask. The detective had parked his car on the crumbling concrete of the forecourt, jockeying for position as usual with the bulging plastic bags which, to judge from their unremitting increase, spent their nights in rumbustious procreation. Up through the layered savours of home he had risen – past the Nappi-San of the O'Driscolls, outside whose front door was garaged a pram destined to block the hallway until Mrs O'D achieved the menopause; the joss sticks of Miss Whistler, the late-blooming spinster on the first floor; the pervasive aroma of slow-simmered underwear, to the dingy love nest whose transformation, Miriam had decreed, was to await his own. Once he became a Jew and they were married, out of the door along with his uncircumcised self would go the gimcrack hallstand, the battered table and chairs, even the brass bed which had jounced like a glockenspiel to so many celebrations, and where tonight – and Christ! how many other nights? – he was doomed to sleep alone.

Remembering what the Professor had told him, he said aloud: 'You're never alone with a neutrino.'

He sat down on the edge of the bed and began to unlace his shoes. Once he became a Jew–! He pulled off the hired bow tie and threw it at the telephone which it ringed like hoopla, only no prizes.

8

In the Haymarket Sir Thaddeus Brigg sat on his plinth
contemplating the skull in his hand with amused affection. The statue looked scrubbed and shining, gener-
ations of pigeon droppings having been removed in
honour of the Tricentennial. Thus refurbished, Sir
Thaddeus – the work of a sculptor well known in the
opening years of the century – looked, for all his full
sleeves and ballooning breeches, less cavalier than
Edwardian, bearing a strong resemblance to his late
Majesty King Edward VII dressed for a slaughter of
pheasants.

As a general rule, the paved square, climbing up the
side of the hill and divided from the Market Place only
by the bulk of St Blaise's, was a well frequented place,
much patronised at lunchtime by the workers in the
surrounding shops, by lovers who could do no better
by way of trysting place, and by shoppers whose feet
were killing them. Lollies and franks, crisps and cokes
were usually on sale from vans parked at the lower end,
food wrappers and greasy napkins carpeting the ground
in a way that was quite deplorable but lent the area a
certain raffish charm.

Racing empty cola tins from the top to the bottom
of the square had become something of a traditional
Angleby pastime, hallowed by the benign, condoning
presence of the author of *Religio Aleatoris* – which is to
say *The Religion of a Gambler*. Good money had been
known to change hands on the result. All in all, a noisy
place, loud with ice-cream jingles and taped rock, the
cries of children, laughter, and Norfolk voices that

turned up at the end of every sentence like the toes of Arabian Knights shoes, as if there were no answers, only questions.

The police had already roped off the square, reporters and television cameramen were in position, when Jurnet arrived to witness the wreath-laying ceremony. The Superintendent had had the delicacy not to require his subordinate, in addition, to look in on the memorial service which, to judge from the sounds escaping from the adjoining church, was already well into its stride. The congregation, the detective was pleased to note, was singing something rollicking: one could hardly be expected to be sad about a man dead for three hundred years. The only melancholy feature of the proceedings, he guessed, was likely to be Dr Spencer Turnbull's eulogy.

A good night's sleep seemed to have defused the Superintendent's worst nightmares about terrorists. The few police constables in evidence hung about in relaxed converse. A formidable woman in a flowered overall whom Jurnet guessed to be from the florist, stood guard over a profusion of wreaths leaning against the railing that hemmed in what remained of St Blaise's churchyard. The only evidence of the unregenerate humankind which ordinarily made the Haymarket its own was furnished by the arrival of two workmen who, without all that much success, were labouring to remove the overnight handiwork of the up-to-the-minute vandal who had decorated Sir Thaddeus's plinth with the slogan, so far impervious to their best efforts: 'UP QUARKS AND ATOM!'

'Enjoy yourself?' the man at the hire service had asked mechanically, as he took back the evening suit with the air of one welcoming home a much-loved child he had never expected to see again. Checking the contents of the box: 'Hey! Didn't you have a bow?'

'Sorry – I forgot!' Jurnet had a sudden vision of the bow looped over the telephone; was seized with a dreadful certainty that if he once removed it, Miriam would never ring again, ever. 'Matter of fact, it was such a good tie, I wondered if I could buy it.'

'Cost you nine-fifty,' the man said, not brazenly, Jurnet was convinced, but because he didn't fancy selling one of his charges down the river. When Jurnet took out his wallet, the man's face fell. He took the money angrily, and let the detective depart without another word.

The bells of St Blaise let out a joyful peal. The doors of the church which opened on to the square were thrown back. Led by the Lord Mayor and the Lady Mayoress, the congregation emerged, every face, after the dim religious light, raised to sun and air in involuntary thankfulness. The order of emergence had obviously been planned, the floral woman in the flowered overall well rehearsed, for as each head of delegation reached the pavement he was rewarded with his own especial wreath before taking up his position facing the statue.

One by one they were handed out, the austere circlets of laurel and the elaborate drifts of roses and carnations. The fragrance of wallflowers – on which Sir Thaddeus had written a famous treatise extolling their all but miraculous ability to restore interrupted menses – lay sweet on the morning. At the end, only one lone wreath, in the shape of a pair of dice fashioned out of white daisy heads and showing a double six made of some dark blue berry, remained unclaimed. The floral woman looked about her, frowning. When nobody showed, she took up her guard at the railings again, not best pleased.

When everybody was in place and even the skittering cameramen still, the chairman of the Angleby Sir Thaddeus Brigg Society, a silver-haired man with a long neck, came forward for his moment of glory. The copy of *Religio Aleatoris*, kept open with a morocco bookmark, trembled in his hands. His voice, however, was steady and resonant as he declaimed the famous words.

'No man who lifts up his eyes in reverence to that night sky where the planets take their majestic courses, can but be assured in his heart, though as yet he hath no worldly proof of it, that He who created the immensities of space must equally – since all things by nature have their exact opposites – have fashioned the converse, a universe small as the other is large, wherein divers atomies, too small for the eye to see, and of so little mass as to be invisible to our crude organs even assisted with the best lens that ever was made, and beside which the smallest mote is as a mountain to the cast of a worm, move and have their being in ways which so far escape us, yet, be assured, are no idle gyrations but part of the divine ordering, full of energy and intention.

'For myself, I conceive no part of this great construction as without purpose, for He who made the world and saw that it was good did not, of a surety, create emptiness, which is a mere nullity without form and void, as it sayeth in the Scriptures, but rather, out of emptiness, created that fullness which is beyond all wonder.

'One day, I do not doubt, with a more practised use of those faculties which God in His wisdom has seen fit to bestow upon us, we shall, by His grace, discover this so far unknown world as it were a new Indies, wherefrom we shall return with treasure whose worth is beyond rubies – to wit, the stuff of the universe itself.

'Let me say in conclusion no more but this, which indeed it is all but invidious to mention to men of reason and faith. It has not as yet been vouchsafed in what wise this knowledge will – in His time, not ours – be revealed to us; only that, ever the gamester, I in the meantime move my piece upon the board

49

with as much subtlety as I am capable of, awaiting in perfect confidence God's answer thereto.'

It was the wives who clapped. From the throats of the physicists, who must have known those famous words by heart, rose, not exactly a cheer, not exactly a sigh; more an exhalation of incredulous gratitude that there they were, the chosen, standing in Angleby Haymarket three hundred years after they were written, gamblers all in a random universe, on the brink, the very brink, of hitting the jackpot, breaking the bank, checkmate.

'Very pretty,' commented Sergeant Ellers, arriving as the wreaths began to pile up at the foot of the plinth, their donors summoned over the microphone by Dr Turnbull in intrepid approximations of French, Italian, German, Spanish, Chinese, Japanese, Hindi: whatever the language, the president of the Tricentennial was game for a try at it. The delays due to misunderstandings as to who exactly was being called did not take up all that much time. 'Almost as good as a funeral, 'cept there's no ham tea afterwards.'

'Who said? There's a buffet luncheon laid on in the Mayor's Parlour.' Jurnet added, smiling: 'Surprised you haven't fixed yourself up a duty in the pantry.'

'I know those civic buffets. That's how you feel afterwards – buffeted. Dab of fish paste on a square of plaster of paris and, *hey presto*, canapés! What did you think of the lamb last night, by the way?'

'Matter of fact, I ordered the chicken after all – '

The little Welshman brought his hands together in a smack which made some nearby physicists look round apprehensively.

'That's a fiver Sid Hale owes me! I bet him you'd be sure to take the chicken once I'd warned you not to.'

'Why should I do that?' Jurnet inquired, genuinely interested.

'Because you're a masochist, that's why, with a deep

50

compassion for the underdog – or, in this case, the underlamb. If I'd said take the chicken, you'd have gone for the lamb.'

'If what you say is true, how come I didn't refuse both and stick to the vegetables?'

'I never said all that compassionate, boyo.'

'It's a load of balls! Didn't get either, anyway. The old chap conked out just as I was going to get stuck in. The whole ruddy lot ended up on the floor.'

'Don't let on to Sid. He might declare no contest.'

'I reckon he saw it all happen anyway.'

'Did he? In that case I'd better find where *he's* got to. After I deliver my message, that is.'

'What message is that, then?'

'The Great White Chief wants to see you.' With no appearance of urgency Jack Ellers added: 'At the double.'

'Know what's it about?'

'Something to do with last night. There was a phone call – who from, I haven't a clue. I was only summoned to the presence after he'd finished talking. All I can tell you is, he looked and sounded in a bloody temper, and told me to round you up soonest.'

In the event, it was not as soon as all that. The last wreath was set in place, the last horrific mispronunciation launched on the unoffending air. No, not the last wreath. The floral dice still waited against the railing, its guardian lady looking ready to lay the damn thing herself if nobody else offered.

Jurnet and Ellers were edging away unobtrusively when Jurnet put his hand on his companion's arm, signalled stop.

Tawno Smith had come into the Haymarket, a dark figure in a dark suit, moving with that balletic grace which had put Jurnet's back up at their first meeting; a proud cleaving of space, so that it was difficult to say how at the same time one knew the man to be transfixed with grief. His fellow physicists watched between sympathy and embarrassment as Tawno Smith went across to the railings and picked up the last wreath.

The lady in the flowered overall – she who, an instant before, had been a vessel of ill-contained wrath – looked at him mistily, touched his jacket sleeve in timid sympathy. It was clear there would always be women to console Tawno Smith when he was feeling bad.

The man took the wreath and came to the centre of the square, walking with the same unconsciously theatrical gait which gave every step significance. Finding the entire space round the plinth pre-empted, he reached up and laid the late Max Flaschner's tribute at the feet of the great Aleator, the man who dared to shoot craps with God in the sure faith that the dice would not be loaded. When it was done, Tawno Smith bowed respectfully to his colleagues and walked away, down the hill, followed, at a respectful distance, by the floral lady.

He was scarcely out of sight before the egregious Turnbull, clasping the microphone, was at it again.

'It is sadly fitting that here, in this place, before the effigy of one I dare to call, in a very real sense, the progenitor of all of us here, that I place on record our communal grief at the sudden, the shocking, passing of our esteemed colleague, Professor Max Flaschner – my old buddy Max, as I personally prefer to remember him – ' and so on and on, killing the man a second time, buried under a load of verbal garbage.

Jurnet said: 'The Superintendent, for Christ's sake.'

The Superintendent was in such a filthy temper that Jurnet, entering his office with its oversize desk which proclaimed, without the need for words, where power lay, knew what the matter must be. Only one thing put the Superintendent in a temper like that.

'You were there!' barked the Superintendent, out of the distance which separated them. 'Within feet – within inches – and you saw nothing! Too busy, were you, tucking into the chicken marengo?'

'If you'll let me know what I ought to have seen, sir, I'll be happy to say whether I saw it or not.'

'Saw it or not!' With a look of loathing at his subordinate the Superintendent rose from his chair, turned his back on the room and its occupant and concentrated his attention on the triangle of Market Place visible from the window. Jurnet, familiar with the ploy, waited; patient but puzzled.

'Bright young casualty officer they have, over at the Norfolk and Angleby,' confided the Superintendent when, the statutory time elapsed, he returned to his seat. The brittle chattiness of his tone was more ominous than any surge of decibels. 'Chap who was on duty last night when they brought in Professor Flaschner. Heart attack, I think you said.'

'Not just me. Everyone – St John's Brigade, the ambulance men. All the classic symptoms.'

'So the young casualty officer thought – at first. Until he looked again.'

Jurnet stared across the width of desk with deepening astonishment. 'You mean there was something funny about the old fellow's death?'

'I wouldn't say funny. What this young casualty officer did,' – the Superintendent referred to a scribbled note on a pad at his side – 'having no authority to do a post-mortem off his own bat, you understand, was pass a tube down the dead man's throat and take a sample of gastric fluid. Next he stuck a needle into the heart to get some blood. He also took a sample of urine and – oh yes! Mustn't forget that – he bundled up the Professor's trousers, which I gather were soaked in orange juice, and sent them post-haste to the coroner's officer – to our old and dear friend Barney Colton – as was only right and proper, for analysis.'

'The smell!' exclaimed Jurnet, beginning to see the light. 'All you could smell was that bloody juice.

Otherwise – ' Full of his own failure, he broke off and suggested humbly, 'With luck we should have the results of the tests by this afternoon.'

'Should we indeed?' The Superintendent was at his smoothest. 'I said he was a young casualty officer. I also said he was a *bright* young casualty officer – one who, as it happened, had, only a few weeks ago, attended one of those seminars Colton runs for hospital staff. Bright as a button, Barney remembers. He recognised Professor Flaschner from a picture they had of him in the *Argus*, and of course he knew all about the Tricentennial – that the junketings would be over in a couple of days, after which the participants would be dispersed to the four winds, never to come together, so to speak, for another three hundred years.' The Superintendent leaned across his great slab of wood in the friendliest way, which was invariably the most dangerous. 'Tell me, Ben. Did it really look like a heart attack?'

'I'm not a doctor, sir. He seemed to be in pain in all the right places – across his chest, round the breastbone, and down his left arm. He had a known heart condition. Everyone seemed to take it for granted – '

'Naturally! If it had happened in the privacy of his home his own GP would have signed the death certificate without a second thought. We lose more murderers that way. What this bright young casualty officer did, despite the lateness of the hour was telephone Barney Colton as the Coroner's Officer, tell him what he feared, and how speed was of the essence; how important it was to get the results of the test before the Tricentennial packed up and went home.'

'Speed of the essence? Dr Colton!'

'Exactly. A *very* bright young casualty officer, destined to go far. As a result – ' here the Superintendent sat up straight in his chair, his eyes bright with anger – anger, as Jurnet knew from their long years together, directed not at him but at the waste and futility of

54

violent death – 'lab technicians were brought hotfoot from their beds, tests have been completed and found positive, Dr Colton has not only done the PM but has actually telephoned me in advance of putting it on paper that the late Professor Flaschner's "heart attack" was a lethal dose of potassium cyanide.'

9

The telephone rang. The Superintendent answered, listened, said: 'Ask him to wait,' before replacing the receiver. He looked at Jurnet. 'Dr Tawno Smith. Asking to see you. Think he's come to make a confession?' Raising an imperious hand: 'Don't answer that! One little matter to get out of the way before we get too enthusiastic – could the Professor have committed suicide?'

Jurnet shook his head decisively.

'Neither likely, nor, I think, possible. He'd ordered the orange juice specially to have it ready when his nephew, or whatever you call him, showed up, and the first thing the fellow did when he showed was polish off a good half of it. So there couldn't have been anything wrong with the stuff at that stage.'

'You have eliminated the waitress from our list of suspects,' the Superintendent observed coldly. 'Who next?'

Ignoring the sarcasm, Jurnet ploughed on.

'The juice was on the table, quite a distance by then from where the Professor was sitting. I can't swear to it, but I'm pretty sure I'd have noticed if he'd stretched out his arm, let alone dropped something into the tumbler. You've no idea what a milling about there was – people popping up and down like Jack-in-the-boxes. When the Professor got out his tablets he looked about for some water to take them with, only there wasn't any, and Tawno Smith picked up what was left of the orange juice and said, never mind, use this instead. So if that's where the cyanide was – '

'No question. The lab did a test on the orange juice spilt on the trousers – '

'Then, as I say, it couldn't have been suicide. It was entirely Tawno Smith's doing – '

The detective stopped short, though not in any sudden, horrified realisation. He had seen too many men and women killed by those who, by all accounts, had cherished their victims above all the world; sometimes going so far as to wonder whether murder, despite its outward appearance, was not, in essence an act of love. A fair man, he did not allow his distrust of Tawno Smith's flamboyant personality to predispose him to assume that the man's open display of affection for his Uncle Max was a sham – or even if it were, not to acknowledge that a pretence was not necessarily sinister, but could be rooted in kindness, a desire to please. 'My Tawno,' the Professor had said, his voice trembling with love.

The Superintendent, looking pleased, or at any rate, less angry, at one more fact established, said: 'So far, then, we know this. Whether accidentally, or of deliberate purpose, Dr Tawno Smith killed Professor Max Flaschner. If it was by accident, then we'll have to consider who wanted to see the drinker of orange juice dead . . .'

'Smith's bound to guess something's up. No death certificate–'

'Lay people seldom see the implications. The casualty officer, as he was bound to do, merely said there were certain things he wasn't quite satisfied about. My information is that Smith appeared to take it to mean that cancer might be implicated in addition to heart disease. He spoke about his uncle's worrying loss of weight during the last six months and wondered aloud if the Professor hadn't had a diagnosis which he had deliberately kept from him to save him grief.'

'*My Tawno!*' thought Jurnet. Just what the old codger might well have done.

The Superintendent picked up the telephone.

'Bring Dr Smith upstairs, will you, Constable?'

Tawno Smith came in quietly. Still, he made an entrance. The bugger can't help it, Jurnet thought charitably, going to meet him, shaking hands.

'I asked for you by name because yours was the only name I knew – ' The man stopped, aware of the presence of a higher authority.

Jurnet introduced the two. The Superintendent invited the visitor to be seated; said, with exactly the right accent of regret, 'Professor Flaschner's death is a grievous loss to the world of science.'

'No,' Tawno Smith returned surprisingly. 'Not to science. He'd done nothing for the last ten years or more. He'd made his contribution. His loss–' the man closed his eyes for a moment. reopened them, dark and brooding – 'is more personal.'

'Of course. If there's any way in which we can be of assistance – '

'If you mean the funeral arrangements, I've a friend lives not far from here, thanks just the same. He's a clergyman, he knows the drill. What I'm here for is to report a robbery. From my uncle's room, that is, in the hotel.' Looking at Jurnet: 'You saw him, didn't you, hand over the keys to me – the car key and the keys to our rooms at the Virgin?' The detective nodded. 'And perhaps you heard what he said when I asked him about the paper I'm due to deliver to the Tricentennial tomorrow?'

'He said it was in a case in his wardrobe.'

'Right. Well – it isn't. I've only just been into his room. I'd been putting it off, but the manager said something. I thought I'd better pack up the clothes, at least. Incredible as it sounds, it wasn't till I slid back the wardrobe door to take his spare suit off the hanger, that I saw the case and remembered anything about my world-shattering paper which was going to put me up there with Einstein, Newton and God. The case was one of those document things, more looks than security. It had been broken open. The lock was hanging off, and my paper was gone.'

Jurnet asked: 'Was anything else in the room disturbed?'

'Not so I noticed. I rang through to the manager and he got hold of the chambermaid who looks after the room – Spanish, didn't speak much English, but enough to make clear she'd gone into it earlier on, expecting to clean up as usual, only of course the bed hadn't been slept in.' Tawno Smith spoke with an effort. He seemed to be consumed with a great weariness. He looked from one police officer to the other, his gaze coming to rest on Jurnet. 'I came because the manager said it would have to be reported, and you and Uncle Max seemed to be hitting it off so well last night – '

'Was there any sign of forcible entry into the room itself?'

'Shouldn't think so. I just unlocked the door without thinking.'

'I'll get over there right away.'

'Take your time.' Tawno Smith rubbed a hand over his forehead, round his face, down to a chin which, dark with stubble, lent a dangerous, anarchic look to his brown face. 'I only came at all, to be honest, because it gave me something else to think about. It's not as if the world is going to be deprived of my new and amazing insight into the nuts and bolts of the universe.

I've two more copies of the paper back home in Cambridge, and as soon as I leave here I'm going to drive straight over there and pick one of them up.' Repossessed by his grief, the man drew a long, quivering breath. 'I knew he had to die soon . . .' He was crying without shame, the dark-lashed eyes wide open, not screwed up like a child's. 'I also knew,' Tawno Smith said, 'that he couldn't die, ever, I needed him so.'

There was nothing the other two could say to that, and they said nothing.

'I also know,' Tawno Smith went on, 'that it's no ordinary thief who comes into a hotel bedroom and steals a pile of typescript when there's an Omega watch and £85 in notes lying on the dressing-table.'

The Superintendent said carefully: 'It is evidently a crime with interesting possibilities – '

'I'll get over – ' Jurnet began again.

'However,' – ignoring the interruption – 'I think the best thing Inspector Jurnet can do for you at the moment will be to accompany you to Cambridge. Detective-Sergeant Ellers can deal with matters at this end. If you'll allow me to say so, I really don't think you are in any condition to drive yourself. Unless one of your friends is available – or, for that matter, can go to Cambridge in your place?'

'Friends.' Tawno Smith repeated the word blankly, as if unsure of its meaning.

Jurnet said: 'Let's get on, then, shall we?'

10

They passed Hethersett, Wymondham, Attleborough, without a word exchanged. The Norfolk landscape ripened calmly in the sun. Only past Thetford, where the road, straight for miles, cut across heath and pine, a different country, did Tawno Smith speak. Addressing himself to the Rover's windscreen, to the shining black ribbon vanishing under its wheels, he said: 'I loved him. I hated him.'

Taking refuge in those all-purpose monosyllables which Norfolk people, from time immemorial, have used as a device with which to gain time, Jurnet observed neutrally, 'Oh ah.'

'People say he rescued me. Do you know about that?'

'He did say something. Didn't he, then?'

'Sometimes I think he did. Sometimes I think he caught me like a fowler might catch a wild bird and put it in a cage.'

'Oh ah?' said Jurnet again. He glanced sideways at the profile presented to him and, once more half against his will, was moved by the man's suffering beauty. 'You should have buggered off along with your mates, you mean, instead of kicking the bloke in the shins?'

'He told you about that too, did he?'

Jurnet remarked with a brusque kindliness, 'See yourself as a gipsy, do you then, instead of a learned doctor? Free as air in your caravan, roasting hedgehogs over the campfire, bit of horse-stealing on the side, all very romantic?'

'Actually no.' The man spoke with a child's directness. 'All I can remember of the gipsy life, if you want to know, is a ruined house – I couldn't even tell you what town it was in – where my mam and I were holed up in the basement. If I ever had a father – as I'm sometimes tempted to doubt – he left no dent on my memory. I can't even remember how my mother looked, her face is a blank, but that basement! I can remember that basement perfectly. Not only how it looked, but how it tasted. Yes, tasted. Whenever I was hungry, as at that time I was always hungry, my hunger and that basement became the only realities. I would break off some of the putty adhering to what was left of the window frame, and chew it. Not swallow; chew. It dulled the pangs, for a little.'

'Did Professor Flaschner get your mother's permission to adopt you?'

'Oh, by then there was no mother to ask, one way or the other. One night, long before the famous shin-kicking episode, three soldiers came.' The dark eyes keeping watch on the rolling ribbon of road narrowed, the voice did not falter. 'I don't even know which army they belonged to: the basement was dark, they never said a word in any language. They took my mother and raped her, one after the other. I hid behind a pile of rubble. I didn't know what they were doing, only that it was something that made my mother cry out like an animal, and that I ought to be stopping them from doing it. Instead, I made myself small, tried not to breathe, in case they did the same terrible thing to me.

'Suddenly my mother screamed out in Romany, "*Plastri lesti!*" which means "Run for your life!" And I ran. Instead of rescuing her I ran for my life.' Tawno Smith put a hand over his eyes. 'Sometimes I think I've been running ever since.'

'You and everybody else,' Jurnet remarked, intentionally deflating. He turned the car on to the road signposted to Cambridge city centre. 'A little kid! What could you have done? Ten to one, if you'd tried, they'd have smashed your skull against the basement wall into the bargain.'

'Probably.' The man sat up straighter in his seat. 'Turn left at the roundabout. I'll direct you from there.' When the detective had followed out his instructions he asked, as one imparting an interesting titbit of general knowledge, 'Did you know that in Romany there's one word for both yesterday and tomorrow? Also the same one word for life as for death?'

'Wouldn't do for us in the Force. The Superintend-ent'd have something to say about it.'

Tawno Smith laughed.

'And there was I, all set to con you with the sheer poetry of gipsy philosophy – the seamless dream where time does not exist, or rather, where nothing exists *but* time! Now I understand why Uncle Max took such a shine to you!' In a cheerful voice, elucidating: 'The word for yesterday and tomorrow is *callico*. The word for life and death is *merripen*.'

'Merry? That's a rum old name for death.'

'It's a rum old name for life.'

The late Professor Flaschner's home was a comfortable house of red brick with facings of rusticated stone and a stone porch too pretentious for the rest of its architecture. It stood in a tree-lined avenue among others of its station. Jurnet drew up at the kerb, wondering what a Cambridge police car was doing parked in the driveway.

As the two men came up the front path, Tawno Smith already fishing in his pocket for the key, the front door flew open, and a woman ran to meet them, a woman past her first youth, but plump and comely; a rosy countrywoman, Jurnet would have said, were not the roses unaccountably faded, the eyelids red and swollen.

'Dr Tawno!' she cried, seizing him by the hands. 'I thought you'd never get here! Is it true, then? Is it true?'

Tawno Smith answered gently: 'It's true, Annie.'

'Oh God!' the woman wailed. 'I knew he should never have driven. I told him a dozen times. But you know him – he wouldn't be told.'

'No, he wouldn't. So there's nothing to blame yourself for. He died as he would have chosen – among colleagues and loving friends.'

(*One of whom had lovingly murdered him*, thought Jurnet, waiting quietly to be introduced.)

'I shouldn't have let him go,' the woman insisted. 'Only you know he could never abide nagging.' The tears overflowed. 'That'll be his last idea of me, I reckon. A bloody nagpot, getting on his nerves!'

Tawno Smith put an arm round the woman's waist; gave the plump body an affectionate shake.

'Don't talk nonsense, Annie! You know how much Uncle Max thought of you.'

The woman found a tissue, mopped her eyes, pushed a strand of hair back from her forehead.

'Yes,' she said bleakly. 'I know.'

Since nobody seemed to be doing it for him, Jurnet introduced himself and asked the woman how she'd known to expect Dr Smith. Had somebody telephoned to say he was on his way?

'Other way round,' she replied obscurely, either not bothering to explain, or at the moment, not capable of explanation. 'I'd phoned earlier, of course, soon as I came in and found the window broken and saw the mess. Phoned the police here, that is, in Cambridge. They said they'd send somebody over at once and I wasn't to touch anything meanwhile. While I was waiting for them to show up I phoned the hotel. Not to the Professor, o' course. I knew the shock wouldn't do him any good. I asked for you, Dr Tawno, an' it were only when they said you were out that I asked to be put through to the Professor, just to ask how he was feeling after the drive and all, and not to forget to take his pills.' With trembling lips that blurred the words: 'Tha's when they said he was dead.'

'What mess?' Jurnet inquired sharply. Tawno Smith gave him an ironical look. Stricken but not surprised.

As for the woman, she made an exasperated gesture, as if the whole blasted business were an irrelevance. Quite right too, Jurnet conceded. What mess, however messy, could compare for messiness with death?

'What you hanging about out here for?' she demanded with anger in her voice. 'Come in an' see for yourself.'

Dr Tawno Smith stood amid the ruins of the study he had shared with his Uncle Max. The room was handsome, with french windows opening on to a comfortably untidy expanse of grass irradiated with the green and gold of high summer. Two substantial desks were placed end on to the garden well, so as to make the most of the light which flowed with impartial grace over smashed drawers and slashed upholstery. On the leather top of one of the desks someone had used a pointed instrument to score a crude representation of the Star of David.

As the physicist and the detective came further into the room, a large man standing looking out of the window turned to confront the arrivals. Just his luck, Jurnet reflected with wry amusement, to run into the one Cambridge cop he wouldn't be in any hurry to fish out of the Cam if he fell in off his punt.

'If it isn't Ben Jurnet!' exclaimed the man, uncovering a glut of teeth in an approximation of a smile. 'What brings you to this neck of the woods?'

'Dr Smith needs to collect some papers.'

'Enough here for him to be going on with.' The other surveyed the wreckage with a proprietorial air. He came away from the window, approached Tawno Smith who awaited him without expression, his gaze roaming the room, from the desks to the shattered screen of the word processor, to the smashed filing cabinet, and back again. It was extraordinary, Jurnet thought, how such a small man was in no way diminished by the proximity of the large detective.

'Detective Inspector Catton, sir,' the Cambridge man introduced himself. 'Nasty business altogether. Vicious. You'll be able to see what's been taken a little later. Just don't touch anything till my prints chap gets here. I'm just hanging on for him.'

Tawno Smith said: 'I know what's been taken.'

'What's that, sir?'

'Two copies of a paper I'm due to deliver at the Thaddeus Brigg Tricentennial. One was in the middle drawer,' – pointing to the desk which had its leather top unblemished – 'the other was in the filing cabinet.'

'Knew what they were looking for, did they? Wondered how they came to leave that case with the medals in it. Gold, are they?'

Tawno Smith closed his eyes briefly. All the strength seemed to have gone out of him.

'It doesn't matter – ' he began thickly.

'Not matter!' Detective Inspector Catton cried. Modulating his tone to one of an oozing sympathy that made Jurnet cringe: 'Naturally you're upset. And the Professor as well . . .' The large man manoeuvred his bulk so as to exclude the Angleby interloper from the action.

Jurnet commented coolly: 'Got in by the window, I see!' Before Catton could object, he went over to the french door, one pane of which had been removed with a skill it was a pleasure to behold: not a sliver left to catch the tell-tale strand of wool or polyester which could give the game away. Cheeky bugger, thought Jurnet, considering all the havoc wrought within, to have left the glass propped so carefully against the outside wall. As much as to say, 'Saved you the price of a new pane, anyhow!'

11

When the Superintendent had finished speaking, Tawno
Smith stayed stiffly upright in the chair to which Jurnet
had shown him. His eyes remained fixed on the police
officer, not in any apparent expectation of more to
come, but as if lacking the strength or the purpose to
look elsewhere. The distant clatter of the Market,
coming through the open window, was suddenly an
intolerable intrusion. The Superintendent got up briefly
from his seat and shut it off, sealing in the silence
which, radiating from the still, silent figure, diffused
itself through the room, changing the quality of the air.
For once, even the Superintendent seemed at a loss.
Then, frowning slightly, he lifted the telephone receiver
and requested tea.

The still, silent man began to laugh.

'Oh you English! First you inform me that I've killed
my Uncle Max and then you give me tea!' The laughter
did not last. Coolly, without hysteria, Tawno Smith
announced, 'I can't bear it.'

Jurnet amended: 'Administered the fatal dose, sir.
The person who did the killing was the one who put
the poison in the orange juice.'

'I should have gone for some water. Uncle Max was
always saying the citric acid would affect the action of
the pills. He just didn't have the strength to refuse. If
I hadn't insisted–!'

'If you hadn't insisted,' interposed the Superintendent, back to full control of the situation, 'and – having
first procured some water for your uncle – had drunk
the juice yourself, as was no doubt intended, the Pro-

fessor, so long as he surmounted his heart problem, would, in all likelihood, be alive today, and you, not to put too fine a point on it, the corpse in the mortuary drawer.' The Superintendent leaned forward in his chair. 'Let me make myself quite clear, Dr Smith. Angleby CID has a murder to solve, a murderer to bring to justice. With the best will in the world, it cannot take on board your personal anguish at having inadvertently administered a lethal dose of cyanide to a much loved relative. Of course,' – with a small smile to accompany a small joke – 'if it was you yourself who doctored the juice and gave it to your uncle with criminal intent, that is another matter.' The smile expanding: 'One you will, of course, expect us to investigate along with all the other possibilities.'

'Investigate away! I plead guilty before you start. Guilty of being glad, even at such a price, that it isn't me who's dead.' After another period of silence, Tawno Smith added: 'Not that even that is the worst thing.'

'How do you mean?'

'I mean, what's the alternative? Round that table in the castle were the people who matter most to me in the world. What you are telling me is that one of them wants me dead.'

'No. Simply that somebody wants you dead. No more than that, at the moment.'

'Simply!' The other sighed. 'As soon as I found my paper gone from the hotel room I should have guessed. When I found the remaining copies gone from Cambridge I should certainly have guessed. What was the good of stealing my work so long as I was still around to replicate it? It had to be me who needed to be put out of the way.'

With a hesitancy which betrayed his fear of finding himself out of his depth, the Superintendent inquired: 'What, in very general terms, is the subject of your paper?'

'You want to know why anyone should go to such

lengths to get their hands on it,' Tawno Smith returned with instant understanding. 'Don't worry, Superintendent. I haven't written a recipe for a bigger and better bomb. I'm a theoretical physicist, a kind of parasite, in a way, battening on other men's work, sucking the essential juices out of it. No,' – rejecting his own assessment – 'more a co-ordinator, a chap with a good eye who juggles such pieces of the jigsaw as are presently available, trying to make sense of them despite the gaps. Trying to predict what the missing pieces must be, and how they fit into the overall pattern. Whereupon' – caught up in his work despite himself – 'the theorist dumps it all back in the lap of the experimenter, saying in effect, "Your move, fellow! See what you can do about making my prophecies come true." ' Tawno Smith sat back in his seat, the compact body remaining tense and watchful. 'And so it goes on,' he finished, changing the metaphor, 'to and fro, the ball first in one court, then in the other. Except that all the time, if you get my meaning, the court, the game itself, moves on a bit, always advancing a fraction nearer – '

'Nearer what?' The Superintendent did not disguise his impatience. 'You still haven't explained what makes your paper so special someone would commit murder for it.'

'When you find him, he'll be the one to ask, won't he?'

The sudden hostility which had sprung up between the two men took Jurnet by surprise. Was it, on the Superintendent's part, rooted in his ill-concealed dissatisfaction with his own ignorance of particle physics? Or had the older man, facing the handsome gipsy across the width of his desk, felt suddenly that sexual jealousy of which he, Jurnet, was only too conscious?

'I fully intend to,' the Superintendent said smoothly. 'Which, however, I'm sure you'll agree is no reason for not canvassing your own thoughts on the subject.'

'You want me to rat on my friends.'

'Only on the one friend – if that is the right word for him, or her – who killed the man to whom, from all I hear, you owe everything. Ah!' he concluded, as a diffident knock sounded at the door and before Tawno Smith, pale and quivering, could say anything, 'The tea!'

12

It wasn't the way out of Angleby Jurnet would have chosen for a country drive. Almost any other of the many roads which radiated from the city like the spokes of a wheel would have had more to offer than this uninspiring expanse of sugar beet and potatoes, diversified only by the occasional square of fallow lying zonked out under its latest fix of superphosphates. Even the measureless Norfolk sky which so often produced its own Himalayan cloudscapes to compensate for any lack of drama down below had withdrawn behind a sheet of yellowed white that looked as if it could do with a good soak in Chlorox.

Detective Sergeant Jack Ellers, manoeuvring the Rover from road to progressively narrower road, each worse paved than the one which had preceded it, slowed at a fork which proclaimed, on both arms of a lichen-stained fingerpost: 'Feldon St Awdry'.

'Christ! As if one way wasn't enough to the end of the world!'

'You want the left one,' Jurnet directed. 'The church. The vicarage is right across from it. It's a good mile out of the village – the present village, that is. According to

69

the vicar, as I recall, the original one was abandoned during the Black Death and, except for the church, left to fall into ruins.'

'A real fun place!' The little Welshman changed down and veered left as instructed. After another mile of winding along a track apparently bent on putting off the moment of arrival anywhere, suddenly, as if unseen stagehands had just that moment manhandled it into position, Feldon St Awdry church showed on the horizon, a small round tower of no distinction, with some equally apologetic masonry tacked on to it. The Victorian vicarage which presently came into view alongside, its crowding chimneys proclaiming an amplitude of hearths if not of fires to warm them, had more authority.

'The church probably looks better inside now than when I was here last,' said Jurnet, moved by some obscure impulse of pity. Since putting into train the long-drawn-out process of conversion to Judaism he had come to feel a fellow-frailty with all religious incertitudes, in whatever form expressed. 'It was all swathed in cloths and scaffolding then. Some medieval wall paintings, or something. The vicar was quite excited about the work going on.'

'Probably hoping God would move back in once the dilapidations were taken care of.' Ellers surveyed the prospect with a dispassionate eye before shaking his head. 'Shouldn't care to take a bet on it.'

The church door creaked open, and again shut. At the sound, the man kneeling at the chancel rail crossed himself and rose to his feet unhurriedly, his cassock resuming its accustomed folds. Hands clasped calmly in front of him, he watched the newcomers approaching up the narrow aisle, one behind the other, stumbling a little over the corrugations of the ancient tombstones which served as paving. Jurnet noticed, as he had noticed at their earlier meeting over the little matter of the stolen plate, that, at home in his church, Simon Maslin did not twitch. The smile, however, all teeth and gum, was unchanged. The man still looked a silly ass.

Not the only one, thought the detective. What about him and Jack, shambling up the aisle with their jaws dropping open, like two village idiots?

The cloths and scaffolding were gone. Boasting no stained glass, the building was full of light. Light which seemed to have concentrated itself on the wall above the simple altar table draped with a tapestry runner which had seen better days. Light which tipped the brass cross in the middle of the table and the candlesticks on either side.

Light which illumined the encounter of Salome and John the Baptist.

The painting had been done in sepia, a vibrant earth which stood out from the cream-washed background with an explicitness at once magnificent and hugely comic. Its creator had had much to learn about the proportions of the human body, nothing as to its potentialities.

Writhing in a series of astonishing convolutions, their veils long discarded, not one but half a dozen Salomes – presumably the nearest a fourteenth-century painter could come to cartoon animation – revolved, limbs intertwined, about an enormous head which lay on a platter garnished with salads and comfits, for all the world like the chef's special. All that was missing was the pile of plates at the side and the cutlery ready-wrapped in napkins. The circling Salomes looked hungry in every sense of the word, alive with eager anticipation.

As for the saint, one could only say that, even minus a body, he didn't look martyred. If appearances were anything to go by, he was enjoying the party as much as anyone, the protuberant eyes bright with lust. High up the wall, regarding the rave-up below with the indulgent eye of a parent happy to see the young ones enjoying themselves, an elderly gent in a long beard held up a hand in benediction; across his lap, like a rug to keep his old bones warm, a headless body that was presumably the rest of the saint's mortal remains. Blood dripping in large, pear-shaped drops from the severed neck traced a pattern down the plaster to unite, with miraculous rightness, the two elements of the composition, the masterpiece.

Jurnet, reassembling his jaw, called out: 'You're going to find yourself up in front of the Bench over that lot!'

The clergyman stood his ground until the two detectives reached him, when he shook hands and gracefully acknowledged his introduction to Sergeant Ellers. 'Splendid, isn't it?' he shook his head smilingly. 'The policeman's eye, if you don't mind my saying so. Expect evil and you will find it. The bishop's been, and the dean, and the chancellor of the diocese, and they were all – enchanted's the only word. A transcendental allegory of sacred and profane love, was what the bishop said: a testimony to the eternal freshness of the Gospel story.' With a boyish enthusiasm: 'The television people are coming tomorrow to make a film – and once people see it! Our local bobby's already been in touch with your traffic branch. They're going to set up a one-way system so that people can come in by the church road and go back through the village.' The vicar sighed. 'I'm afraid we shall lose some of our wonderful peace and quiet, but, on the other hand,' – the man's face glowed – 'we shall be going back to a service every Sunday – perhaps even two, if there is sufficient demand! – instead of just one in four.'

'It sounds all go,' said Jurnet, wondering how the impending pilgrims, facing that east wall, were going to be able to keep their minds on the sacred aspects of the allegory as against the only too visible onslaughts

72

of the profane. He explained: 'We rang the bell at the vicarage. Mrs Maslin seemed to be out – '

'She's gone into Angleby to try and persuade Tawno to come back with her. When he phoned last night to tell us the dreadful news, she begged him to come to us, but he said no. We want him out here for his own safety, if nothing else. After all, whoever tried to kill him may well try again.'

'Very likely. We did offer him a degree of police protection but he turned it down flat. He's got guts, I'll say that for him.'

In the vicarage kitchen, a cavernous space haunted by the ghosts of Edwardian skivvies – a room, thought Jurnet, for which a covey of Salomes cavorting on the khaki walls would have done wonders – Simon Maslin, back to all fingers and thumbs once off the church premises, made tea for his visitors, sloshing the water on to the tea bags, filling the mugs to the brim and over. Jurnet, refusing sugar in an oblique homage to his absent love who had strong opinions on the subject, stirred the beverage notwithstanding, adding an additional pool of brown to the one already soaking into the deal table.

It had not taken long to elicit the information – if you could call it that – that the clergyman, at the castle banquet, had, or chose to say that he had, noticed nothing significant relating to the cyanide in the orange juice. Indeed, or so he asserted, he had not even observed the glass of juice on the table, Tawno being the cynosure of all eyes and everyone gathered about him in a jostle of pleasure and excitement.

'We were all so happy,' Maslin protested, the pale blue eyes opening widely. 'It is Tawno's special gift. When he is present, it is suddenly more sweet to be alive.'

'All happy?' The detective seized on the phrase. 'Even the joker who dropped death into the glass? You're a churchman, sir. In the way of business you have to be a bit of a psychologist. Think hard. Wasn't there something you noticed, something out of character, something even in the smallest degree unusual or disquieting?'

The answer came back as before.

'We were all so happy.'

Jurnet stirred his tea again.

'I suppose, after you and your family left the castle, you all joined Dr Smith at the Norfolk and Angleby?'

'Hardly joined. We went there, of course, Adam and Nina Pender with us. By the time we got there, though, it was all over and Tawno was just leaving. He looked so awful we wanted to go back to the hotel with him, but he said he'd rather be alone. He said that the Ahilars – the Israelis, you know – had already come by with the same suggestion, and he'd turned them down too.'

'Dreadful thing to happen,' Jurnet commented vaguely. Then, in a confiding manner not free from calculation: 'I'm in a funny position, sir, and I'm hoping you can help me.'

'I'm not sure.'

'It's like this, sir. Whenever we – the Force, that is, the CID – find ourselves with a case of murder on our hands, the first thing we need to know, the first person rather, is the victim. What kind of man was he? What in his life marked him out for a violent end? Unfortunately, in the general way of things, we can't ask the person most concerned. He's lying in the morgue, not giving interviews to anybody. In this particular case, though we're up against something out of the usual run. Professor Flaschner, poor old gentleman, is dead sure enough, but in a sense – if we're correct in our assumption that the poisoned juice was intended for another – he isn't *our* victim, just the bloke that got in the way.'

'Tawno – '

'Exactly!' the detective concurred heartily. 'Dr

Tawno Smith. 'Now,' – leaning across the table – 'you might think that ought to make things easy. For once our *corpus delicti*, so to speak, is still walking around and breathing the air. For once we can question him directly, find out who wanted him dead.' With a shake of the head: 'It doesn't follow by any manner of means. The bloke may not have a clue as to who harbours homicidal intentions against him. He may even be under the delusion that the killer is his best friend.'

Simon Maslin echoed: 'His best friend.'

'Could be!' the detective confirmed blandly, as if the other had been the one to make the suggestion. 'A case like this, I don't mind admitting, is a bit of an object lesson. Number of times I've looked down at a body with its skull bashed in and thought, if only the dead could speak. And yet here I am, with the dead, as you might say, alive and kicking, and still I have to go round cap in hand to those who knew, who know him.' Jurnet drank deeply of his tea, and replaced the mug with precision on the ring it had already made on the table top. 'Rum old world, sir.'

The clergyman smiled his foolish smile. His words were not foolish.

'You are wondering, Inspector, are you not, how somebody like me, with nothing to recommend him, could possibly call a man like Tawno Smith friend.' Jurnet saying nothing either to confirm or deny the allegation, the man continued, amusement and affection alike in his voice. 'You could not be more surprised than myself. You may possibly think it is because Tawno, like all kings of men, needs a court jester, and I, God knows, was born to fill that role – but you would be wrong. Just as you would be wrong to think it is because he sleeps with my wife and I am what I believe is known as a complaisant husband. Though he does the one, and I am the other. We are friends because we find ourselves bound together by those bonds of love which are, of all its manifestations, the purest and least self-interested, based as they are on mutual respect unsullied by sexual jealousy or other forms of greed.'

There was a sputter of rubber-soled footsteps hurrying down an uncarpeted stair, quieter along a flagstoned floor. A door opened and banged to. The clergyman's smile intensified, the teeth, or so it seemed, multiplying.

'Christopher,' he explained. 'He'd meant to go in to the Tricentennial, only he was too upset by the news about Uncle Max. I expect he's gone for a run – I hope so. It will do him the world of good. Do you run, Inspector Jurnet?'

'Only if someone's after me.'

'A pity. It's the best restorative in the world.' The clergyman got up from his seat, went over to the window and peered out. 'Ah, there he goes, into the spinney. He'll be doing the four-mile round, unless he turns off to the quarry, and makes it six. Splendid!'

Overlaying Simon Maslin's foolish smile was a tenderness of fond reminiscence.

'That's how I came to be Tawno's friend, actually – by running. I knew about him before, of course. He was already one of the great men of the college, indeed, of the University. I knew him as one might know the Queen or the Prince of Wales by standing on the kerb, watching them drive past. He didn't know that I existed. Why should anyone want to know me, poor, shambling creature that I was, with nothing to recommend me but an undiscriminating love of my fellow men? I had had a lonely childhood, Inspector, an only child, my parents elderly, my father the priest of a remote parish in the fens where people were twisted with the damp and their own dark imaginings. I only started to run – running as a crucial part of my life, I mean – because, when I was fourteen, one of those same people, a big man with a small head and eyelids that were always half-shut, came after me. I had no idea what purpose he might have had in mind, only

76

that I was frightened silly and ran away, along one of those raised paths you find fringing the dykes in that part of the world. I ran faster and faster in an ecstasy of fear, until – I hardly know how to describe it – something happened. Suddenly, I wasn't frightened any longer, and I moved with none of that awful awkwardness which seemed to be programmed into me. Through God's grace I was vouchsafed a vision not of the divine but of the wonderful possibilities of my own body. Marvellous! So marvellous that I turned and ran back past my pursuer, even smiling at him as we bumped elbows on the narrow path.'

The clergyman stayed quiet for a little. Then he said: 'I don't think I could have got through my first year at Bilney without running. Every morning, soon as there was a glimmer of light in the sky, I was up and out – none of your miserable jogging, but running at speed; running for my life, literally, out of the college, out of the town, out into the fields misty with the rising dew. By the time I got back I had garnered the strength to endure another day.

'The funniest thing,' said the Revd Maslin with a chuckle, 'was that the day I got to know Tawno – or, to put it more accurately, that day he got to know me – there he was, running beside me for a good fifteen minutes before I even noticed he was there. Later he told me that, an early riser himself, he had often looked out of his window and seen me crossing the quad, and that particular morning, on an impulse, and because I always looked as if I were enjoying myself, he decided to join me – waited for me, in fact, and then, when I emerged from my stair, simply fell into step as though that was what we had been doing together for donkeys' years.

'You won't believe this, but it must have been at least ten days running together before we exchanged so much as a word.'

Jurnet said: 'I can believe it. You get caught up in the rhythm.'

'That was it exactly! Are you quite sure you don't run? The rhythm!' The clergyman rolled the word on his tongue. 'So that when we *did* begin to communicate – in words, that is: our bodies were already old friends, comfortable with each other – we were able to dispense with the meaningless preliminaries. And we have stayed friends ever since.'

'Still running?'

'I can't speak for Tawno. Christopher and I go out every morning. He's a kind boy who moderates his pace to that of his aged parent.' Simon Maslin said with utter simplicity: 'When I wonder what will become of me when I can no longer run, I console myself with the hope that the Lord will find some other use for this poor, ageing carcass, though I can't for the life of me think what.'

Jurnet said: 'Now tell me about Mrs Maslin.'

With a great and obvious effort, Mr Maslin became still. Breathing with care so as not to disturb this precarious equilibrium, he said: 'I've already told you all you need to know.'

'Not all.'

Well, perhaps not all,' the other conceded. He looked across the table to where Sergeant Ellers, as discreetly as he could contrive, sat poised with notebook at the ready. 'I can see I shall have to tell you the rest, such as it is, otherwise you will send me to the top of your list of suspects. You will think the theft of Tawno's paper just a red herring to put you off the real scent.'

'Give us credit for having already taken that possibility on board.'

'Of course. You are the professionals.' Forehead creased: 'My difficulty is that telling you what you are pleased to call "all" may only confirm your suspicions, and I shall find myself in one of your dungeons at the precise time when Claire left orders, if she wasn't back, for me to put the casserole in the Aga. Forgive me.' The clergyman rose to his feet, his busy shoulders and arms disturbing the calm folds of his cassock. 'If I'm being frivolous, it must be because I am frightened. I feel a great need to run and know I must not.'

'Later,' said Jurnet kindly. 'There'll be plenty of time later.'

Simon Maslin said surprisingly: 'There were at least three other cars parked at Roudham Cross. The people in one of them were eating their lunch. Somebody's bound to have noticed me.'

'Roudham Cross?' asked Jurnet.

'Where the Peddar's Way crosses the A11.'

'I've heard about the Peddar's Way.'

'I'm sure you have,' the vicar responded courteously. 'The old Roman road that slices across Norfolk to the north coast. A lovely, lonely green way that I occasionally treat myself to – or a few miles of it at a time, anyway – as a change from Feldon.' The tombstone teeth exposed themselves briefly. 'There must have been better ways of passing a free afternoon than positioning myself a good half-way to Cambridge on the day Professor Flaschner's house was broken into. To say nothing of my gross ineptness in stopping off at the dry-cleaner's in Angleby on the way back.'

'What was that for?'

'To get Uncle Max's evening suit. He'd left it here ages ago, after he'd been down for a weekend – left it deliberately, because he hated dressing up and it made a good excuse to be able to say, truthfully, that his evening clothes were buried in the wilds of Norfolk. But for the Tricentennial there was no getting out of it. Only when Claire took the dinner jacket out of the cupboard where it had been hanging it smelled damp, the way I'm afraid all our clothes here get to smell if they aren't worn regularly. So Claire left it off at the cleaner's, and I picked it up on my way back from the Peddar's Way, and took it over to the hotel.'

The man paused and Jurnet commented: 'That doesn't sound all that incriminating.'

'You ain't heard nothing yet!' The foolish smile flashed out in all its glory. 'At the hotel desk they told me Uncle Max had already arrived and left instructions that he wasn't to be disturbed until six o'clock. I explained about the suit. It was only wrapped in one of those polythene covers and the clerk grabbed it as though it were a sack of coals. I didn't like the way he handled it at all. Uncle Max hated dressing up but when he did he was quite a dandy. So I took the suit back and said I'd prefer to take it up to Professor Flaschner's room myself. The fellow didn't want to let me, but I gave him a couple of pounds and promised to slip in and out as quiet as a mouse. And that's what I did.' Simon Maslin looked from Jurnet to Ellers and back again. 'Uncle Max was fast asleep, breathing heavily. I tiptoed over to the wardrobe and hung the suit up whilst the chambermaid who had let me in waited outside. Outside,' he repeated. 'Tawno told Claire his paper was stolen out of a briefcase left in that same wardrobe.'

'That appears to have been so. When you hung up the Professor's suit, did you see any signs that the case had been broken into?'

The clergyman shook his head.

'I didn't even notice there was a case there. But then I would say that, wouldn't I, if I was the one who stole it?'

Jurnet replied smoothly: 'Sergeant Ellers will have got it all down.' He waited, a man not to be put off.

Simon Maslin asked with resignation: 'Claire?'

'If you please.'

'She's talented,' said Simon Maslin, 'as well as lovely to look at. Even all those years ago, before she'd even finished her training, she was beginning to make a name for herself. Liberty's had a display of her earrings when she was still a student.'

'Was that when you met her?'

'Later than that. I'd just begun my first curacy. At Culverton, that was, near St Neots. I don't know whether you know it? Delightful church with a splendid font cover, a real treasure. Claire herself comes from Wimbledon, actually, but at that time she was working for some jewellery people with a place just outside Cambridge on the Huntingdon road. As a matter of fact, she still designs for them, on a freelance basis. They think the world of her.'

Jurnet inquired patiently: 'So you met her in Cambridge?'

The vicar looked surprised.

'Haven't I said? She was living with Tawno.'

'With Dr Smith?'

'Well, not exactly living. Not cohabiting, which I believe is the technical term. Tawno lived with Uncle Max at Heathcote Avenue and Claire had a little flat in Trumpington, but – well, let us say they belonged together.' The man's face shone. 'It was a very beautiful thing to see.'

'So at the time you weren't yourself in the running?'

'Running?' Simon Maslin looked amused. 'In the running for Claire's affections, you mean? Even I, who in those days could run like the wind, couldn't run fast enough for that. Let us say that, whenever I visited them – and I was a frequent and, I dare to hope, welcome visitor – I basked in the reflected sunshine of their happiness.'

With calculated brutality Jurnet asked: 'So how come, then, she's Mrs Maslin, not Mrs Smith?'

'What a pity it is you don't know Tawno better!' If the man showed any sign of taking umbrage it was all on behalf of his absent friend. 'He's a free spirit, he won't be bound, even in the most loving bondage.

81

Neither will he engage himself, he who is so full of love, to love one to the exclusion of all others. Do you know what the word *Camo-mescro* means in Romany? Tawno told me. It means "lover". *Cam* is the Romany word for love – and Tawno lives in Cambridge! Isn't that a remarkable coincidence!'

'Amazing. May I ask if the lady was happy with the arrangement?'

'The lady was – the lady is – very happy.'

'Christopher,' said Simon Maslin. He went over to the window for the second time. 'I expect he'll have gone round by the quarry, it's such a super afternoon. They're old quarry workings, actually: flooded, the water unbelievably clear. On a day like this the reflections of the sky – ' He broke off, came back to the table, said again, 'Christopher. That's the answer to your question, Inspector. You see, Claire became pregnant.'

'And still Tawno wouldn't marry her?'

The clergyman shook his head in amusement.

'How refreshingly old-fashioned you sound! Claire was going to have an abortion. When I went to see them they both spoke about it quite openly. It could have been an appointment with the dentist. It didn't seem to have occurred to either of them that, as a priest, I was bound to take the news badly. It simply hadn't occurred to them that anyone could feel so strongly on the subject. It was quite a disgraceful performance on my part' – the man smiled, a little shyly – 'because, as I went on and on, mouthing the usual platitudes about the sacredness of human life, I felt a nasty vein of self-interest beginning to take over. I suddenly saw how I, the impotent – yes, Inspector, impotent – clown they tolerated out of the goodness of their hearts, bless them, could become an integral part of that happiness in which those two lived, moved and had their being. For once I found myself possessed, if not by that gift of tongues

82

which transformed the Apostles, by an eloquence equally beyond my normal halting efforts. By the time I had finished I had persuaded them both that not only was it an act of criminal irresponsibility to abort a human foetus, but that the resulting child had a God-given right to a life in a secure and socially acceptable environment. Preaching unselfishness out of the depths of my own selfishness, I did the one thing in my life of which I am unashamedly proud. I left the way clear for Christopher.'

Jurnet digested this news for a moment, then asked: 'And the boy? Does he know?'

'The boy does not know. Had he turned out black-haired and brown-skinned, he would have needed to be told. Fortunately he is fair like his mother and the problem did not arise.' A sudden concern bleaching the colour out of the man's cheeks: 'You understand that I give you this information in total and absolute confidence, never to be divulged in any circumstances?'

'I understand.'

Only partly reassured, Simon Maslin cried: 'He's *my* son, you understand? Mine!'

'I understand.'

'Mine and Claire's, that is, but chiefly mine. Claire's a good mother and Christopher, I'm quite sure, is conscious of no deprivation of mother-love. But always, in the way of things, he has had to come second in her heart and mind. If Tawno and Christopher were in the same house together and it caught fire, and Claire could save only one, it would be Tawno she'd choose, even if she had to sacrifice her own life to do it. I accept that. It's part of the bargain.' After a short silence he added: 'If I'm to be completely honest, I even welcome it. It makes Christopher all the more my son, and I his father.'

In some agitation, and with a clatter which threatened their survival, Simon Maslin cleared away the mugs. Back from the sink: 'Think what my life would have

83

been without them! Buried alive and alone in an obscure parish, unloved, I fear, even by the God I seek to serve with heart and soul. Instead of which' – the clergyman's face glowed – 'I have a family to love, and a family to love me.'

'And Dr Smith? Is he content to back off completely? Christopher looks as if he has all the makings of an exceptional young man.'

The other responded lovingly: 'He has been full of promise from babyhood. Not surprising in one who has Tawno's brains and Claire's beauty and artistic sensitivity. From somewhere – humbly, I may have done a little towards it, sown a seed – he also has a sense of divine purpose, a faith which is strong and positive. Tawno recognises Christopher's qualities, loves him, takes an interest in everything he does – but no more. The two of us are not in competition. As he has told me more than once, other than biologically, he is not one of nature's fathers.'

Jurnet leaned back in his chair, and said easily: 'Just the same, I don't suppose he'll be sorry if the youngster goes in for physics, same as him.'

'Tawno will be glad if he goes in for whatever makes him happiest.' But the man sounded less sure. 'Zero hour!' he explained, taking avoiding action. 'The casserole – and I think I'll whip up a lemon meringue pie for dessert while I'm about it. Christopher can cheerfully put away half of one at a sitting, if he gets the chance!' The foolish smile no longer looked so foolish to Jurnet. 'If, by your last remark, Inspector, you meant to suggest that I might easily kill Tawno if I felt he was pressuring Christopher into doing physics when the boy has a God-given vocation for the priesthood, the answer is yes, I might kill him. But not easily.'

13

Back in Angleby, Jurnet had Jack Ellers drop him off at the castle bailey. He fancied a word with the museum curator.

'He was there at the table, part of the crowd milling round the gipsy baron. I remember thinking at the time, what's he want?'

'Want me to run you up to the bridge? It must be nearly time for them to knock off for the day.'

'Good!' responded Jurnet, who had taken an admittedly unreasonable dislike to Alistair Tring. 'Buggers in a hurry to get off are buggers off guard. I'll get out here, ta. I could do with stretching my legs.'

After he had gone, dodging the traffic across the road, Sergeant Ellers waited a little before driving away; watched as Jurnet began the ascent, part path, part stair, that zigzagged up the castle mound towards the plateau where the great keep squatted like a giant toad, stonily regarding the city below. The long legs moved effortlessly, the pace unfaltering, even when the steps became steep and shallow, mere toeholds hacked out of the hillside.

'Up yours, Valentino!' The chubby Welshman smiled as he slipped the car into gear.

Arrived at the top, Jurnet, who had felt himself under observation all the way up, leaned against the railings with lungs bursting, wondering who the hell he was trying to impress, and why.

The commissionaire at the turnstile, with a satisfaction he made no attempt to disguise, said: 'Closing time in five minutes.' When the detective produced his ID card and asked for the curator, he looked as if an unfair advantage had been taken of him. Whilst the man phoned through for instructions, Jurnet noted that Diana was back in the lobby, the marble nipples taut, apparently none the worse for her recent ordeal in the Gents. Further down the corridor the great black Buddha sat empty-lapped, enigmatic as ever.

The commissionaire came back and said, above the fretful buzz of the electric bell announcing the imminence of closing time, that Dr Tring was in the Exhibitions Gallery, down the corridor, third on your right. 'You'll have to ask him to let you out,' the man warned, in a tone which suggested it was by no means certain that permission would be granted.

The room was the nave of a cathedral, lit only by the light filtering through glass coloured in patterns which somehow awakened correspondences. The room was nothing of the kind, Jurnet corrected himself, recovering from his initial shock of pleasure and discomfort. It was a perfectly ordinary gallery hung with pictures illuminated by strip-lighting. As to what the pictures, with their multi-coloured swirls against a black background, signified, that was another matter. *The Art of the Bubble Chamber and the Particle Detector*, proclaimed the notice over the entrance.

A voice out of the gloom commented: 'Not bad, eh?' Alistair Tring's little beaked face was aglow with self-satisfaction. 'Finest museum display of the year, if I say it myself! We're a bit late getting it all together, but if anything in this bloody shindig was worth waiting for, this is it. What the hell do you want, anyway?' The last words were appended without animosity. It was clear that, in his present mood, the curator of Angleby museum welcomed any spectator of his triumph.

'What are they supposed to be?'

'Be? Subatomic particles or something. Things that go bump in the night. Does it matter?'

'Who painted them then? Or are they photos?'

Enlarged hugely behind his outsize spectacles, the curator's eyes sought the ceiling.

'Does a copper have to have everything tagged as Exhibit A before he can trust his own judgement? Suppose I told you they were the trails of rockets going off, or the tracks of tropical snails? Would that make them any more or any less beautiful?'

Jurnet maintained doggedly: 'I like to know what I'm looking at.'

'Fuck you!' Alistair Tring said, and touched a wall switch. The gallery sprang into brightness, the pictures retreated, their magic gone. Abstract art, not Jurnet's cup of tea at all.

'These the ones to tell me all about it?' the detective persisted, nodding towards a pile of leaflets on a table by the door. 'I'll have one of those.'

'They're 35p,' the other said sharply, pocketing the proffered coins. 'We're closing now.'

Jurnet put the leaflet in his pocket and said: 'Actually, I came by to ask why, at the Tricentennial banquet, you went over to Professor Flaschner's table.'

'To put cyanide in Tawno Smith's orange, why else? Also to ask him if he'd do the official opening bit for this exhibition. Where he goes the press and TV follow, and I wanted all the coverage I could get for free. As it was' – with an undisguised distaste – 'all those bosoms and bums . . . You talk about my going over to Flaschner's table, but I never got within a mile of it.'

'Oh ah? I'd fancied myself you were closer than that. Still, you didn't happen to notice anything – anything out of the ordinary in any way?'

Alistair Tring said, the high red in his cheeks brightening further with the excitement of uttering something it were wiser not to say: 'There was a boy. I thought he looked divine.'

'Ah!' Jurnet countered with determined stolidity.

'That'll be young Christopher, the Reverend Maslin's son. That's the lot, then?'

'That's the lot, unless you want to include the foreign-looking guy with a bush of hair the birds could nest in.' The curator's hand, unaware, smoothed the curator's own thinning locks back from the curator's brow. 'One of those.'

'Got it in one. Mr Ahilar does come from Israel.'

'Reckoned he must, when I saw him with the glass of orange juice in his hand.'

'In his hand!' Jurnet did not grudge the man the flash of pleasure behind the spectacles. 'Drink any?'

Alistair Tring shrugged his shoulders.

'Not unless he snufled it up his schnozz. The glass was only half-full and he had that long Jewish proboscis of his poked in so deep that when, eventually, he took it out, he had to polish the bloody thing dry on his table napkin.' The man finished blandly: 'I took it to be an old Semitic custom.'

Let out of the castle by a door used mainly, to judge from the cartons and bags piled outside, for the expulsion of waste from the castle cafeteria, Jurnet walked slowly round to the arcaded west front of the keep which, like an actress insisting on being photographed on her best side, was the one which was always shown on the picture postcards. From below rose the evening noises of the city: cars, buses at peak-hour density, voices, footsteps, churned into a syncopation of Angleby throwing off its daytime shackles. What matter if the coming dark held out little more than the prospects of snores in front of the telly? The moment of release remained one of infinite promise.

Jurnet looked down on the streets he loved. A fine city, so the tourist publicity went, with a Norman cathedral and more churches than you could use up in a month of Sundays. Also – though this tended not to get into the glossy brochures – villains and ponces, and drugs that went *crac!* in the night. Also orange juice that old gents like Professor Flaschner quaffed before dropping dead on the spot.

The memory of the pictures he had just seen still stayed with him, got between him and the reality below, their lovely lines spiralling upward into the air that shimmered above the red-pantiled roofs. A little ashamed, he blinked to dissolve the fantasy, and concentrated his attention on the flesh and blood crowds he could see below hurrying home to their teas.

So the world was just a bowl of subatomic particles, was it? Big cheese! Did particles have feelings? Could they taste the pains of death, the joys of love? *Physicists!* he thought indulgently. Children playing with marbles.

Back at Headquarters, the duty sergeant, not one of Jurnet's favourite people, beckoned him across to the desk as the detective attempted to make his way unobtrusively upstairs.

'Not your day, Ben,' the man announced. 'Two smashers in to see you, and you have to be out.'

'You could have told the Superintendent.'

'I could have told the Chief, but oh no! Nobody but Detective Inspector Jurnet would do!' The duty sergeant rolled his eyes in the kind of mime he was convinced made him one of the most popular chaps on the Angleby establishment. Jurnet swallowed hard and managed, amiably enough: 'Did they arrive with each other?'

'The one with the blonde hair and the baby face – some baby! I've got the names and the times here – she'd been waiting a good twenty minutes when the dark one showed. *Olé!* A pair of castanets and some clicking heels and it could have been Benidorm any Saturday night.'

'Did they leave together?'

'Know who they were, do you?' The man was irrepressible. 'Some people have all the luck! Yes, they left together. Seemed a little embarrassed to find the other one here. I got 'em both a cup of cha. The dark one give me a smile – phew! That's a hot number, as I don't suppose I have to tell you. The other looked a bit peaky, I thought. In the end, said they couldn't wait any longer, and they'd be back tomorrow. Told them to take my advice and phone for an appointment, you were in such demand.'

The duty sergeant's merry laughter followed Jurnet up the stairs, where the detective found the Superintendent on the point of transferring his gold fountain pen from his desk to his pocket, unfailing sign that he was about to call it a day. First thing every morning he placed it reverently in front of him, a kind of mini-mace, to signify that the house was in session. Feeling bloody-minded after his encounter below, Jurnet said without preliminaries: 'That man Ahilar, the Israeli. There could be an espionage angle.'

Alarm showed on the Superintendent's face before the safety curtains of sardonic humour descended, as usual.

'MI5, would that be, or MI6?'

'Both, probably. The man was seen with a half-full glass of orange juice in his hands. Sniffing at it.'

'Probably grows them himself back home and wanted to assess the competition.' The Superintendent, back in control, got to his feet. 'When you interview him, no doubt you'll ask him if he spies for a living.'

'Bit difficult at the moment. He and his granddaughter went to the hospital. When they heard Professor Flaschner was dead, Ahilar offered to accompany Dr Smith back to his hotel, an offer Smith refused. My information is that Ahilar then left to catch a train back to London, in order to get to Heathrow for his flight home to Israel.'

'The granddaughter accompanying him?'

'I understand she's now in Cambridge.'

'Ah. Good-looking girl, is she? We can't have a spy

story without a *femme fatale*.' The Superintendent sat down again. He didn't actually take the pen out of his pocket; only, when he spoke, it was with a change of tone equally significant.

'What on earth can there be in that paper of Smith's?'

'Whatever it is, it won't be long before the whole scientific establishment knows – so long as Dr Smith stays alive to do it over again. If it *was* Ahilar who stole it, or had it stolen, he must have understood, the minute he saw that it was Professor Flaschner who was dead, that he'd killed his dearest friend to no purpose.'

'Dearest friends, were they? They're always the most lethal.'

'Yes, sir,' agreed Jurnet, thinking of Miriam and assailed with a sudden intense desire for extinction in her arms. Aloud he said: 'They were in Treblinka together. The concentration camp.'

'I know what Treblinka was!' the Superintendent retorted. Subsiding: 'No, I don't. Any more than you do. Any more than anyone does who didn't actually go through that particular hell.' As if questioning himself rather than the other: 'Having survived Treblinka, how could you possibly bring yourself to kill someone who had survived with you?'

'We've agreed that the cyanide was intended for the Doctor.'

'Yes. Of course.'

Jurnet said, not hamming it up this time: 'Might be as well, just the same, to check whether the Smiley boys have got anything on him.'

'Fancy a jaunt to the Holy Land, do you?' the Superintendent inquired with delicate malice. Such oblique inflections were the nearest he allowed himself to expressing an opinion on his subordinate's so far unsuccessful efforts to become a Jew. Miriam being a tacitly agreed taboo subject between them, Jurnet's superior officer had no idea that she was, at that very moment, in Israel; no sense of the way Jurnet's heart strings jangled at the sudden prospect of a reunion there, how-ever brief.

The Superintendent understood better, perhaps – it was part of the compulsive game of hate and love, no winners, no losers, the two of them played obsessively – why the other chose (or perhaps did not choose, did it without thinking) to throw away all possible personal advantage by informing him, then and there, that, as it happened, that was where his fiancée was working at that very moment: and yes, in the circumstances he wouldn't be at all unhappy if his own work took him to the near neighbourhood.

The Superintendent received the intelligence without apparent interest. 'For heaven's sake, Ben, let's keep it simple, shall we? You know as well as I what those undercover jokers are like – only waiting for retirement and the sale of their memoirs to the *Sunday Times*. We're under no obligation to provide the scenario.'

'No, sir.' Having burnt his bridges to no purpose, Jurnet smiled at the instrument of his undoing. 'Not Jerusalem, then. Cambridge OK?'

'Cambridge OK.'

Jurnet sat at his kitchen table in his shirt sleeves eating the ham sandwich he had bought at the delicatessen on his way home. He had asked for ham deliberately, a little uncertain, though, towards whom his small defiance was directed – at Miriam, Judaism in general, or the telephone squatting on the bedside table beside the unmade bed.

As usual when he went out of his way to make gestures, this one rebounded on himself alone. The ham, despite its craftily enrobing mustard, was defi-nitely off. Jurnet dropped what was left of it into the waste bin under the sink and made himself a mug of tea to take the taste away. Lemon tea – natch. That ought to put things right with the Lord God of Hosts, mighty in battle.

The apology for a meal finished, he gave the mug a perfunctory rinse and fished the museum leaflet out of the jacket hanging over the back of the kitchen chair. He took it through to the living room and sat down in the armchair whose springs, at one with his mood, went *clunk!* in a terminal way.

The leaflet started off promisingly with a definition of the second law of thermodynamics which struck a chord of delighted recognition. So it wasn't just him: the best brains in the world were agreed that every day the whole bloody universe was sliding slowly but inexorably into chaos. You didn't have to be an Isaac Newton to work that one out. Any copper on the Angleby beat could have told you as much, without giving it a fancy name like entropy either. Except that, it seemed, entropy had a foreseeable end, an eventual state of equilibrium which was as far as you could go, the end of the line. More than could be said for the decline of law and order in his native city, which held out no such prospect of ever calling it a day.

It didn't take Jurnet long, however, to decide that a 35p pamphlet was not really enough to reveal the structure of the universe, let alone account for it. Electrons, quarks, positrons, protons, neutrons – to say nothing of those old pals, Professor Flaschner's neutrinos – they came at Jurnet from all directions, sliding down sunbeams, spinning like tumble dryers, swinging from star to star like demented acrobats.

The detective was aggrieved to discover that the pictures on the gallery walls were an elegant con, their jewel-like colourings added by clever processers, and the sprays and spirals which had struck such a mysterious resonance deep within his heart and brain not the real McCoy at all, but only the signs of its passing. The footprints of the yeti, not the real thing.

Jurnet went back into the kitchen where he deposited the leaflet on top of the remains of the sandwich; then, on second thoughts, fished it out again, on the chance it might at least furnish some names to flash around with careful casualness in his never-ending joust with the Superintendent.

He was under the shower when the telephone rang.

Leaping from the bath, he ran for the bedroom, leaving wet trails across the carpet, water from his hair dripping down the back of his neck. He flung himself at the phone, wrested the receiver from its base. Panted 'Hello!'

Wrong number.

14

The flat was in a rundown shopping street, its entrance between a Tandoori take-away and a pet shop where goldfish in a tank in the window goggled at passers-by as if they couldn't believe their eyes. A square of card, taped to a door which could have done with a lick of paint, said, the names listed one below the other: 'Anthea. Hats etc. Knock once. Mrs J. Piercy-Gibbs. Two knocks. Tracy Marberger. Thrice – and give me time to get down those damn stairs.'

Jurnet knocked three times. Despite having just come away from a cosy chat with DI Jim Catton, calculated to give anybody the runs, he felt at ease. He liked the street with its faint air of sleaziness, blessedly unlike the groves of Academe along the banks of the Cam, where even the trees, to the detective's jaundiced ear, rustled in a superior way, as if they too knew something denied to the common herd. After a while he knocked again, resisting an impulse to stop after the first knock in order to ask Anthea of 'Hats etc.' what the etc. stood for.

He had no fear of Catton's having pointed him in the wrong direction. The man knew his job. One day, when they were both old and grey, the two of them would get together over a beer and try to puzzle out why they hated each other's guts.

Overhead a sash window was pushed up, and a voice called. 'Who is it?'

Jurnet stepped back on the pavement so that Esther Ahilar could see him, and so that he could see the lovely face looking down.

'You are the policeman – '

'That's right, miss. I'd like a few words, if that's all right.'

'It is not very convenient.'

'I've come all the way from Angleby, miss. I'm sure you want to help the police with their inquiries into Professor Flaschner's murder . . .'

The girl stared down for a little. Then she said: 'I'll come down and let you in.'

'In October,' Esther Ahilar said, sitting on the divan in the poky little room, arms bare in her yellow shift, knees pressed as tightly together as if she feared for her virtue, 'when term begins, I shall live in the college.' Something, possibly nervousness, had made her accent more marked than the detective remembered it. 'This flat is lent to me by a friend who is now in America visiting her family, I have to do some preliminary reading so that when lectures begin I shall not be left behind.'

Contemplating her beauty but even more the strength that lay behind those dark eyes, Jurnet thought, you, doll, you'll never be left behind by anything or anyone. Out in front, in love or in war, carrying banners.

As if to give the lie to his pretensions to insight, the same eyes suddenly filled with tears.

'Uncle Max! I try to put him out of my mind, but then you have to come and remind me. Why, instead, aren't you out finding his murderer?'

'We're working on it, love. What else do you suppose I'm here for?'

'If you think I killed him, you're quite mad!'

'Did I say anything of the sort?' Jurnet responded peaceably. 'Only, look at it my way, Esther.' The girl looked up sharply at this use of her first name, searched the detective's face, and then let her gaze slide away, apparently satisfied. 'If I don't go about asking questions how am I ever going to find out anything?'

'What do you want to know?'

'That's more like it!' The detective, who had perched himself precariously on the high stool which, apart from the divan and several floor cushions covered with oddments of kelim, offered the only seating in the place, slid off and walked thankfully about the room, a couple of strides in any direction bringing him to window or wall. 'First, then, the dinner. At table. After Dr Smith arrived. Did you notice anything at all out of the ordinary? Anything at all?'

'Only Mrs Pender,' the girl returned, with a flash of humour that made her youth explicit. 'I'd never seen anyone like her. I'm sorry. I know you don't mean anything like that. And anyway you said "*after* Dr Smith". After he arrived, I didn't see anything after that.'

Anything or anyone apart from Tawno Smith: that's what you mean, isn't it? Aloud Jurnet said, 'Did you notice if anybody beside Dr Smith and your Uncle Max so much as touched that tumbler of orange juice?'

'Only Zeider did.' At Jurnet's uncomprehending stare she explained: 'It's the name he called his own grandfather when he was a boy in Lithuania. He is in the orange business. He knows more about oranges than anybody. He smelled the juice and said it was from Cyprus.' She finished endearingly: 'You have to be very good to tell Cyprus from Israeli.'

'He didn't say it smelled peculiar, unusual in any way?'

Esther Ahilar shook her head.

'Just Cyprus. He's always picking up glasses of juice. He does it automatically.' Red welled up under the golden skin. 'If you ask him and he says no, he never picked it up, that won't mean anything sinister. Just that he did it without thinking.'

'I'll bear that in mind.' The detective took out his notebook and made a business of writing something down. What he actually wrote was: 'Give the Super credit for guessing right about the oranges.' The notebook closed and returned to its place, he continued: 'When you and your grandfather left the castle, did you go straight back to your hotel? The Cotman, wasn't it?'

'Yes, the Cotman – and of course we didn't go straight back! We went to the hospital.' Again the eyes were bright with tears. ' And why am I crying now, for goodness' sake? Uncle Max was old, he was ill. I've seen a busload of Israeli soldiers blown apart by an Arab bomb and I didn't cry. Young men with their lives still in front of them. I felt many things, but not tears. So why should I cry for the death of one sick old man?'

Because you love Tawno Smith and are grieving for his grief, Jurnet thought to himself. Aloud, he said: 'Very natural, I'm sure.'

'And poor Grandfather! They were like brothers, you know. Not just because of the concentration camp numbers. They shared a past they couldn't share with anybody else. He was always popping over to England on business – so he said. But we all knew the real reason was to spend time with Uncle Max.'

'And you? Did you ever come with him?'

'Oh no! This is my first time in this country.'

'You speak English so well I assumed – '

'Thank you.' The girl inclined her head prettily. 'That is because my mother was English. She came to Israel in her university days to stay on a kibbutz, met my father, and never went back.'

'Ah!' Then: 'If you were never here before, then, to know your Uncle Max so well, he must have come to Israel?'

'Of course! Before he became ill, he came many times.'

'And Dr Smith with him?'

Esther Ahilar grew quiet, eyes cast down, the long lashes dark against the golden skin. She said softly: 'Once he came.'

'Tell me about it.'

'Uncle Max always talked so much about him. A scamp, he said, a genius: a strange and lovely creature a little bewitched. True or false, I made my picture of Tawno out of the things Uncle Max said.'

'When he came, were you disappointed?'

'I never saw him.' The eyes lifted from their rapt contemplation of the worn linoleum. 'I was away in the army, camping in the desert. The day I got my mother's letter to say he had arrived, was actually staying in our house, sleeping in my bed, I walked out into the desert and raged at God. I couldn't believe He could be so cruel.' The girl looked at the detective with something like pity. 'It isn't easy to speak of love to someone who – ' she stopped in embarrassment.

'Hasn't experienced it himself?' Po-faced, Jurnet finished for her. 'How right you are.'

Jurnet commented, not without guile: 'Your grandfather must have been glad to have you with him at such a time . . .'

The girl shot him a quick look.

'He had a plane to catch from Heathrow. My grandfather is a strong man, Inspector. His life has taught him to endure. There was nothing he could do for Uncle Max by staying on. Of course,' she added, 'if he'd known at the time that it wasn't a natural death, it would have been different.'

'Different in what way?'

Esther Ahilar said calmly: 'If he'd known, he would have remained in England, found out who was the murderer, and killed him.'

Jurnet observed, 'It shows a commendable confidence in the English police, I must say. You think we should ask him to come back and show us how to go about it?'

'Oh!' the Israeli girl did not even try to hide her contempt. 'You would drive him mad with your habeas corpus, identity parades, and whether or not you have evidence that will stand up in court – '

'We call it justice,' the detective interpolated mildly.

' – and in the meantime, while you are busy filling in the forms, the killer will get clean away.'

'More than your grandfather would do, if he started taking the law into his own hands. I'm afraid you'll just have to put up with us fuddy-duddies, bumbling on, asking questions, and questions, and more questions. Such as, for example, where did *you* take yourself off to, once you had seen Grandpa safely on the train to London?'

The girl took a long time answering. Long experience told Jurnet, from the way she bit her lip, glanced at the door as if willing some improbable deliverance, that she was adding up the pros and cons of lying to him. The detective found himself awaiting the outcome with an anxiety beyond the call of duty: and when at last, the issue decided, she squared her shoulders and looked him straight in the eye, he smiled back at her with something of the encouragement of a proud parent for a child who had done well.

The girl said: 'I went to the Virgin. To Tawno.'

Esther Ahilar said: 'I can't be sure if I went to the Virgin to comfort Tawno or to seduce him. Both, probably. I was quite crafty. When I asked at the desk if Dr Smith had come in, the receptionist looked at me in a certain way. I'm sure it is a very respectable hotel, and for a woman to ask for a man at that time of night is not respectable.' She gave a little laugh. 'I suppose he thought – well, you know.

'At first he didn't even want to telephone up to Tawno's room, saying the Doctor had left instructions he wasn't to be disturbed – but I made out it was about his uncle, who had just died, something important. I spelled out my name for him. Miss Ahilar: it sounded more respectable than Esther. In the end he did ring, and when Tawno answered, after a long time, the man said, "Room 314? There's a Miss Ahilar down here at the desk – " and so on, pronouncing my name in such a peculiar way that it could have been anybody. But now I knew the room number.

'Tawno must have said something like "Didn't I tell you I wasn't to be disturbed?" because the receptionist threw me an angry look. He put back the receiver and told me, grinning all over his face, that Dr Smith had said that whatever it was it would have to wait till the morning. I said thank you and left. The lift and the staircase were both in full view, so I went out of the front door and round to the back, where the car-park was. When I'd parked my car I'd noticed there was a door with a sign over it: *Staff Entrance Only*. I pushed the door open and there were some narrow stairs, not at all like the grand staircase in the front. I went up the stairs to Room 314.'

'Go on.'

'I knocked and I called through the door who I was, and after a long time Tawno came and unlocked it. He was wearing the silk dressing-gown Grandfather had given Uncle Max for his birthday. He looked like a little boy who had been dressing up in his papa's clothes. In spite of everything, I could not help smiling.'

The girl went on, tremulously: 'He wasn't at all pleased to see me. He'd been crying and perhaps he thought it wasn't manly to be seen with tears on his face. When I say that he wasn't pleased' – she amended carefully – 'I mean that his intelligence, whatever you care to call it, wasn't pleased. But the too-large dressing gown had fallen open, and I could see that his body – you understand what I'm saying? – was very pleased. For a little I thought it was going to be all right. But then, suddenly, he pushed me away, called me a word in Romany, a bad word, I could tell by the way he said it. He went to the dressing table, picked up a key and threw it at me. They key to the next door room.'

'Room 315. The Professor's.'

'Yes.' Esther Ahilar gave the detective a sombre look. 'I slept there, if you can call it sleep, lying on the bedspread, hoping against hope that Tawno would realise how right it was, how Uncle Max would have approved, that we should spend that night of all nights together. I took off my clothes so that if – when – he came I would be ready for him.' She said, with neither false modesty nor foolish pride, 'I am a virgin, Inspector Jurnet. They are still quite common in Israel among religious Jewesses, but I am not religious; and there have been times, I will not deny it, when I could have taken pleasure in performing the act of love. Except that there would have been no love about it. You will think me very sentimental,' – she leaned forward, as if the detective's opinion mattered to her – 'keeping myself pure for my true love the way they do in old-fashioned novels, but it was not like that at all. Only that, without love, it seemed not worth the doing.'

'Yes,' said Jurnet, who seemed to be hearing the story of his life. With deliberate insensitivity he demanded: 'Those clothes of yours – did you hang them up in the wardrobe?'

'I – I don't think so. I threw them down on a chair.'
She finished dully: 'He never came. In the morning,
soon as it was light, I dressed, went down the back
stairs again: got into my car and drove here.'

'That car,' said Jurnet, not sorry to have done with
the bedroom. Too many things didn't happen in bed-
rooms. Phones didn't ring, lovers didn't show. 'I got
the impression you and your grandad had only just
flown in for the Tricentennial?'

'That's right. We arrived that morning. Originally
Grandfather had decided to go to Bonn, but as I was
planning to go up to Cambridge early, and Uncle Max
had sent him a pair of invitations to the dinner, he
decided a little detour was in order.'

'And the car? A hire job?'

'No. The car is my birthday present, two months in
advance. Grandfather is wonderful to me. As soon as
he heard I'd been accepted at Cambridge he put in the
order, with all the documentation, and arranged for it
to be waiting for us at the airport.'

'So you drove straight from Heathrow to Angleby?'

'Almost straight. It was lovely. Even in summer
England is so green, isn't it? We were on the M11 when
there was this sign which said Cambridge, and we had
plenty of time. So I said, why don't we go there, long
enough to show you my college.'

'It was definitely *your* idea, then?'

'I think so. Does it matter? We'd been cruising along
through the lovely green country, the car going like
velvet.' The girl smiled with remembered pleasure. 'I'd
never had one before, all to myself. Somehow the idea
of Cambridge just developed naturally. Grandfather
said, "Uncle Max shouldn't be driving. Why don't we
pick him up and give him a lift to Angleby?" '

'So, then. What time did you and your grandfather
actually get to Cambridge?'

Esther Ahilar wrinkled her brow.

'Half-past two? Three? Something like that. Before

we did anything else, we found a phone box and rang Uncle Max up, but there was no reply. We tried again from the college, but he must have started out already. We were both upset we hadn't thought to telephone from Heathrow.'

'Were you and your grandfather together all the time you were in Cambridge?'

'I've already told you.'

'No time when he went off on his own, even to go to the Gents?'

'Why are you asking such things?' The lovely eyes flashed. 'He did go and get some petrol, if that's of any possible interest. He'd told them at Heathrow to have the car ready with the tank full, but for some reason they only put in four gallons. I gave him the car key and while I signed on in the college library, he went and got it filled up.'

'How long was he away?'

'If I'd known that an English policeman was going to ask such a question I would have made a note of it! All I know is, I filled in the form at the library desk, waited for them to make out a ticket, then I browsed along the shelves a bit. I took down an encyclopaedia from the reference section,' – colouring delightfully – 'I wanted to see what it said under "Gipsy" – I read what it had to say until Grandfather came back.'

'I see. I don't think you've told me the name of your college?'

'Magdalene.'

'I see,' Jurnet repeated, mentally calculating the distance between Magdalene Street and the Professor's house in Heathcote Avenue; how much time needed for the double journey, the careful removal of the pane of glass, for the slashing of upholstery, the making of an unholy mess. The girl's distrustful gaze upon him, he inquired in a lighter tone: 'And what did the encyclopaedia tell you about gipsies?'

Esther Ahilar answered with a sombre satisfaction:

'That they're a persecuted race just like the Jews. Wanderers the way the Jews have been forced to be wanderers, and, like them, holding fast to their own integrity. Braver, really, because unlike Jews they didn't have the promise of Zion to give them hope.' She ended with a childlike pleasure, 'Tawno and I have a lot in common.'

'It wouldn't surprise me. Have you seen him, since you got to Cambridge?'

'How could I? I phoned this morning and the housekeeper told me he was staying on in Angleby until the Tricentennial was over. In case you don't know, the housekeeper is called Mrs Venables. Uncle Max often spoke of how well she looked after him. By the way he spoke, I think perhaps she was his mistress.' A hand to her mouth: 'I shouldn't have said that, should I? It's only my thought, none of my business.'

'I didn't hear it,' Jurnet said, smiling. Then: 'Will your grandfather be coming back to England for the funeral?'

The girl shook her head.

'I shouldn't think so. Zeider doesn't set much store by funerals. He says they went out with the Holocaust, and, ever since, for a Jew there remain only two responses to death – silence or revenge.' She shivered momentarily. 'I expect he'll say *kaddish*, the prayer a man recites after the death of a child or a parent or a sister or a brother – not because it's a prayer about death, but because it isn't. It's a prayer about life, full of praise and hope. But he is not a religious Jew.'

15

At first glance it had been hard to understand how the man could ever have rated the nickname Dandy. With imagination, however, you could pull back the sagging shoulders, flatten the belly, excavate a face still young and cocky out of the surrounding flab. Even with things as they were, coming into the airless cubicle designated by DI Catton an interviewing-room, the man moved with a residual zest, one of the boys.

'Jesus!' exclaimed Dandy Venables. 'Look what the wind's blown in! Valentino and Taffy Chubbycheeks!' Sergeant Ellers, seated in a corner with his notebook at the ready, acknowledged the salutation with a grin. Jurnet pressed his lips together – *bloody hell!* – annoyed even though aware that to the seasoned denizens of the nick nothing was unknown, not even the secret name of God.

Without waiting to be invited, Venables sat down on the one unoccupied chair, facing the detective inspector across the table.

'Wha's on yer mind, cock?' he inquired cheerfully. 'What you got in mind fer me to confess to today? Rape, arson, sell me little sister to an A-rab sheikh? Take yer pick. Fer ol' times sake I'll be happy to oblige.'

Jurnet said: 'You're slipping in your old age, Dandy. Robbery, yes, but brainless vandalism?' Shaking his head apparently more in sorrow than anger: 'What did you want to go slashing those chairs for?'

'Oh Gawd! Here we go again. How many times I got to say I didn't do nothing to no chairs? Would I be likely to pick out the very place where my old woman's working?'

'I don't know. It would depend on the circumstances.'

'You mean, such as her carrying on with that curly-haired gippo of hers while I'm sweating it out doing porridge?'

Concealing his surprise at this turn in the conversation, Jurnet commented coolly: 'It would provide some kind of explanation, certainly.'

Dandy Venables laughed.

'Annie can screw the Prince of Wales, for all I care. Me sayin' "I do" at the altar were one o' them fatal slips anyone's prone to tha's taken a drink too many. You could bite yer tongue the minute you've said it, on'y what can you do, the wedding guests grinning like hyenas, an' three bran'-new brother-in-laws, every one of 'em wi' muscles like King Kong? What's more, the bloody clergyman were RC, like Annie. Marry you fer ever, no getting out of it till yer number's up, if then.'

'You could have got yourself a civil divorce.'

'I'm talkin' about Annie. It suits me, mate. Suits me down to the ground. Always a home to come back to, meal on the table, warm bed 'cause it's a mortal sin to deny your wedded husband his conjugal rights even if he is a criminal pain in the arse. If you think I'd do anything to risk Annie getting the push, you're barmy!'

'I understand from Detective Inspector Catton that you called in at Heathcote Avenue the morning you were let out of gaol?'

'On'y to pick up my key to the flat an' let Annie know I were back in circulation.'

Jurnet said: 'It was a very neat job, Dandy. Too neat for your own good. Dabs apart, it had to be Dandy Venables to take out a window pane like that.'

'Dabs?' The man dropped his pose of amiability and glowered at the detective. 'You tryin' to set me up or something? All I did in that bloody room was take a gander while Annie was answering the phone. If she'd given me the key straight off I wouldn't have hung about even that long. Once she handed it over I said ta-ra an' left, leaving her still talking.'

'And were you home when she got back, later?'

The man shifted in his seat.

'How you do go on!' he complained. 'I may have gone out for a couple of jars with old friends. Catch up on the news, an' so on.'

'Or, on the other hand, having kept watch to make sure your wife had left the Professor's house, you could have gone round to the back and effected an entry in your usual tidy way, removed Dr Smith's papers as per your instructions – also mucking up the room generally, as you'd been told to do.' Jurnet regarded the man on the opposite side of the table with a quizzical air. 'How much they pay you for the job?'

Dandy Venables said: 'Go shit yourself!'

Mrs Venables had lost her comfortable look. Eyes sunk deep in their sockets, she peered out at Jurnet in an absent-minded way as if trying to decide whether he was, or was not, the milkman.

Jurnet said briskly: 'Detective Inspector Jurnet, Angleby CID,' and watched a reluctant recognition seep into the woman's face.

'I remember you now. Dr Smith's not here.'

'I didn't come to see Dr Smith. It's you I wanted to have a few words with, if it's not inconvenient.'

'Me?' The woman's voice sharpened in unison with the alarm that showed in her eyes. Not one used to deception, Jurnet decided; and no bloody good at it. 'What you want to speak to me for? Nothing I can tell you you don't already know.'

'I expect you'll find there are a few things.' Smiling with conscious charm and a little annoyed, despite himself, at deploying his wares to such small purpose: 'Only, do we have to chat on the doorstep?'

The housekeeper opened the door without welcome; turned away, leaving the detective to shut it behind him. 'You'll have to come into the kitchen. I'm getting some soup on.'

Jurnet followed the woman to the back of the hall, through the baize-lined door she made no attempt to hold open for him, into a kitchen whose Edwardian origins lay submerged in the latest in domestic gadgetry. Jurnet, who, weaving his fantasies of married life with Miriam, occasionally paused in front of department store windows to price displays of worktops and peninsulas, hobs and spit-level grills, exclaimed with unfeigned admiration: 'Now that's what I call a kitchen!'

A pale smile illlumined Mrs Venables' face before a stronger misery quenched it.

'He wanted me to have the best,' she said. She looked at the vegetables heaped on the table, with sudden hatred. 'I must be mad. Who do I think I'm making that for?' She found a basin, scooped the vegetables into it, and emptied the lot into the bin; rinsed the basin out, dried it and returned it to a cupboard. The action seeming to bring her some obscure comfort, she turned to the detective as if seeing him properly for the first time, and commanded, 'Sit down. I'll make us both a cup of tea.'

It was over his second cup that Jurnet let it be known that he had had a word with Dandy Venables. The burglar's wife did not look surprised.

'Thought you'd be bound to. Once I heard – ' the woman's voice fragmented, reconstituted itself with effort – 'once I heard that the Professor hadn't died natural, I knew it would all have to come out. About me being married, and who to.'

'Professor Flaschner must have known, surely?'

Annie Venables shook her head.

'I always meant to tell him.' She looked at the detective, unsure of his response. 'You'll say, why didn't I, for Christ' sake – what was stopping me? When I first answered the ad in the paper and said I was a widow, that was different. I'd found out the hard way you don't get taken on if you say, "I'm married, only my husband's in prison at the moment, I'm sorry to say." But after all the years I've worked here, and him being the kind of man he was, I knew I could have told him the truth without it making a penn'orth's difference. It was simply that I couldn't bear to let him know I'd started work for him with a lie.'

'Man he was, you could have told him right at the start and it wouldn't have made any difference.'

The woman cried out bitterly: 'How was I to know that? I wanted desperately for him to take me on, not only because I needed the job. In just those first few minutes of speaking, I sensed he was kind, kinder than anybody who had come into my life so far. I couldn't take the risk of mucking up my chances.' She sat quietly for a little, her hands in her lap. Then she said: 'He left me £80,000. Did you hear about that?'

'No, I didn't know. We've been waiting to hear from the solicitors.'

'Dr Tawno told me.' She raised her head and looked directly at the detective. A tremulous smile curved her lips. 'In crime stories, they always look at the will first go off, don't they, to see who'll benefit? In case you're thinking I had something to do with the Professor's death, I better let you know at once that I'm thinking of not taking it.'

'What's the point of that? He wouldn't have left it to you if he hadn't wanted you to have it.'

'I'd have got it with a lie.'

'You aren't the first to tell one. You won't be the last.'

'But not to someone you love!'

Jurnet said, low: 'Most of all to someone you love.'

Jurnet said: 'Take my advice. Don't let on to Dandy. He won't be able to get down to the betting shop fast enough.'

'I don't know.' Annie Venables inclined her head with a weary humour. 'Maybe he's turned over a new leaf. This last time, he never asked me for a penny. Usually, it's the first thing. The minute I see him I get out my bag. This time, all he wanted was the key. He said his financial worries were a thing of the past. Nowadays, he said, prisons had moved with the times like everything else. They were like a regular Stock Exchange, and he was on the point of making a killing.'

'Didn't you ask him what he was on about?'

'I was scared stiff the Professor'd come downstairs any minute and want to know who I was talking to. I'd just taken him up some soup and crackers and made him promise to rest in bed till it was time for him to leave for Angleby, and he said he would, but you never knew what he'd do next. When Dandy turned up I got myself in such a state, I can't tell you. For one thing, I forgot to turn off the iron and nearly burnt the Professor's dress shirt I was ironing. He'd left his evening clothes down in the country, on'y he said as how Mrs Maslin'd never be able to turn out a dress shirt the way I did.' The woman's breasts heaved as she enumerated the crowding anxieties of that morning. 'What with the shirt, and getting the Professor's case packed, and all the time worrying at him insisting he was going to drive Dr Tawno's car no matter what, and the doorbell ringing and it was Dandy, I hardly knew what I was doing. On top of it all, just at that moment the cleaners phoned about the carpets – they were going to come in and steam-clean them while the Professor was away – and while I was speaking to them I saw Dandy go into the study – '

'How long was he there on his own?'

'Only as long as it took me to run across the hall and order him out. I didn't even wait to tell the cleaners to hold on. I found my bag, gave him the key. I told him I'd have his tea on the table at half-past four, and practically pushed him out of the house.'

With a sigh Mrs Venables recovered from the remembered breathlessness of that moment. 'Not a minute too soon, either. As I turned away from the front door there was the Professor on the landing in his underwear shouting down to know what in heaven's name I'd done with his socks.' The housekeeper cried briefly, wiped her nose on a tissue which she returned to her apron pocket. 'By the time I thought to get back to the phone, the cleaners were having fits.'

'What time did the Professor leave for Angleby?'

'It must have been about two, I reckon, give or take a few minutes.'

'And you yourself left the house immediately after?'

'I wouldn't say immediately. I tidied up the Professor's room first, straightened his bed. When I went into the study to make sure the windows were locked, I saw something there that worried me more than anything that had happened that morning. On the mantelpiece was a glass with a little whisky still in it. Whisky! I reckon, in his heart, the Professor was as afraid of that Porsche as I was – but there! If Tawno wanted it in Angleby, Tawno should have it. The sight of that glass! I took it into the kitchen and smashed it in the sink. Silly, really, breaking up a set like that. No call for it.'

'We all do things we're sorry for afterwards. What did you do then?'

'I put on my coat, picked up my bag, locked up and went out to the shops to buy a kipper for Dandy's tea. 'He's weak,' Dandy's wife said. 'You've had to do with him. You know. And no sense of danger. Watch him cross a six-lane highway and it could turn your hair white, the way he plunges in regardless.'

Noting that, despite all, Annie Venables seemed still to retain a residual affection for her delinquent spouse, Jurnet remarked: 'He hasn't been charged yet.' Voice and manner hardening, the detective demanded: 'Did anyone you know, out of those who were present when the Professor was taken ill, know about you and Dandy?'

Blood rushed into the housekeeper's pale face. She stared at Jurnet.

'Only Dr Tawno.'

'You don't have to worry about the doctor. We checked his travel times from Switzerland, and the lecture he gave in London. Even on the assumption that, for some reason we haven't yet fathomed, it suited him to arrange for a break-in staged in his own home, there was no way he could have got at Dandy, to set it up.'

Annie Venables had gone pale again. She said faintly: 'Mrs Pender is a prison visitor.'

In the study, Jurnet crossed over to the fireplace and stood with furrowed brow examining the silver-framed photograph which occupied the centre of the oak mantelpiece. Mrs Venables stood shivering, although the room was warm, not to say stuffy, the windows shut and the heat of the sunwarmed garden hammering on the glass. Jurnet saw that the missing pane had been replaced.

The housekeeper looked at the mutilated chairs with as much loathing as if they themselves were the intruders.

'I can't wait for the upholsterers to pick them up.' Then suddenly, explosive, as if there were something she needed to get off her chest and have done with it: 'Tweren't me told Dr Tawno about Dandy. Dandy did it himself. Waited outside the laboratory one day, collared hold of him and told him who he was. Told him he knew what was going on between him and me, and asked for money to keep his mouth shut.'

'Oh ah?' Jurnet turned from his contemplation of the photograph. 'And did Dr Tawno give him any?'

'Give him any?' The detective recoiled a little at the outrage encapsulated in the three words. 'What d'you, mean, give him any? Dr Tawno nearly split his sides laughing. He told me all about it when he come home. I'll tell it to you in his exact words.' Mrs Venables took a deep breath. 'He said, "That husband of yours picked the wrong one – eh, Annie?" '

Jurnet said, as delicately as he knew how: 'I take it the right one was the Professor?'

'You take it right for once.' For the first time since Jurnet had entered the house, the housekeeper looked happy. Grief slid off her like the sloughed skin of a snake. 'He was old, he was ill. If they were giving out prizes for what you do in bed he'd have come away with the booby prize. They say in his day he was a great one for the ladies. Before my time.' Annie Venables paused; considered the lost possibilities and dismissed them without regret. 'All I know is that he was loving and tender. He made me feel somebody. He made me warm and comfortable and safe. Yes, safe!' she repeated fiercely, as if the detective had ventured a contradiction. 'Safe, though I'd cut myself off from my church and from external salvation. I couldn't go and confess to Father Donovan that I was committing adultery, could I, because he'd only have told me to stop it, and I wasn't going to stop it, not for Heaven, not for all the devils in Hell. Whatever it says in the Bible, it wasn't a sin, me and the Professor together, and I wasn't going to listen to anybody, not even a priest – not even God – saying different. It was good and beautiful.' For a moment she was transfixed by the memory of happiness before grief wafted back like an enshrouding fog.

'And Dr Smith knew about your relationship with his Uncle Max?'

'Course he knew! He'd have had me himself other-

113

wise. He's a lovely man, if it hadn't been for the Professor I don't suppose I'd have said no. But do anything against his uncle? He'd never! I belonged to his uncle: that was that. I think he liked me all the better for making the Professor happy. And I did! You ask Dr Tawno if I didn't!' Now the tears were running down the woman's cheeks unchecked. She wrung her hands, not for her own loss but for her dead lover, deprived of the light. 'There were terrible things in the Professor's past that still haunted him. Sometimes at night he'd cry out in his sleep: the names of people who had been killed in the concentration camps. He seemed to think he had no business being alive when they were dead. When he called out like that I'd wake him up and rock him in my arms like a baby till he fell off to sleep again – '

Jurnet turned back towards the fireplace with a puzzled look on his face.

'Yet he kept a photograph, an autographed photograph, of Goering on his mantelpiece. One of the worst Nazis.' Jurnet cocked his head to one side, straining to pronounce what was written obliquely across a lower corner. '*Unverge* something – '

' "To my never-to-be-forgotten friend" – that's what it means.' Annie Venables joined the detective on the hearthrug. 'The Professor told me. It was a joke, he said. The man was going to be hung, only he took poison first. You probably read about it. What he meant by *never-to-be-forgotten* was that there wasn't going to be time for him to forget the Professor, or anybody else, for that matter. The Professor was an interpreter at Nuremberg, at those war trials – didn't you know? He told me that for some reason, even though he knew he was a Jew, Goering took a shine to him.'

'Putting his photo on show over the fireplace – he must have taken a shine to Goering.'

'He always said he put it there to remind himself.'

'What of?'

'I'm not sure,' Annie Venables returned slowly. 'He never said and I never thought to ask.' The reddened eyes filled afresh. 'And now it's too late.'

16

'A single dab on the doorknob for which he has no difficulty accounting.' Detective Inspector Catton sat on a corner of his desk, one leg dangling. Not bothering to conceal a smirk of satisfaction, he announced, 'We're going to have to let the bugger go.'

'Fine!' applauded Jurnet; at which the smirk, like the pieces of a child's kaleidoscope when shaken, instantly re-arranged itself into an expression composed of equal parts of pique and distrust. Abandoning his carefree pose as inappropriate to the changed circumstances, the Cambridge man seated himself behind his desk, acting the man in charge for all he was worth. Jurnet, who had the example of his Superintendent by which to measure lesser pretenders to the seat of power, was sunnily unimpressed.

'Can't see what's fine about it,' Catton growled, making no bones about where, in his opinion, responsibility lay for the failure to produce a credible charge.

'I said fine because now we'll be able to check up on the contacts he makes – and on who contacts him.'

The smirk back in place, Catton said: 'If you think we're going to put a tail on the likes of Dandy Venables you've got another think coming. We're not New Scotland Yard, you know.'

'I realise Cambridge is a small town,' Jurnet returned

unabashed. 'I just hadn't realised how small. Still, you must have guys on the establishment, official or unofficial, who keep their eyes and ears open, and report back what they hear or see.'

Catton said: 'If there's anything sensational to tell, we'll send you a postcard.'

Jurnet crossed King's College quad, passing the Chapel with an expression which concealed in equal parts an involuntary uplift of spirit and a disapproval rooted in remembrances of the Baptist chapels of his childhood, temples to a God who wouldn't be seen dead in such radiance of stone. Sergeant Ellers was waiting for him, plump forearms resting on the parapet of the pretty little bridge which was their designated rendezvous. Jerking his head in the direction of the river, he demanded of his superior officer, 'That what I pay my taxes for? To keep those layabouts afloat in the style to which they're accustomed?'

Below, slim-waisted young men, enjoying the picture they made against the backdrop of grassy banks and weeping willows, punted young women, most of whom were rounded in the right places, up and down the Cam. The young men handled the long poles with a careless skill born of long practice.

'Not students,' Jurnet decided. 'Too well dressed, for one thing. Too good at it, for another. Plumbers, washing-machine repairers, taking their lunch hour. Term doesn't begin for another couple of weeks.'

The detective leaned against the balustrade, enjoying the hazy sunshine of late summer or early autumn. The prospect was pleasing: calm and privileged, but benign. Miffed, nevertheless, by the inbuilt condescension of the place, Jurnet said, more abruptly than he intended: 'Get anything?'

Looking a little surprised, the chubby Welshman pulled out his notebook, riffled through a few pages.

'Holbride and Tate,' he announced then. 'One of the

oldest firms in the business. Going since Tubal Cain and still carrying on in the old traditional way. Which includes' – pause for effect – 'extracting gold and silver from finely ground-up ores by dunking them in a solution of – wait for it! – sodium or potassium cyanide.'

'There had to be somebody involved in the case who had access.'

'Access and how! Not just through the precious metals department. Seems the firm is branching out into cutlery, of which Mrs Maslin is doing the designing, surprise, surprise. She's been going about the works learning all the processes involved in electroplating and the case-hardening of steel.'

'And cyanide comes into them, too?'

'Chap who showed me round, been with the company twenty-seven years, showed me the stuff – sodium cyanide, it was – white, crystalline, used in electroplating. "Tablespoonful of that, sprinkled on their cornflakes, kill a regiment," he said as if it was something to boast about. To harden the steel, what you do is drop it into a very hot bath – 800 degrees centigrade, I think he said – of 60 per cent cyanide in sodium chloride. All in all, at Messrs. Holbride and Tate, there's a lot of it about.'

'You didn't let on Mrs Maslin was the real object of the exercise?'

'What d'you take me for? Made out I'd given my old woman one of those Claire Maslin pendants for an anniversary present and it had positively taken her breath away. Lucky the geezer didn't know what a detective sergeant gets paid or he might have got suspicious. As it was, he positively simpered. Offered to ring through to the switchboard to find out if the lady was on the premises, so that I could have the thrill of meeting her personally. I said, alas, I had to be getting on, and left hurriedly.'

From below the bridge came the lazy swish of punts

moving through the water. High overhead, a jet laid
its vapour trail across a bleached-blue sky.

Jack Ellers asked lazily: 'Shall we be seeing Mrs
Maslin, then?'

Jurnet answered: 'We'll be seeing her.'

The girl at the reception desk in the Institute lobby was
refreshingly human. Jurnet, who had half-expected to
be challenged by a computer-brained hologram programmed to do anything from demanding his creden-
tials to, if necessary, felling him with a karate chop,
smiled back at the smiling face framed in hair that was
only a little less glorious than Miriam's, at features
which, if they didn't come within a mile of Miriam's
beauty, were pleasing enough to an eye unspoilt by
perfection. The accompanying software (not too soft,
so far as the detective was able to judge) filed away
decorously under the pink sweater, appeared to be a
reasonable facsimile –

'You were saying?' the girl reminded him, not displeased at the effect she was having on the darkly handsome inquirer.

'Dr Pender. He arranged to meet me here ten minutes
ago.'

'I'll let him know you're here,' said the girl. 'Who
shall I say it is?'

'Detective Inspector Jurnet, Angelby CID.'

The girl said in a friendly way: 'My dad's a policeman.' Getting an answer to her summons, she spoke
into the mouthpiece: 'Detective Inspector Jurnet, waiting to see you.' Disconnecting the call, she reported:
'He'll be right down.' Adding with a giggle: 'What's
he done? Hit his Nanny over the head with his teddy
bear?'

'What's that supposed to mean?'

'Just my joke,' said the receptionist, and busied herself with an incoming call.

Adam Pender put his hand into the pocket of his corduroy jacket, took out a packet of cigarettes; looked at it unhappily and put it away again. On the white-painted wall of the lobby were several outsize representations of lighted cigarettes with a diagonal red line drawn through them.

Jurnet suggested obligingly; 'We can go outside, if you prefer.'

'Not worth it. There's nothing I can say to help you. I didn't see anything. Christ!' – lower lip suddenly trembling – 'is it really necessary to rehash that trauma all over again?'

'I'm afraid it is.'

'In that case' – the man got up from the leather-covered couch on which the two had seated themselves – 'perhaps we'd better go outside after all.'

Outside, on the car-infested tarmac which surrounded the Institute, the light, hazy as it was, was enough to make clear that Adam Pender was not the young man he looked in kinder light. Even his corduroys and plaid shirt, a young man's clothes, seemed to distance themselves from their wearer.

The physicist led the way to a patch of grass furnished with a teak bench and a couple of young women stretched out in the sun. At the men's approach the young women got up, tugged at their skirts and blouses, and moved away with a nod, back to the Institute. Ensconced in a corner of the bench, Jurnet waited until Pender had his cigarette alight, had taken the first sustaining drag. Then he began without beating about the bush: 'Everything points to Dr Smith having been the intended victim. Would you care to tell me what your quarrel with him was about?'

'Such diplomacy!' Adam Pender exclaimed. To Jurnet's surprise he looked suddenly unperturbed: if anything, relieved. 'You were there when I complained to Uncle Max. You know very well what it was about.'

'I don't want to jump to conclusions. I got the

119

impression you were of the opinion that you'd been denied your just share of credit in the work Dr Smith was currently engaged on. Is that right?'

'Bang on! I was livid. Angrier than ever after the way Uncle Max brushed my protests aside. Of course I knew Tawno could do no wrong in his eyes, but Uncle Max was a just man, he had always been so kind to me.' Pender sat silent for a moment. Then he said: 'But then Tawno arrived – '

'Yes?'

The other drew deeply on his fag, then threw it away, three parts unsmoked. Immediately the packet was brought out of the jacket pocket again, a second cigarette selected, lighted: the long draw, the slow, luxuriant expulsion of smoke. It took the detective a little while to realise that the man was crying.

Jurnet waited. Presently Pender got his feelings under control; murmured, 'Sorry about that. I can't seem to get used – '

'Nothing to be ashamed of. You said the old man was kind to you – '

'I loved him like a father – more! When my own father died – he kept a newsagent's and confectioner's in Balham – what I remember most was my mother phoning to ask what she ought to do about an order of Mars Bars that had been delivered that morning. Did I think she could ask the wholesalers to take them back? I thought she'd lost her marbles, ringing me with a question like that. "What on earth do you want them to take them back for?" I asked, and she answered, "Because Dad's just died. Didn't I say?" '

The second cigarette went the way of the first. When Pender had accommodated himself with a third, he ventured: 'I expect, after that illuminating anecdote, you think I'm a dreadful snob.'

'We're all that, one way or another.'

'I don't think I am, not really. I was just so besotted with joy to be asked into a house where there were

120

books as a matter of course, paintings on the walls, and conversation that gave you a whole new perspective on the uses of language. I wasn't the only one of his students the Professor asked round – he wasn't one of those dreary dons who deliver a lecture, say "good morning, gentlemen," and can't get back to their sherry in the Senior Common Room fast enough – but I was the only one he told to call him Uncle Max. And Tawno – Tawno treated me like a kid brother.' Adam Pender smiled, a smile of pure happiness. 'I can't convey to you what they were like, those early years in Cambridge. I felt ten feet tall. The realisation that the universe wasn't, after all, a piece of real estate where all the buildings had been completed, give or take a few plots still awaiting planning permission, but instead was a pulsating web of which I myself was a part, a pattern of probabilities leading to knowledge hitherto undreamed of – I can't tell you how wonderful it was to be young and clever!' The smile faded, the happiness with it. 'The trouble was, that I just wasn't clever enough – somebody who could run 100 metres when 1500 was what was called for.' With a deprecatory gesture: 'There are still days when I tell myself, I'm a PhD for Christ's sake. I *must* be brainy!'

'What was the Professor's opinion of your capabilities?'

'Oh, he was the first to cotton on. He was very sweet; sweet and merciless. It was always his philosophy that the truth had to be faced, however painful. He did everything he could to soften the blow – landed me this job here, where I sport a title on my door commensurate with my paper qualifications, but am, in fact, a kind of glorified office boy.' The bitterness subsided, the face retrieved a modicum of its lost youth. 'I don't think I could have taken it, if it hadn't been for Nina.'

Jurnet said: 'Tell me about her.'

'You'll need to be told,' Adam Pender said. 'Otherwise

you'll think what everybody else thinks – everybody, that is, except the three who know better.'

'And what is that?'

'That I'm either purblind, or impotent, or a cuckold. That Nina and Tawno are lovers.'

'And why should I think that?'

'Come off it, Inspector!' The man waved his hand and the long column of ash fell on to his trousers. He looked down as if surprised to see the stub still in his hand; opened his fingers and let it fall to the ground. 'You were at the table when Tawno arrived. You saw how she carried on.'

'It seemed to me that everybody carried on when Dr Smith arrived.'

'There was that too,' the other conceded. 'Tawno makes waves. But just the same, don't tell me you didn't jump to certain conclusions?'

'Jumping to conclusions is precisely what a police officer's trained not to do.'

'Only proceed on a basis of evidence, eh? So when I tell you, as a matter of evidence, that Nina is chronically shy and introverted, that the way she gets herself up, the reputation she invites, is nothing more than a theatrical persona she's created to defend that pathetically vulnerable self, what do you say?'

Jurnet hesitated, then decided to say it.

'The first thing that occurs to me, frankly, is that you must be a saint to put up with it. Either that, or a born doormat.'

Adam Pender laughed. 'Not a saint, that's for sure! A masochist, a doormat, maybe; though not, I think, a born one.' After a moment's consideration: 'There *is* a third reason, Inspector.'

'Oh ah?'

'That I love Nina. More important, that we love each other.'

Repressing the envy which surged through him in a

hot flush, Jurnet said, very matter-of-fact: 'You understand I'll have to listen to what Dr Smith has to say?'

The other returned confidently: 'Tawno would never
let Nina down by denying they slept together.'

'You call that letting her down!'

With affecting simplicity Adam Pender said: 'I'm
sorry that I haven't made you understand.'

17

On the road back to Angleby, Jurnet had Jack Ellers
stop at the Peddar's Way.

'Let's see where the Revd Maslin comes for a bit of
peace and quiet.'

Obediently, the little Welshman turned the car off
the A11 on to a wide track that looked as if it led
straight into the heart of nowhere. Ahead, a shut level-
crossing gate promised the imminent passing of a train;
and even as the sergeant parked by the crossing keeper's
cottage the Angleby-Birmingham Intercity streaked
past, sending a convention of local rooks into near-
hysteria. From somewhere too close for comfort came
the snap, crackle and pop of machine-gun fire.

'Trains to the right of me, battle-training to the left
of me, bloody vultures overhead shitting themselves
silly.' Jack Ellers chortled. 'Peace, perfect peace!'

Jurnet got out of the car, surveyed the ground on the
further side of the railway line, the track bisecting a
wall of conifers black against the sky. He suggested
without conviction: 'Maybe it gets better further on.'

'Got the red flag up,' announced the crossing keeper,

coming out of his cottage. He looked pleased: a solitary man, by the look of him, one who cherished his privacy. Nothing kept hikers away like a good burst of gunfire. 'Nato,' he said. 'Bin bangin' away for a fortnight. You should 'a read the notices,' He finished: 'No parking here.'

Jurnet produced his ID card and explained pacifically: 'We just wanted to take a look.'

'Oh ah? Not bodies again, is it? Anyone disappear for fifty miles around an' they always start off by lookin' here.'

'No, no. Just looking, like I said.'

'Lookin' for what? There han't been anything to find here since that rape, two year ago last April.' Grumbling, the man turned back to his front door. 'It's gettin' like a ruddy Piccadilly Circus.'

As always, Jurnet came back to his native city convinced there was nowhere else which came within a million miles of its beauty, its exquisite rightness as a machine for living. What was Cambridge, after all, but a small town which had got above itself? In Angleby, at least, they'd had the sense to stick their university outside the city limits where it didn't get in the way of grown men with a proper job of work to go to.

The good feeling persisted as far as the ring road roundabout, where he began to wonder exactly how he was going to account to the Superintendent for the way he had spent his day.

Back at Headquarters, the latter greeted him with a cordiality which completely threw him, until he realised its cause.

'Mrs Maslin was here,' said the Superintendent. 'Charming little woman.'

That 'little' said it all. Fluttering and helpless, preferably blonde – perhaps because Mrs Superintendent was brunette and could make mincemeat of her husband on

the golf course without even driving off the ladies' tee
– was how the Superintendent liked them.

Getting his blow in first, Jurnet said: 'I suppose she
came about the cyanide.'

The Superintendent did not look too pleased at this
stealing of his small thunder. 'You've been to that firm
she works for, have you?'

'Jack was there. He'll tell you.'

'Holbride and Tate, sir,' the chubby Welshman came
forward and confirmed promptly. 'Sodium and potassium cyanide both. Enough on the premises to wipe
out an army. Properly stored and accounted for, but
definitely there. And Mrs Maslin particularly, because
of her work connected with cutlery, is, you could say,
a bit too close for comfort.'

'Hm.' The Superintendent at his desk shuffled a few
papers and remarked sourly, 'Extraordinary hair!' He
spoke as though an unfair advantage had been taken of
his good nature. Arching his fingertips together in a
gesture his subordinates, for sufficient reason, knew
boded no good, he leaned back in his chair and
enquired, 'What else has emerged?'

'Bit of a ragbag, so far.' Jurnet made clear by his
tone that he was not apologising. 'Pointers, though. A
beginning. I'll set them all out in my report.'

'Titivate my appetite with a few hors-d'oeuvres.'

'Yes, sir. Briefly then – Mrs Venables, the Professor's
housekeeper, turns out to be married to Dandy Venables. You've had to do with him, I think. Chap who
specialises in beautiful break-ins – ' The Superintendent
listened impassively to the end, then shook his head.

'I don't like it. The housekeeper and the old man,
the gipsy charmer, the Penders, the Maslins, that Israeli
girl – there's altogether too much love in the air for
comfort.'

Jurnet nodded, on the same wavelength.

'Know what you mean, sir. Where there's too much

love there can be too much hate – the swing of the pendulum.'

'Exactly!' The Superintendent stood up, Jurnet and Ellers instinctively straightening their own shoulders at the sight of that elegant, erect figure. 'Swing of the pendulum reminds me. Time I was going home. Busy day tomorrow.'

Ellers, in his motley as court jester, ventured: 'At least we'll be kissing goodbye to our visiting geniuses.'

'A distinguished body of men it has been a privilege for the city to entertain,' the Superintendent responded severely. 'Tomorrow should bring down the curtain in a fittingly dignified manner. The ceremonial depositing in the University's archive of the papers presented in the course of the Tricentennial – it promises to be an impressive occasion. Their publication will be the first undertaking of the newly formed University of Angleby Press.'

Jack Ellers offered cheekily: 'Bit of Hamlet without the Prince, though, won't it be? I mean, without our gipsy charmer's *pièce de résistance?*'

'Not at all. By the time the rest of the book is ready to go to press they hope to have Dr Smith's contribution ready for inclusion with the rest. It'll be a marvellous feather in Angleby's cap. Dr Brant, the Vice-Chancellor, told me he'd heard from Dr Smith to say he didn't expect to keep them waiting long – he just has to rework some of the equations he's not completely satisfied with.' The Superintendent declared: 'That's important. I've advised the Vice-Chancellor to state it loud and clear, so that the media pick it up.'

Jurnet cottoned on at once.

'You mean, let the villains know they don't have the final version? That way, in case they've still got ideas about eliminating Tawno they'll hold their horses at least till he's made his improvements. If his paper's worth committing murder for, it must be worth waiting a bit longer to get the latest update.'

126

'Precisely.'

'By which time, with luck,' finished Jurnet, pursuing a pleasing fantasy of villains massing in ambush well outside the borders of Angleby police territory, 'it could be somebody else's responsibility.'

The Superintendent's eye was cold as he observed: 'Let me remind you, Inspector, that the apprehending of Professor Flaschner's murderer remains ours.' *Here it comes*, thought Jurnet; and here indeed it came, the inevitable gambit. 'Know what, Ben?' the Superintendent said in the friendliest possible way, 'You're going to need some help.'

'Not tonight, ta,' said Jurnet, in answer to Sergeant Ellers' invitation. 'Kiss Rosie for me and tell her ordinarily I'd go through fire and water for her steak-and-kidney, only I already arranged to meet this old school chum – '

'Where you eating then?' The little Welshman's tone indicated that he did not believe a word of it.

'Romano's.' Which was a daft thing to say, Romano's being in Assembly Street, just the other side of the Haymarket; which, in turn, meant he could not plausibly, under his colleague's sceptical eye, take his car out of the car-park in order to drive to a no-parking-at-any-time street two minutes' walk away.

The colleague, pitiless, waited in full view to check that Jurnet was indeed headed in the direction he had asserted was his goal. Touched by his friend's concern, the detective was nevertheless relieved to turn the corner into the Haymarket, shutting off sight lines. A short wait until Jack Ellers was on his way, and then he too could retrieve his car and make his way home for another evening of intelligent conversation with a telephone which for all they went on about the benefits of privatisation, seemed only to know people who wanted to talk about insurance or double-glazing.

The Haymarket was empty except for some pigeons,

diligently employed despite the lateness of the hour in returning the refurbished Sir Thaddeus Brigg to the statue they knew and loved. People had been about earlier, though, as a sprinkling of crisp bags and other detritus attested. The physicists' wreaths, still piled at the foot of the plinth, looked, with their dropping petals and drooping leaves, apter tributes to a 300-year-old death than they had in their original perkiness. Tawno Smith's wreath – or was it the Professor's? – had come off worst, the berries which had formed the numbers on the floral dice having vanished – down the pigeons' gullets, at a guess. Double six had become double blank. Must be a lesson in it somewhere, Jurnet thought desultorily. Higher up the plinth the dread graffiti-hound had struck again: '*God is ex-directory.*'

When it seemed safe to go back and get his car, Jurnet drove home though the deepening dusk, anxious to get there in case there was a letter from Miriam, putting off his arrival as long as possible in case there wasn't. At the entrance to his block he ran into the O'Driscolls who, in the interest of getting to the movies in time for the main feature, had regretfully to cut short his deeply interested inquiries as to the latest O'Driscoll's weight, number of teeth and who did he take after? On the first floor landing the smell of joss sticks was power-ful enough to justify a one-man raid – *where's the ganja, baby?* – if the detective hadn't been dead sure that on the other side of the door Miss Whistler was doing nothing more inimical to the peace of the realm than sitting in the lotus position knitting the curate a scarf.

When he could dream up no further excuse for delay, Jurnet unlocked his front door and found a postcard from Miriam on the mat. On one side was a coloured picture of a lot of sand. On the other, Miriam had written: '*I love you.*'

18

The physicists who had presented papers at the Tricentennial filed into the lecture hall, where their fellow-
delegates and the faculty of the University of Angleby
were gathered with the Vice-Chancellor, awaiting
them. To Jurnet's unromantic eye, the little procession,
robed in its Sunday best academicals, looked pathetic,
caught in a time warp. Either that, or like amateur
actors of no great talent taking part in some grotty
costume play.

To the polite applause of their confrères they slowly
processed the length of the brash, bright room and
mounted the dais at the further end, each carrying under
his arm a handsome leather folder containing, it had to
be surmised, the sacred typescript. These folders, after
a somewhat clownish exchange of bows and doffings
of caps and bonnets with the Vice-Chancellor and with
Dr Turnbull and the chairman of the Angleby Sir Thaddeus Brigg society who supported him upon either side,
were deposited upon a table where a single folder of
the same kind already rested. The television crew did
their stuff. Dr Turnbull turned his best profile to
camera. Their mission accomplished, the learned doc-
tors descended to ground level again where, with a
rustle of stuff as they pulled their gowns about them,
they took their seats in the first row, left empty for the
purpose.

In the muted ripple of sound that filled the brief
interval before the Vice-Chancellor rose to address the
congregation, Dave Batterby, the living and breathing
manifestation of what the Superintendent meant by

help, slipped into the seat next to Jurnet's. Jurnet acknowledged the newcomer's presence with a small nod, nothing too encouraging.

Convinced that his brothers in arms saw him as he saw himself, a future Chief Commissioner, Dave Batterby needed no encouragement.

'Had a word with that Turnbull bugger. Says he was nowhere near the goddam table. If he had been, he'd have moved away double quick because the slightest whiff of orange triggers off his migraine. Also says his wife does not and never has slept with Tawno Smith, and if he ever finds out the name of the lying bastard who started the rumour that she had and does he'd – he couldn't seem to make up his mind exactly what he'd do, but it would definitely be something.'

The man went chattering on although the Vice-Chancellor had begun to speak and physicists in the adjacent seats were miming disapproval. Keeping his own voice down, Jurnet instructed his helper: 'Get hold of him again after the party breaks up and ask him to explain quantum physics to you. Don't let him get away till you understand the subject from A to Z.'

'Is that necessary?'

'Vital!'

'As myself a historian,' – the Vice-Chancellor, in full flow, bent over the table and extracted the folder which had lain there before the arrival of the others – 'a member of a discipline whose concepts of time and reality, if you will forgive me for saying so, have come in for a severe mauling at your hands, I might perhaps be forgiven a certain ironic satisfaction at receiving, amongst these other distinguished christening gifts to our infant press, one consisting entirely of blank pages.' Opening the folder at random and displaying the double spread thus revealed, so that the gathering could appreciate its unblemished virginity, he went on: 'Ladies and gentlemen, I take no such pleasure. The events of the past week have shocked and saddened us

130

all. The police, we may be sure, are straining every nerve to bring the miscreant, or miscreants, to justice, and we can only wish them well in that most worthy undertaking. To Max Flaschner, that great man, we have already paid our collective tribute, and I propose, therefore, to say no more here than that the eventual publication by the University of/Dr Tawno Smith's delayed contribution to our proceedings will be the best answer we can make to the dark forces of barbarism and ignorance which threaten to overwhelm us. May it be ready soon!'

Tawno Smith disengaged himself from the group gathered about him in the University refectory and came over to where Jurnet was wrestling with a prawn salad. The prawns were winning by the look of it, the detective not being much of a hand at eating with his plate on his knee.

'I thought you might be wanting to speak to me before I went back to Cambridge. Save you a journey.'

Jurnet found a window sill to abandon his plate on.

'I didn't mean to interrupt your lunch.'

'Had all I want, thanks' – to say nothing of remembering, a bit late in the day, that prawns were no dish of choice for an apprentice Jew.

'Then let's get ourselves some coffee and go out in the air, shall we?'

Outside on the terrace, the concrete ziggurats of the University at their backs, in front of them the land falling away sweetly to the river, Jurnet inquired: 'You off today, then?'

'Soon as Christopher shows up. I'm taking him back with me to stay, to give him the chance to get to know his way about the town before term begins.' Tawno Smith's mouth, the full, sensuous lips, twisted in self-deprecation. 'That's what I kid myself. The truth is, I can't bear the thought of going back to Heathcote Avenue alone.'

131

'Mrs Venables was expecting the upholsters to pick up the chairs – ' It was a poor attempt at consolation, but the physicist acknowledged the intention with a grateful nod. His eyes had lost their cheerful mischief.

'Let me be truthful in one thing at least. Whether you wanted to speak to me or not, I wanted to speak to you. In fact, since Uncle Max died, you, in a funny kind of way, are the only person I *can* talk to. You're the only one who, like me, is completely involved in his death to the exclusion of everything else.'

With Miriam's card in his jacket pocket – the detective put his hand on it, fingered an edge, just to make sure – Jurnet could confirm with a clear conscience: 'I'm involved all right.'

'*Completely*'s the operative word. I know you're a policeman, you do it for a living. Just the same, I sense that completeness of commitment – ' the man broke off. His smile was so attractive that Jurnet hardened his heart as a precautionary measure. 'Or am I being too ridiculous?'

'I'm involved all right,' Jurnet repeated carefully. 'Only, we're not likely to find out today who killed the Professor, nor, in all probability, tomorrow or the day after. If you're excluding everything else in the meantime, what's happening about that paper of yours?'

'You see what a humbug I am!' Once again Jurnet found it necessary to steel himself against the man's charm. 'I've already warned Christopher I'll be fully occupied with the rewrite once I get home. He'll have to find his own amusements.'

'I don't suppose he'll find that too difficult, not with Miss Ahilar in Cambridge too.'

'Esther? Is she really? That's wonderful! We'll have to find out where she's staying.'

'I understand she rang up Heathcote Avenue and left a message with Mrs Venables.'

'Ah! You've been speaking to Annie.'

132

'And to Esther.'

Tawno Smith said: 'I imagine she's told you about coming to the Virgin?'

'She told me. I must say, I'd rather have heard it from you first.'

'I didn't want you to know that she'd passed the night in the room where my paper was – or rather, where it had been. It must have been taken long before she put in an appearance. I didn't want to put her in an invidious position, that's all.'

Jurnet said severely: 'Everyone who'd been in or near your uncle's table was already in an invidious position.'

'I wasn't really in any condition to think. I'm sorry I didn't say anything.' The curly head came up, the black eyes that met the detective's so transparently honest he had to suspect them. 'Almost as sorry as I am for not letting her into bed. If she *had* passed the night in Room 314 instead of Room 315 it would have obviated any suspicion you might have of her, and it would have been – comforting.' The man set down his cup and saucer on one of the green metal tables which dotted the terrace. 'Do you know what gipsies do when there's a death in the family – on the very day of the death, before the corpse has had time to settle comfortably in the grave? I'll tell you. They go to bed and make love, more passionate love than at any other time of their lives. If it is a woman who has lost her husband, never mind. She takes a lover for the night, a husband the same. They can take their pick of the tribe and no one will say no. It is a necessary compulsion, an affirmation that *merripen* means life as well as death, and that, of the two, it is life that will always prevail.' He finished: 'The children of such couplings are invariably beautiful and mysterious, knowing secrets.'

'I suppose you could call young Christopher beautiful.' Jurnet kept his voice carefully devoid of expression. 'As to what good he is at knowing secrets, I couldn't say.'

Tawno Smith looked at the detective with a lively interest. 'You *have* been asking around!' The bright eyes clouding. 'You haven't said anything to Christopher himself?'

Jurnet shook his head.

'Thank you for that.' The other's countenance cleared. 'Fatherhood seems to be something that's creeping up on me.'

Jurnet pointed out repressively: 'Christopher and Mr Maslin seem to hit it off wonderfully well.'

'Dear old Simon! Blessed are they that run! Just one of the crackpot ideas he's filled the boy's head with.'

'Like going into the church, you mean?'

'The boy has a natural bent for mathematics, Inspector: a talent – it may be a genius – it would be criminal to frustrate.'

'Mr Maslin appears to think he has a natural bent for holy orders.'

'Mr Maslin thinks! Mr Maslin doesn't think! Nobody's asking Christopher·to make a choice between God and science, for Christ's sake! It's perfectly possible to take both on board, if you're that way inclined. Uncle Max was a practising Jew, but he didn't feel he had to become a rabbi, any more than Christopher is called upon to fritter away his great gifts visiting the sick or debating how many angels can dance on the point of a pin.'

Tawno Smith screwed up his eyes against the sun. 'You think I'm selfish, don't you?' he challenged. 'Selfish because Simon's had all the hard work of bringing Christopher up and it's only now, when he's house-trained and fit for civilised society, that I propose calmly to walk in and take possession.' With a shake of the clustering curls: 'It isn't like that at all – simply that Simon's job has come to its natural end. Christopher has outgrown him.'

'Don't we all outgrow our parents?' Pressing on: 'Christopher is clever and handsome. Would you feel the way you do if he were plain and stupid?'

'I don't suppose so for a moment.' Tawno Smith looked Jurnet full in the face, tilting his own to the other's height. 'If you're just the detective hound who's nosing about in my neck of the woods, you'll write me off as beneath contempt. If, as I hope and believe, you are my friend and my protector, you'll believe me when I say that, just as Uncle Max, I'm quite sure, would have died for me if necessary – Hell! he *did* didn't he? – I would die for Christopher.'

The boy came out on to the terrace, the sun turning his pale hair to a brasher gold. He screwed up his eyes against the light and Jurnet saw the gipsy in him. Why, knowing what he knew, the resemblance, glimpsed for an instant and instantly gone, should nevertheless have taken him by surprise, the detective could not have said. But surprise him it did.

Christopher, in turn, showed his surprise in finding the object of his search in company with the fuzz.

'Thank goodness! I was beginning to think you'd cleared off without me.'

'You know I wouldn't do that. What have you done with your luggage?'

'I left it with the porter in the front hall.'

'Fine! I'll bring the car round and pick you up there.' The man shorter than the boy, the two stood smiling at each other, neither quite at ease.

'You remember Inspector Jurnet, of course.'

The boy nodded slightly, looked out over the terrace.

'Brilliant day. Wish you'd let me drive.'

'The Porsche! I didn't even know you'd passed your test.'

'I haven't, as a matter of fact.' With a challenging glance in the detective's direction: 'But I know how.'

'All this in the Inspector's hearing! You want to get us arrested?'

Christopher said with spite: 'He's not much good at arresting. He hasn't arrested whoever killed Uncle Max.'

The physicist looked upset and discomfited. Jurnet said equably: 'Don't worry. They all have to go through it, cheeking the cops. Part of the rites of passage.' He reached into his pocket for his notebook, scribbled a few words on the pad, tore the page out, and held it out to the boy. The boy blushed, unsure of the right posture to adopt.

'Take it,' Jurnet urged him. 'With luck, it'll give you a better opinion of the guardians of law and order.'

Christopher Maslin took the paper with reluctance, glanced at it and blushed deeper.

He mumbled, 'Thanks.'

'What's going on?' Tawno Smith demanded. 'What have you given him?'

'Only Esther Ahilar's address.'

19

Jurnet drove out to Feldon St Awdry unaccompanied. Apart from anything else, he wanted to take another look at the wall paintings in the church, something more satisfactorily accomplished, he fancied, without the inevitable running commentary from Sergeant Ellers.

Running. As if the word were of itself enough to conjure up the reality, the detective became aware, ahead and over to his left, of a figure in shorts and singlet heading away from him across the fields with a fluidity of movement it was a pleasure to behold. He stopped the car and watched as the Revd Simon Maslin dwindled into the distance. The sugar beet had been harvested, the lumpy land not yet harrowed, yet the man moved as unfalteringly as on a fine cinder track. In one field, the beet tops had been left on the ground as fodder for a small flock of sheep who wandered among the wilted greenery with the air of creatures used to better things. Complaining, they moved slowly out of the way as the runner passed through their midst; stood for a moment with heads up looking after him before returning to their joyless banquet.

Judging from the empty road, the empty land, the pervading sense of being at the world's end, the media had not yet launched the dancing Salomes on to the tourist circuit. At the fork, as before, both ways pointed impartially to Feldon St Awdry. This time, Jurnet chose the route through the village, which turned out to be an unrewarding place built mostly of a brick the colour of green bacon. Claire Maslin was out in the vicarage garden cutting chrysanthemums. A great swathe of them already filled a trug of spliced willow.

'They're for the church,' was her greeting, 'and they were here before we came. I can't stand them personally.' Throwing down her scissors, she pulled off rubber gloves and straightened up, pushing her ash-gold hair back behind her shoulders. Her beauty, thought Jurnet, was, like everything else about Feldon St Awdry, equivocal. Now you see it, now you don't. One minute an enchanted princess spellbound in a Victorian vicarage: the next, a stupid bint who couldn't see it was time to put her hair up and act her age.

'It's the smell,' she explained. 'They smell like incontinent old women. Oh, leave them where they are,' she instructed, as the detective bent to pick up the trug. 'I

137

can't bear them in the house. Simon's out running. Was it him you wanted to see, or me?'

'You, actually. I shan't keep you long.'

'As long as you like. It's lovely to have someone to talk to.'

She led the way down the hall into a sitting-room which, with its bay window framing a view of the garden and the churchyard beyond, could have been a pleasant place, if anyone had cared enough to make it so. As it was, too many armchairs covered in dingy repp, too many small tables consisting of circular brass trays set down on a criss-cross of some Indian wood, stood about as if newly deposited there by the removal men, waiting for somebody to arrange them into a home.

Mrs Maslin curled herself up in one of the armchairs, kittenish, looked up at the detective through her lashes, and asked sweetly: 'Is it to do with the cyanide? I called in at the police station to tell you about it, only you were out. Not that I've ever had anything to do with it. The very thought of poison scares me stiff.'

Jurnet plunged in. 'As a matter of interest, did you ever invite anyone of your family or your circle of friends to visit Holbride and Tate's, to see something of your work there?'

'You mean' – the woman crisply stated the question for him – 'could anyone who was at the castle dinner have had the chance to steal some?' She uncurled herself, moved to the edge of the chair, pulling her skirt modestly down over her knees. The skirt was printed with splashy flowers, the colours a little tired. Summer clothes when summer was over. Like its wearer, Jurnet thought.

'They've all been there, one time or other,' Claire Maslin replied, unfussed. 'Except Tawno and Uncle Max, of course – they were always too busy. I'm a bit of a show-off, Inspector. It pleases me to let people see I'm somebody on my own account, not just the vicar's

138

wife.' The woman clasped her hands round her knees and asked like a good little girl: 'Anything else you'd like to ask me?'

'There is one thing. Before the dinner, when the Professor was sitting on that Buddha – remember? What exactly did you understand him to mean when he thanked you for everything?'

'What *exactly?*' Mrs Maslin stood up. 'I'll tell you,' she said. 'I'll tell you what that slippery old fraud was thanking me for. He was thanking me for letting myself be manipulated like the silly ninny I used to be in those early days when I first knew Tawno, when everything I did was what the great Uncle Max thought best for his darling. No tantrums about the other women the young genius went to bed with, no demands that he marry me, not even when I became pregnant.' She broke off and regarded Jurnet with a look that held in it something of contempt. 'I suppose you swallowed whole Simon's story about his talking me out of an abortion?'

'Not true, then?'

'God, no! Though I dare say he's talked himself into believing it is. It makes Christopher that much more his, to kid himself that he alone saved him from being washed down the nursing-home sluice. I *chose* to become pregnant. Not out of any great maternal feelings, I admit, but because I hoped Tawno might marry me, once he knew a child was on the way. And he *would* have, if it hadn't been for Uncle Max!'

'How did the Professor stop it? And why should he want to?'

'Which d'you want me to answer first? He wanted to stop it because he didn't want to let Tawno go, that's why. Not to me, not to anybody. A little lechery on the side was fine – Uncle Max was no slouch in that department himself – but a lifelong commitment to anybody but him, the one who'd rescued him from the rubbish dump, who'd brought him up, loved him above anything a mere woman had to offer – that was different!'

Claire Maslin's face, twisted, stared incongruously out of the flowing hair. Jurnet asked mildly: 'Didn't Tawno have anything to say?'

'Oh, Tawno!' With a loving exasperation: 'Tawno loves everybody. It's strange, because sometimes I've wondered if he has a heart at all, things don't seem to touch him the way they do other people. Yet how can anyone love who hasn't a heart? All I know is that he loves – he loved – his Uncle Max best. Sometimes I've even wondered – I know it's wicked, but there it is,' – the woman's face had flushed a deep red – 'if they went to bed together, there was so much passion to their love for each other. More like lovers than father and son.'

Claire Maslin considered a moment what she had just said, shrugged her shoulders, and left it at that.

'It didn't take me long to find out I had to share Tawno with a lot of other women. It took longer to stop being hurt by it, but I did reach that point eventually. Muslim women, I used to tell myself, are brought up to know they'll have to share their husbands with goodness knows how many other wives and concubines, so it can't be against a woman's nature, just something she has to get used to. Tawno's so good at making love it's no wonder women fall for him like a ton of bricks. And if, in time, as they all do, they come to realise that they have been loving, not being loved, and drift away, they never forget the marvellous time they've had while it lasted.'

'You didn't drift away – '

'You forget I haven't got a husband – not what you could call one – to drift back to. And besides, there was Christopher.' With a wry smile: 'It's funny, isn't it? All the years Christopher was a little boy, Tawno couldn't have cared less about him. It's only now that he's grown up he's begun to take notice – '

Jurnet said: 'You still haven't told me how Professor Flaschner stopped Tawno from marrying you.'

'Easy! All he had to do was remind Tawno of his own past – of the father who deserted him, of the mother raped and screaming out "Run for your life!" How could anyone with that weight of memory willingly assume the responsibility of a wife and child? And I'll tell you something else,' – now the woman's face had grown sly – 'how do we know any of it is true? It could all have been a pack of lies that Uncle Max cooked up because it gave him such power over Tawno. Things were in such a mess in Germany after the war, anything could have happened – '

'But Dr Smith remembers being in that cellar with his mother – '

'How much can a child of four or five *really* remember, especially if it's something that's been dinned into his head over and over? "*Remember how you kicked me in the shin? Remember how the soldiers came into the cellar and did things to your mother, and how she cried out in Romany and you ran away?*" '

'You really did hate Professor Flaschner, didn't you?'

'I'll tell you something else.' The woman did not bother either to confirm or deny the allegation. 'Tawno's circumcised. I've looked up everything I could find about gipsies, and there's nothing about them practising circumcision. It's Jews who are circumcised, so isn't it more likely that Uncle Max picked up a poor little Jewish orphan? A lot of Jews look the way Tawno does.'

'But why should the Professor want to make up such a story?'

'I've told you – power! I know people see Jews as outsiders, and I suppose they are, in a way. But in another way they're the exact opposite. They belong to a club, they really care for each other in a way other people don't. So long as there are other Jews in the world no Jew is ever completely alone, the way Uncle

Max wanted Tawno to be, dependent on him and him only.'

Jurnet hazarded: 'Could be – assuming you've guessed right – that he wanted to protect the child. Figured he'd already suffered enough anti-Semitism to last him the rest of his life.'

'*Could be!*' the vicar's wife repeated with ironic emphasis. 'It's easy to see you fell for the famous Fla-schner charm like everybody else! Who knows what Uncle Max really wanted? I used to say to myself, he's a scientist, truth is what scientists live by, so I must be wrong. He can't possibly be a scientist and at the same time such a dreadful liar. But then I came to understand that science – his brand, anyway, and Tawno's too – isn't like the science I learned at school, all laws and certainties. It's full of change and chance, and as little to be relied on.'

Jurnet asked: 'Have you ever discussed any of this with Dr Smith?'

Claire Maslin returned with a bleak simplicity: 'I have never discussed anything with Dr Smith. Dr Smith is the man I have given my body to, and bodies do not discuss. They touch, they absorb, they enter into each other. They become one, so how could they discuss? It would be talking to oneself.'

'You've been talking to me, at any rate,' said Jurnet, getting up. 'I'm grateful.'

'Grateful for what? For letting you know what I really thought of Uncle Max? What an awful humbug you must think me for putting on such a show of affection! Are you quite sure you aren't going to ask me to accompany you to the police station to help you with your inquiries?'

'Quite sure,' returned Jurnet, unsmiling. 'Not just yet, anyway.'

Claire Maslin said: 'That's good, because I want to move to Cambridge. I've already phoned a couple of agents to arrange appointments to view. Uncle Max didn't want me there permanently: it would have taken Tawno away from Heathcote Avenue. But now he's dead' – she looked about the room unseeingly, as if already she had willed it out of existence – 'there's nothing to stop me.'

'Does Mr Maslin know?'

'Oh, Simon!' The slender shoulders shrugged in irritation. 'Simon is so bloody forgiving! Do you know what he said when I told him? Not a word about not going on his account. All he said was, he didn't think Christopher would like it. At Christopher's age, he said, boys want to get away from their parents, that's why they go to universities at the other end of the country when there may well be a perfectly adequate one right on the doorstep in their home town.'

'Something in that, I shouldn't be surprised.'

'For God's sake!' the woman cried. 'As if Cambridge isn't big enough for both of us! First, it's Uncle Max, now it's Christopher. When am I going to be allowed to do something because it's what *I* want? And what I want is to be near Tawno all the time, so long as I live.' The dark eyes darkened further. Remarkable, thought Jurnet, unmoved but admiring, against the blonde skin, the ash-gold hair. 'I tell you this, Inspector – not sentimentally, like a silly female who reads too many women's magazines – I tell you because it's true. If Tawno had drunk that poisoned juice, I would have put out my tongue and licked the last drops off the sides of the glass, so as to be dead with him.'

Jurnet pushed open the church door with a feeling that in so doing he was giving in to temptation. Was this, he wondered, how the archetypal bloke in the dirty raincoat felt as he made for the back of the porn shop, seeking the choice items which were kept under the counter?

Nothing under-the-counter about the six Salomes. Their blatant sexuality, made manifest in the colour of

143

dried blood, so assaulted the detective that in voluntary self-defence he closed his eyes, reopening them only when he felt fairly sure the minxes were back on their wall and it was safe to come in.

As before, the attention of the naked dancing figures was concentrated on the severed head looking up at them with unbridled lust. That was to say, the attention of all but one. For the first time Jurnet noticed that one of the Salomes, having caught sight of the bearded gent sitting at the top of the wall with the headless body of the saint draped across his knees, was unmistakably giving God the glad eye.

Jurnet laughed aloud, the sound rumbling comfortably round the little church. He felt in his pocket for the postcard from Israel and promised himself the pleasure of bringing Miriam to Feldon St Awdry the minute she returned to England and he had found out who had killed Professor Max Flaschner.

The unpredictability of either consummation in the moderately foreseeable future sobered the detective instantly. Since leaving the vicarage he had felt, without exactly knowing why, optimistic: on the verge of understanding. Now, he felt suddenly dulled and diminished by the shame inseparable from the necessary obscenity of probing other people's secrets: a kid poking a stick down a drain, all on the chance of turning up a hard little pebble called truth out of the enveloping gunge.

A man was dead – the wrong man, it seemed; which must have given those ruddy physicists no end of joy, the random universe behaving randomly. If only the old man had snuffed it of natural causes, as he had seemed on the point of doing! Yet, when you came down to it, what was more natural than murder? It wasn't something you caught, like flu or Aids. It was there dormant all the time, an intrinsic part of the human make-up, programmed into you by that cock-eyed God who, having created it along with everything else, couldn't wait to try out His new invention. Only four people on earth – the business, you might say, scarcely beyond its planning stages – and He had to goad Cain into killing Abel. Twenty-five per cent of the entire human race wiped out at one go. No doubt about it, it worked!

20

It was six o'clock in the morning when the phone rang, rousing Jurnet sufficiently to answer it, if not enough to identify a voice whose inflections of mockery he nevertheless dimly sensed as not unfamiliar.

'I conned the duty sarge into giving me your home number,' said the voice of Detective Inspector Jim Catton. 'I knew you'd be wanting to be put in the picture without wasting time going through channels. Make my apologies to that gorgeous bird of yours if I've woken her up from her beauty sleep or interrupted anything interesting.'

Jurnet banged the receiver back on its cradle. After a few seconds he lifted it off again and laid it down on its side on the bedside table so that Catton wouldn't be able to get back. After a further few seconds given over to an inward struggle in which, to his glowering self-contempt, he was the uncontested loser, DI Benjamin Jurnet reconnected himself to a world which might conceivably have need of his services, and waited for the phone to ring yet again. Which it promptly did.

'As I was saying,' said Catton, 'when we were rudely interrupted, we found him in the river, not feeling the cold one little bit. Not along our beautiful Backs, either. Down by the gas works, a different country, brother, except that the water's just as wet along there, and just as drowning.'

Jurnet said nothing. Waited until the other demanded, measurably less cocky: 'Don't you want to know who it is?'

'Don't you want to tell me?'

What children they were! 'Sod you!' the Cambridge copper's voice came down the line, acknowledging defeat. 'Dandy Venables has bought it.'

'Where's the fire?' Jurnet demanded, as Sergeant Ellers turned on the siren and let the Rover have its head on the long straight of Thetford Warren. Stands of Norwegian spruce galloped towards them like the charge of the Light Brigade before receding into the instant past: carpets of heather announced themselves and were gone. The car precipitated itself across the junction with the Peddar's Way at a speed to scare the pants off any spectral centurion unlucky enough to be crossing.

The little Welshman turned off the noise, slowed down with a cheeky grin.

'Though you wouldn't want to be late for the PM. The Super said – '

'I heard what the Super said.' *How many bloody post mortems had the Superintendent attended in the last five years?*

'Get hold of – what's the name of their police surgeon – Hutton? Humphrey, that's it, while you've got the chance,' the Great White Chief had ordered, grumpy to have had his breakfast interrupted. 'Next to him our dear Colton is greased lightning, and you know what *he's* like.'

'Yes, sir. Catton didn't seem to think there was necessarily any villainy. Said the fellow had had several skinfuls before they stopped serving him at the last

146

pub he visited, just before closing time. The Cock and Battledore, that was, only a block away from the river, at a point where there aren't any railings, just some small workshops directly on the waterside. Took the wrong turning, Catton reckons, down one of the slip roads, and was too far gone to do anything about it.'

'Perhaps we should leave it to Detective Inspector Catton and be done with it,' the Superintendent observed sourly, 'and then the rest of us can go back to bed. If it's because you're fearful for the fate of your eggs and bacon, Ben – '

'Not bacon, sir,' Jurnet returned brightly, reflecting that his swiftness to take offence must be a sign that the conversion process was at last beginning to take. 'Oysters and black pudding, actually.'

'Oh ah,' remarked the Superintendent, pronouncing the two syllables, that essence of Norfolk, as if they belonged to some quaint foreign lingo.

Just as well, thought Jurnet, as the Rover proceeded, slower now – just as well his breakfast had in fact consisted of a cup of instant and a single matzo cracker, a leftover from Passover discovered in a corner, as it might be a last year's Christmas card. Thus provisioned, he could face the post-mortem with nothing showing that a seasoned police officer should be ashamed of. Nothing to give away his absurd sensitivity to a skull with its top sawn off as if it were an Easter egg so well packaged you couldn't get at the goodies inside any other way. Nothing to let on how a dead face which had nothing to tell him could be more eloquent than the living faces he daily confronted, full of secrets; nor why the liver and lights produced like rabbits out of a hat from a torso slit from gullet to gusset, should constitute a probing more violating than the most merciless cross-examination. Nothing, above all, to betray the cosmic anger which invariably surged through his being in the presence of violent death.

Jack Ellers had timed it well. By the time the two

detectives came into the PM room Dandy Venables had been returned to his refrigerated cubbyhole and Dr Humphrey was scrubbing up at the washbasin in the corner. An orderly was sluicing down the metal table and the floor. The smell was certainly less obtrusive than it must have been earlier.

Jim Catton greeted them merrily. 'You've missed all the fun!'

The pathologist, who looked tired, pursed his lips, made as if to speak, and thought better of it. The Cambridge detective, with a jovial hand flung out in the doctor's direction, proffered: 'These are the two nosy parkers from Angleby I was telling you about.'

The result of this introduction was to render Dr Humphrey – who had the air of a man more at home with the dead than the quick – more accommodating than might otherwise have been the case. He actually shook hands with the newcomers, and asked after Dr Colton. It was high time, he intimated, that he and old Barney got together for a good old chinwag. Jurnet did not permit his mind to dwell upon what the two police surgeons might find to chinwag about.

'You'll have to wait for my report, of course, Inspector, as well as the lab report on the contents of the stomach. However, I do not anticipate any difficulties. It all seems quite straightforward.'

'Accidental death, you mean?'

With a touch of reproof: 'That will be a matter for the coroner's court. All I can state at the moment and off the record, is that the deceased died of drowning, probably between ten p.m. last night and two a.m. this morning. The man was alive when he went into the water. No injuries, apart from a few superficial scratches caused, possibly, by bumping against the river bank or by the branch with which, I understand, he was found entangled. Shortly before death he had consumed a large quantity of alcohol.'

'In other words,' Jim Catton said in his jolly way, 'a thoroughly uninteresting run-of-the-mill death.'

Dr Humphrey shrugged on his raincoat, did up the buttons with a painstaking attention to the task. Picking up his case, he nodded to Jurnet and Ellers. At the door, a hand on the old-fashioned porcelain knob, he turned and looked at Catton. In a voice as grey as the rest of him, he said: 'I'll try and do better next time.'

'A barrow-load of laughs,' asserted Detective Inspector Catton, ushering the nosy parkers from Angleby into his room at the police station. He was referring to Dr Humphrey; and incredibly, Jurnet, for the first time in their fraught acquaintance, found himself drawn to the man. Nobody with such an engaging confidence in his own good standing with the world could be all that bad.

Sergeant Ellers looked on with an air of demure mischief at his superior officer making himself comfortable over coffee and sandwiches; at the two DIs calling each other by their first names. It would seem that Dandy Venables, poor bugger, had not died in vain.

Jim Catton leaned across his desk, gesturing expansively.

'I warned you I couldn't undertake to have the guy tailed. You won't deny I said that, Ben.'

'You said you'd keep an eye out – '

'Which we did. How else d'you suppose we know so much about the deceased so soon? Let me tell you how Dandy, God rest his soul, spent his last day on earth. He went in two betting shops, had a good day – won a total of £175.15. After which, understandably enough, he started celebrating, first at the Bussey Arms, then the Bag o' Nails, ending up at the Cock and Battledore. No trouble anywhere – quiet as a lamb, they say, at all three places – only by the time he turned up at the Cock and Battledore, the landlord, who's had plenty of experience in that line, summed him up as having had enough for one day. He told Dandy to be a good boy and get off home while he still had the legs to carry him.'

'He didn't happen to notice if anyone else left at the same time?'

'Do us a favour! We only been at it a couple of hours. We'll go back and ask, OK? Anyway, Dandy didn't leave by the front door. He said he needed to take a leak and went out the door that leads to the pisser. When he didn't come back into the bar the landlord sent his barman to make sure he hadn't fallen down the hole, but the fellow comes back and says as there weren't no sign of him. There's a door to the car-park next to the lav and he reckoned Dandy must have left the pub that way.' Catton swallowed the last of his coffee, belched delicately with hand over mouth, and said 'Manners!'

'Anyone see him after that?' asked Jurnet, in a voice measurably less matey.

'No one we've turned up so far. The lane at the side of the car-park leads straight down to the river. One blooming lamp post at the corner and that's it. Could have happened to anybody.'

'Hm.'

'Naturally you don't want to commit yourself. The Flaschner connection, eh? Personally, I'd put my money on accidental death without a second thought. If it wasn't for the money.' Catton looked so pleased at springing the surprise he had kept until the end that it was impossible, Jurnet found, not to be pleased for him.

'What money's that, then?' he asked, acting the stooge to perfection.

'£175.15 won on the gee-gees – right? An unknown amount spent on booze. Take one from the other, it still oughtn't to add up to the £515 found on the body, wouldn't you say?'

'£515!' The detective's whistle gave great satisfaction. 'He could have won more than you thought?'

The Cambridge man shook his head definitively. 'Not a chance. We know as a fact that Dandy never patronised anywhere bar the two shops I've mentioned. £515, mostly in fifties.' Catton belched again, sat back with the complacent expression of an actor who feels he has performed his part well. 'What's your theory, Ben, of how Dandy came by that little windfall?'

21

The Penders lived in a street that had once been well-heeled, had gone down in the world, and was on the way up again, though not to its former spacious gentility. Ranks of buttons at the side of every front door attested to the fact that the premises had been born again, converted, with property developers the unlikely source of missionary endeavour and central heating and fitted kitchens the signs of grace. The doors themselves, lacking their original grained oak or mahogany, were, with a fashionable perversity that invariably put Jurnet's back up, painted in 'off' colours – blues, greens and browns, all of them, by some modish alchemy of chromatology, sliding into grey. Beside them, to the detective's prejudiced eyes, the few remaining houses in the street whose doors sported no paint at all to speak of, were oases of reality in a pseud's world. Directly across the road from the Penders', a derelict chapel which, in the circumstances, could have been forgiven for taking a different stance, maintained on a tattered poster: GOD IS LOVE.

Mrs Nina Pender was less a pseud than a sphinx.

Clad in a djellabah patterned in whirligigs of black and white, she welcomed the two detectives into her drawing-room with all the unabashed avidity of a spider greeting a couple of likely flies. The parlour was little less disturbing than its chatelaine. There was a lamp that looked like a spring trap set to catch one of the larger cats, a coffee table consisting of plate glass balanced on intestines made of chrome. Unframed slabs of spatter on the walls hinted at meanings it were safer not to pursue too closely. Most threatening of all was the sofa, its purple upholstery blowsy as a bordello.

'What was it you wanted, exactly?' Mrs Pender inquired in a tone which insinuated her readiness to provide whatever it was, no matter how far off the beaten track. 'Do please sit down.'

The two detectives sat down on the edge of the sofa, the little Welshman moderately comfortable, Jurnet feeling a right berk with his knees up near his chin. For her part, Mrs Pender sank gracefully down on to a cushion at their feet, her painted face upturned, her painted lips slightly parted, the neckline of her exotic garment considerably more so. A vamp of the 'Twenties would have exhibited more finesse. Repressing an impulse to laugh, Jurnet was already engaged in looking for some sign of the shy introvert of whose existence her husband had assured him when the dire thought struck: what if the vamp was intended to be seen through, a red herring to confuse the trail? How could one be sure that the smoke screen did not obscure merely another smoke screen, which in turn – Christ! How many skins did you have to peel off to get to the ultimate Nina Pender?

The ultimate anybody.

In self-protection as much as anything, the detective took out the list with which Dave Batterby had provided him.

'Christian Aid, Oxfam, Royal National Institute for the Deaf – ' he intoned.

Mrs Pender, red flooding into her face, sat bolt upright on her cushion, reacting to the inventory of her good works with the dismay of a vestal Virgin faced with incontrovertible proof of her sexual hanky-panky. At the end of it she got up, without much grace, but regaining her cool as she did so. 'Proper little do-gooder, aren't I?' With a leer which was the optical equivalent of a sideways dig in the ribs: 'Alibis, my dear Watson! You have no idea how busy charities are! Committee meetings are a positive obsession. All I have to say to Adam is, "I've a committee meeting on today, darling. I don't know what time I'll be back," and off I can go, without a care in the world, to Heathcote Avenue and Tawno.'

Jurnet referred to his list again. 'I see that among your other voluntary activities you are a prison visitor at Angelby gaol.'

Nina Pender made a face. 'Was, you mean. That was when we were living in Angleby, when Adam was at the University. They were starting an experiment – women visitors visiting men, something they'd never done before. It sounded like fun. And besides – '

'Another alibi?'

'Exactly!'

'Yet' – Jurnet feigned puzzlement – 'here's a funny thing. Both the prison chaplain and the chairman of the Visitor's Committee have, within the past week, stated that you continue to be one of their most conscientious volunteers, one on whom they can unfailingly rely.'

Mrs Pender ran a hand over her sleek black bob. 'Oh well. I didn't think you meant *that*. It's a bit different, isn't it, from flag days and bring-and-buy. You meet some really interesting characters –

'Such as Dandy Venables?'

Nina Pender took the news of Dandy Venables' death badly. A good deal worse than his newly fledged widow, if Jim Catton was to be believed. According to

Catton, Annie Venables had taken one brief glance at her drowned husband, said, 'That's him,' and gone frozen-faced away, refusing the offer of a lift to Heathcote Avenue on the ground that she had a bit of shopping to pick up on the way back. Mrs Pender began to cry, without artistry, unless it was artistry of a high order: an intermingling of lipstick, blusher and mascara which lent her face fleetingly the pathos of a clownish child.

The news that Dandy had gone drunk to his last rest was received with a horror beyond tears.

'That will have been my fault,' she whispered. 'He wouldn't have had the money if it hadn't been for me.'

'How's that, then?'

'The grant. I got him a grant from the Willington-Rideout Foundation. They're specially interested in the rehabilitation of discharged prisoners. It was to keep him going while he learned glazing.'

'Glazing!' For the life of him the detective could not hold back a grin. On the sofa Sergeant Ellers was doubled up over his notebook as if with a sudden cramp.

'The restoration of stained glass, actually. At Ely. All the cathedral glass needs attention, and the Foundation's put up the money for a special workshop.' Tears filling her eyes anew, Nina Pender went on: 'It seemed a wonderful opportunity for a sensitive, artistic man who had never had the chance to express that side of his personality, to acquire a skill which would stand him in good stead for the rest of his life. From the way he talked, he seemed to have a real affinity for glass.'

'I think you could say that,' Jurnet agreed. Jack Ellers, on the sofa, sucked in his breath noisily. 'This grant you speak of – how was it to be paid?'

'A sum down, to set him up when he came out, give him back confidence in himself and in the world, that it wasn't a place where every man's hand was turned against him. The rest was to be paid as wages, with

154

the prospect of a rise after three months if he showed promise.'

'I see. This sum down. How much was it?'

'£400.'

'And paid how – when?'

Nina Pender said: 'He said he couldn't cope with banks and cheques, and could I arrange for it to be in cash: he'd put it in the Post Office. We were in Angleby anyway for the Tricentennial, so I met him in the Haymarket – at Sir Thaddeus Brigg's statue as it happens – and gave him the money. Six fifty-pound notes and the rest in tens.'

Jurnet reflected a moment. Then: '£400. You're sure that was all you gave him?'

'Of course I'm sure.'

'You didn't by any chance put him in touch with any of your friends in Cambridge, or elsewhere?'

'By no chance.' The woman looked at the detective uncomprehendingly. 'It wasn't a side of my life I cared to have talked about. It could give people the wrong idea.' From habit, perhaps, she made the sentence sound rich with sexual innuendo. 'I didn't even tell Adam.'

'Nor Mrs Venables either?'

'Annie?' the woman stared. 'Oh, because she was Dandy's sister-in-law, you mean? No, I never did. Dandy said she'd always looked down her nose at him even when her husband was alive, thought she'd married beneath her by marrying into the Venables family Once his brother was gone, he said, she'd cut off all contact with the lot of them. He said if he let on he'd come into a bit of money, she'd suddenly get friendly, he shouldn't wonder. I said I didn't think Annie was like that at all, but he said you never could tell what anyone was really like until you knew them through and through, the way he knew Annie, and often enough, not even then.'

'Sister-in-law, eh?' commented Jurnet. 'So that's

what he told you! Did you, in fact, ever discuss Dandy with Mrs Venables?'

Nina Pender shook her head. 'I'd noticed the similarity of name, of course, right from the beginning. I was going to ask if by any chance there was a connection, but then I thought, the man's in prison, I don't want to embarrass her. Maybe she doesn't even know he's in gaol, and won't thank me for telling her.'

'You needn't have worried. She knew all right. Women usually know what their husbands are up to.'

'You've got it wrong,' the other proclaimed confidently. 'Not husband. Brother-in-law. Dandy was her brother-in-law. Annie is a widow.'

'She certainly is,' agreed Jurnet. 'Ever since her hubby ended up in the Cam, that is.'

There was a brief, unbelieving silence. Then: 'You're joking!'

Mrs Pender prowled about her drawing room, her op-art draperies swirling about her.

'The news appears to upset you.' The detective's tone was not sympathetic. 'Did you and Dandy have a relationship?'

'In the interview room at Angleby gaol? Out in the street in the Haymarket? It's the lie!' Nina Pender, throwing herself down on the cushion again, this time without coquetry. 'I can't bear lies! I can't bear them!'

'I'm glad to hear it. As someone who can't abide lies, did you ever discuss the Professor or Dr Smith with Dandy, or tell him anything about the paper Dr Smith was due to deliver at the Tricentennial? Did you ever recommend Mr Dandy Venables' services to a friend or acquaintance who was looking for the right person to do a temporary job that would pay well?'

Eyes owlish with smudged mascara, Nina Pender said: 'I don't understand you. This isn't about Dandy at all, is it? It's about me. The funny thing is that I called in to see you in Angleby to ask your advice about his grant, only you were out. I thought you looked sympathetic. And now you're trying to connect me with Uncle Max's murder!'

Jurnet shook his head.

'I'm trying to connect the murderer with the murder. Nobody else. And I think you understand me very well indeed.'

Out in the street a nasty little wind had come up. GOD IS LOVE flapped the notice on the board of the derelict chapel, close by where the two detectives had left the Rover. Somebody up there, thought Jurnet, settling thankfully back into the car, could do with a change of agency. What kind of a slogan was that to sell the product? God is Reason, perhaps, or Justice – but love, that crazy consumer of energy to no purpose?

As if to give the detective right, the wind caught a tattered edge of the poster and slit it smartly from top to bottom. The G had lift-off, planing down the street until impaled on a spear-topped paling, where it fluttered like a bill waiting to be paid. OD IS LOVE, proclaimed the poster, adapting to changed circumstances.

Jurnet nodded in complete agreement.

Very odd.

22

Looking grey and depleted, Annie Venables answered their ring.

'Not you again! What is it this time? There's Doctor Tawno here, and young Christopher. You'll have to come back later – that is, if you have to come back at all, which I can't see why.'

'Visitors as well, I see,' Jurnet remarked pleasantly. He nodded in the direction of Esther Ahilar's little car, parked in the driveway.

'I've got to go. They're waiting for their coffee.'

'We shan't keep you long,' Jurnet promised, a foot inside the door, on the doormat. 'All I really wanted was to say how sorry I was to hear about Dandy.'

The woman's face, normally so soft and rosy, turned from grey to a frozen rage. With a pointed glance downward at the intrusive foot: 'Right! Well, you've said it! Ta very much. Goodbye!'

'Don't be like that, Annie.' Jurnet turned the charm full on. At his side, Sergeant Ellers was the only one to register admiration at the performance.

'Don't be like what, for Christ'sake?' The house-keeper's lips twisted. 'You tell me, Mr Know-all! Me, Annie Venables, so mixed up she don't know whether she's coming or going or gone stark raving bonkers. Oh come in, blast you!' With a wail, opposition unex-pectedly collapsing, 'That coffee won't be fit for drinking!'

She hurried away. The two detectives followed, Ellers carefully closing the front door after them, and nipping across the hall in time to hold open the baize-lined one to the domestic quarters as the woman reap-peared carrying a loaded tray. The two awaited her return in a kitchen redolent with the smell of home baking. Biscuits were still cooling on a wire tray.

'Not up to Rosie's,' pronounced Jack Ellers, taking one and nibbling with the air of a connoisseur. To Mrs Venables, returning free of her burden, he rec-ommended: 'A pinch of nutmeg, love, along of the cinnamon. You try it next time. It'll work wonders.'

The housekeeper sat down at the kitchen table with a sigh of exasperation. 'Get on with it,' she said to Jurnet. 'Spit it out and get it over and done with.'

'I didn't mean to get in your way,' Jurnet said in all sincerity. 'I'd have gone to your own place, except I was sure I'd find you here. Better to keep working than sit staring at four walls.'

The woman leaned her head on her hand. 'This here *is* home from now on, if you want to know. The only reason I ever kept on that bloody flat was for Dandy to have somewhere to come back to. If I never see it again it'll be too soon. Especially after that Inspector Catton and his mates give it a going over.' She looked at Jurnet with a sharpened interest. 'They were looking for Dr Tawno's paper, weren't they? As if Dandy would have hung on to something that could be turned into ready money! Next thing you know, they'll be saying I waited behind after the Professor had driven off, to give Dandy a hand. If they haven't said it already.'

'They couldn't say that,' Jurnet reassured her. In fact, Catton had said that very thing, more than once. 'If you were there, there wouldn't have been any need to take out a window pane.'

'Something in that.' The woman did not sound particularly grateful for the let-out. 'How much nutmeg?' she demanded, as Ellers helped himself to another biscuit.

'Forget it, love,' Ellers answered. 'I was wrong. They're perfect the way they are.'

Annie Venables got to her feet and looked about the kitchen as if for something to do. She settled for washing up the metal sheets on which the biscuits had been baked. At the sink, arms plunged to the elbows in the hot, soapy water, she banged the tins together like cymbals, the two detectives sitting quietly watching, waiting. Even so, Jurnet was unprepared when, the tins stacked to dry on the draining board, the woman turned back to him, her cheeks as pink as her arms, handsome and challenging.

159

'Do you know what I hate most about this whole bloody business?' she demanded, not as if expecting an answer. 'That it makes me feel myself important, which I'm not an' never will be. The two men in my life dead – one of 'em, maybe both, murdered – it's awful enough as it is, without the other something I reckon even you clever dicks don't know about. That I can't help feeling proud, flattered to be at the centre of the drama, like someone out of a play or a grand opera. Next thing you know' – her voice hard with self-loathing – they'll be knocking at the door from the *News of the World*, offering big money for my life story. Dandy would have bust himself laughing. He always said he was going to leave me a wealthy widow.' She came back to the table and stood looking down at Jurnet with a mixture of aversion and pleading. 'For pity's sake, what's the truth of it? Did someone kill Dandy? The same one as killed the Professor?'

'As of this minute, Annie, I honestly can't give you an answer. Let's just say we're keeping an open mind.'

In the sitting-room, a comfortable place, they seemed moderately glad to see the detective. Tawno Smith exclaimed, 'You must have some coffee!' Esther Ahilar took her eyes off Tawno Smith long enough to smile a greeting, Christopher Maslin his off Esther Ahilar long enough for a non-committal nod.

Jurnet sighed inwardly, felt for the postcard in his pocket. *Tell me the old, old story.*

Love.

Tawno Smith said: 'These youngsters are just off to the cinema. So if there's anything you want to ask them – '

'It's only a show put on to get freshers to join the Film Society.' Esther Ahilar put in at once. 'We don't have to go.' Christopher Maslin looked stricken. 'I mean,' the girl amended, taking pity in a maternal way whose dire import, lost on the young man, restored the light to his eyes, the glow to his cheeks, 'it's not something where you have to be there on the dot.'

'Actually,' Jurnet explained, 'I called by to have a word with Dr Smith, and to pay my respects to Mrs Venables.' Smiling at the girl: 'You and I, Miss, have already had a little chat.' Turning to Christopher Maslin: 'Time I was over in Feldon St Awdry you'd taken yourself off for a run.'

'Had I?' The boy spoke with a lack of interest not far short of insult. 'It wouldn't have made any difference if I hadn't. I didn't put poison in Tawno's orange juice and I didn't see anybody else doing it either. Honestly! If I *had* put it in, you don't suppose I'd be owning up to it, do you?'

Tawno Smith interposed gently: 'Inspector Jurnet needs all the help he can get.'

'Sorry!' the boy mumbled, his bad temper seeming to surprise even himself. 'It's just – oh, I don't know!'

I do, thought Jurnet. Dead's dead, and you're alive and in love.

'And now there's Annie,' the boy went on, as if it were really too much. 'We didn't even know she had a husband alive, let alone one dead in the river. Well, Tawno did, apparently, only he never let on.'

The latter observed mildly: 'I can't remember Annie's private life coming up as a subject of conversation.' The bright black eyes liquid with sympathy, the physicist continued: 'She shouldn't have come in this morning, poor soul. I offered to drive her back home, but she said no: she was better off getting on with her work as usual.'

Jurnet said: 'Understandable.'

'As a matter of fact, she asked if she could move in as resident help from now on – said she couldn't stand that council flat of hers a day longer. Naturally, I was only too pleased.' He looked from one to the other of the two young people, seeming to sense their distaste for the way the conversation was going. Funny,

161

thought Jurnet, equally taking in the closed young faces, how death, the one certainty left in a changing world, was the one remaining dirty word it wasn't manners to come out with in company. Radiating charm, Tawno Smith inquired: 'Will you let these infants off the hook, Inspector, and send them on their way? No grilling? No third degree?'

Jurnet said, smiling: 'Not at the moment, anyway.'

'If you're sure . . .' Esther Ahilar seemed in no hurry to leave. She leaned over the tray on its low table, flicked open the lip of the coffee pot, peered inside. 'You never had your coffee,' she reminded the detective. 'I don't know if this is still hot enough.'

'Not for me, thanks. Detective Sergeant Ellers and I had a cup in the kitchen with Mrs Venables. He's still in there, having an additional word.'

'Oh.' The girl looked disappointed. Speaking to the gipsy, appealing almost: 'If you think we ought to stay . . .'

Tawno Smith responded lightly, 'It's up to the Inspector.' The way the man's glance slid off the girl, a careful non-looking that didn't miss a thing, told the detective more than words.

'Enjoy the film,' Jurnet said.

The study looked different, no longer serious: a utilitarian desk, a couple of armchairs upholstered in a nondescript blue, a new carpet on the floor equally undistinguished. Only the garden, insistent through the uncurtained windows, remained vibrant, slatternly and familiar.

Jurnet observed: 'You've changed things about a bit.'

Tawno Smith surveyed the new decor with only a partial satisfaction.

'Not enough. However much I try to disguise the place, I can't fool Uncle Max. He hangs about like a *bavol-mengro*, a windfellow, a ghost as you Gorgios call it, stopping me from getting on with the rest of my life.' Unashamed tears in his eyes, the man admitted: 'I can't tell you how much I miss that maddening old man.'

'Maddening?'

The other laughed, a swift recovery, white teeth glinting in the brown face. He motioned the detective to an armchair.

'Trust a policeman to pick up the operative word! Have I, I ask myself, set you wondering afresh if it wasn't me, after all, who dropped the cyanide into the orange juice?'

Producing a smile to match, Jurnet said: 'That would be to assume I'd ever stopped.' Adding courteously: 'Among all the other alternatives, naturally.'

'Naturally.' The physicist bent his curly head in acknowledgement. 'And if I told you further – as I do, what the hell? – that I spent a good part of the day Dandy Venables was found in the river in bed with his wife, does that set you wondering even more?'

'Wondering's what I get paid for. Only, one thing at a time, if you don't mind. In what way did you find the Professor maddening?'

Tawno Smith moved across the room to the fire-place, to the mantelpiece where, Jurnet now noticed, the silver-framed photograph of Goering still kept its place.

The detective remarked, 'I should have thought that would have been the first thing to go.'

'Oh, positively not! An ever-present reminder, Uncle Max always said, of the seductiveness of evil. No home should be without one. Also' – studying the portrait with close attention – 'of the persistence of vanity. It must have been taken years before he put on all that disgusting fat. Can you imagine having a supply of pictures of your young, heroic self on tap, even in Nuremberg? Yet Uncle Max – can you credit it? – said he had never met a man of more delicate under-standing.'

'Was that the kind of thing that got up your nose?'

'Not especially.' Tawno Smith sat down in the second armchair, swallowed up by it. A small man, Jurnet reminded himself: the strength, the self-containment, misled you. 'Simply that, for all the affection between us, we were as different as chalk and cheese, he brought up in the rigid order of the Mosaic code, me, lawless Ishmael. With backgrounds like that we were bound to see the world differently.'

'Generally, d'you mean, or in your scientific work in particular?'

'Science, everything! What makes you think you can hive science off as if it were something only specialists need to take account of?' The physicist's face had become quite rosy with earnestness. 'Frankly, I'd given you credit for more sense.'

Jurnet, taken aback, mumbled something about never having been much good at it at school.

'And so you discarded it, along with your school uniform and your football shorts, the day you left! How rude I am!' The charm resurfaced, the passion remained. The detective thought: 'It's not only women you're gone on. 'I simply can't understand,' declared Tawno Smith, 'how people can move about the world so *unaware*, treating creation as if it were no more than a painted backdrop put up to add interest to their dim little charades. Just because the sun rises and sets every day without any apparent help from you doesn't mean you aren't involved.'

Jurnet pointed out, reasonably enough, 'Can't see there's much I could do about it, even if I wanted to.'

'Now you're laughing at me. I deserve it.' The man's smile did not cancel out the underlying seriousness. 'What I'm trying to get over is the fallacy of treating human beings as separate from the physical world, instead of being part of it. They penetrate each other like a man penetrates a woman, a mutual giving and receiving which is probably the nearest we shall ever get to a definition of reality.' Tawno Smith looked at the detective intently. Then he said: 'Let me tell you about my paper.'

'Physicists – theoretical ones, at any rate – are not creators. They are more like explorers. They discover what is already there, only hidden in inaccessible places. They make up equations which are partly works of art and partly coded instructions, like Chinese calligraphy, having meaning only for the initiates.

'Scientists are never satisfied,' said Tawno Smith. 'It is their function always to want to know what is on the further, the hidden, side of the hill. Over the centuries they constructed what seemed at the time an ideal solar system – the sun, the moon, the stars, the planets – everything in its place and a place for everything. A noble Palladian mansion of a universe, magnificent, determinate, but not exactly comfortable for daily living – no room for endearing untidinesses, no coffee stains, so to speak, on the immaculate table linen. It wasn't really surprising that presently there were other scientists who began to yearn for a universe more consonant with their anarchic selves, one where, as in life, everything was not all cut and dried and where chance and probability took their proper place in the scheme of things.'

Frowning with the effort of compressing much into a small space, Tawno Smith said: 'Physicists of genius eventually uncovered that new universe of which they had dreamed dreams: a subatomic world as infinitely small as the other was infinitely vast, composed of the particles which are the building-blocks of the universe.'- They physicist eyed his visitor a little uncertainly. 'Can I hope to convey to you the excitement simply of knowing it to be there?'

'I'm out of my depth,' Jurnet admitted frankly. 'And that's what your paper's about?'

The other burst out laughing.

'My dear Inspector, that was only the introduction! Here beginneth the second lesson.' Tawno Smith squared his shoulders, as if confronting some solid obstacle that blocked the way. 'There are in nature – you'll have to take my word for it – four fundamental interactions, forces if you like, upon which nature itself depends. They are called the strong force, the weak force, the electromagnetic force, and the force of gravity; and the greatest prize in theoretical physics today is to uncover the underlying symmetry which has to exist between them. Not the old unity, mind, inflexible as marble, but a new one which takes account of the chanciness of the universe and comes to terms with it. Getting gravity to fit in with the other three has been the biggest problem awaiting resolution.

'And I,' said Tawno Smith, not boastful – if anything, with a certain sadness, as if, a little, he regretted having reached the end of a delightful quest 'have done just that. Solved it. You wanted to know what my paper is about, and now you know.'

'I hear what you say,' Jurnet agreed. His old science master, he thought would have recognised the tentative tone instantly, the agonised striving after comprehension. 'But what does it mean? How is it so important that somebody was prepared to kill for it?'

'I don't know.'

'You must do!'

'I don't know,' Tawno Smith repeated. 'I'm not having you on, truly. I told you, I'm a theoretical physicist. The practical applications are out of my star. The most I can say is that another hill – well, perhaps a small mountain – has been climbed, and the view across the further landscape that has been revealed to the human eye for the first time has to be interesting.' He extricated himself from the armchair in one lithe, seamless movement and went to look out at the sun-drenched garden. 'Phaeton, they say – ' addressing the window panes – 'took the chariot of his father, the Sun

God, and tried to drive it across the heavens. He couldn't control those four horses breathing flame from their nostrils and they plunged to earth, taking him with them.'

His back to the light so that the detective could not make out his face: 'As I said; Inspector, I don't know but I can guess.' The man's voice was at once exultant and appalled. 'Can you imagine what power man may have in his ordering once he holds gathered in his hands the reins that control the four forces which in turn control the universe? Will he be Phaeton, falling out of the sky, burning up the earth with the heat of his fall, or will he be Phoebus Apollo the god, coasting majestically from horizon to horizon, the four wild horses docile as grazing cows beneath his masterful hand?' With a humorous shrug and an instant change of mood: 'Don't ask me! All I do in my paper is give general directions, not provide a detailed map of the way to go.'

'All!'

'Yes, all.' Tawno Smith came back to the centre of the room. 'I know my limitations, Inspector Jurnet. An old *dukkerer* – a fortune-teller – once told me no one would be more loved, no one more hated, and that I would end up in what she called "the highest place". What did she mean, d'you suppose? The Nobel Prize, dead on Everest, or strung up on some super-gallows especially constructed for those who are too clever for their own good?' He threw out his arms like a dancer striking a final, triumphant pose. 'And now, I suppose' – eyes shining with mischief – 'you want to ask me about Annie Venables?'

Jurnet said: 'About Esther, actually.'

23

The Superintendent was looking grey. It took Jurnet, coming into the office, a moment to realise that this greyness was not a matter for solicitude, but a reflection. The fellow had the damnedest way, when it suited him, of taking on, chameleon-like, the coloration of his visitors.

The visitor, as it happened, was dressed in navy pinstripe, with a pink shirt the same colour as his face, and a tie that was fairly showy. His hair was sandy, his little moustache sandier, stained with nicotine. Piecemeal, there was nothing particularly grey about the man, unless it was his teeth which were a poor colour and were perhaps the reason he spoke with barely parted lips. Nevertheless, grey was what the total package added up to. The chap carried greyness with him like a snail its shell; a personal fog into which, Jurnet did not doubt, he could retreat whenever the occasion called for a quick getaway. When the Superintendent, effecting introductions, pronounced 'Major Coxon-Barringford', the name, hyphen and all, drifted greyly down the air like a dead leaf. Fixing his subordinate with a stare that dared him to make something of it, the Superintendent said: 'Major Coxon-Barringford's here to help us over Efrem Ahilar.'

'Glad to answer the call,' the Major said austerely, leaving no doubt where the responsibility lay for his presence in Angleby. 'Extraordinary fellow, had him on the books for donkey's years – well, naturally, considering the trouble he gave us under the Mandate. But ever since they proclaimed the State of Israel – amazing!

Enough orange juice to float a navy, otherwise sweet Fanny Adams. Anyone who can preserve his cover like that, all those years, has to have his head screwed on right.'

The man crossed his legs, bringing into view expensive shoes whose bows, tied double, did nothing to endear him further to the detective. In his book, people who felt a compulsion to anchor their shoelaces twice over proclaimed themselves by that distrustful act niggling and ungenerous.

Jurnet suggested, 'Maybe orange juice is all there is.'

'Ha!' barked the Major, whether in appreciative laughter at the other's sally or scorn for its provincial artlessness it was impossible to say. 'That's a good one! And now, on top of everything else, we hear there's a johnny in the Cam, husband of the late Professor Flaschner's housekeeper – '

'That's right,' Jurnet confirmed. 'Dead drunk. Probably an accident.'

'Bit simplistic, wouldn't you say? Axiomatic in our neck of the woods that when it looks like an accident, that's the time to watch out!'

'An excellent working principle, if I may say so,' the Superintendent put in. Only Jurnet, who knew him like another self, could possibly have been aware that his chief was struggling to contain his mirth. 'Particularly applicable in this case, which seems, from start to finish, to be one of murder by accident. There seems little doubt that the poisoned juice was intended for Dr Tawno Smith.'

'Ha!' the Major ejaculated again, this time openly sceptical. It dawned on Jurnet that, whatever proposition was put forward, the Major was committed to shooting it down on principle. 'The gipsy genius! At least, from what I gather, that gentleman, at time of going to press, is still all in one piece.'

Jurnet said: 'Dr Smith reckons nobody's going to make a move till he's finished tidying up his equations.'

'Does he indeed?' commented Major Coxon-Barring-ford. 'And what do *you* reckon, Inspector?'

Jurnet replied evenly, aware it was a formula he was a bit too keen on, 'I'm keeping an open mind.'

The Major tut-tutted. 'Let me give you a piece of advice, young fellow – to wit, that minds are not made to be open, like a whore's bed airing off between clients. An open mind is no better than an open sewer – fast as something flows in at one end, something else slithers out unnoticed at the other.'

'And if' – this from the Superintendent, contriving to look immensely grateful for the insight – 'it turns out you've made up your mind and got it wrong, what then?'

'Why, so much the better!' the Major shone with a beautiful certainty. 'It means you've tested one idea to breaking point and can go on to the next one knowing you've cleared at least one set of possibilities out of the way.' The Major jack-knifed his thin body at the waist, apparently moved by a sudden need to check that his laces remained double-tied. Reassured, he straightened up and resumed: 'This Efrem Ahilar, for example – take it from me, you're barking up the wrong tree. It's the lovely Esther who knocked off the Professor and unloaded Venables into the drink. Did you know she's a karate black belt? Well, she is; and as of now she is in the process of seducing Dr Smith so as to be in the best possible position to snatch his world-shaking manuscript the instant its revision is complete.'

Jurnet, keeping his voice carefully neutral, asked: 'And is she planning to kill Dr Smith once she's got her hands on it, to make sure he can't produce yet another version?'

'Got it in one,' applauded the Major. 'You see how it all falls into place.'

'Except that Tawno Smith will have nothing to do with her.'

'Are you in love?' Tawno Smith had asked, poised on the balls of his feet in front of the empty hearth. Even at rest, the detective thought, the man looked about to take off for distant horizons, action implicit in every line of the neat, compact body. 'I recognise that this is an impudent reversal of roles. You are the one to ask the questions.'

Besides being none of your bloody business! His hand in his pocket, fingering Miriam's postcard, Jurnet said in his most formal tone, 'I can't think my personal feelings are relevant to this inquiry – '

'Don't be so stuffy, man!' The physicist's white teeth shone briefly in his brown face. 'It's purely a matter of semantics. If we're to communicate, you and I, we have to be sure we're speaking the same language. L-O-V-E – an odd-sounding little word, a little more than one syllable, a little less than two. Nothing to do with mere pleasure. Women and I have played delightful games together. But love – !' Tawno Smith shrugged his shoulders.

Jurnet said: 'We're talking about Miss Ahilar, of course.'

The other inclined his head in agreement. 'The beauteous Esther. We are also talking about my son, Christopher.'

'Oh ah.'

'The all-purpose cop-out! I need help, Inspector, not animal imitations!' The man pushed his black curls away from his forehead and complained like a sulky child: 'It's Uncle Max I blame, actually. When he was around I felt no compulsion to bind myself to people in this terrible, demanding way. I was my own man. But now' – the face the gipsy turned on the detective was less suffering than rebellious – 'now he's gone and left me at the mercy of four little letters with ideas above their station – '

Cutting to the heart of the matter, Jurnet proffered:

171

'It's not the first time a father and a son have fallen for the same woman.'

'Ye Gods! Did I say that? You've got it all wrong, man! I have not, as you so elegantly put it, fallen for Esther – fallen for her, that is, in any other way than to believe that in different circumstances we could share some pleasant times together. Alas for me, however, she's a girl who takes that little word *love* a great deal too seriously. And Christopher's another. I'm caught between the two of them like the filling in a sandwich, unable to get away from either.'

'I don't see that,' Jurnet demurred. 'It's not as if she's given the lad any encouragement. If Dr Tawno Smith didn't exist Christopher'd still get nowhere with her. He's young. He'll get over it.'

The other sighed.

'I don't think he will, you know. When you look at my son, Inspector, you see an English schoolboy – yes? – beautiful but a bit retarded, the way they all are, even these days with sex education and whatever else they teach them in the name of something or other. And Christopher, with that so-called father of his pumping him full of religious poppycock from the day he was born, is more backward than most. But that isn't all he is, by a long chalk.' The pride in the voice was touching, if self-congratulatory. 'He's a young man of great gifts with a single-mindedness I have to respect even when it scares me stiff. He loves Esther and – take my word for it – however many women he may go to bed with, he'll never love anybody else. I've already turned his life round sufficiently by persuading him to read mathematics, not divinity, and I owe him something.

'For that reason, if no other, I have to decline Esther's only too explicit offer. I can't let him see me succeed where he has failed – '

The Major repeated on a note of incredulity: 'Nothing

172

to do with her? Can't imagine where you picked that one up, chummy. The fellow's a notorious womaniser.'

'I picked it up from the fellow himself.'

'Well, then!'

Looking pleased, Major Coxon–Barringford checked up on his bows again, and, finding all in order, gave one of them an affectionate tweak. The double bow became instantly a single one. The Superintendent and his subordinate watched in silence as the visitor repaired the fault.

'As to Jaffa Joe,' the Major resumed, a little out of breath, 'I can't promise, after all this time with no action, that his file is fully operational, but we'll always supply an up-date any time it suits you to call for one.'

'You've been most helpful.' The Superintendent spoke briskly, discarding his reflected greyness without ceremony, as if stuffing into a laundry basket an overall which had served its purpose. 'Marvellous idea of the Chief's to get you down here to give us the benefit of your expertise, but fortunately we won't need to put either you or your department to that trouble – ' His eyes everywhere but on his junior officer, his voice gathering strength and sparkle, the Superintendent ended the sentence – 'since Detective Inspector Jurnet here will be leaving for Israel the day after tomorrow.'

24

The road climbed upward without compromise, striving towards a thinner air and a thin blue sky so suffused with heat that its blueness was more of an intellectual assumption than something actually perceived. The sky, not to put too fine a point on it, was yellow, the land was a yellow skin stretched over a yellow skeleton, bits of which had broken off and lay about the surface like ancient bones turned up by the plough. The driver, a young man with a Birmingham accent and, to judge by his driving, an utter confidence in the God of Israel's concern for his personal survival, remarked with a deep contentment: 'In spring, when the almond blossom's out, it's even more beautiful.' Passing a cement factory, its gritty starkness exquisitely attuned to its surroundings, the boy said: 'This is the old road. We get back to the other at Beth Shemesh. I wanted to give you a better chance to look around.'

And for you to play your games of Russian roulette with oncoming traffic, thought Jurnet, but did not say: only, 'Very thoughtful of you.'

When, feeling obscurely that the man had a right to know, he had gone to Rabbi Schnellman's flat above the synagogue to impart the news that he was on the point of taking off for that land to which God, for His own inscrutable reasons, had led the Israelites, the joy which transfigured the rabbi's face had added a further dimension to the detective's private exhilaration.

'But that's marvellous!' Rabbi Schnellman had exclaimed, grasping Jurnet's hand. The words tumbling out as if he hardly knew what to mention first, he had begun to speak of orange trees and olive groves, of deserts that at sunrise and sunset flared with all the colours of the rainbow. Mostly, though, he had spoken of Jerusalem the golden, and the spiritual enhancement it brought to every Jew simply to stand on that hallowed ground, to breathe its unique air, bask in its incomparable light: slot himself into that invisible space which, no matter how far he had wandered from the faith of his fathers, was always there, awaiting him.

The good man's enthusiasm had been contagious; so much so that Jurnet had neglected to inquire where he, a mere candidate for conversion, stood amid the general euphoria. Never had he felt so nearly a Jew, an excitement which had lasted through the journey to London, the hassle of Heathrow, the landing in a strange land where he felt he ought by right to feel immediately at home.

Going up to Jerusalem he did not feel at home. He felt Abroad. The Costa Brava, the Algarve, those bloody Greek islands – all the places Miriam had dragged him to on holiday – and now, God help him, Israel. Just one more Godforsaken hole where the green of Norfolk was completely lacking and the sun shone hot enough to frizzle your balls. Going up to Jerusalem, his self-communing intermittently interrupted by some heart-stopping piece of brinkmanship on the part of the boy from Birmingham or some answering lunacy from other traffic on the road, Jurnet found his eye and his heart growing progressively colder.

It was a cooling off that made even the longed-for reunion with his lover seem less probable, even something less to be desired In his mind's eye he saw Miriam searching his face with those great eyes of hers in which, however joyous the occasion, a residual melancholy always lingered. He saw her turn away, the sadness explicit. The Norfolk dumpling, she would be thinking, the narrow-minded provincial for whom not even Jerusalem the golden could come within measuring distance of Angleby.

Well, wasn't it the truth? Eyes narrowed against the glare, Jurnet studied the landscape, conscientiously seeking something to praise. The boy from Birmingham was talking about how this was his last job before going into the army. He gunned the Merc ahead of a taxi as if practising a military exercise, and swerved to regain the nearside a matter of inches from the radiator of an oncoming bus.

'Mr Ahilar said to say his apologies for not being able to see you today as arranged. He had to go out of town unexpected and won't be back in Jerusalem till late tonight. Said, if it's OK with you, I'm to pick you up nine sharp tomorrow morning and drive you over to him.'

'It's OK with me. Thanks.'

'He said, if you want, I'm to be at your disposal the rest of today.' Racing a Swedish-registered Volvo to the next bend and reluctantly giving way only when confronted with a truck laden with avocados coming from the opposite direction: 'Anywhere you want to go, just say the word.'

Repressing a stray qualm that, in view of his underling's driving, Afrem Ahilar's generosity might have a more sinister connotation, Jurnet replied: 'Very kind of Mr Ahilar, but if you'd just give me a few minutes to drop off my bag at Meyerson's Hotel, and get a wash and brush-up, then take me to Police Headquarters, I shan't need to trouble you any further.'

'Police Headquarters, eh?' In a leisurely, offhand way the young man swivelled round in his seat so as to study his passenger's face. Though it had to be said that the Mercedes, apparently untroubled by this withdrawal of supervision, continued its journey at uninterrupted speed and seemingly no better and no worse driven than before, the manoeuvre made Jurnet feel nervous. Perhaps it was some communicated suggestion of unease which made the young man, at the end of his examination, declare: 'Don't tell me you're a cop! You don't look like one.'

'Maybe you've forgotten what an English copper looks like.'

'Me, forgotten!' The other laughed. 'Me and the Brit fuzz, chum, bosom pals! We sent each other Chanukah cards every Christmas. Whenever business was slack down at the nick or they were feeling in the mood for a spot of aggro, "Le's call round an' have a word wi' young Danny," they'd say. "Let's go an' see what he's bin up to." An' of course I always had bin up to something or other. Juvenile delinquent of the year, that was me – '

'And here in Israel, I suppose, you're a reformed character?'

'Tha's right,' said the boy, not smiling.

Jerusalem was all right. '*All right!*' Jurnet visualised Rabbi Schnellman's consternation, the plump face reddening, the generous mouth screwed up into an O of outrage. '*Is that all you've got to say about it?*'

OK. Substitute 'interesting', if it makes you feel better. Jerusalem was quite interesting, if old buildings and old religions turned you on, and people in the streets who, for Jurnet's money, almost made the place worth a *petit détour*, as they said in the French guidebooks, so long as you had time and it wasn't all that out of your way. Deducting the parties of tourists being led like sheep from shrine to souvenir shop and apparently finding it increasingly hard to distinguish one from the other, the variety of human beings out taking the air was still astonishing. It was not merely a matter of clothes, the detective decided – an Arab's robes, a priest's kaftan, the wide hat and black suit of antique cut sported by the well-dressed Chasid. Rather a factor of being, the way they moved, inclined their heads when they spoke. A calm certainty, as if each carried with him his own Jerusalem.

The city went about its business at several decibels above what would have been considered normal in England, the citizens piling on to buses with the ungenerous urgency of alpine villagers fleeing an impending avalanche. They greeted each other with cries of joy and parted as extravagantly as if they never expected to meet again this side of the grave. But underneath the surface excess – underneath the tension which Jurnet, as a copper, had sensed almost immediately in the crowded streets and even more in the narrow alleys full of dark corners – there beat, as it were, an encompassing

177

rhythm, a communal awareness of the place not merely as something old and therefore entitled to the respect due to age, but as a fount forever renewed and renewable; of today and tomorrow, until the end of time.

It pierced Jurnet, the would-be Jew, to the core to perceive this special quality of Jerusalem whilst perceiving equally that he was not, and never could be, part of it. If God had chosen that moment to lean out of His heaven and announce His intention of wiping either Jerusalem or Angleby instantly from the face of the earth and it was up to Ben Jurnet to choose which, the detective knew what his answer would be.

And where did that leave him with Miriam?

It was a pity, in a way, he couldn't just have stayed quietly, waiting for his appointment time with Efrem Ahilar to come round, sitting comfortably in Jerusalem Police Headquarters in Sheikh Jerach Road, for it was blessedly cool there and it felt like home: the same air of commitment, the same sprung vigilance.

Not that it looked like home, especially the dark-eyed beauties in chic two-pieces garnished with lanyards and epaulettes, and the casually dressed, casually mannered men who were, so far as the detective could judge, the equivalent of his own CID. On the other hand, Yacoov Ben-Peretz, the recipient of his courtesy call, was too much like home to be true, a typical fair-haired, blue-eyed Englishman, you would have said, discounting the foreign flash of three stars on the shoulders of the short-sleeved light blue shirt, except that Englishmen nowadays so seldom looked like that outside the covers of Mills & Boon romances.

The two had shaken hands and stood a little longer, smiling at each other, both of them – Jurnet was convinced – amused by the ethnic irony of their encounter: the dark, Mediterranean Brit and the Anglo-Saxon Israeli. Then the Chief Inspector had spoken, not in the clipped public-school accents his appearance demanded, but something heavily based on Brooklynese, and Jurnet was back in Jerusalem again.

Though it had all been arranged in London, the proprieties had to be observed.

Jurnet said: 'Very good of the Commissioner to let me have a word with Mr Ahilar.'

'As many as you like, since I understand that Mr Ahilar himself has raised no objection. And besides' – the Chief Inspector's blue eyes darkening perceptibly – 'here in Israel we're at least as keen as you are to nail the guy who bumped off Professor Flaschner. A great man and a very good friend of this country.' The Chief Inspector picked up some papers Jurnet recognised. 'We appreciate your sending us such a full summary.'

'Only fair you should know what it's all in aid of. In fact, if, having read it, you have any thoughts of your own on the subject, I'd be glad to hear them.'

The other laughed in an understanding way: one cop to another. 'Only thought I have is to be thankful it's not my baby.' The man quietened, frowned. 'You're not banking on fitting up Efrem Ahilar for the role of killer? I've asked around. Everyone says the two were like brothers.'

'I'm not banking on fitting up anybody, except the man – or woman – who actually did it.'

'Sorry! Slip of my American slang. Let's see if I can't make up for it – '

The Chief Inspector got up, went over to the window, and, turning his back on his visitor, looked down into the street. The whole so exactly corresponded to the Superintendent's habit that Jurnet, his momentary annoyance forgotten, almost joined him there, if only to check that it really was Jerusalem on the other side of the glass, not Angleby Market Place.

'What I can do for you,' the Chief Inspector went on, 'is let you into the difference between an Englishman and an Israeli.' He came back from the window and resumed his seat. 'Maybe, you think, there isn't

179

any that matters. We're all human beings, after all, and we're a nation now, like all the other nations, not a bunch of starry-eyed screwballs who came here to bring to reality the dream which has kept Jews alive through centuries of rejection and persecution. We've grown up. Today we not only glory in all the usual perks of a democratic state – the parliament, free press, and so on – we also possess the other apparent indispensables – pimps, prostitution, drugs, all the accepted markers of a sophisticated society.'

'And murder?'

'That we have too. And that's what I want to let you in on – well, not so much murder as the Israeli attitude to violent death, because that will tell you more about the kind of people we are than almost anything else. We've had to fight, if necessary kill, for this land of ours: to get it, make it, keep it – unlike you English, who were lucky enough to have got your own dirty work over and done with before there was television and the media to take it all down and angle it whichever way suited them. You guys who have had your nation-hood handed to you on a plate may have got the impression that we here put a lesser value on individual life than you flatter yourselves you do in the West – '

'No.' Jurnet interrupted. 'No less and no more.'

'Your sentiments do you credit,' said Chief Inspector Ben-Peretz with a little nod of acknowledgment. 'But you're still wrong, my friend. We value it more. What you've left out of your calculation is the Holocaust, the six million who died in the concentration camps. Why, indeed should you remember them more than forty years later, except as a terrible statistic which must never be allowed to recur? With us, on the other hand, it's different. With us, you see, it's not six million at all, a convenient round number, but one and one and one and one, my brother and my brother and my brother – ' The Israeli police officer broke off. 'Do I make myself clear?'

'I think,' said Jurnet, 'you're telling me that you don't think Efrem Ahilar killed Professor Flaschner.'

The Chief Inspector laughed outright. He looked across the desk at his English counterpart with something close to affection.

'Is that all I've been telling you?'

'Not all.'

In the lobby, one of the dark-eyed beauties – a sergeant, to judge from the three stripes on her sleeve – received the English detective's stumbling inquiry with sympathetic attention. Was there anywhere in Jerusalem an office, some kind of organisation perhaps, which looked after the affairs of a desert settlement called Tel Tzevaim? He asked because he rather hoped to get in touch with an old acquaintance of his who was staying there for a while, maybe pay a visit to the place if there was some easy way of getting to it and back again. Always assuming, since he was only in Israel for a couple of days and he found the time, it wasn't too far from the city –

'Tel Tzevaim!' Police Sergeant Shoshana Kishon repeated, glowing with the pleasure of imparting good news. 'You are in luck! It was in the paper only yesterday. My mother works in occupational therapy and she said she was going to take time off work to go and see it, it sounded as if they have done wonders – oh!' In the face of her inquirer's evident bewilderment: 'My English! It is so bad! I will speak it over again, more slowly.'

'No. It's very good,' Jurnet contradicted. 'It's me. What's this about luck?'

'There is an exhibition at the Kronberg Hall,' the policewoman began again, with an endearing frown as she took time getting her tongue round the alien syllables. 'It is not more than fifteen minutes' walk. Isn't that a wonderful coincidence? It is possible,' she added, without batting an eyelash, 'you will find the young lady is already here in Jerusalem, waiting for you.'

'What's happening in this Kronberg Hall, then?'

'There is an exhibition. It is five years since the settlement was established, and they are celebrating the birthday. According to the newspaper, in that short time they have already done remarkable things. There are many handicapped people, and some are mental – mental – '

'Mentally retarded?'

'Thank you, mentally retarded. Some Falashas too, from Ethiopia, who have many problems. But the papers said just the same the quality of the work' – achieving the end of her recital with a flush of achievement – 'is quite exceptional.'

Jurnet felt vaguely depressed. A bloody craft fair. Miriam presiding over a display of woven baskets and woolly mitts – some hopes! There might, of course, be somebody he could give a message to. (Such as what, for Christ's sake? *Come back at once. I'm dying of love for you?*) He recognised, amid the misery, an enjoyable touch of malice to think of her astonishment at hearing he was actually in Jerusalem, leading his own exciting life without any help from her.

The sergeant said: 'Today is a big party. The Major will be there and important people who have given the money – '

'Ah well, thanks very much.' With a studied lack of haste Jurnet prepared to leave. 'I may drop by for a slice of birthday cake if I can spare the time. Kronberg Hall. I'll remember that.'

Sergeant Kishon produced a street map and spread it out on the counter.

'I will show you exactly where it is.' With a jab of an immaculately tended fingernail: 'There! You see it is not far, though if you wish there is a bus, number 9, which stops outside the door.'

'You've been very kind.'

The lustrous eyes twinkled. Sergeant Shoshana Kishon said, in the deadpan voice of a police officer reporting back to his superior, 'Besides the Mayor and the people with the money, they are bussing the entire settlement in from Tel Tzevaim for the occasion. They will all be there, you may be sure of it. Even your old acquaintance.'

Jurnet did not wait for the bus. He needed to walk, to run, to take great leaps into the air. Having nourished himself for so long on the diffuse possibility of seeing Miriam again, the knowledge that it was actually about to happen, the lovely image made fresh, was almost more than he could bear.

He hurried through the streets, crossing and recrossing, at peril to life and limb from the ebullient traffic, from sun to deep shadow and back again to sun, whenever he spied a space that, for a delusive moment, promised a faster rate of knots. The estranging strangeness of the city was submerged in his happiness. What was Jerusalem to him or he to Jerusalem? It was enough that it was the place which contained his love.

Even with two unintentional detours he bettered the dark-eyed sergeant's projected time by a good two minutes; came out into a square filled with sunlight and heat and people who all seemed to be talking at once, whilst, on the steps of a moderately imposing building labelled unmistakably Kronberg Hall, a smiling man in white sports shirt and slacks – whom Jurnet, used to the civic mummery of gold chains, gathered incredulously was the Mayor – in no way put off his stride by the noise battering against him, was making a speech. Several coaches decked with bunting were already parked empty in the square where others nosed their way in, the crowds giving way with nonchalance only when it seemed they must inevitably be crushed beneath the chariot wheels, and re-forming instantly a little more tightly packed and no less vociferous.

They let the foreigner through good-humouredly. Burning with impatience, Jurnet waited while the coach driver left his seat and joined the four young women who were helping the passengers to alight. At the same time, a posse of young police constables, appearing as if from nowhere, cleared a passage to the front door of the Hall with an efficiency that threatened to dislodge the Mayor along with the other obstacles in their path. The Mayor, unruffled, moved aside a few inches and went on speaking.

The passengers, most of them young adults with Down's syndrome, their broad faces bright with excitement, went into the hall, their minders accompanying them – women who were young and comely, but were not Miriam. No good, Jurnet realised, looking for the cloud of bronze hair which ordinarily made his lover recognisable from afar. Out of respect for the city which had once held the Temple and would, when the Messiah came, hold it again, the girls wore kerchiefs on their heads, knotted with a modesty that made it hardly possible to tell if they were dark or fair. At the thought of Miriam with her head covered out of respect for Jerusalem, Jurnet's happiness receded a little.

The Mayor finished his speech. Everybody except Jurnet clapped, still talking nineteen to the dozen. As the detective hesitated, wondering whether Miriam might not have come in on one of the earlier coaches and be already in the hall, the feeling of strangeness, of not belonging, of never being able to belong, began to seep back, rolling in like a fog to chill his heart and blight his foolish hopes. Desperately seeking a point of reference, Jurnet reminded himself that this city which so contemptuously rejected him was also the city of Calvary and Gethsemane.

No use. He had already gone too far down another road, too late for turning back.

Another coach came into the square; like its predecessors creating for itself a space in which to pull up and set down its load. This coach, Jurnet noted, was specially adapted, with a slide-back door on one side, and a ramp to be let down in place of steps.

One to each wheelchair, a fresh group of young women, their kerchiefs equally hiding their hair, carefully manoeuvred their charges down to ground level. Safely arrived, they settled the twisted bodies, smiled down into the trustful faces smiling up at them, before making for the further ramp the policemen had laid over the steps leading up to the Kronberg Hall portico.

Confronted with this evidence of an inscrutable providence, the onlookers in the square fell, not silent, but aware; shaken by a murmur full of love and pity. The cripples in their wheel chairs, heads sunk between shoulders, useless arms and legs dangling, regarded them with compassion.

Miriam was the last to descend from the coach, piloting a wheelchair occupied by a wizened little creature who might have been a child were it not for the eternity of pain stamped on the tiny face. Jurnet, who wanted with every fibre of his being to look at his love, absorb her presence into every corner of his consciousness, found himself compelled to look instead at this casualty of time. *Suffer little children.* Bugger both of you, he thought angrily, at last tearing his eyes away.

Miriam had never been more beautiful. She had changed, Jurnet saw – thinner, the eyes set deeper in the suntanned face. The body in the unassertive, long-sleeved dress, whilst no less made for delights, had lost its explicit voluptuousness. Jurnet also saw that these outward modifications were of no consequence beside the changes in the essential Miriam. Gone was the haunting melancholy, the air not so much of discontent as of incompleteness. Her lover realised, with something of a shock, that never before, not even in bed, whether in the transports of passion or in the calm that

185

came after, had he seen her, as now, unequivocally happy, all defences surrendered.

A wheel of the chair had wedged itself into a space between the old paving-stones, Miriam bent down to release it, tugging with one hand, steadying the chair with the other. The effort was too much for the kerchief, which slipped from her head, the hair cascading forth like a bronze waterfall. Tears came into Jurnet's eyes.

A mere matter of feet away, he still did not feel able to make his presence known. Miriam herself was too preoccupied to look about her. One of the young constables sprang to her assistance only too willingly, the detective thought sourly; glad when, despite all efforts, the wheel still did not budge. Miriam said something in Hebrew at which the policeman nodded, and then, undoing the strap that held the crippled child/woman in place, she lifted her from the chair. Cradling the damaged soul in her arms, she turned towards the shadowy portico. The little creature nestled against her breast with a sigh of contentment.

And Miriam? Jurnet gazed long and hard, lovingly and despairingly, at the glory of Miriam's face. Then he turned his back, ploughed a path for himself to the edge of the square, and, with many unthinking errors of direction, found at last his solitary way back to his hotel.

25

Efrem Ahilar lived in Rehavia, not far from the Knesset;
the home of a wealthy man in a golden city where
domestic space equalled gold, plenty of it. As if to
flaunt this precious commodity, Efrem Ahilar's home
was full of empty spaces, the few pieces which stood
about the large living-rom severely functional, rough-
hewn pieces that looked as if they had just come from
the carpenter's bench. It was, thought Jurnet, waiting
for his host to come in from his balcony, the perfect
home for the quintessential Jew. Sling a few things into
your knapsack and you'd be ready to leave at a
moment's notice, before the Cossacks arrived or the SS
men kicked in the door. Roots, the room seemed to
proclaim, were dangerous. Was it possible that Efrem
Ahilar felt that corroding insecurity even here in
Jerusalem?

The man came in, quickly sliding the glass door to
the balcony back into place to keep out the heat, already
quickening in the early day. He wore shorts and a T-
shirt that revealed well-muscled legs and arms and a
strong neck that belied the grizzled hair. The face, however, deeply furrowed, seemed older than Jurnet
remembered it.

Efrem Ahilar said: 'Before we get down to business
you must tell me whether you have seen my Esther
lately, and how she is looking.'

'I saw her a couple of days ago. She looked fine.'

'I am very glad to hear it. Her letters – forgive me!'
the man came towards Jurnet with outstretched hand.
'I forget my manners. There will be coffee in a moment.

This is your first time in Jerusalem, I think you said?' Jurnet nodded. 'We have a Hebrew blessing to celebrate such a joyful consummation. After we have spoken I will teach you the words, and then your visit will be crowned with every kind of success.'

Jurnet, omitting to say that Rabbi Schnellman had already primed him with the appropriate formula to be addressed to the Almighty on first catching sight of the City of David, nodded with every appearance of gratitude.

'Almost I envy you!' Efrem Ahilar exclaimed. 'To experience that unique lift of the heart which comes when you see Jerusalem for the first time! Jew, Christian, Muslim, it is all one. One day, I promise myself, I will make a scientific experiment. I will bring back an Indian from Tierra del Fuego and a head-hunter from Papua New Guinea and then you will see how people who have never even heard of the city will be uplifted by that same joy of homecoming.'

A girl, young and slender, brought in the coffee, set the tray down on a low table and almost ran from the room. Efrem Ahilar said, with affection in his voice: 'She is like a young deer. She takes fright if a leaf moves.' He poured the coffee into cups made of a thick pottery that looked like petrified cream. The coffee was Turkish, thick and sweet and foreign. Jurnet got it down somehow.

'I will be frank with you,' Efrem Ahilar said. 'I worry about my Esther. So excited to go to Cambridge – but now, her letters are not cheerful. Can it mean, I ask myself as now I ask you, that she has not yet gone to bed with that young devil, that not-so-young devil, Tawno?' The graven lines of the man's face softened in a wry smile. 'I see that I shock you a little. This is no way for a grandfather to talk, hey? Especially a Jewish grandfather who should want for his granddaughter a nice Jewish boy, a lawyer or a chartered accountant.' With a humorous shrug of the broad shoulders: 'What would be the use? She could be standing with just such a one under the *chupa*, the marriage canopy, and in would walk Dr Tawno and crook his little finger, and she would be off like the wind, her wedding veil billowing out behind her, her bridegroom left standing there like a silly ass, a *nudnik*.' Efrem Ahilar sighed. 'She has loved him since she was a child.' With a chuckle: 'Cambridge! An English degree! How solemnly we weighed up the pros and cons as if we didn't, both of us, know that to her Cambridge meant only one thing – Tawno and Tawno and Tawno again.' Brows knitting: 'And yet, now that she is there, she does not sound happy.'

'Young Christoper Maslin is in love with her.'

'There will always be men who are in love with my Esther. When she is an old woman they will still die of love for her. So what is Christopher Maslin? A child Esther could never – '

'No. But he's Dr Smith's godson. And, as I understand it, Dr Smith wouldn't want to queer his pitch.'

'Godson!' Efrem Ahilar hooted. 'But that is ridiculous! What is godson to that heathen?'

'From what I've observed, it seems to be quite a lot. He doesn't want the boy humiliated.'

'Ridiculous!' the other repeated. He strode about the room, filling up the expensive spaces with his impatience and his patent concern. 'If Max were still alive there would be no difficulty. I could use him as an excuse for being in Cambridge. Now, if I turn up, it will be fussy grandpa who can't trust his darling to manage her own life without interfering.' He came close to the detective, halted with a smile that transformed his rugged features. 'I have it! All you have to do is arrest me and take me back to England to face a murder charge. I will waive all that extradition nonsense. When, as must happen, you have to let me go for lack of evidence, I shall go to Cambridge to recuperate from my ordeal. What more natural?'

Jurnet said stolidly: 'There was a death in Cambridge as well, as a matter of fact. Perhaps you've heard.'

'Annie's husband, you mean?' Efrem Ahilar nodded. 'Esther telephoned me. She keeps me informed of every particular – or did, until recently, when she sends only scratchy notes which, saying nothing, say only that something is wrong.'

'Did she tell you that Venables was found in the Cam?'

The other nodded. 'Drunk, she said. Terrible for poor Annie. That woman was good to Max, good *for* him. Esther said it would be necessary to wait for the verdict at the inquest before coming to a definite conclusion.'

'Very proper,' the detective agreed. 'The man was drunk, certainly. Whether that was how he came to be in the river is another matter.'

'You mean it's another murder? There's a connection with what happened at the castle?'

'It's always possible,' said Jurnet, answering both questions at once and, in effect, answering neither. 'Did you yourself never meet Dandy Venables?'

'Dandy! Now that *is* a name! I never even knew Annie had a husband alive.' But Efrem Ahilar's face was suddenly alight with a mischievous humour. 'Unless, of course, I met him by appointment while Esther was signing in at her college and I went – or rather, *said* I was going – to get petrol.'

'That's one scenario,' the detective concurred easily. 'The way that window pane at Heathcote Avenue was removed looked remarkably like Dandy's handiwork. One thing's certain. If he did in fact effect an entry into that study for the purpose of stealing Dr Smith's paper, he didn't do it for himself. A lecture on the forces that hold the universe together isn't a commodity your common or garden villain'd be interested in. Someone must have hired his services.'

The Israeli put his hand into the pocket of his shorts and drew out a scrap of paper.

'Keep that carefully, Inspector,' he adjured, handing it over. 'A photostat of the receipt from the Cambridge garage. For the moment I retain the original. I am a careful man, you understand. When I go abroad I keep a strict account of all my expenses.' With a laugh: 'Perhaps you will think too careful for my own good. Haven't I read in your English detective stories that the innocent never have alibis?'

'Musn't believe all you read.' Jurnet studied the faintly inked print-out, making out the heading Herbert Robinson Ltd, Newmarket Road and the date. 'Not, I'm bound to tell you, that this is worth all that much in the alibi line. You had time for more than just filling up.'

'So I did! Plenty of time, if I hurried, to get to Max's house, meet my accomplice, break in and take the paper without wasting a moment.' The man reflected, one sandalled foot idly tracing the grain of the wood-block floor. Then, looking up with a serious air: 'Even though your native security services may perhaps have aroused in your mind some ungentlemanly suspicions of me, I will tell you how to know it was not I who stole Tawno's paper. Let's face it, given who I am, what I have been, I might well have bought this man Venables, I might well have removed those pages containing a new vision of heaven and hell. I might even, later in the day, have dropped poison into Tawno Smith's orange juice. Yes, even the fact that my Esther loves him would not have saved him if the interests of my country had demanded it. That is the kind of man we have had to be, we who fought to rescue the remnant of our brothers and sisters from the gas chambers and bring them safely to the Promised Land. What I would not have done, however, in any circumstances, was slash my dear old friend's favourite chairs.'

Efrem Ahilar remarked, with no evidence of anxiety: 'You have my fingerprints on the glass, of course.'

'Naturally the glass has been the subject of examination,' returned Jurnet rather awkwardly. The detective saw no reason for letting on that the sole identifiable prints recovered from its surface were those of Tawno Smith and the waitress who had fetched the orange juice from the kitchen.

'Mine and Mrs Pender's, that is,' the Israeli amended. 'The lady wanted a lesson in how to identify orange by the nose. I handed her the glass, and she took it and sniffed, though what could she hope to learn, the silly woman? But she insisted. I will tell you this, though,' the orange juice expert went on, 'in case it is of any assistance. When I sniffed that juice, the poison had not yet been added.'

'You're saying the smell of orange couldn't have drowned out the almond smell of cyanide?'

'For Max, probably, yes. For Tawno. But not for my educated nose which could distinguish a speck of dust dropped in, a grain of sugar.'

Jurnet looked at Efrem Ahilar's nasal organ, large and commanding. Some buggers, he thought, have all the luck: a single, simple piece of apparatus programmed to do all the work, smell its way unerringly to a solution of every difficulty.

The detective said: 'Good of you to let your police here take your prints for sending on to us.'

The Israeli grinned. 'How would it have looked if I had refused?' He sat down and poured himself another cup of coffee, gestured an offer of the same to Jurnet, who shook his head in refusal. 'Have I now told you all you want to know?'

'There *is* one other thing. At the castle dinner, as I recall it, you – or maybe it was the Professor, I'm not sure – mentioned something about taking his messages back to Israel for him.' Jurnet took out his notebook, poised pencil at the ready. 'What I'd appreciate knowing is who those messages were addressed to, and whether they were written or verbal. If I could trouble you for the names – '

'Only one name, my friend, and only one address, though the latter, I'm afraid, is no more than an accommodation one. Put your notebook away,' said Efrem Ahilar. 'I doubt if the person concerned would be in if you called or left a message on his answering machine. Max's messages were all in writing, and all to be forwarded to the same address: to God, at the Western Wall.' At the sight of the detective's disconcerted expression the orange merchant added kindly: 'You have doubtless heard of our quaint old custom?'

'The Wailing Wall, is that what you mean?' Jurnet pulled himself together. 'I've read about people poking requests and prayers into the cracks between the stones – '

'That is the place. All that remains of the Second Temple. Only, the Western, not the Wailing, Wall, if you please, even though people of simple faith still assert that the dew which nightly falls on those hallowed stones is made out of the tears that, over the centuries, have been shed there for the destruction of the Temple and the sufferings of the Jewish people.' The man finished the last of his coffee, returned the cup and saucer to the tray. 'The practice of leaving prayers and supplications, to which you refer, still persists. Whilst you are here in Jerusalem you must certainly go and see for yourself, if you have not already done so; even leave your own *kvittel*, as we call it. As they say, you never know! For many visitors, it is the first place they make for: of all the landmarks in the city the most ancient and the most holy. But then' – the gleam of curiosity in the deep set eyes was not to be disguised – 'you are not a Jew.'

'No. I am not a Jew.'

'It is funny you should ask me about this,' commented Efrem Ahilar, dowsing the spark, 'because it is

only two days since I carried out Max's instructions for
the last time. Since I got back to Israel I've been rushed
off my feet. Every morning I've said to myself, "Today
I must go to the Wall," and, every evening, "I must
be sure and go tomorrow." Not that I feel unduly
guilty. By now, I am sure, Max will have delivered his
message personally. He was not a good man – far from
it – only a great one. But if the Master of the Universe
likes a good laugh – and one has only to look around
one to be certain of it – He could not deny Himself the
pleasure of my rascally old friend's company.'

'I suppose,' ventured Jurnet, despising himself for
asking, but asking nevertheless, 'you didn't yourself
happen to look at that last message?'

'Read it, do you mean?' The detective bowed his
head without resentment at the contempt in the other's
voice. 'Of what possible interest could it be to me to
do any such thing – and even more, if I may say so,
to you? Do English police, today, hide even in the
confessional?'

'I couldn't help wondering' – Jurnet pressed on
regardless – 'whether the Professor might not have
made some reference – something which might give us
a pointer – '

'Come between a man and his Maker?' Unappeased
Efrem Ahilar resumed his walking to and fro. He
reminded the detective of a caged animal, one of the
large cats, blank-faced but dangerous.

'I tell you,' he said at last, his voice blandly chill. 'I
placed the message where I always placed Max's messages, between the first and second courses of stone –
you would need to be a giant to reach higher – and
four, no, five blocks from the barrier which divides off
the women. The upper block at that particular spot is
eroded into a little arch, almost architectural, and there
is a deep niche. You will have no difficulty in recognising it, any more than you will have difficulty in recognising which, of all the papers deposited there, is

Max's. Most of them are little more than scraps. People are modest, they realise that God is kept busy with great affairs. They state their own small business in as few words as possible. But Max!' Affection warming the cold voice: 'The *chutzpah* of the man! Sometimes, when I saw the size of the package he was deputing me to deliver, I would think, he is not asking but telling – telling the Lord how to run His own creation!'

'Was the last one like that?'

'The last one was like that.' The temperature had dropped abruptly. 'Several pages, at a guess, sealed into a narrow business envelope, manila. You will have no difficulty recognising it. You should have little more difficulty in taking it away.'

Jurnet stared, speechless.

'Why do you look surprised? Isn't that what you want? At the Wall', the man went on implacably, 'people's attention is fixed on the two most important things – themselves and the eternal. The police and the army, for their part, are too busy keeping their eyes open for terrorists to bother about worshippers. If you are reasonably dextrous, as I am sure that you are, no one but God will notice what you have done. I should perhaps add,' the Israeli finished, his tone dry but somewhat less unfriendly, 'that Max once told me he invariably addressed the Lord in Hebrew, the language of the Torah. He felt it to be an elementary courtesy. But no doubt you will be able to get it translated.'

It was a wall, Jurnet told himself, as if the telling of it alone confirmed its existence. A wall, nothing more. High, fifty feet at least, with tufts of vegetation sticking out here and there for all the world like mops hung out to dry. For devout Jews, if you believed the guidebooks, the holiest place in the holy city of Jerusalem.

Standing in the crowded square, Jurnet stared at the wall and thought about Miriam; how he had done the right thing in letting her go without a word spoken.

No, he corrected himself: that was to put it the wrong
way round. It was she who, all unknowing, had let *him*
go, retreated into the inner sanctuaries of this bloody
holy city, this bloody holy land, where he could not
follow her. Where he saw a shabby, shaggy old wall
she saw – what did she see? – the Temple, Solomon in
all his glory? *You tell me*, he demanded, neither expecting a reply nor getting one.

Where had he got the idea that becoming a Jew was
something simple, almost as simple as taking up golf,
say, or snooker? You bought the prescribed gear,
learned the rules, hired a coach to give you some idea
of the game, and *presto*! you were in, you'd joined the
club.

Some hopes!

The detective felt in the pocket of his slacks and
brought out the *kippah*, the little skullcap crocheted in
black wool, which Miriam had brought back from an
earlier trip to Israel. He put it on his head, where it
settled itself unobtrusively among the thick dark hair.
Thus dressed for the part, he moved towards the golden
limestone, counting off as he went the number of blocks
from the fence which divided off the women's section.
Eyeing the barrier, he shook his head in sad bafflement.
What did Miriam, when she came to this place, make
of being hived off as a second-class citizen? But then,
his Miriam of Angleby, the committed feminist quick
to take offence at real or fancied affronts to her gender,
was not the Miriam of Jerusalem, cradling a cripple in
her arms.

Close to, the size, the sheer density of the wall was
discomforting, a contemptuous commentary on the
people who buzzed about its base like so many flightless
flies. The niche of which Efrem Ahilar had spoken was
unmistakable, the late Professor Flaschner's communi-
cation to the Almighty equally so. All that remained
was to grab it and run – or rather, not run: act as if
you were praying, even repeat the prayer Rabbi Schnell-

196

man had taught you. No harm in paying your respects to the god of the place. Then, after a decent interval, the letter safely bestowed, turn and walk slowly away. *Out of Zion shall go forth the Law, and the word of the Lord from Jerusalem.*

Big deal.

A few feet away, an old man stood by the Wall, praying. Jurnet could see his lips – the red, perpetually moist lips of an old man – moving, hear the inarticulate hum of what he was saying. The old man, bony and with bowed shoulders, was dressed in heavy black clothes that must have been devilishly uncomfortable in the sun, for every now and again he pushed the wide-brimmed, low-crowned hat up on his forehead and mopped his face with a large handkerchief, yellowish white like his scanty yellowish white beard. It took a little while for Jurnet, who had been stealing cautious glances in the old man's direction to make sure he was not observed, to realise that his neighbour was crying.

The old man cried without moving his features, his parchment-skinned face with its high-bridged nose seen in profile, like the illumination of a medieval manuscript. The hand that held the handkerchief trembled, the one pale blue eye that Jurnet could see, disconsolate as a child's with a broken toy. Was it possible, Jurnet wondered incredulously, that anyone in his right mind could actually shed tears, real tears, over something that had happened under the Ancient Romans? The old boy had probably lost his missus or his money or something.

Or something.

Jurnet suddenly felt convinced – he could not have said how – that the old man was indeed lamenting the destruction of the Temple in AD 70. Why this should have affected the detective one way or the other, he could not have said either. He reached out a tentative hand and touched one of the stones of the wall, not the one with the niche, the next one along. The stone was warm in the sun, its surface striated like the trunk of an ancient tree. As he moved his hand, exploring its grooves, Jurnet had the strangest feeling that the hand was still, it was the stone that moved, responding to his touch, alive.

The movement, it seemed, was a signal, making him aware of the men who had first levered that stone into place. Good workmen they must have been, to lay stones, so scarred by time and events, and still so true. Jurnet thought admiringly, you'd have to go a long way today to find buggers who could lay stone like that.

The stone was warm, the sun hot, too bloody hot; the absurd little *kippah* no protection from its pitiless rays. Jurnet found himself swaying, the same way, funnily enough, the old geezer further along was swaying, knees slightly bent, shoulders sagging. Probably, the detective told himself, they both had a touch of the sun.

The incandescent circle overhead expanded until it filled the entire sky. It confused, consumed him, making him momentarily uncertain as to where he was, who he was. He and the sun and the stones became one – he and the sun and the stones and the old man weeping salt tears for the destruction of the Temple.

For a moment Jurnet felt that at last he understood what Jerusalem was about – what the city stood for: what it meant to be a Jew, not just a Jew anchored to one brief speck of time, but a Jew through the ages, participating in all that the word Jew stood for in transient suffering and enduring joy.

For a moment.

Cool in its shadowed niche, the murdered Professor's letter to the Author of his being awaited Jurnet's taking. The detective looked at it, blinked: it was still there. He fished out of his pocket Miriam's postcard that said '*I love you*', snatched off the *kippah*, Miriam's gift:

tossed both into the niche, retrieving nothing in exchange, and walked away.

26

Detective Sergeant Ellers announced: 'Peddar's Way.'
He depressed the accelerator a trifle and the Rover
leaped across the metalled interruption of the ancient
trackway. On the common beyond, the heather was
purpling a treat.

The little Welshman looked about him with a proprietary air.

'Bet you didn't see anything to beat that on your
foreign travels.'

'You win hands down.' Jurnet stretched out his long
legs and smiled out at the landscape. Imperial purple.
Had the sight of the heather carpeting the chill northern
earth lifted up the hearts of the Roman soldiers far from
home, much as the sight of it, that very moment, was
lifting up his own? Norfolk, he thought: yellow corn,
purple heather, a city that, in place of being golden,
was rosy with brick and sharp with the flash of flint.
He could not remember when he had enjoyed a car ride
more.

Feeling magnamimous, he said: 'True, they had a
bloody drought on. They say it's beautiful in the spring,
when the almond blossom's out.'

'Oh ah?' The Norfolk syllables, even pronounced
with a Welsh accent and half taking the mickey, made
Jurnet doubly content to be home. 'Have to fix yourself
up a return visit, then, won't you, if this blasted case

still isn't sewn up. Specially if Miriam's still out there.'
If this last was said with intent – as transparently it was
– his colleague did not rise to the bait. 'Rosie's been
dying to know how she's been making out,' Jack Ellers
continued, brazenly putting his curiosity on to his wife.
'You never said.'

'She's fine. Looking marvellous.'

'When doesn't she?' Taking unaffected pleasure in his
friend's good fortune, the little Welshman said with
relish: 'Some reunion that must have been!'

'It was, rather.'

For the umpteenth time since setting out from Angleby,
Jurnet reached into the dashboard cubby-hole, picked
up the envelope he had placed there, carefully flat:
levered out the postcard-sized object from within.

Jack Ellers asked: 'What was that name you said?'

'Micrograph. So I've been told, anyway. All that
means is writing done very small, not necessarily in
circles, like this one is. Can you imagine anyone having
the eyesight and the patience, let alone the skill, to get
down a whole book of the Bible, round and round, in
a total circumference of less than four and a half inches?'

'Must have been barmy to try.'

'Rabbi Schnellman said it was an old tradition.'

'Oh,' – disparagingly – 'tradition.'

Jurnet did not add the rest of what the Rabbi had
said – that the little square of paper was, in effect, an
offering – one proffered out of thankful joy for the
God-given dexterity that resided in the scribe's hands.
Now, in the moving car, looking down at the concen-
tric circles of text, at one moment spattered with tree
shadow, at the next bright with sun, the detective could
easily fancy that the microscopic Hebrew letters themselves jumped for joy.

'Book of the Bible, eh? S'pose there's no doubt that's
what it is?'

'Not controller's instructions to agents in the field, if

that's what you're afraid of.' Jurnet laughed, not very convincingly, having thought the same thing himself and felt guilty for the thinking of it.

Rabbi Schnellman had set his fears at rest.

'It's a *megilla*,' he had confirmed, raising his head, plump face aglow, from the magnifying glass which he, unlike the unknown writer, had been obliged to make use of. 'The Book of Esther. Perfect. The first of its kind I've seen without a single correction. Where in the world in Jerusalem did you come by it?'

'I congratulate you.' Over the hotel phone the voice of Efrem Ahilar had sounded warm and uncomplicated.

Jurnet, in no mood for *politesse*, had growled in reply: 'I don't know what you're talking about.'

'The Wall,' said Efrem Ahilar. 'I repeat, I congratulate you: as, I must confess, I congratulate myself on my own perspicuity. You did not, after all take Max's letter away with you. I guessed you would not, but I couldn't be sure.'

Anger rising hot within him, the detective demanded: 'You're been there to check up on me, have you?'

'Not necessary,' came back the cheerful answer. 'Danny was on the spot all the time, watching you. The boy who brought you from the airport.'

'Him? At the Wall? I never saw him.'

'That was the idea.'

'You've got a nerve.' Jurnet fought down his irritation. 'What is this – testing?'

'Let's just say you passed with flying colours. I gather you're leaving us at midday tomorrow.'

'I never said so.'

'Let's just say I gathered. It is so, isn't it?'

'Tomorrow,' Jurnet admitted with reluctance.

'That's settled, then. Danny will call with the car to drive you. Early – ten-thirty, so that you can take your time.'

'Better tell that to Danny.'

Efrem Ahilar laughed.

'I'll do that.' After a short pause he began again, on a different note. 'I spoke to Esther on the phone an hour ago. She sounded depressed. I would like you, please, to take back and deliver personally a little present from me to cheer her up. Danny will bring it when he calls for you.'

'What kind of present?' asked the detective, instantly on his guard.

The other laughed again.

'Don't worry, Inspector. Not cocaine, I promise you, nor anything else either contraband or against the law. I shall leave it unwrapped, so that on the journey you can, if you wish, go over it with a fine-tooth comb. It's a *megilla*, if you know what that is.'

'As it happens, I do. The Book of Esther.'

'Bravo!' the Israeli applauded. 'You are, as you English say, beginning to learn our lingo. The story of how a brave woman saved Israel. You will do this for me, Inspector? I shall be very grateful.'

With a copper's suspicion of all favours, whether given or received, Jurnet attempted evasive action.

'I can't promise when I'll next be in Cambridge. It could be some time.'

'You will do it, then!' The man pounced on the hesitation, overbore it. 'I want you please to give it – you yourself, Inspector, nobody else – directly into Esther's hands. She speaks well of you, and I am uneasy. If there is something, you will find out what it is, and if there is nothing you will, I hope, be kind enough to put a doting grandfather's mind at rest. My Esther used to be as lion-hearted as that other one, the bride of King Ahasuerus, but now – '

Jurnet said: 'Don't worry, I'll see she gets whatever it is. And thanks for the offer of the lift. But – ' a sudden monstrous thought striking him: it seemed he was never to be on terms of simple good fellowship with this Israeli Nell Gwynn in drag – 'a test, you said. How do I know that letter you stuck in the wall really was the Professor's? How do I know you or your precious Danny didn't stick it there, stuffed with blank paper, waiting for me to play patsy?'

'That's easy,' said Efrem Ahilar. 'You don't.'

'Shan't be long,' said Jurnet, getting out of the car with Esther Ahilar's present. 'Tell Catton I'm on my way.'

'I'll do that.' Sergeant Ellers looked out through the windscreen at the swirl of tourists round King's College Chapel.

'Where do they all come from, for Christ's sake? Don't they know summer's over and other people have work to do?' Through the open window of the Rover the little Welshman smiled up cheekily at his superior officer. 'Pity the young lady didn't get an eyeful of that sexy Middle Eastern tan you've brought back with you. She'd have asked you up to her pad, not made it the great outdoors.'

'Oh ah. Said she needed some fresh air. I'm meeting her other side of the bridge. It's quieter there.'

The meadow on the other side of the river was a whole lot quieter. Round Esther Ahilar, sitting under a tree, her back against its trunk, the quiet was complete, a cordon she had drawn about herself, a princess under a spell of her own casting. Jurnet, approaching across the grass, hesitated before breaching that invisible obstacle: held back, too by the girl's beauty, which was greater than ever, and very disturbing.

Feeling he was getting too old for that kind of thing, the detective lowered himself gingerly on to the rubble of beech mast and fag ends that littered the tree's base. The Israeli sun, he decided, had done more than give him a tan. It had dried up such juices of youth as had, until that exposure, still coursed hopefully through his ageing veins.

Handing over the gift: 'With your grandfather's compliments.'

'How kind of you to act as his messenger boy!' She put the envelope down beside her. 'I'll read it later.'

'It's not a letter. A present.'

'A present!' The childish anticipation which lit up the girl's face reminded the detective how young she was. He watched indulgently as she opened the little packet, following his admonition to proceed carefully.

'It's a *megilla*,' he said unnecessarily, when at last she held the micrograph in her hands. 'The Book of Esther.'

'I can see what it is.' The girl gazed down at it unsmilingly. 'It makes me dizzy to look at it. The Book of Esther with the words running round and round like rats in a cage, chasing each other's tails.'

'It's a work of miraculous skill!' the detective protested, genuinely outraged.

'It's horrible! Here,' – she held out the scrap of paper as if anxious to be rid of it – 'you take it, since you admire it so much.'

'It's a present from your grandfather, to cheer you up.'

'Dear Zeider!' the lovely face blushed rosy with shame. 'How awful of me, to go on like that! He loves to give me treasures.' She brought the unwelcome treasure back closer to her. 'You won't tell him what I said?' Seemingly forcing herself to concentrate on the tiny print: '*Vayehi bi'me achashverosh* – "Now it came to pass in the days of Ahasuerus – " Isn't that a wonderful beginning? Much better than "Once upon a time".'

Jurnet saw tears in the enormous eyes. He said: 'I can't understand what you don't like about it.'

'It's the way it goes round and round,' Esther Ahilar answered. 'Going nowhere. Like me.'

Esther Ahilar said to Jurnet: 'Do you know what you are like? You are like an agony aunt in the women's magazines. "*My boy friend has smelly feet. What shall I do? Dr Tawno Smith will not go to bed with me. What shall I do?*" An agony uncle.'

'Not a bad description for a detective,' Jurnet conceded, carefully evading the specific question directed at him in his new incarnation. 'Except a copper asks a hell of a lot more questions than he provides answers.'

The girl nodded in grave comprehension.

'So this time it was Grandfather's turn. How did he make out? Did your trip to Jerusalem get you any nearer to finding out who killed Uncle Max?'

'I got to know Mr Ahilar a lot better than I did before. Whether that was worth the price of the fare, only time will tell. One thing I learned,' said Jurnet, 'is that he's worried sick about you.'

'Dear Zeider!' Esther Ahilar's voice was warm with love. 'He's a wonderful man. He's led this marvellous, dangerous life. Did you know, during the war, he literally stole dozens of Jews from under the very noses of the *kapos*, the concentration camp guards? I'm not being fair to him.' The girl shook her head in self-rebuke. Her dark hair swung against her pale cheeks. 'What he wants most for me is to be happy. If he could buy Tawno for me the way he bought the Book of Esther, he would do it without a second's hesitation. Only Tawno's not for sale, any more than King Ahasuerus. Just me, going round and round – '

Esther Ahilar did not give the impression of going round and round. She continued to sit relaxed, her hands loosely in her lap. Under the tree in her long dress, surrounded by green distance, all she needed was a daisy chain about her lovely neck to turn her into one of those sentimental Victorian paintings you see on Christmas cards or calendars.

As if she had plucked something of Jurnet's thought out of the air she said, with a sad little laugh, 'I'm really very Victorian, you know. You wouldn't think, would you, that a *sabra*, a child of a brash new country, could be so old-fashioned – the young lady keeping herself pure for the Mr Right who is bound to come along one day? Only, in those novels there is always a happy ending, isn't there, instead of Mr Right saying, "If you want to make me happy, take my godson instead!" '

Jurnet offered inadequately: 'He's very fond of young Christopher.'

'No,' the girl contradicted in a firm voice. 'I'm the one Tawno is very fond of. Christopher is the one he loves. For a little, you know, I wondered if, perhaps, he wasn't bisexual. Not that it would have made any difference to me. There were all those other women – I didn't mind them, so why should I mind if he liked boys as well, so long as he loved me, too? But then I thought it couldn't be, because if he loved Christopher with a sexual love, he wouldn't want me to go to bed with him. He would be jealous.' She looked at the detective with a kind of feverish calm. 'Suddenly it came to me that he worries about Christopher exactly the way Grandfather worries about me, so perhaps he is Christopher's father. He is old enough, Mrs Maslin has loved him for a long time, and Mr Maslin is not an attractive man. It seemed to me possible.'

'Did you talk over the possibility with Christopher?'

'Of course not! I went to Tawno and asked him.' Tears came into Esther Ahilar's eyes. 'He was angry. He is never angry, but then he was angry with me. Did I think, he said, that if Christopher was his son he would have been ashamed to say so, instead of boasting of it to the whole world? He called me a trouble-maker. How would the Maslins feel if such a story got about, how would Christopher feel? I cried a lot, I swore that I had never said a word to anybody. He made me feel terribly sorry I had ever asked, but also terribly glad I'd been wrong. It meant, don't you see, that whatever else it was, I wasn't coming between father and son. It gave me more of a chance.'

Jurnet said, drawing in his breath: 'Yes. I see that. Though, if you'll excuse my saying it, the youngster must know how you feel about Dr. Smith. It's there for anyone with eyes in his head to see.'

Esther Ahilar shook her head.

'Christopher doesn't have those kind of eyes. He's very self-contained. Sometimes I wonder he ever noticed me enough to fall in love with me in the first place.'

'No surprise to me.'

'I mean it,' the other insisted. 'There are times when, for a little, I make up my mind that I *will* go to bed with him after all, that this virgin stuff is really too ridiculous in this day and age. It will please Tawno and also, perhaps, it will be better for me in the long run. From all I've heard, making love is something you have to learn. You aren't usually much good at it first time round.' Calm and candid, she inquired: 'Has that been your experience, Mr Jurnet?'

Flinching inwardly under an instant surfeit of reminiscence, Jurnet responded with a pretence of lightness: 'Nothing to write home about, I'll admit that.'

'There you are then!' The girl nodded as if that was the answer she had expected. 'But then, when I've thought about it a little longer, I always change my mind again. I can't do it. And I tell you this, Inspector,' – the girl sat up straight, daylight between her back and the tree trunk – 'even if I did what Christopher is always begging me to do, I don't think it would make him happy either.'

'Now you're talking daft! The lad's head over heels – '

'In one way,' the girl interrupted. 'In another, I sometimes wonder if he doesn't hate me. *Because* he loves me, if I can make you understand what I'm saying. I get in the way of his religion. In his inmost heart, I think, he would rather be a monk and love only God.'

Esther Ahilar got to her feet, resuming the vertical in one lovely rhythmic line. Feeling a graceless lout next to such harmony, odds and ends of vegetable

207

debris stuck to his trousers, Jurnet picked up the Book of Esther which the girl had left on the ground and stood up.

'Here. You mustn't forget this.'

'No.' She took the micrograph without looking at it. 'You know what I've found out, Inspector? That love isn't the gentle thing I'd always imagined . . . It's pitiless, a possession by demons.' She turned her large, sad eyes on the detective. Jurnet noticed that her slight foreign accent had become more pronounced. 'Everyone says that *sabras* are not easily frightened. They are too arrogant.' Voice breaking: 'I do not feel very arrogant at this moment.'

Jurnet riffled through his repertoire and selected his hearty mode.

'The trouble with you, young lady, is, you're feeling sorry for yourself, when the truth is, there isn't a girl in Cambridge wouldn't give her eye teeth to change places with you. You're young, intelligent, beautiful. Everything and everybody's going your way.'

'Everybody except Tawno.'

'Just as well someone's got a ha'porth of commonsense! Think of the difference in your ages! When you're not yet into your forties, the prime of life, he'll be an old man.'

'I've loved him as long as I can remember loving anybody. It's too late to change now.'

The detective said: 'I promised to let your grandfather know how I found you.'

'Please! Nothing to make him worry.' The girl moved out of the shadow of the tree on to grass that was green in the English way, a gift of nature, not a conquest wrung from it. Jurnet, his spirits rising, rejoiced anew in the Englishness of England.

Under the English sun Esther Ahilar's beauty was breathtaking. She pleaded: 'You must tell Zeider I'm a little homesick, but otherwise – marvellous! Say how interesting I find the lectures, how romantic the surroundings. How happy I am – yes, happy! I'm not just saying it. There are many different kinds of happiness. Tell him I told you I would not be anywhere else for all the world.'

'Not depressed, then?'

'Not depressed at all.' Smiling brilliantly up into the suntanned face of the detective: 'Merely desperate.'

27

'It's in the air,' Detective Inspector Catton announced in tones of disgust. 'I put it down to all these bloody philosophers we got here in the colleges, always proving things aren't what they seem, or, if they are, they got no business to be.'

Jurnet, concentrating on getting down his tea, typical nick tea with its unmistakable undertaste of iron filings, wondered what philosophers could possibly have to do with the return of an open verdict on the body of Dandy Venables. Conceding the possibility that coppers in an ancient university town might be vouchsafed insights denied to yobs from redbrick Angleby, he said nothing, awaiting enlightenment.

Sergeant Jack Ellers harboured no such inhibitions.

'Always thought philosophers were for telling you what things were, not what they weren't.'

'Fat lot you know!' DI Catton returned with a contempt excessive in a host. 'Here in Cambridge, I tell you, it's in the air, like exhaust fumes. Bloody health hazard you don't know about till it's too late.'

Mystified, Jurnet decided to intervene.

'What exactly are we talking about?'

'Philosophy. Philosophers. That bugger Venables.' The Cambridge man warmed to his theme. 'Ever heard of a bloke name of Wittgenstein?'

'*Gesundheit!*' Ellers responded cheekily. 'Can't say I have. What did he go down for?'

'Didn't go down for anything, though I'd've made it life, if I'd had any say. One of those ruddy philosophers, here in Cambridge. Foreigner, as you might have guessed. Know what he said? He said, "The world is everything that is the case." ' He looked from one to the other of his visitors as if satisfied he had made his point.

Sergeant Ellers, having thought about it, ventured judiciously, 'Well, it is, isn't it?'

DI Catton snorted. 'So what? To be a philosopher all you got to do is jot down any old garbage that comes into your head and next thing you know they're handing you out a Nobel Prize or a Companion of Honour. The trouble with Cambridge,' he proclaimed, 'is people are a damn sight too clever.' Favouring Jurnet with what the latter, charitably but with some effort, took to be a humorous smile: 'Not like good old Angleby, eh? Everybody thick as two planks and none the worse for that.'

'That's right,' the Angleby copper agreed amicably. 'What I don't see is what it has to do with the verdict on Dandy.'

'Open!' declared Catton. 'That's what it has to do! Here's a geezer so tanked up, anyone come near him with a match and he'd've gone up like a sodding rocket, and still they call it open! On'y thing open about it was opening time. Anywhere else it'd be Accident or Misadventure and Bob's your uncle. But not here! Here, in this seat of Higher Learning, it's not enough to prove Dandy was pissed enough to've walked on the bloody water, let alone drowned in it. You have to ask yourself, what would that bugger Wittgenstein have said?'

'Hard lines,' sympathised Jack Ellers, putting his finger on the root of the other's discontent. 'You mean the file's got to be kept open.'

'Tha's exactly what I mean! Anyone'd think we got nothing else to do! Not to say that, even if we *do* turn up something that links the dear departed to your fucking Professor, your lot will get the credit after we've done all the work. As to your Dr Gippo Smith,' – carried away by the excess of his emotion, Detective Inspector Catton downed the best part of a cup of tea at a gulp – 'keep an eye on him, you said.' He wheeled round so as to confront Jurnet eyeball to eyeball. 'Know what he did?' Jurnet shook his head, wondering what was coming next. 'Only rings up to say he's just caught a suspicious character hanging round the house, that's all, and would we please come over and collect him. Says he's had to tie the guy up, gag him and lock him in the coal cellar to keep him quiet. Russian, he thought, judging by his red socks, even though, before he'd got the gag on, the man had insisted he was Cambrige police. "But then, he would, wouldn't he?" he says, cool as a cucumber.'

'And was he?' Jurnet asked, keeping as straight a face as he was able . . .

'Joe Burley,' the other confirmed, disgustedly. 'Detective Constable. Always told him he'd get into trouble one day with that hosiery.'

'Levantine,' said the Superintendent. He sounded displeased.

'Sir?'

'I said Levantine,' the Superintendent repeated, louder. 'That tan you've come back with. Couldn't you have got yourself a hat?'

For one ridiculous moment Jurnet thought of telling his superior officer about the *kippah* still, presumably, reposing in the crevice of the Western Wall. Instead, he remarked non-committally: 'It *was* very hot.'

'All you need is a couple of rugs over your shoulder and you could be in business.'

'I'll have to see what I can do. Was there anything else, sir?'

'Damn it, I apologize!' The tone of the Superintendent's retraction was such as to indicate that it had done nothing but add an additional item to the ever-burgeoning list of his subordinate's shortcomings. 'The Chief's been handing me out a packet. I showed him your report but he seemed more interested in your expense account – as well he might be. I've assigned Dave Batterby and Sid Hale to other duties. We're not getting anywhere, Ben!'

That, at least was better than '*You're* not getting anywhere.' Jurnet, on the point of permitting his unacceptably brown face to relax its Red Indian impassivity, stiffened afresh as the Superintendent resumed this threnody. 'Trip to the Holy Land, everything found, and what have we got to show for it? A suntan!'

'Cambridge,' Jurnet said smoothly, 'was pretty hot too. Greener, though. Less Levantine.' Allowing no time for a comeback: 'One thing I learned is that our Dr Smith's a pretty accomplished liar. When the Ahilar girl, putting two and two together, asked him outright if he wasn't young Christopher Maslin's father, he blew the roof off at the very suggestion.'

'And that was worth wasting time and money going to Cambridge for?' The Superintendent was implacable. 'To find out that somebody connected with the death of Professor Flaschner was lying? If you'd come back telling me you'd discovered somebody out of that cosy little coterie was actually telling the truth, that'd be another matter.'

Jurnet reminded his superior officer that he and Detective Sergeant Ellers were there primarily to have

212

a discussion with Detective Inspector Catton over the Venables verdict.

'Open!' exclaimed the Superintendent, in precisely the same tone the Cambridge copper had used, an open verdict being only one more example of the administrative untidiness he deplored above all else. With a further unconscious echo, the Superintendent being an Oxford man himself. 'It's something I've always noticed about Cambridge. Shilly-shallying. A chronic inability to make its mind up one way or the other.'

'Too much philosophy, would you say, sir?' Jurnet put on his most innocent expression. 'An overdose of Wittgenstein?'

The Superintendent stared, then burst out laughing.

'Good God, Ben! Don't tell me you've enrolled in the Open University! Now then,' – their interminable game suspended for the moment, good humour restored to the satisfaction of both – 'suppose you let me know what the good Catton proposes to do with this *carte blanche* which the coroner has handed down to him.'

'Tuck it away in the furthest corner of his filing cabinet, I shouldn't be surprised, and make out it's got lost in the post. What I'd be tempted to do myself, in his shoes. There are still only two things that appear to connect Venables with the murder – the way that window pane was removed, and the fact that Annie Venables was his wife.'

'Not much to go on,' the Superintendent agreed, 'except that two coincidences in the same context always tempt one to think that neither can be a coincidence after all. You called in on Mrs Venables, no doubt?'

'Not this time. I couldn't see any point. Nor on Dr Smith either. I wouldn't have minded a few words with young Maslin, but when we drove over to Bilney College, the porter said he'd seen the young gentleman go out in shorts and trainers, ten minutes before, off for a run.'

'*Mens sana in corpore sano*, eh?'

'Wouldn't know about that, sir, only that it made me specially sorry to have missed him. Running's something he's got from his dad – from the Revd Maslin, I ought to say – along with his religion. I got the impression the two were mixed up together somehow, and one was as important as the other. Whenever you've got something on your mind, to Mr Maslin's way of thinking, you've got two alternatives. Either pray to God or else run, rabbit, run. Either way, all will be made clear. I'd like to have caught up with the lad before he got going.'

A poster, glimpsed when he was stopped at the traffic lights at the top of Shire Street, induced Jurnet, homeward bound, to alter his plans. '*Last Day Wednesday*' screamed a sticker slashed diagonally across an advertisement, not, as one might have hoped or feared, for the end of the world, but to signal the imminent demise of Alastair Tring's contribution to the Sir Thaddeus Brigg Tricentennial. Today was Wednesday. Tomorrow *The Subatomic World: The Art of the Bubble Chamber and the Particle Detector* would be no more.

When the lights changed the detective set the car in motion, round the one-way system, up the slope which led across the old cattle market to the castle bridge.

'Closing in ten minutes,' said the commissionaire at the turnstile. Recognising Jurnet, he smiled broadly.

'Five minutes more than I need.'

The detective paid for his ticket and hurried to the Exhibitions Gallery. There was nobody about except, unlike last time, a girl sitting at the table with the leaflets. Jurnet forked out 35p for a second copy, convinced, as ever in such circumstances, that she would only think him close-fisted if he were to say that he had bought one already. On closer examination, the girl had a pleasing appearance, ingenuous but not foolish. She might have taken his word for it, at that.

'I'm awfully sorry, but we're closing in a few minutes.'

'That's all right. I've been here before. Just wanted a last look.'

The girl favoured the detective with a look of pleased understanding.

'Know what you mean,' she said. 'When they first put me here on the door I thought, God, I'll die of boredom. I'll positively die! Too dark to read, nothing but these meaningless scribbles to look at. But now' – with a self-deprecating smile at her own foolishness – 'I feel that, when they go, they'll take a part of me along with them.'

She left the table and came, as if it were the most natural thing in the world, to stand with Jurnet in front of an exquisite multi-coloured spray that stood out with surprising boldness against its black background. Strands of yellow, purple, blue and red reached up towards an infinity situated beyond the frame. Near the base of the central stalk, which was coloured gold, a small green shoot curled in a spiral which reminded the detective of Esther Ahilar's Book of Esther, going round and round. '*Now it came to pass in the days of Ahasuerus . . .*'

'Grasses of fairyland,' the girl said softly.

Jurnet read aloud from the card tacked to the wall at the side of the photograph.

'*A high-energy proton (yellow) enters from the bottom and collides with a proton at rest. The small electron spiral (green) shows that negative particles curl anticlockwise and positive particles clockwise. The collision produces seven negative pions (blue) and nine positive particles (red)* – ' Breaking off with a smile: 'They should have given you the job of writing the captions.'

As the two moved from picture to picture, caught up in the gyrating circles and spirals, the veils that

215

drifted across the dark surfaces like cosmic dust in the Milky Way, the girl, to Jurnet's surprise and delight, took his hand. He felt mysteriously happy; not just, or even primarily, because he was walking hand in hand with a pretty girl, something he hadn't done since Miriam went away, but because, against all the probabilities, he discovered that he had learned something momentous. Something to store along with all the other bits and pieces. Something that, once he had deciphered the code, would explain why Professor Max Flaschner was dead.

The electric bell began to buzz for closing time.

Because he had been brought up to distrust happiness, Jurnet said: 'You know, of course, all this is faked. They're just the souped-up tracks of particles, not the real thing.'

'Tracks *are* the real thing,' the girl responded, undisturbed. 'There are people who can construct a dinosaur from the footprint it left on a patch of dried-up mud.' She stared at the photographs with shining eyes, memorizing them. 'If those are tracks,' she said, 'imagine what the things themselves must be like.'

'I can't imagine.'

'Neither can I,' said the girl. 'That's the wonder of it. To be beyond imagining.'

Home greeted him with its familiar affirmations – the rubbish bags leaning companionably together on the little forecourt, never growing less in number however many times the dustman called; the smell of slow-simmered underwear and joss sticks. On the ground floor the O'Driscolls were having their evening row, the passion in their warring voices, Jurnet felt sure, only to be assuaged by the act of love, and, probably, the advent of yet another little O'Driscoll nine months later.

The last of the magic left over from the subatomic world evaporating, Jurnet made his way up to his own

216

front door, wondering why the hell he hadn't asked the girl in the exhibition gallery to have dinner with him, to go to bed with him, to play Scrabble or Trivial Pursuits. Anything to keep loneliness at bay.

'You'll have to go now,' the girl had said; and, smiling up into his face with an unselfconsciousness which could only betoken a husband or lover hanging about in the wings, if not a couple of kids into the bargain, 'Don't *worry!*'

Good thinking, he thought, perched on the edge of his armchair, levering off his shoes and worrying what not to worry about.

Not his supper, that was for sure. Having already turned down Jack Ellers' invitation to share the ballotine of chicken Régence with which Rosie proposed to regale her spouse that evening, he had not been unprepared for the Superintendent's intervention on the same subject, delivered in characteristic style.

'Crime in Angleby hasn't come to a halt, Ben, while you've been getting yourself a liberal education in Cambridge.'

'No, sir.'

'So – if we don't want to lose one of our DIs, which, in the circumstances, we can ill afford,' – with a look which implied that, in other circumstances, the verdict might have been different – 'you'd better treat yourself to a decent meal tonight however much it goes against the grain.'

'I was thinking of going to Mario's.' Jurnet produced the first name that came into his head.

'You'll do better at the Chop House. Good English beef to stick to your ribs – and I mean ribs! If you take much longer clearing up this Flaschner business, it'll be the first murder in the history of the British police to be solved by a walking skeleton.'

'The Chop House isn't a bad idea,' Jurnet agreed, the words emerging with an ungraciousness which altogether concealed the detective's lift of the heart that the other was concerned for his wellbeing. Love was a ticklish thing, in whatever form it thrust its trouble-making spoke into the works.

After a moment, the Superintendent had added with a studied obliquity, it being a silent covenant between the two of them that the name of Miriam was never to be mentioned outright in their conversations: 'Must be three years now since Mary went to visit her brother in Vancouver. Away three months. First time we'd been apart in twenty years. Missed her dreadfully, of course, but one thing I discovered. That – selected with a careful discrimination, mind you – there exist, even in Angleby, consolatory ways of filling in the long blank spaces – '

'Yes, sir.'

The bugger! Not that Rabbi Schnellman hadn't been just as bad, in his way.

'Of course you saw Miriam!' he had declared, as one stating the obvious.

'Just a glimpse in the distance.'

'How come in the distance?' the rabbi had demanded, dismay mantling his plump face.

How distant was distance, Jurnet now asked himself, carefully not attempting an answer. It sounded the kind of problem Jewish scholars, pondering every word of the sacred writings, might toss to and fro, from one learned authority to another, like children tossing a ball, never once dropping it.

So, was it all over, then, between him and Miriam? In the uncompromising light of Jerusalem it had certainly seemed so. In Angleby, though, with the first presages of autumn already blurring the hard edges of the city, the outlook, like the weather, was more unsettled. *On the one hand* – as those same scholars were fond of saying, striking a delicate balance between possibilities – *and on the other* –

Hell!

218

The detective went into his kitchen and found the remains of a loaf, of which only the outside was mouldy; also a small round box containing three of the foil-wrapped triangles of cheese spread of which Miriam was unaccountably fond. Jurnet trimmed the bread, made himself a cup of instant coffee, and sat down at the kitchen table to de-foil one of the sections of cheese. As usual, the mechanics of this seemingly simple operation first irritated, and then enraged him: at which point he chucked all three portions into the bin, prised the metal/cheese amalgam off his fingers under the tap, and sat down moodily to enjoy, if that was the word, his evening meal.

What the bloody hell was he to do with the rest of the day? Take the Superintendent's delicately tendered advice, go out and find himself a whore – selected with a careful discrimination of course? Watch the telly?

He wandered into the bedroom where the television set, still in its wrappings, was installed facing the bed. Miriam had bought it as a parting gift, a substitute for the black-and-white antique in the living-room which hadn't worked for years, bless it.

Jurnet went to strip off the encasing polythene, then desisted, overwhelmed by superstitious fear. Let him once put the virgin set into commission and that would be the end. Miriam would never show and he would be left, under the baleful eye of the digital clock with which his up-to-the-minute love had replaced his dear old wind-up alarm, condemned to an eternity of *Dallas* and *News at Ten*.

For lack of any better idea of what to do with the spasmodic dollops of time which the clock persisted in meting out to him, Jurnet went early to bed, lying naked on the duvet and peopling the interval before sleep with Tawno Smith and his women, with Esther Ahilar and Christopher Maslin, young and beautiful and still not satisfied, with the Salomes on the chancel wall of the church at Feldon St Awdry, dissolving erotically one into the other and out again. In a desultory, inchoate way, the detective wished he had had a word with young Christopher, though what about, he couldn't remember. Always seemed to be out for a run, anyway.

Funny how many of them in this case ran, beginning with the kid Tawno obeying his mam and running for his life. Drowsily, Jurnet asked himself how it could have happened that, looking at the photographs in the museum gallery those twiddles and twirls running at near the speed of light, he had felt, just for a moment, that he knew why Max Flaschner had been murdered. Answer came there none, and he thought, the hell with it.

Why, at parting, had that pleasant girl at the gallery adjured him not to worry?

Who was worrying?

28

Dr Tawno Smith came into Jurnet's room at Police Headquarters so cheerily pleased with himself that the detective, in spite of reservations activated anew by the man's presence – the bugger was too cocky by half! – had to smile. Ignoring the proffered seat, the physicist stood looking at Jurnet with shining eyes. Vibrant with energy, he asserted nevertheless: 'I'm falling asleep on my feet. I've been up all night. But I wanted you to be the first to know.'

'Can I get you a cup of black coffee?'

'Nectar or nothing! I wanted you to be the first to

know because, after myself, you are the one best placed to profit by it. It's finished. *C'est fini, fertig, finito*. As we gipsies say, *Jaw si*, so it is.'

'The famous Tricentennial paper, would that be?'

'The famous Tricentennial paper, what else? Hang about for another three hundred years and see how they celebrate *my* Tricentennial! Before I came here I went first to the Post Office and then to the bank. One copy, by registered post to the University Press, a second deposited in the bank vaults for safekeeping. The two of us have been set free!'

'You've had something a bit stronger than coffee.'

'Me – a Romany! You should know better. A libation of orange juice poured out on the ground to the memory of Uncle Max, that's all. Well?' Tawno Smith demanded, coming close enough to Jurnet to put a hand on the detective's shoulder. 'Aren't you going to congratulate me?'

Unaccountably uncomfortable under the friendly touch, Jurnet twisted his body round.

'That depends on what's in it,' he said.

Tawno Smith first looked mock-reproachful, then shouted with laughter. The electric excitement which possessed him was such as to make Jurnet feel positively relieved to have disengaged himself from physical contact.

'Don't tell me you've forgotten your lesson already! The four forces, remember? The weak, the strong, the electromagnetic and gravity – '

'I haven't forgotten. They sounded more like the four horsemen of the Apocalypse to me.'

'I come to announce the completed symmetry of the universe and all you can do is quote some demented mystic! You disappoint me, Inspector. I had taken you to belong to our brave new world, not to the old one whose skin we sloughed off at the turn of the century. You talk as if, were it possible, you would un-invent relativity.'

221

'Only wish I knew how.'

'Incredible!' Tawno Smith shook his curly head in disbelief. 'An intelligent man who doesn't believe in progress!'

'I don't believe in putting matches within the reach of children.'

'And I was going to invite you to my party!'

The other grinned. 'It's off, anyway. I decided it would be too melodramatic, too much like Agatha Christie. I was planning it all the way from Cambridge. How I'd get together everyone who was round that table at the castle. Even Uncle Max: I'd be sure to leave a chair for his ghost. And somehow' – the tone of roguish mischief, for a wonder, scarcely faltering – 'by the time my guests had finished eating and drinking and throwing their arms round me and each other in an ecstasy of love, I would know which of my dear friends had killed that darling man and I could kill him – or her – bid the others good-night and go happily to bed.'

Jurnet said: 'Just as well you had second thoughts.'

The physicist made a comical face.

'The truth, Inspector Jurnet, is that I'm getting too old for such capers; getting ready to settle down in slippered ease, even – would you believe it? – in matrimony. Yes, now that I've told you I shall be perfectly content to celebrate my world-shattering achievement by driving home and going, quietly and comfortably, to bed with Annie – another legacy from Uncle Max, bless him. Everything good I have in life comes from that man.'

'Lucky for you Mrs Venables is a widow now.'

'A barbed observation if ever I heard one,' the other remarked with no apparent disquiet. 'I gather you saw Esther.' Jurnet nodded. 'I don't know what you said to her but it's had a marvellous effect. She's been so sweet to Christopher it's unbelievable. Claire, who's gone back to Feldon for a few days, has given him the key to that place she's taken out at Comberton. Oak beams, low ceilings, roses round the door. The perfect venue for the consummation of young love.' Tawno Smith laughed. 'You see what a romantic I'm becoming in my dotage! Claire, who knows what things are really important, has filled up the freezer there with all kinds of lovely nosh – '

Jurnet said: 'And you, I suppose, are off to Feldon to let the Maslins in on the good news?'

'I told you – I'm going home. Besides, it's the first time Claire's been back to Feldon for quite a while, and I don't want to butt in. The bishop's due to consecrate the Salomes in a couple of weeks' time and Simon wants Claire's advice about this and that. They'll hear about my paper from Christopher. He's the one who will understand its significance better than anybody.' Face alight with paternal pride: 'I ran into Masham – he's one of the biggest bugs at Bilney – a few days ago and you should have heard what he said! If he were a betting man, he said, he'd put his last penny on Christopher turning out to be one of the mathematicians of the century.'

'Has he quite given up all ideas of the cloth?'

Tawno Smith frowned slightly.

'There are days when he's moody,' he admitted, 'plagued with self-doubts. But' – brightening up – 'a natural modesty. Better than being big-headed, the thing Uncle Max was always slapping me down for. With indifferent success, I may say! It's all mixed up with Esther, anyway – I'm putting great hopes in that key! Once the boy's made it with her, he's going to be in too much of a heaven on earth to worry about that other one up in the sky.'

'Unless,' Jurnet suggested carefully, 'she sleeps with Christopher solely to please you.'

'I don't care if she does it to please the Great Cham of Tartary, so long as she does it! Don't they have a tag in your line of business – *res ipsa loquitur*, "the

223

thing speaks for itself"?' Tawno Smith smiled. 'Let me presume to give you a word of advice, Inspector. If a woman comes into your bed, and it isn't done for money, the only inference you're entitled to draw is that she's there because she wants to be there, the same as you are. Start probing further and you'll deserve all you get.'

'Ta,' said Jurnet, the thought of Miriam suddenly constricting his throat and making it difficult for him to speak. 'I'll bear it in mind.' With an effort, he managed: 'I take it you've already been in touch with Detective Inspector Catton?'

'Annie's promised to phone. I didn't dare.' The gipsy's eyes sparkled with urchin glee. 'He'll know soon enough, anyway, once the media get hold of the story and turn me and my paper into bedtime stories to scare the kiddies.'

'Not only the kiddies.'

'You're beginning to sound like Uncle Max! Time I was off. I'll see you get a photostat once it's in print. You won't understand a word, but never mind. You can cut it up into little pieces, sprinkle it with holy water and make a bonfire, going three times round it widdershins – '

29

Jurnet came out on to the forecourt to find that the prolonged Indian summer was over at last. There was an unmistakable smell of autumn in the air, of dry rot flexing its biceps, of carbon dioxide trapped beneath lowering cloud. Being the contrary cuss he was, he did not find this overnight change of ambience entirely melancholy. On the contrary. Summer, that delusive softness, that promoter of failed dreams, had gone on too long, a damn sight too long. That was the trouble with deserts, he thought, as he pulled the car's choke out to its full extent, finding a pleasurable difficulty in getting it to start in the chilled air. No winter: no Miriam.

An equinoctial energy appeared to have got the desk sergeant at Police Headquarters on the move beyond the call of duty. The moment he glimpsed Jurnet coming through the door into the lobby, he left his post and came running.

'I've been wearing my finger out trying to get you on the blower – '

'Where's the fire?'

'You tell me.' The desk sergeant jerked his head in approximate indication of direction. 'I've put the bugger in the first-aid room. PC Bly's in there with him.'

'With who? Who've you put in the first-aid room? And what's wrong with him?'

'It was on account of the blood.' The desk sergeant was patently enjoying his tease. 'Not to worry, though. When I hiked up his T-shirt to have a gander I saw it wasn't his.'

Christopher Maslin sat on the edge of the high examination couch with a blanket round his slumped shoulders. The morning sun, peering through the window, picked out the golden hairs on his legs, bare from brief shorts to white ankle socks. No blood to be seen, not even in the boy's face. PC Bly, not much older than his charge, stood awkwardly by, unequal to the agony inscribed on that colourless mask.

Jurnet took one look and sent the young PC thankfully away in search of hot, strong tea with lashings of sugar. Not until the door of the first-aid room had closed behind him did the detective address the motionless figure, look directly into the empty eyes. When the boy spoke at last it was one word only.

'Esther – '

The word was the key, like the key to the cottage at Comberton, so suited to the consummation of young love. Words gushed out incontinently: a gabble, of which, alas, it was only too easy to make sense. To all appearances cheerfully cool, Jurnet felt his heart contract with pity. Summer was over all right.

When the tea came, and PC Bly sent away again with orders to locate Detective Sergeant Ellers and point him in the direction of the first-aid room, the detective seated himself at the boy's side. Putting an arm round the trembling shoulders, he held the cup gently but insistently to the pallid lips. Christopher Maslin did not want to stop talking, perhaps could not. He turned his face away from the steaming liquid, shouted 'You don't want to hear what I've got to say!'

'Yes, I do,' said Jurnet. 'And I will. Now drink.'

The boy drank. The blanket slipped from his shoulders, disclosing the white T-shirt, its front stained – soaked – with blood. The boy looked down at the blood and began to scream. Jurnet set the half-empty cup down next to the telephone on a small glass-topped table. He tried unsuccessfully to ease the T-shirt over the boy's head. The boy stopped screaming and said with a dreadful clarity: 'It won't come off, so you might as well stop trying. I shall have to wear it till the day I die.'

'If you say so.' The detective pulled the shirt down again, using the opportunity to make sure the torso beneath, though mottled with blood which had permeated the fabric, was indeed whole and unbruised.

Christopher Maslin shut his eyes and announced out of the horror that lay behind them: 'Somebody must have told you she doesn't have a face. It isn't something

226

you could pass by and not notice. All gone, except for one eye watching for me to come back.'

Feeling cold and old, Jurnet inquired in the most ordinary of voices: 'Come back from where?'

The eyes opened, regarded the detective with a tired surprise. 'From my run, of course. Not a good idea, as it turned out. Not at all like Norfolk, Cambridgeshire. Tankers, tractors – incredible! Couldn't find anywhere to get off the road. Only track I found led to a field where some men were dipping sheep. No way through.' The boy smiled, a smile that was worse than the horror. 'Stupid thing to do, wasn't it, after a night of being so close together, touching, to go off like that. What I should have done was get up and make tea and biscuits, taken them in to her in bed, on a tray with a pretty napkin on it, and one of those roses from outside the front door.' Chattily: 'You've no idea how many different kinds of biscuits Mother left behind in the larder. Rich tea and chocolate digestives and I don't know what. Only you see, she was still asleep and I didn't like to wake her. Also' – confidingly now – 'I was a little shy. She'd been so sweet and kind, when I hadn't really been very good.' Subsiding, uncertain: 'At least, I don't think I had been. She said I'd done everything right, but I don't know. I'd never done it before, so I hadn't anything to compare it with. It was so strange, lying there between a girl's legs, not at all what I'd expected. In a way I was quite relieved when it was over. Am I saying something awful?'

Jurnet answered heartily: 'We've all gone through it, first time round.'

'Really?' But the boy continued to look doubtful. 'I must have been awful to make her kill herself. She'd brought the gun with her from Israel and she told me she took it with her everywhere. She said it was a habit she'd got into in the army.' Christopher Maslin went back to his own personal investigation. 'I don't know if she was only saying what she said to make me feel good, or because she really meant it. I meant to ask her when I got back to tell me honestly, only by then' – the boy finished, the words chosen with a painstaking attention to every syllable – 'it wouldn't have been any good asking, because you can't talk without a mouth, can you, and she didn't have one any longer – '

Jack Ellers, who had slipped quietly into the room, his notebook at the ready, exchanged nods with his superior officer before slipping quietly out again, the page still virgin. Jurnet knew without being told that he had gone to alert Cambridge, to send DI Catton, siren whooping, weaving in and out of the tankers and tractors fouling up the Comberton road, to the cottage with the roses round the door.

In a sudden surge of panic, the detective wondered how he himself could have waited so long before setting the wheels in motion. Was it possible that Esther Ahilar could still be alive? At the same time, at a deeper level of consciousness he knew very well it was for that very reason he had delayed picking up the extension on the glass-topped table. If his information was correct and Esther Ahilar alive was Esther Ahilar without a face, Esther Ahilar dead was a mercy. Christ! What had the girl done to herself? Unless it was this snivelling kid here, shivering in a shirt stained with Esther Ahilar's blood, who had stage-managed the whole thing. Gone running, had he? A likely story!

Jurnet thought of Tawno Smith in bed at Heathcote Avenue with his comfortable Annie Venables, and gritted his teeth with rage. He thought of Miriam and the God-awfulness of love, and his anger expanded to encompass the universe. He thought, *how the hell am I going to tell Efrem Ahilar?*

At the same time as he thought all those things, he asked Christopher Maslin, 'What decided you to come all the way here? You should have gone to the police in Comberton. There must be a phone at the cottage. You could have phoned.'

'Could I?' The boy looked up, apologetic. 'I'm sorry, I never thought. All I thought of was getting away. I didn't think Esther would want me to hang about. I thought she would rather be private, looking like that. I'd have kissed her goodbye if there'd been a mouth to kiss, only there wasn't; only a black hole and some threads of flesh hanging down. Her car was outside and I got into it. I remember what you said about having a licence, but it was all right, you don't have to worry. I've just passed my test. First time. That's good, isn't it?'

'Very good.'

'If it hadn't been for the traffic I'd rather have run. But as it was – '

'You couldn't have run all the way to Angleby.'

'Couldn't I?' The boy considered the possibility and maintained politely: 'I think I could, you know. I'm in pretty good condition. As it was, I'd have driven on to Feldon only I knew Mother was there, and I didn't want to tell her just then what a mess Esther had made of her pretty bedroom . . .' Worriedly: 'I suppose the bedclothes can go in the washing machine, but the wallpaper – it had little bunches of flowers – the wallpaper was so pretty – ' Tears rolled down the boy's cheeks. He said brokenly: 'Esther was always saying how much she liked you, Mr Jurnet. How you were somebody to be trusted. How you knew a lot more than you let on – '

Jurnet stayed silent.

'You aren't the only one,' the boy continued. 'God also knows a lot more than He lets on. I pray all the time, but He never says anything back. My father says that's how it ought to be, that even to expect an answer is a failure of belief. But it would be very comforting if He did, just once in a while at least. What do *you* think, Mr Jurnet?'

'I think your father knows a great deal more about God than I do.'

229

'Because he's a priest, you mean? I wanted to be one myself, only Tawno says it's my duty to God to use the gifts with which He has seen fit to endow me – '

'Is that what Dr Smith says?'

'He says science *is* God's answers, that a perfect equation is better than a psalm because it both praises God and extends man's understanding at one go.' Christopher Maslin picked up the blanket and huddled himself in it, head and all. Out of its puny shelter he announced: 'I shall have to ask him – '

'Tawno or God?'

'Both. I shall have to ask both of them what's the perfect equation for Esther without a face?'

'In all my years in the Force,' declared the Superintendent, 'I've never before known a woman put a pistol in her mouth and squeeze the trigger. Not even an ugly one whose looks, or lack of them, you might have thought, were a key factor in deciding her to make away with herself. And this one, you say, was quite a looker – '

Jurnet, in a gruff voice, said: 'Beautiful!'

'Extraordinary! You're both quite satisfied the Maslin boy isn't involved?'

This time it was Jack Ellers who, after a quick sideways glance at his friend's face, took up the story.

'He was involved all right, sir, only not directly. He didn't kill her. DI Catton had his lot into Comberton at the double, and not one of 'em had any doubt but that the poor girl'd done herself in. They turned up a couple of sheep-dip men who confirmed seeing young Maslin running up their lane spick and span, no blood, and telling him he'd have to go back to the road the way he'd come. That was a good five miles out of the village and within five minutes of the time Mrs Maslin's neighbour – a Mrs Wolsey, her husband works for the Gas Board – heard the shot. She'd just been making her hubby's sandwiches and she'd had her eye on the hard-boiled eggs, so she knew the time to the minute. The cottage is one of a pair, and she was so sure at first it was a shot that she came out of her back door and stood looking at the next-door windows, wondering if she ought to knock and ask if everything was all right. She'd seen the red sports car arrive the night before, knew there was a young couple staying. Quite taken with them she was, so lovely to look at, him so fair, her so dark. Everything was so quiet and peaceful in the early morning – bar that one bang, that is to say – and she thought they wouldn't thank her for disturbing them if they were at it, if you knew what she meant, when all it was, probably, was a car backfiring or a chap out in the fields after a rabbit.

'Hm.' The Superintendent frowned at Jurnet and said: 'I can't say I'm happy with the way things keep happening to the people you've lined up in the Flaschner inquiry.'

'No, sir,' agreed his subordinate, meekly shouldering the blame, to the other's manifest annoyance. The Superintendent, Jurnet knew from long experience, preferred a hard target to a soft one for the anger which – his invariable reaction to the senseless waste of a life – was, at that very moment, welling up inside that superbly tailored exterior.

'I gather the girl didn't have a licence for the gun.'

'No, sir,' Jurnet again corroborated, earning himself a second dirty look. 'Israeli army issue. Young Maslin said she told him she took it about with her everywhere. She said it made her feel safe.'

'Safe! Where did she think she'd come to? Chicago?'

Jurnet said: 'At any rate, she's safe now.'

30

The Maslins, summoned from Feldon St Awdry, had, as requested, brought with them a change of clothing for Christopher. Simon Maslin, his face calm, his usually unbiddable limbs working in perfect co-ordination, had dressed the unresisting boy – unresisting, that is, until the clergyman had tried to remove the blood-stained shirt.

Jerking away, Christopher Maslin explained, in the tired tone which had characterised all his discourse, 'I have to keep it on. I know it needs a wash, but I have to. When I leaned over to kiss her, I was nearly sick. I was disgusted. She killed herself because of me, and I was disgusted!'

'Of course you must keep it on,' Simon Maslin returned, as if the connection were obvious. 'When the time comes to take it off – well, you'll know when that is yourself, won't you? Let's just see what we can do with this blazer, shall we?' And, a moment later: 'Look at those sleeves – half-way up to your elbows! Incredible how much you've grown in a couple of months – ' Chattily, lovingly, as his wife and the detectives looked on without speaking, Simon Maslin dressed his son. Yes, thought Jurnet, on the verge of a mental correction, his son. The fellow's earned him.

The five of them were jammed into the Rover, half-way to Cambridge, before Claire Maslin spoke for the first time. Her little-girl voice sent a shiver down the detective's spine. Fearing hysteria, he had been both relieved and disconcerted by her self-possession and her appearance. The fine lines which had been in evidence at the corners of her eyes, the slight slackening of tissue either side of her chin, all the discreet advertisements that the woman was no longer a girl, had disappeared, nature itself collaborating in the fugue from reality.

'Will we have to stay in Cambridge?' she wanted to know. 'Because if we have to, I really ought to have phoned Annie to let her know we were coming, in case there's anything she needs to get in. That woman's a real treasure. I don't know what Tawno would do without her . . .' She half-turned to look at her son where he sat wedged between her and her husband, head lolling. The concern in her eyes, Jurnet saw in the rear mirror, was no pretence; merely swamped by a greater one. 'Tawno's going to be so upset,' she said, confirming the detective's diagnosis. 'And just when he'd been feeling so much better – happier than he's been since Uncle Max died. His paper's finished at last, did you know, and gone to the printer's.' The word 'paper' ringing a bell: 'I do hope there won't be anything in the *Cambridge Gazette* about Esther before we can break the news personally.'

Jurnet did his copper bit, official. 'Detective Inspector Catton shouldn't keep the lad long. Everything seems perfectly straightforward.' ('*Perfectly straightforward*' an inner voice echoed sardonically.) 'Shouldn't be more than a few days to the inquest, depending on the press of court business and how soon Mr Ahilar gets here – '

Jurnet would have preferred not to think about Efrem Ahilar, even though he remembered less the man's words when told of his granddaughter's death and the manner of it, than the long silences between, which had seemed filled with a dreadful keening which was beyond the range of the human ear, yet occupied every nook and corner of perception.

'I gave her the gun,' Efrem Ahilar said, his voice over the wire slower than Jurnet remembered it. 'I smuggled it in.'

233

'I didn't know if it was her or you.'

'It was me. Meet me at Heathrow with handcuffs. Leg irons.'

'If it hadn't been the gun it would have been something else – '

'But it was the gun. And I gave it to her – ' In a harsh voice, Efrem Ahilar began to chant something in Hebrew. It sounded more like a curse than a prayer. Jurnet waited for the noise to end, then asked, as gently as he knew how – how could you ever make such a request gently? – that the Israeli get hold of his granddaughter's dental records and bring them to England with him.

'We have to have a formal identification – '

'Don't worry. I shall know my Esther.'

'The records could save you additional pain – '

'What additional pain? I have used up all there is, already.'

Judging by the meal she put on the table, Annie Venables had had no need to get in anything extra. Grateful for her calm assumption that the fuzz needed sustenance no less than the quality, Jurnet and Jack Ellers succumbed without protest to the balm of salmon *en croute* with raspberry meringue to follow, unsurprised – for they had noted it often enough – by the appetite with which the bereaved attacked their victuals. Even Christopher, lying back against his father's shoulder, and exhausted from the strain of answering DI Catton's questions, put away a good meal without prompting. Every now and again, with an unselfconsciousness lovely to see, Simon Maslin brought a fork primed with a specially luscious morsel to the boy's lips, which opened obediently to receive it. Tawno Smith, who had cried noisily and without shame at the news of Esther's death, sat watching the two with a grave pleasure, no jealousy. All in all, conceded Jurnet, made mellow by the food and a glass of hock that smelled

234

like flowers and tasted like liquid joy, he was, as the Irish said, a lovely man.

Annie Venables looked magnificent. No longer the housekeeper whose proper place was the kitchen, she sat at one end of the table facing Tawno Smith across the length of polished mahogany, indisputedly the hostess. The Penders arrived as coffee was being served by Millie, a bright little stick-insect of a woman whose presence, more than anything else perhaps, demonstrated the erstwhile housekeeper's changed status.

The retelling, for the benefit of the new arrivals, of the news about the dead girl, engendered a fresh catharsis of lamentation. Tawno, wiping his eyes, left his place, travelled the length of the table and leaned over Annie's chair. Placing a hand on her shoulder he whispered in her ear, something that evoked a nod and a tremulous, 'If you like – '

'Please let's try not to upset Annie,' Tawno Smith admonished his friends. 'It won't help Esther and it won't help her. She's pregnant, bless her, we only got the results of the test yesterday, and the doctor says she has to stay calm and collected.' Over the gathering murmur of surprise and delight he ended, with a sob that even the sceptical Jurnet accepted as completely genuine: 'Keep the good wishes, which I know you have for us, for a happier occasion. Today belongs to Esther.'

Today might belong to Esther but still, tears and all, the friends left their chairs and gathered round the happy couple, Nina Pender and Claire Maslin, Jurnet noted, apparently as content with the news as the rest. Only the Revd Maslin, benevolently smiling, kept his seat, an arm on the boy who slumbered fitfully against his chest.

Adam Pender disengaged himself from the throng and came to join the two detectives. He looked pale and harassed.

'Has it got anything to do with Uncle Max's

murder?' he demanded. And, accusatory: 'You still haven't found out who's responsible!'

Jurnet said, 'Sorry about that.'

'I didn't mean – ' The man ran a hand through his hair, and began again. 'That wasn't what I wanted to speak to you about. Did Tawno tell you he's completed his paper?'

'He did.'

'Did he tell you, as well, that he's put my name on it as co-author?'

'He never said anything about that.' The detective did not disguise his surprise. 'You must be over the moon. It's what you were complaining about, wasn't it – being left out?'

'That's right. It's what put me at the top of your list of suspects – for all I know, has kept me there.' Adam Pender took a deep breath. 'Look, Inspector,' – his voice taking on a note of pleading – 'a mention, that's all I wanted, and all, in justice and friendship, I expected. A small acknowledgement of a small but genuine contribution. Not something for nothing – certainly not my name bracketed with his at the top of the title page! Everyone who's in the know, anyone in particle physics, will know it's ridiculous – '

'Looking a gift horse in the mouth, aren't you? A pal offering you immortality on a plate – '

'But why? Why?'

'I'm sure you've asked Dr Smith that very question.' The other nodded glumly. 'What did he say?'

Pender shrugged his shoulders in angry bewilderment. 'That he thought it would make me happy. That it would get me a university chair. That if it landed a Nobel Prize I could probably find a use for half the cash – '

'And you don't find those reasons convincing?'

'How the hell can you tell with Tawno?' With a wry smile, swiftly gone: 'I suppose I judge by myself – who else can you judge by? – and I can't see myself handing out half the glory, to say nothing of half the loot, just like that.'

'Just like what, then? You're a hard man to please, Mr Pender, if I may say so.'

'Hanged if I know! Punishment, perhaps? Blackmail? Maybe he's made up his mind I'm the one who stole the original and he's going to make me pay for it in his own devilish way by hoisting me into company I'm not equipped to keep up with, and where I'm bound to fall flat on my face. Perhaps' – with an expression which made clear that this possibility was the most dire of all – 'I was wrong about Nina all the time. She and Tawno have been having it off and now that he's settling down to be a respectable married man this is her severance pay, for services rendered – '

Christopher Maslin woke up crying out, 'Esther!'

'Hush!' Simon Maslin rocked the weeping boy in his arms. 'He's overtired,' he apologised to the others. 'Ever since he was a little boy he's had bad dreams whenever he's overtired.'

'Let's get him straight to bed, then.' Annie Venables' voice was warm and maternal. 'Keeping him up this long after all he's gone through – I don't know what I could have been thinking of.'

The boy pushed aside the clergyman's restraining arms and stood up. 'I want to go home,' he announced, swaying on his feet, his hair golden as an angel's in the sunshine coming through the window. 'I want to go home and see God.'

Nina Pender breathed: 'What is he talking about?'

Claire Maslin explained: 'He means those paintings in the church. He and Simon have got them on the brain.' She came close to the boy and, lifting his hand to her mouth, kissed it. 'We have to stay on here for the inquest, darling. Too much of a fag to drive all the way to Feldon and then back again. Your father has to go, to see to things because of the bishop, you know

237

all about that. You and I will stay here and let Annie spoil us, the way she always does.'

The boy turned towards Simon Maslin, still sitting down, still smiling.

'Will you go and see God for me, then?'

'Of course I will, old chap.'

Christopher Maslin nodded, as if satisfied. 'You'll know what to say, better than I can.'

'I'll do my best, you can depend on it.'

'Come along, love,' Claire Maslin insisted. 'Let's go upstairs.' After a little, as the boy stood unmoving, she asked, without apparent pique: 'Would you rather your father went up with you? Or' – after another interval, a longer one – 'Tawno?'

Christopher Maslin shook his head at the three expectant figures.

'The policeman.'

Jurnet came forward feeling embroiled beyond the call of duty. 'OK, young 'un,' he said, covering up his embarrassment with the jolly manner which filled his mouth with the bile of self-disgust. 'Rarin' to go.'

'Second door on your right on the landing,' came Annie Venables' housewifely instruction. 'Warm towels in the linen cupboard.'

The three of them, the rejected ones – Simon and Claire Maslin and Tawno Smith – followed the pair out into the hall, where they stood at the foot of the stairs, watching the slow ascent. They were still there, a good ten minutes later, when the detective re-emerged on to the landing, still wondering why he had been chosen. Beyond 'Good-night', the boy had not said a word.

Jurnet looked down at the upturned faces, pale in the dim light: one gipsy; one fairy-tale princess, slightly used; one clownish priest. Not three – reminding himself of something Chief Inspector Ben-Peretz had said, back in Jerusalem: one and one and one. They stood there looking up. Lovely people who scared the pants off him.

238

31

Jurnet rose from his chair and came across the room to shake hands, as Efrem Ahilar was ushered in by PC Bly.

Esther Ahilar's grandfather did not look unduly altered by his loss. The lines of body and face were, if anything, stronger than ever. There was a weightiness, not to be measured in pounds or kilograms. It was as if that force of gravity whose taming Tawno Smith was so chuffed about, had chosen to enfold this one individual out of all others in an extra wrapping, as it might be a protection, or a shroud.

Jurnet said: 'I looked for you after the inquest, but you'd gone.'

'You should be glad of it.' The man had not forgotten how to smile, although the smile, like everything else about him, seemed to have acquired a disproportionate mass. 'Your English law, I think, would not look kindly on a defence based on killing a man for *not* seducing your granddaughter.' Putting the matter to one side, as if he had said all that needed to be said on the subject, 'I'm here primarily to say thank you, Mr Jurnet, for the way you gave your evidence – for what you did not say, as much as for what you did. I am very grateful.'

'I only said what was true. That she was depressed and homesick.'

'Of course she was homesick! Nobody who comes from Jerusalem can be free of homesickness every hour he spends away. If only that had been all!' For a moment, a crack disfigured the composed exterior.

'The pathologist, too – what a feast the newspapers would have made of the semen on the thighs! It was kind of him to omit all mention of it.'

'There was no need. She was *virgo intacta*. It spoke for itself.'

Efrem Ahilar shook his head.

'You are mistaken, Inspector, with your office jargon. *Virgo*, if you like, but not *intacta*. I believe that my poor girl, in every other particular so clever, so self-reliant, never before had a man between her legs. I am certain she never even realised the boy Christopher had not accomplished what he set out to do.' A deep sigh, an upwelling of grief instantly repressed. 'Not that it would have made any difference, you understand. She would have felt equally soiled. Esther was not a girl to make use of a technicality to extricate herself from a situation to which she saw only one way out.'

The silence prolonged itself until the detective ventured gently: 'You should have put in that dental record and left it at that – '

The other shook his head. 'Part of one's continuing education, my dear sir. Every death is a preparation for one's own. I had to look at her' – the tone, remaining calm, belied a certain wildness in the eyes – 'not just to make sure it really was my Esther lying there in a mortuary drawer far from Jerusalem. Not just to remind me either, as if I needed any reminding, of the absurdity of love. To remind myself that it was my gun which had turned her into that mangled offal. Did you know', Efrem Ahilar interrupted himself, 'that when it was all over, a police officer approached me with the pistol in his hand, still with your official tag on it? If he would only shoot me, I thought, what a marvellous thing English justice would be! But no. It was simply to return my property, on my undertaking to take it out of the country forthwith, and would I please come to the desk and sign for it?'

'We're also awaiting your instructions about Esther's car.'

'Sell it for your police charity. I will send you the necessary documents.'

'That's very generous of you.'

'No,' Efrem Ahilar said. 'Only tying up a few loose ends. I am not a generous man. I am going home and taking my Esther with me. Once I have put her to rest in the soil of Erez Yisroel I can mourn, not before. Then, for a week, I shall sit on a low chair in carpet slippers, not shaving, and my friends will come, bringing cake and sweet biscuits and, most of all, their company. We shall sit and grieve and gossip and drink lemon tea together, say the prayers at the prescribed intervals. We Jews have had plenty of practice in how to deal with bereavement, we have brought it to a fine art. And at the end of the week, I shall go back to my business purged, but completely unreconciled to the God who, for His own unfathomable reasons, let it all happen. For reconciliation', he finished calmly, 'it will be necessary to be first revenged.' The Israeli leaned forward in his chair and inquired in an interested voice: 'How are things going with you, Mr Jurnet? Are you any nearer to finding out who killed my old friend Max?'

'The investigation is being wound down,' the detective said. Uttered by himself for the first time, the words made the position not only real, but incontrovertible. 'Not one of my most brilliant feats of detection.'

'Is it permissible to proffer a little advice to an English police officer?'

'Any help gratefully received.'

'Two things, then.' The Israeli settled himself in his chair as comfortably as its unforgiving contours allowed. 'One. When there are no other clues, look for your clues in the human heart.'

241

Thank you for nothing! 'And the second one?' Jurnet asked.

'Drink orange juice. Believe me when I say I do not say this because it is my business. South African, Florida, will do equally well. There is nothing better for making the mind receptive to new thinking. You think I am joking? I am not joking. When I get back to Israel I will send you a case of Jaffa oranges for you to squeeze fresh yourself.'

'Very kind of you to offer, but no thanks.'

'It would not look good, is that it? A gift from a suspect – bribery and corruption! In that case,' Efrem Ahilar got up to go, 'I will have to think of something else.'

'Orange juice!' snorted the Superintendent, taking in his subordinate's report. 'The fellow must be off his rocker.'

Jurnet said: 'His granddaughter's death has hit him hard.'

'No doubt.' Softening the merest fraction: 'I'm glad at least he appreciated the way the inquest was handled. Never hurts to give foreigners the opportunity to see the English approach in action.' Impossible to decide, from the well-bred countenance, giving nothing away, whether the observation was to be taken ironically or at face value. 'Gives 'em a standard to aim for. Though, from what you tell me, young Maslin deserves at least part of the credit, breaking down and getting himself excused at the crucial moment – '

Jurnet compressed his lips and returned a repressive 'Yes, sir.' He would have preferred to have left unresurrected the image of the boy in the coroner's court, muttering inaudible answers to questions, the dark eyes in the white face haunted by remembered horror. Lucky for the lad that when he keeled over altogether, the Revd Maslin had been there to catch him before he cracked his skull open on the courtroom floor.

'I don't care much for this talk of revenge,' the Superintendent was saying with a petulant air. 'Usually, I'm not too happy to see a suspect in a murder inquiry take off for foreign parts where we can't keep tabs on him, but I won't be sorry to learn that Mr Ahilar has left our sunny shores.'

'Yes, sir.'

'Cheer up, Ben!' With a smile whose sweetness contained no more than the irreducible minimum of adulterant additive, the Superintendent said: 'We aren't supermen. We can't win them all.'

'No, sir,' agreed Jurnet before exploding, rejecting consolation. 'They're all such good friends, that's what gets me down! There's so much sweetness and light it makes you want to throw up. There they are, going round and round the great Tawno like here we go round the mulberry bush, a closed ring an outsider hasn't a dog's chance of breaking into – '

A deep breath. Self-control regained: 'Do you know what Smith says, far as I can make out? What we now know about the physical world that we never knew in the old days is this random element – particles jumping about all over the place, only you never know which specific one is going to jump next. And that's me to a T,' – the detective turned to go – 'without a clue which of that bunch is going to be the one to jump. Could just as well be the old dead Professor himself for all the chance I've got of ever finding the answer.'

32

The packet lay on the detective's desk, awaiting him. More than a letter, less than a parcel. Detective-Sergeant Ellers looked up from what he was doing, and grinned across the space between.

'Go easy on that lump in the middle, I should. Thought I'd leave it for you to open, boyo, just in case it's lethal.'

'Oh ah?' Jurnet picked up the packet, studied the superscription, put a tentative finger to the lump, small but unyielding. The chubby Welshman went on, irrepressible: 'Desk sarge says it was brought round by a pageboy from the Cotman, said his instructions were to deliver it into your fair hands and no other. When the call came through I said you were closeted with he-who-must-never-be-disturbed, and the lad would have to wait.'

'Which I gather he didn't?'

The other chuckled. 'Probably frightened it would go off. Seems the geezer who gave it him did it just as he was checking out from the hotel. The cab was at the door to take him to the station. The kid had already got his tip and didn't reckon the bloke would be back to make sure he'd dotted every i and crossed every t.'

'Cheeky bastard!' Jurnet murmured absent-mindedly. He had recognised the handwriting on the packet.

'Dear Mr Jurnet,' wrote Efrem Ahilar,

'I owe you an apology. When you called on me in Jerusalem I made you feel uncomfortable. I was also crude and rude enough to doubt your integrity. I sent

Danny to the Wall to spy on you. So far from taking away, you yourself left something behind. Like the Romans – eh, Mr Jurnet? – who always, in a foreign country, took care to propitiate the god of the place. And why not?

'When, more forthright – more English, should I say? – you were rude in your turn, suggesting I might have read my old friend's letter to God before sending it on its way, I chose to act insulted, to mount my high horse, as they say.

'Did I really make you feel small, Inspector? If so, I am sorry for it. Because you were quite right.

'I read it, Mr Jurnet. I read Max's letter.

'To redeem my credit with you a little, if that is possible, let me say that this was the first and the last time I ever came between him and his heavenly correspondent; and that I did it, not out of vulgar curiosity, but because of its enclosure which – assuming you have got this far reading my covering note – must now be close to your hand. *What can it be?* I imagine you thinking, your suspicions aroused, even as were my own.

'In the last months of his life, I must tell you, my old friend became increasingly irascible. He was a very sick man. Over the telephone – and we spoke to each other frequently – he would often make statements I couldn't make head or tail of – which shouldn't have been surprising since they seemed to be about physics, of which I understand less than nothing – except that their tone was somehow wild and threatening. I would put the phone down after such a conversation, feeling sad at what I took to be the decay of a great intellect.

'Obviously, once I realised, that last time, that there was something enclosed with the letter, I could not allow it to be placed in the Wall unexamined. Who could say what quirk Max's deceased mind might have seized upon? Small as it seemed to be, for all I knew to the contrary the object which I could feel through the envelope might be an explosive charge designed to finish off what the Emperor Titus had begun two thousand years before – bring down the Western Wall and complete the destruction of the Temple. I could not think how my old friend could contemplate committing such an obscenity, but I could not take the chance of doing nothing.

'In short, I took out Max's letter and read it through – as now, in photostat, I pass it on for your perusal, together with the enclosure, which I decided to remove as not being appropriately housed in that holiest of monuments. Should legal proceedings require it, I will send you the original manuscript. I enclose also a translation which I am sure you will have checked for accuracy. If there is a rabbi in Angleby he will have no difficulty. Max wrote a pure and beautiful Hebrew, a pleasure to the eye and the understanding.

'A possibility which has doubtless sprung to your mind even as you read is that I send you herewith a forgery: that, for my own purposes, I have set the whole thing up. There is no need to trust me. The matter is easily decided by the experts you will bring in to pass on the genuineness or otherwise of Max's handwriting. At Heathcote Avenue there must be many examples which can be used for purposes of comparison.

'I fear, Mr Jurnet, you will be angry with me for another reason. Why, if, as I assert, I am only an innocent bystander, did I stand by without comment while you were casting about this way and that, like an angler in a stream which I, at least, was aware contained no fish? Why, immediately I read the letter and gathered its import, did I not do what any true-blue Britisher would have done, and turn it over to the police?

'Mr Jurnet, I scarcely need to remind you that I am not a true-blue Britisher. I am Max Flaschner's oldest friend. I loved him. I value his good name. Even at this stage of the game I find it despicable in myself to have to abuse his confidence as I now abuse it. If Esther were still alive you would never have heard from me. But as she is not alive – '

The last sentence broke off unfinished. A brief post-script at the foot of the last page stated that a further copy of the translated letter had been sent to Dr Tawno Smith for his better enlightenment.

The little silver box had a well-handled look about it: small scratches that could have been made with a thumbnail; a dent or two signifying where, at a guess, coins with milled edges had shouldered it in a pocket. Picking it up with some disinclination, Jurnet was surprised by the pleasure transmitted in the feel of it, the way the perfect oval lay nested in his hand.

'Pretty little bit of rubbish.' Jack Ellers came over to look. 'What you reckon? Snuff box? Powder compact?' Indicating the hairline crack which alone suggested a possible point of entry: 'That's what I call workmanship! They don't make them like that any more. Whatever "them" are supposed to be.'

'Could be anything.' Jurnet took the box back and sat frowning down at the single word engraved on the top, its decorated script at odds with the uncluttered purity of the basic shape.

'Foreign,' Jack Ellers opined unnecessarily. 'Somebody's name, d'you suppose?'

'Your guess is as good as mine.' Jurnet unearthed a magnifying glass from a drawer, and used it to examine the elaborate curlicues more closely. Eventually he decided, pronouncing syllable by syllable: '*Ein – tritts – geld.*' Raising his head in sudden recollection: 'Hold on! Didn't you once tell me you did German for 'O' Levels?'

'That right!' the chubby Welshman assented cheerfully. 'Did for it good and proper. It's never been the same since.' Taking another look: ' *–geld* Doesn't that mean "money" That and *auf wiedersehn*'s my lot.'

After some moments of unsuccessful effort, Jurnet

desisted; replaced the mysterious little object on the desk and looked at it. It was very beautiful. The detective felt curiously unwilling to do as his colleague suggested – take a knife to that gleaming perfection, pry the two halves apart. It seemed to him not only vandalism, but an enforced entry into a secret he wasn't sure he wanted to be made privy to.

The little silver case caught the sun coming in through the window and transformed its yellowness into an eye, cool and lunar. With the absurd feeling that he was under observation, Jurnet picked up Professor Max Flaschner's letter to God.

33

'As the Master of my being, You will know better than I that this is the last missive I am likely to address to You *poste restante*. "Why bother, then, to write at all?" You may well ask. A little patience, and I shall have all eternity in which to put my point of view.

'Lord, forgive my importunity. I am a clever man, as You know, and also a great fool. All my life I have repeated the Shema, proclaimed 'Hear O Israel, the Lord thy God, the Lord is One", but only now that I near its end do I realise that in all this time I have learned nothing of this One in whom I have unthinkingly placed all my hope: no conception of this eternity in whose depths I am willy-nilly to be submerged like a non-swimmer who had never before ventured into water above his ankles.

'It is not, as I hope You will do me the courtesy of

believing, that I have begun belatedly to worry about the quality of accommodation You have in mind for me beyond that turnstile into the unknown – how many stars, whether or not there is central heating and air conditioning, television and tea-maker. Jews have always had enough to worry about here on earth without bothering overmuch about the nature of heaven and hell. Though I have every confidence that in this universe of infinite possibilities You have devised some other, and doubtless superior, alternative to a sheet of stationery inserted into a chink in a wall, I cling – whilst I am still around to cling to anything – to my childish picture of my pen-friend in the sky; One to whom (even whilst another part of my consciousness accepts that He already knows all that there is to be known) I can impart my news, my aspirations and reservations, as to an old crony who will find them novel and surprising: One who, though He never replies to my letters in kind, has His own way of letting me know that my effusions have been read and their contents noted.

'Well then.

'As You will see from the letter-heading, I am writing this at the Virgin, in Angleby, where I arrived this afternoon from Cambridge, and where I am taking a little rest until it is time to go to the castle for a dinner that is to be held in honour of the three hundredth anniversary of Sir Thaddeus Brigg. By the time my old friend Efrem brings this letter back to Jerusalem with him and tucks it into its usual resting-place, You will, I am sure, have been made aware that I went to that splendid Norman monument high up on its hill to do more than put away a lot of fancy food I shall later be sorry for.

'I shall have committed murder.

'Dare I presume to imagine that, knowing me as You do – that is, as a quick-tempered man – You are still surprised, even bowled over? Let me explain the how and the why of it.

'First, then – what I've done so far. I left Heathcote Avenue this afternoon, driving Tawno's car and fussed off the premises by Annie Venables who, quite rightly, didn't think I should be driving at all, let alone a fancy sports model. In the back of the car was the bag she had packed for me, also a document case containing all three copies of the paper Tawno, who is travelling to the Tricentennial direct from London, is scheduled to deliver to the conference as the high point of its proceedings. It would be true to say that the delivery of this paper, of whose probable contents rumours have been going about for months, is awaited with an anticipation which incorporates elements of admiration, envy and the direst foreboding.

'Annie, that good soul, thought she had seen me on my way when I nosed the Porsche into the road and drove off with an insouciant wave of the hand. What I actually did was turn the next corner and park. I got out of the car and walked back to the road junction where, screened by a convenient hedge, I watched and waited until I saw her push open the garden gate and, as is her invariable custom, hurry away in the opposite direction.

'When the coast was clear I went back to the house, to the study Tawno and I shared, and where we have spent too many fertile hours exchanging ideas about that maddening and mysterious cosmos in which it has amused You to deposit us. It was quite extraordinary how little effort was needed to reduce our calm and lovely sanctuary to a shambles! A few slashes across the upholstery, the middle drawer of one of the desks stove in with the poker: a Star of David incised with a compass on the leather top of the other: the filing cabinet smashed open and files strewn higgledy-piggledy over the floor. At first, as I began to wreak this necessary havoc, tears came into my eyes, I wept like a baby. For a moment it seemed almost that the destruction of my bits and pieces, my *lares et penates*, was a crime more dreadful than my projected extinction of a human being; but in a little – You will understand better than I the mechanics of the human psyche – a kind of exhilaration seized hold of me. When the job was done I stood panting with both the effort and the enjoyment. I had had a wonderful time! I went over to the mantelshelf, intending to tear up my signed photograph of Hermann Goering as a fitting finale to my demolition, but when I saw that extraordinary face, that oh-so-suave evidence of the paper-thin membrane which divides civilisation from inhumanity, I left him to preside untouched over the ruin.

'My next step was to manufacture evidence of the forcible entry which must be assumed to have preceded such an orgy. Keeping on the gloves with which, in the best traditions of practical criminology, I had provided myself, I went outside and carefully removed one of the panes from the french windows. I had never before removed a window either with or without felonious intent, but I discovered I had a real talent for it. I leaned the glass against the wall with a feeling that I had missed my vocation, and a certain regret that I had left it too late to make a change now.

'Back to the house, then, for a last look at the carnage I propose to come upon with appropriate expressions of horror upon my return from Angleby. Annie, poor dear, will be the first to discover the mess. I hate to thank of the distress it will cause her – but there! By then, if all goes according to plan, she will have something more important to cry about.

'By the time I had finished the job, the exhilaration was wearing off a little, so I poured myself a drink – more than one, actually: more, I am quite sure, than the police allow for people in charge of cars. I am sorry about this last because, for all that I am about to commit a murder, I am essentially a law-abiding citizen, loath to transgress the rules of an ordered society. It's a wonder – unless I have You to thank for it – that I wasn't run in on the way to Angleby for driving under the influence.

'I sit here with Feldreichmarschall Goering's bequest to me at my elbow, open so that with a slight swivel of the eye I can see the two compartments inside, one empty, the other still occupied by the cyanide pill which lies bedded in its white satin as if it were a jewel of infinite price – which perhaps it is. I shut the case and read again the inscription on the outside – *Eintrittsgeld* – "entrance money". To where? Valhalla, Hell? Oblivion?

'How smooth he was, the devil, all those years ago in Nuremberg, the execution scheduled for the following day! Most of the fat gone, the skin hanging in yellowed pleats like an old sheet that has been stored too long out of the light, and yet still debonair. A monster I looked upon with loathing and admiration.

' "You have worked very hard, Max," he said to me. You notice the familiar address? How his eyes, still, despite all, a pilot's eyes, used to scanning the heavens, danced with mischief at my stiff and stammering reaction. "I would like to leave you a gift, to show my appreciation, except that I have nothing left to give." When I made the slight bow that was the most I dared by way of acknowledgement, he turned away with: "Maybe I'll think of something."

'When, after the man had killed himself, they brought me, one cyanide pill short, the case he had somehow managed to conceal from his gaolers, I was touched, I admit it, flattered that, monster or not, he had taken the trouble in those last moments to write a note which said it was to be given to me "in friendship". Today, though, I find myself wondering how it comes about that I have never got rid of that second cyanide pill, that it is here, sitting on a hotel dressing-table, waiting to be put to use. At that time, remember, I had not even heard of my little gipsy on his rubbish heap. I did not even know that he existed.

'Someone knew, didn't He, Lord?

'*Someone* knew. What else remains for me to tell you, before I make myself beautiful to go to the castle in order to kill my darling Tawno?

'A little north of Thetford, just before you cross the ancient track they call the Peddar's Way, there is a pond in a hollow, not far back from a lay-by. That is where I got rid of all three copies of Tawno's paper. My original intention had been to burn them, but when I saw how dry the heather was, how brittle the bracken, I was afraid of setting fire to the entire heathland.

'Fortunately, somebody had discarded a large brown-paper bag there. I tore the papers up very small and put them into the bag with some stones to weigh them down. Even though it was only a little distance to the pond, it was tiring for an old, sick and drunken man to push his way through the heather, and when I came to the edge the water and the vegetation began to shake and shimmer so that I could easily have fallen in, me and the papers together.

'Were you watching, Lord? Did You see me there teetering, longing to tumble in so that, despite my carefully laid plans, I could die and my Tawno live? The pond was full to the brim despite the dry summer, black with a scum of oil, or perhaps pesticide, floating on top. For all its nastiness it looked to me as inviting as if the Lorelei herself were seated there naked on a rock, her arms and legs spread wide in invitation. For several moments I staggered about the brink like the drunk I was, the sun, the sky, the water reeling in sympathy. Just at the glorious point of extinction a merciless hand grasped me in a band of iron, and a young voice, bright with concern inquired, "You feeling OK, Dad?"

'It was the voice of a young hiker who, in khaki shorts and sturdy boots, his knapsack on his back, was walking the Peddar's Way. He accompanied me back to the Porsche, where he was extravagant in his admiration of its sleek beauty, and needed a bit of convincing that I was well enough to drive.

'Were you giving me a last chance, God, or presenting me with a final temptation? How I yearned to agree with the young hiker that I was indeed not well enough, offer him money to drive me back to Cambridge, forget about the whole thing! With a great effort I pulled myself together and said that I was feeling perfectly all right, thank you. When the young hiker finally took my word for it, he said a perky "Cheerio, then!" and walked away with a springy stride that was a pleasure for the eye to follow. At least, he looked like a hiker. He hadn't any wings that I could see.

'Well, here I am, Lord, as You see, safe and sound in my comfortable room at the Virgin, though how I managed it, You know better than I. How the Porsche ended up perfectly parked in that impossibly difficult car-park – a miracle! I could never have done it sober.

'Do You know, Lord, by what name the gipsies call You? Of course You know, You who know everything, that it's Devel, or sometimes Dibble, or Dubble. In other words, variations of Devil, unless it's a coincidence, in which case it is a very odd coincidence indeed. I can't tell You with what eagerness I look forward to hearing the truth of it. If God and the Devil are one and the same, that would explain many things that have so far eluded my muddled understanding. My Tawno has a pet phrase he often uses with a smile on his face. "My dearie Dubbleskey," he exclaims, which means "For my dear God's sake".

'For my dear God's sake, I am going to kill my Tawno.

'I lie. Not only, nor even primarily, for my dear God's sake. Not even for the sake of this peerless creation of Yours, whose beauty and ingenuity continually challenge my poor comprehension, but for the sake of

254

the men and women, those knowing imps with whom You have been pleased to people it, and whom, with the indulgence of a loving father, you have allowed to become altogether too clever for their own, and everybody else's good.

'I can well understand that if, for the sake of argument, a man, not a god, had made the universe, he would demand to be accorded credit for his achievement. "It was nothing," he might say, mock-modestly. "Just something I dreamed up on a rainy afternoon." But is it possible that God too is similarly hungry for praise, and that to gain our applause He lets us into more and more of His secrets, without thought of the consequences?

'Lord, I cannot believe this of You. Either this is a world fit for creatures made in Your image, or it is a clever conjuring trick, all done with mirrors, and on which it is time – more than time – to bring down the curtain. Somebody has to cry *Halt!* to this impulse of self-destruction, and I now cry it. Believe me, God, we cannot afford the luxury of any more Einsteins.

'Or any more Tawno Smiths.

'Don't tell me that there will inevitably be more of them; that by destroying Tawno and his precious paper I effect only a temporary postponement of what people are pleased to call the march of progress: that others will come along who will replicate all Tawno's insights and more. As a Jew I am only to well aware that there is no such thing as an ultimate danger: there is always another round the corner. But just because the traffic never stops, and you may one day get run over crossing the road, that's no reason for running out without looking.

'Once, long ago, Lord, you called upon Abraham to sacrifice his son Isaac. It was a test, and Abraham having passed it, you let the boy go. In sacrificing my Tawno it is I, Lord, who am testing You. When I have finished writing this letter, I shall open Goering's legacy once again, take out the cyanide, and put it in my pocket. This evening, at dinner, when nobody is looking, in the middle of all the love and laughter that always surround Tawno wherever he goes, I shall drop it into his orange juice. My darling gipsy! The suffering will be very short. Pray God, let it be short!

Hear, O Israel, the Lord thy God, the Lord is One.'

34

The turn of the year had done nothing to improve the quality of the countryside in the vicinity of Feldon St Awdry, merely adding a further dusting of exhaustion to the already knackered soil. The spuds had gone, the sugar beet lay about wilting, an unconvincing promise of sweetness if ever Jurnet saw one.

'Season of mists and mellow fruitfulness my Aunt Fanny,' commented Sergeant Ellers.

There were, nevertheless, the two detectives had to acknowledge, signs of life on earth that had been missing from earlier visits. Somebody had tidied up the pulpy excrescences which, like toothless gums, were all that remained of the hedgerows. The traffic department had crept out betimes and decked the telegraph poles with blue one-way arrows and blue-and-red no-waiting signs. Boards lettered in an ersatz Gothic directed putative pilgrims 'To the Wall Paintings'. Where the road divided, left fork to the church, right to the village, a lone motor-cycle cop bestrode his charger, a knight to challenge all comers.

'Anderson, isn't it?' Jurnet leaned out of the passenger

window with that friendliness which procured him friends in the Force despite his foreign-looking mug. 'Any idea what time the balloon goes up?'

'Ten more minutes. We got the media there already, snapping away like they can't believe their eyes.' Then, 'Seen the pictures, have you?'

'What about 'em?'

'Anywhere but a church,' said Anderson, who was chapel himself and Pentecostal at that, 'they'd close the place down before you could say knife. As it is, they got the bishop coming to bless 'em, to say nothing of the Lord Mayor and Lady Mayoress.'

'Wonder the Super didn't decide to tag along,' Ellers observed, as he set the Rover in motion again. 'As our resident culture-vulture you'd have expected – ' After a pause for reflection, the little Welshman finished: 'On second thoughts, perhaps not.'

Not on your nelly, Jurnet confirmed inwardly, settling well down in his seat, thus blocking out the sugar beet. If there was one thing he could bank on his superior officer preferring not to know about, just at the moment, it was anything that impinged, however distantly, on the death of Professor Max Flaschner. The detective had the idea that were so much as a card with a picture of Sir Thaddeus Brigg to arrive at the Superintendent's classy neo-Georgian overlooking the golf course, it would be returned unread to the postman: '*Not known at this address.*'

'It's so bloody unreasonable,' pursued Jack Ellers, who seemed to be following his colleague's thought telepathically. 'A murder that turns out not to be a murder after all – if only they were all like that! You'd think he'd be over the moon. One less for the statistics, serfs freed for new assignments. But he takes it as an insult to him personally.'

Jurnet, who loved the man as his mate did not, and who therefore knew his weaknesses (without which,

257

indeed, he would have loved him less) as well as his strengths, had been less surprised. Standing to one side whilst the Superintendent read the dead man's confession to a murder he had not lived long enough to commit, Jurnet had noticed the fine-cut features darken, first with astonishment, then reproof, and finally anger: anger, as he must surely see it, that he had been made a fool of. The likes of the Superintendent did not, by definition, go barking up the wrong tree; and if, by some hitherto unheard of contretemps, he was heard so to do, heads must be expected to roll for it.

The Superintendent had just about simmered down, reconciled himself more or less to a reappraisal of the case in the light of new information, when a call to the effect that Dr Tawno Smith was below, seeking audience, had set the pot boiling with renewed energy.

'What does he want?' he demanded irritably. 'Nobody's ever suggested he killed Flaschner on purpose.'

'He must be thanking his lucky stars he killed him by accident, considering the probable alternative. He doesn't have to feel guilty any more, either. Nothing like knowing your nearest and dearest are plotting to kill you to make you reassess your original feelings of love and affection.'

'Psychologists are all we need,' the Superintendent observed sourly, the aristocratic features setting into lines of a remote and embittered obstinacy. 'Ahilar should have known better than to send the fellow copies of the correspondence without first consulting us. He should have left it to us to decide what was the proper line to take.' With unction, discovering pity as a weapon of policy and pouncing upon it pitilessly: 'All said and done, it was a pretty heartless thing to do – deliberately to knock the bottom out of the trust and devotion of a lifetime.'

'Revenge. Ahilar makes no bones about it.' At the thought of the dead girl, the detective found himself experiencing an increasingly familiar disgust with the human race. 'Do you want me to see Dr Smith on my own, sir? Or shall I tell them to bring him up here?'

Tawno Smith had looked different. Well, naturally. You don't find out that the benefactor who has rescued you from a rubbish dump and brought you up as a surrogate son has in fact planned to kill you and damn near brought it off, without looking different.

Except that Tawno Smith's difference had been different.

The man had put on weight. Not enough to blunt that sharp, balletic elegance which was so instantly attractive, or dull the flashing mischief of those dark-lashed eyes; but enough, as it were, to soften the focus. You could envisage, as you could never have envisaged before, the emergence from that plumper chrysalis of a butterfly of a quite different brand of distinction – a public figure, a pillar of the Establishment. Someone you could easily imagine on the box, one of the great and the good and just the teeniest bit vulgar.

'This must be a terrible shock for you,' said the Superintendent, shaking hands with an appearance of sincerity Jurnet could not but admire.

'Well, yes,' the other agreed before, to the astonishment of both detectives, breaking into delighted laughter. 'Who would have thought it of the old devil? Out of luck, wasn't he, the dear old sod – I mean, having one of his attacks come on just at the moment of truth.' Sobering only a little: 'What he must have thought when he saw that orange juice coming closer and closer, and he hadn't the strength to push it away!'

It was the one and only time Jurnet had seen his superior officer at a loss.

Jurnet said: 'He opened his eyes at the last minute. I saw him. He opened his eyes and looked at you.'

'So?'

'So – ' Moved by some obscure sense of loyalty to

the dead man, the detective pressed on. 'So it could equally be that, knowing only too well what you were offering him, he took it just the same, because when it actually came to the point of killing you, he couldn't bear to go through with it, he loved you too much. Better him than you.'

'What a born romantic you are, Inspector!' Tawno Smith's good humour appeared undented. 'You'll be telling me next that Uncle Max actually believed all that guff about saving the world from the consequences of another Einstein. You didn't know Uncle Max! Jealousy, my friends, the green-eyed monster – that's what it's all about. Jealousy that I'd got where he'd been trying to get for a lifetime, without success.' With a laughingly bemused shake of the head: 'How I hadn't the nous to see it before, I'll never understand. All the time I was working on the paper, all those hours spent mulling it over together, he did everything he could think of to point me in the wrong direction. All told, I must have wasted a couple of years dutifully chasing after the false clues he craftily laid down for me to follow. The old fox!'

'Professor Flaschner says himself he was afraid of the possible consequences of your discoveries. How can you be sure it was jealousy?'

'Of course I'm sure! Just as you're sure I've got it all arsy-versy.' Tawno Smith spread out his arms in a gesture which struck Jurnet as unneccessarily theatrical. 'Was the late lamented Professor a senile buffoon, a dog-in-the-manger loser, or a posthumous saviour of mankind? We'll never know. But now I look back with hindsight I can see that all I had to do was offer to put his name on the title page alongside my own, just as I did with Adam – preferably putting his first – and there'd have been no cyanide in the orange juice, I promise you!'

Bright-eyed, Tawno Smith looked from Jurnet to the Superintendent and back to Jurnet again. 'It never occurred to me, or I'd have done it like a shot. You see, I loved the old bastard. Still do, if you want to know. He left me a legacy for which I'm eternally grateful.'

'I heard he was a wealthy man – '

'Not money, you idiot! Annie. My darling Annie Venables who, Thursday after next, *kek dosh* – as we say in Romany, meaning "may no harm come to it" – will become Mrs Annie Smith. Congratulate me!'

It was the Superintendent who said, after an interval but with a creditable pretence of enthusiasm, 'Congratulations!'

'Thank you!' A smiling acknowledgement. 'As Mr Jurnet knows, she's expecting. Blooming like the rose, and her cooking's better than ever. Uncle Max made a mess of it with me, and I – I fear – have made a mess of it with Christopher. But hang about another few months and I'll show you the proper way to bring up a son!'

'A rum 'un,' pronounced Jack Ellers, edging the Rover round a pile of sugar beet that had spilled over from the verge on to the roadway. 'Still – better than having the bugger collapsing in tears on the threshold. The Super must have been glad of that, at least.'

'Not a bit of it! Not to give a tinker's cuss – those were his very words – it wasn't gentlemanly. He could hardly bring himself to say goodbye. Fortunately for the future of particle physics the good doctor was hardly out of the room before a call came through from the Chief that made our hero really blow his top. Seems that Secret Service drip with the shoelaces – what was his name? – had been on the blower to pass on a tip from his masters. Let sleeping dogs lie. Apparently the Department of What's-it doesn't think it will make a good impression for word to get about that the scientific supermen upon whom the future of the planet

261

depends may be sodding assassins no different from the rest of us.'

'What a lot!' Sergeant Ellers drove for a little in silence. Then he pondered aloud: 'At least we can make pal Catton's day. Send him a billy-do to say he can now file Dandy Venables away for keeps, give him Christian burial. The Professor made it clear he'd never heard of the guy, could do his own windows very nicely, thank you.'

'Poor old Dandy! After all that, just another legless drunk in the river. It's the end of an era. There'll never be another like him to take out a window pane – '

'Professor Flaschner just about fooled you – '

'Well, he's gone too, hasn't he? I tell you – breaking and entering, it's becoming a lost art.'

Feldon St Awdry church was well in sight before Jack Ellers spoke again: a tentative sounding out of opinion.

'That bugger Smith – laughing like that. You reckon it was genuine? No on with the motley, hiding a broken heart?'

'I wouldn't know,' muttered Jurnet who, ever since Tawno Smith's visit to Headquarters, had been plagued by that very question. 'Christ, I wouldn't know.'

The two passed the white-coated volunteer waiting self-importantly at the entrance to a field evidently designated as a car-park; drove on to the vicarage, passing little knots of cameramen who, after a cursory glance, dismissed them as non-people, without newsworthiness. In the vicarage driveway two women, heads down against the breeze which flapped the brims of their special-occasion hats, were levering a large tray of canapés out of a shooting brake, taking care no mayonnaise or piped salmon mousse got on to their best frocks.

Claire Maslin came out of the vicarage door, stood watching the pair for a moment before coming across to coo in that voice which was several sizes too young for her: 'You *are* clever! How absolutely marvellous!'

The women accepted her tribute with modified rapture, and passed indoors with their burden, their large hips moving beneath their polyester florals. Not the most popular vicaress in the business, Jurnet surmised. No hat, no gloves, that ash-gold hair spread girlishly on her shoulders – nothing you could put your hand on doctrinally (Mrs Maslin was too clever to be caught out that way) but . . . Just because Salome was up to you-know-what on the chancel wall didn't make it OK for the vicar's wife to enter the House of God with her nipples showing for all to see through the fine silk of her blouse.

Looking pleased to see them, the vicar's wife came towards the two detectives as they got out of their car.

'I'm so glad you got my message. I'm going back to Cambridge once this is over, and I wanted to be sure you knew about Christopher.'

'How is the lad?'

Mrs Maslin clasped her small hands together. 'I think the lad is going to be all right.' Her eyes shadowed: 'You can't imagine how awful it's been. Grief – well, I may be wrong, but I think, sooner or later, one can come to terms with grief, don't you? One has to. But grief compounded by an unreasonable hate!' She breathed the air deeply. 'He wouldn't go back to college, he never so much as opened a book, wouldn't even go running with Simon. Just sat about – in the church mostly, but not praying, far as I could tell. He could have had his eyes turned inside out for all the notice he took of anything. He didn't eat enough to nourish a sparrow.' The hands clasped each other tighter, each taking comfort from the other. 'He kept on repeating, "If only Tawno had made love to Esther, it wouldn't have happened." When I pointed out that the only reason he hadn't was out of consideration for him, Christopher, he told me not to be silly: "Tawno goes to bed with everybody. He even asked me if I thought Tawno was anti-Semitic and that was why he wouldn't have anything to do with a Jewish girl. In the end I couldn't stand it any longer, hearing Tawno so maligned. It was so unfair. I told Simon there was only one thing to do – tell Christopher the truth.'

'Was Mr Maslin of the same opinion?'

'He was not. He didn't want me to say anything, especially after we heard about Annie being pregnant. How would Christopher take it, Simon wanted to know, once he knew the way Tawno had refused to take on the responsibilities of fatherhood towards *him*?' Looking earnestly up into the detective's dark face, Mrs Maslin asked: 'What do you think, Mr Jurnet?'

Jurnet said uncomfortably: 'I need notice of that one.'

'It doesn't matter any more.' The woman unclasped her hands and clapped them softly together. 'Because I told him. I was so sure it was the only thing which would get him back on an even keel. Bad enough, I suppose, not to know who your real father is, but to hate him out of ignorance – it was too much! I said how much Tawno had come to love and admire him when he saw what a fine, clever young man he'd grown into: how he was full of plans for his future. And, most of all, how Esther was the biggest proof of the way Tawno felt for him, because he had actually fallen in love with her himself, and only held off when he realised the depth of Christopher's own feelings, for fear of hurting him – '

She was silent, looking out towards the church. There were a good many cars in the car-park now, and people were moving slowly up the path to the church door, where a robed, composed Simon Maslin stood to welcome them. When it seemed she had nothing further to say, Jurnet asked: 'And did it work the oracle?'

'It was wonderful!' The woman's face lit up. 'He made me repeat what I'd said, as if he couldn't take it in first time. We put our arms round each other. We cried together a little. If only Tawno could have come into the room at that moment, how wonderful it would have been!'

'Mr Maslin must be feeling a little – ' Jurnet hesitated over the right word and finally settled for 'sad.'

'Not at all! He's admitted I did the right thing. If anything, it has deepened his relationship with Christopher, not harmed it. They went for a run together this morning, just like old times – the long round, by the quarry – and they came back laughing and fooling about like a couple of schoolboys. You never saw anything like it.'

'Christopher over at the church now, is he?'

'He's gone to Cambridge, to fetch Tawno. You know he passed his driving test? Annie has to spend a couple of days in hospital, having tests, and Tawno's on his own. The Porsche's being serviced and he was on the phone this morning moaning like a banshee, everyone had deserted him, so Christopher had this sudden, marvellous idea, to go and fetch him for the dedication. Both Simon and I were very touched. They should be here any minute.' Mrs Maslin glanced down at the dainty platinum and diamond watch on her wrist, a bauble too expensive to have been a gift from her husband. 'We ought to be making our own way over. I do hope they aren't going to be late.'

35

The little church was crowded, the bright clothes of the women and the scent of flower arrangements sprouting from every corner. Coming in from the bitter-sweet freshness of summer's end, Jurnet sniffed the air with some disapproval: chrysanthemums were not his favourite flower either.

Leaving Mrs Maslin to her calm progress up the aisle to a front seat among the VIPs, the two detectives, with difficulty, found places for themselves at the back of the nave, where a few rows of well-worn benches – borrowed, at a guess, from the village school – had been squeezed in between the rear pews and the font. A jolly-looking woman in outsize checks moved up to make room for them, giggling as she did so.

'Thought I'd better spread myself out and cover it up.'

Jurnet looked down at the space revealed, at the message carved into the battered wood: 'Sarah Anne Carr only fucks on Thursdays.'

'Bully for Sarah Anne Carr,' he commented, sitting down. 'Good to know someone still exercises a little self-control.'

An elderly man was playing something on the small organ wedged into a niche adjoining the chancel rail: playing pretty well, the detective thought, something cool and classical. Self-important young men in their Sunday suits distributed the order of service. A starched gaggle of choirboys, full of ill-suppressed laughter, waited outside the door to the vestry, transmogrified for the day into the bishop's robing room. The tele-

266

vision crews and the photographers hung about with ill-concealed impatience. One of them removed a half-smoked fag from behind his ear and contemplated it with a hungry passion before putting it unlit between his lips, where it hung dispiritedly.

On the white eastern wall Salome, all six of her, danced the dance she had danced before King Herod. John the Baptist's head was hidden by the intervening heads of the congregation. Now, for the first time seeing the daughter of Herodias divorced from the bloody sacrifice below, Jurnet was surprised by the realisation of the latter's essential unimportance in the total composition. Whatever else Salome was doing, she was not dancing to excite a male lust which was not only tedious but downright risible. Self-absorbed, she moved in the figures of a ritual rooted deeper than sex, deep in the primitive roots of being.

With an effort, the detective raised his eyes towards the God who sat with the headless body of the saint across his knees, only to have his attention ambushed en route by the outsize drops of blood frozen in their progress down the wall. Subatomic particles, he thought confusedly: the radioactive fallout of love.

The bishop had done them proud. Resplendent in cope and mitre, attended by lesser clergy and by the choirboys, awed into silence by the sudden solemnity of the occasion, His Grace progressed the short distance from the vestry to the high altar, where the Reverend Simon Maslin, who had stood there awaiting his coming, gave way with respectful dignity.

The clergyman's face was radiant. He did not, Jurnet thought, look at all like a man who had just lost his son. Maybe Mrs Maslin was right. What she had done was what was needed all along; a new beginning free from the corrosive burden of acting out a lie.

To a theme of Thomas Tallis, the bishop, with gestures of a grave and sacerdotal beauty, consecrated the wall paintings to the uses of Feldon St Awdry church.

Taking as his text a phrase from Ecclesiastes – 'A time to mourn and a time to dance' – he contrived gracefully to suggest that, in the case of such a wonderful work of art, the two times were not necessarily irreconcilable opposites; that one's heartache over the barbarous death meted out to the saint could properly coexist with an appreciation of Salome's talents in the dancing line. It was only when His Grace went on to praise the 'transcendent spirituality' of the work that Jurnet sensed the eye of his checkered neighbour upon him, and fielded a broad wink. 'They're so unworldly, bless 'em,' she whispered.

'*Except the Lord build the house*,' sang the choirboys, in voices of unexpected sweetness, '*their labour is but lost that build it.*'

Simon Maslin was so much at home in his pulpit that it seemed a pity, Jurnet thought, he ever had to come down from it. Serene, authoritative, his physical and mental awkwardnesses forgotten, he seemed the model of what a parish priest should be. Even the times he frowned a little, his gaze wandering over the heads of his congregation to the curtain which hid the church door (wondering what the hell's keeping Tawno and Christopher, was the detective's guess), in no way loosed his authority, his loving hand on the helm. Jurnet, assailed by thoughts of Miriam and Rabbi Schnellman, was the awkward one, dropping the order of service so often that finally he let it lie where it fell, among the embroidered kneelers worked by the Ladies's Guild.

The Reverend Simon Maslin said: 'Let us pray.'

Going down on his knees – Jack Ellers and the checkered lady participating enthusiastically to right and left of him – was the worst of all.

'*Give us this day our daily bread* – ' came the voice full of a calm certitude. '*And forgive us our trespasses, as we forgive them that trespass against us. And lead us not into tem-'*

Later, Jurnet could only think that the reason he hadn't heard the church door open, nor the sound of the curtain rings swishing along their rod, must have been that he had been concentrating on how soon it would be OK to get up. It astonished him not to have heard the iron latch being raised, nor the sound of it falling back into place again.

High up in his pulpit, the Reverend Simon Maslin had broken off in mid-stream, mid-word, his flock carrying on automatically for a little, until their voices too, unshepherded, petered out uncertainly. By that time the boy was a good way up the aisle, well past the back pews, and the detective's first reaction to the sight of the slender back, the shoulder-blades prominent through the white knitted fabric, had been one of a disapproval which surprised himself. You'd have expected a parson's son to show a bit more respect than to barge into church in running gear, especially on such a special occasion. Jurnet's second thought was, so Tawno Smith hadn't come after all. Just as well, perhaps. It was, after all, Simon Maslin's day.

By the time the detective had arranged these random feelings into some sort of order, a kind of group uneasiness had begun to stir among the people at the front of the church, all of whom – with the exception of a few still obstinately waiting for the prayer to be brought to its proper conclusion – had risen from their knees. Tall as he was, Jurnet still could not make out what it was that Christopher Maslin was carrying with such care. It looked like a large silver serving-dish. For a second the detective wondered whether the youngster's entrance was not a planned part of the proceeding's: the ladies at the vicarage sending him over with a tray of their posh titbits to keep the bishop and his missus going till lunch was served.

The noise increased. Over the intervening heads

Jurnet caught a glimpse of the mitre bobbing about. A woman suddenly cried out piercingly.

At the sound, with one accord and without consultation, Ellers and Jurnet launched themselves into the aisle, which by then had become clogged with spectators trying to see what was going on.

'Police! Let us through, please!'

The request met with small response. The noise had become a little demented. A cameraman perched on a flat-topped tomb suddenly let his camera slide from his shoulder, whence it disappeared with a crash of glass on stone. On the brink of initiating more actively physical measures, Jurnet found that, by chance, the crowd had divided, enabling him momentarily, before it closed ranks again, to see along the remaining length of the aisle, past the chancel rail, all the way to the east wall.

With his back to the body of the church, Christopher Maslin was setting his tray, or whatever it was, down on the altar, positioning it in front of the brass cross and at a careful equidistance between the brass candlesticks at either end. So far as the detective could make out, a cloth of some kind covered the contents of the dish, and this the boy now removed, letting it fall to the floor. When it was done, he turned back to face the congregation, and the detective saw for the first time what it was that had aroused their alarm. The front of the boy's T-shirt, as well as his shorts and his bare legs, were soaked with blood, more blood than on the day Esther Ahilar had shot herself. His hands were red too, his arms splashed with crimson.

Christopher Maslin watched expressionless as hysteria took over. On the altar of Feldon church, directly beneath the painted head of John the Baptist, another severed head, this one three-dimensional, lay on a silver dish. The head of Dr Tawno Smith, come to rest, as the gipsy fortune-teller had prophesied, in 'the highest place', the high altar of Feldon church.

Clotted blood had stiffened its fetching curls, dripped

into the eye-sockets, obscuring pupils and irises alike. Viscid strings of God knew what hung from either nostril. None of this was as terrible as the whole lemon which had been stuck into its mouth, the way a lemon is stuck into a roast boar's head, to make it smile.

'Christ!'

As the two detectives lunged forward, heedless now of the susceptibilities of those who stood in their way, the gap closed up again. Just for an instant, before Christopher was cut off from view, Jurnet glimpsed, or thought he glimpsed, a bony, long-fingered hand outstretched towards the boy, and the boy taking it in his reddened paw. Jurnet glanced up at the pulpit. It was empty, a black gown draped limply over the Jacobean panelling.

By the time Jurnet and his companion had fought their way through to the chancel, the open space in front had become filled with a milling of choirboys, trying at one and the same time both to look and not look at the grisly trophy on the altar. The bishop, his face in his hands, prayed aloud in long, sobbing breaths. Next to him, Mrs Maslin, her long hair lying like silk on her shoulders, sat bolt upright in her seat, screeching like a crow.

Jurnet seized the little man who had played the organ.

'Which way did they go?'

The man tore himself free in an elderly tantrum, but pointed a shaking finger at the little door which opened from the chancel direct into the churchyard. The door was open.

Jurnet ran to it, halted on the threshold by the sheer surprise of the day outside, sweet and untroubled. A gentle breeze rippled across the uncut grass, making it appear by turns shiny and matt. The last of the poppies dropped their petals like drops of blood. In the distance a tall, thin man in clerical grey and a tall thin boy scrambled with what seemed a light-hearted ease over a stile, and dropped down to the footpath beyond.

'Jack!' Jurnet looked round for his friend and found him at his heels. 'Get the car! Get hold of someone who knows the way to the quarry – the old quarry, that is, in case there's more than one. It has to be quicker by road.' With a disregard he knew he'd be sorry for later, he tore off his jacket and tie and thrust them at the little Welshman. 'I'll see you there. For Christ's sake, hurry!'

Jurnet ran. All three of him. One, the classic figure of retribution, stony, calm, inexorable, moving with measured tread. Two, the out-of-condition cop, wishing he had the nerve to drop his trousers; get rid of the cloth that caught at his knees, chafed his inner thighs, and gave him less than a hope in hell of overtaking the Maslins before they reached whatever was their goal.

The third Jurnet ran because, to run was to run was to run. Once he had got his second wind he found himself caught up in the mesmeric rhythm of which Simon Maslin, once upon a time, had given him some inkling. He ran dream-like with the turning world, not so much cleaving the landscape as marking time whilst trees and brambles, the dark pine and the heather that edged the path, backed silently towards him and receded into history.

Every now and again he caught sight of his quarry ahead; each time with the distance between him and them widening. 'My quarry is going to the quarry,' he found himself panting foolishly.

He observed that wherever the path was wide enough the two Maslins ran side by side, holding hands. Some of the blood on young Christopher's hands must have transferred itself to the clergyman's.

The path swept round in a wide curve and became steep, for Norfolk, the line of its summit bounded by a sky of faded blue. No sign of the runners. By now, Jurnet thought, the magic evaporating a little as the gradient sharpened, Jack Ellers must surely have found his way to the quarry, have done the necessary. He would find the three of them sitting in the Rover waiting for him, silent in the shared embarrassment which always seemed to attend an arrest. By now, very likely, the little Welshman, like the other two, would have Tawno Smith's blood on his hands.

Jurnet breasted the slope and saw the flooded quarry spread out below him, a peaceful or a sinister place according to one's affinity for or allergy to such secret places; an expanse of liquid sky empty save where a bloodstained T-shirt floated serenely on the surface, its short sleeves spread out in a truncated cross, a thalidomide one that had lost the best part of its arms, and its head besides. Unless it was some trick of the light, the shirt appeared paler than when the detective had last seen it, some of the blood, he assumed, having washed out into the water, though certainly not enough to taint that untroubled blue.

The quarry was an almost perfect circle, its sides everywhere steep and sheer save at the point where once, during its working life, the traffic of the place must have gone in and out – a slash through the cliff wall which had been sufficiently patched up with concrete to make a leakproof basin to contain its new element. Nowhere else in the circumference, Jurnet noted, was there easy access to the water. Any search for the missing father and his son – yes, his son, the detective insisted stubbornly – would have to begin there.

The Revd Simon Maslin, Jurnet remembered, had praised the water in the quarry for its transparency. If so, the detective thought, it was ganging up on him now, the interloper presuming to put his nose in where it wasn't wanted. The T-shirt barely moved. Apart from a spasmodic ruffling of its upper skin, conjured up by a trapped breeze struggling without much success to get out of the hole into which it had fallen, the water could have been solid. One could more easily envisage the missing pair, after their leap from the heights – still holding hands, Jurnet did not doubt – lying on the surface stunned by the impact than having passed cleanly through to the depths.

Jurnet lowered himself on to his stomach, head projecting over the quarry edge, wondering vaguely how safe it was to entrust himself to the crumbling rim masked in heather. *Detective, Vicar and murder suspect found drowned together*: – it would be a long time before the *Argus* got itself a headline to compare. More to the point, what would the Superintendent make of the heroic denouement, played out against that outsize puddle in the ground? *Detective-Inspector gives his life in vain attempt to arrest suicidal murder suspect*? Some hopes! More likely: *Last words of Angleby CID man: 'I didn't dare to return to Headquarters with the news that I'd let yet another one get away.'*

With an effort, Jurnet purged his mind of such protective facetiousness. Precariously prone, he had at least established that he was not quite alone in that benighted place. Immediately beneath him, at the water's edge, two mallards, a duck and a drake, were having a whale of a time, diving over and over again and coming up with – what? Jurnet averted his eyes, choosing not to see. As the drake's rump up-ended itself preliminary to yet another reconnaissance, its curlicued tail feathers, new-fledged after the annual moult, proclaimed, perky and iridescent, that summer was well and truly over.

The Rover, protesting up the ruined track in low gear, made its presence known ahead of its arrival. Jack Ellers, his face a tracery of scratches, jumped out, took in the situation at a glance, and ran up the slope to join his superior officer.

'We overshot!' he panted, not one to find his salvation in vigorous exercise. 'They've grown a bloody thorn hedge across the entrance, so it wasn't all the chap's fault. The job we had getting through! Couldn't blame him for saying he'd had enough. Wait till the Super sees the bill for the respray!'

Jurnet edged himself carefully backward, rolled over, sat up. He said nothing, merely looked down at the T-shirt lying on the water. Jack Ellers followed the direction of his gaze.

The garment looked darker, wetter. In fact, water-logged. As if it had only been awaiting the arrival of the CID sidekick for independent confirmation from a second party that it had ever been there at all it slowly, with a kind of luxurious sluttishness, abandoned its cruciform mode, slumped itself into a shapeless rag, and sank.

Jurnet, he could not have said why, uttered a little cry of protest. Ellers, who knew and loved the man, waited a little; looked down at the still, the empty water. Then he ventured: 'Reckon we better call out the divers – '

'Yes. Reckon we better had.'

36

Quietly, their shoes making little or no sound on the soft track, Simon Maslin and his son came over the brow of the hill, still holding hands, still running. At the sight of the detectives standing frozen with an almost angry disbelief, the two slowed down, went into a long deceleration, as if it was not all that easy to stop running once you had got well and truly into your stride. Even then, the boy did a little jig in addition, a brief running on the spot before he subsided, finally still.

The clergyman called out in a jolly way: I *said* this was where you'd be! Didn't I say so, Christopher?' – turning his face, his whole body, lovingly, to the boy by his side. 'Didn't I?'

'Yes, Father.'

The boy's voice was low, but composed. His body was bare to the waist, very lovely in the slender strength of youth, very calm. There was not, after all, all that much blood on his running shorts, almost none at all on his limbs, subsumed, presumably, into his perspiration.

Grim-faced, Jurnet kept the distance between himself and the pair. 'I saw the T-shirt. I thought – '

Simon Maslin's disclaimer came swiftly. No difficulties of enunciation, no silly-ass rictus.

'You thought wrong, Mr Jurnet. Self-murder is not an option open to Christians. Christopher and I were running, not away from life as you seem to have decided, but towards it – weren't we, Christopher? Towards a new horizon, and beyond, to a new understanding of God's purpose.' With a deprecatory smile: 'It's hard to put into words. If only you ran, my dear sir, you would understand so much more easily.'

'I *do* run,' Jurnet contradicted. 'Or I did. All the way from Feldon church to this God-forsaken neck of the woods. And still it wasn't vouchsafed to me how Christians who wouldn't for a moment think of killing themselves can – quite cheerfully, it seems, so long that is, as they are runners – go about killing other people. Killing them, what's more, in a particularly foul way.' As the detective spoke, he could taste the familiar ferment of violent death rising hatefully in his gullet. Deliberately turning his back on the older man, he spoke to Christopher Maslin. 'I must ask you to accompany us to Police Headquarters – '

'That's all right,' the boy responded quickly, before

his father could intervene. 'I want to. I've been wanting to tell you, ever since it happened.' He left Simon Maslin's side, moved towards Jurnet with hands outstretched. 'Don't you want to put on the handcuffs?' And, when the detective, retreating from contact, shook his head brusquely, 'Or perhaps you think, in my case, it ought to be shackles, just in case I start running again?'

'You won't get far this time.'

'I don't want to get anywhere. I just want you to understand!' The boy, a note of mounting urgency in his voice, reached for Jurnet's hand; held on to it, so that the detective could not withdraw it without making a hoo-ha. 'I just want you to understand that I'm *not* somebody who goes about killing people, not even Tawno. I want to be a priest and a priest doesn't go about killing people. It was Tawno *made* me do it!'

Jurnet disengaged his arm with an ungracious wrench.

'Let's be on our way.'

'I mean it!' the boy persisted, clutching, this time, the detective's shirt in order to detain him. 'I meant it about going to Cambridge to bring him back for the dedication. I just thought Father would be glad – he wanted the day to go well and Tawno was always so good in company, making people laugh, and all that. I know Mother thinks I hated him on account of Esther, but I didn't, truly.' With an undertone of peevish spite: 'Esther was the one I hated, if you must know – silly, moony Esther who thought you couldn't love anybody except by going to bed with them, and then, if it didn't turn out just right, you had to go and blow your bloody brains out and make a mess all over my mother's bedroom.' The boy's chest was heaving, his voice had risen to a shout. 'Do you really want to know what my first thought was when I found her lying there on the bed without a face? I thought, "Serve you right, you stupid bitch! Bloody well serve you right!" '

Sergeant Ellers took off his jacket and draped it round the boy's naked shoulders.

'Take it easy, Sonny.'

Christopher Maslin continued to shiver uncontrollably; but he did not stop talking.

'Tawno knew all about my knowing he was my true father. Mother must have rung up and told him she'd decided to let the skeleton out of the cupboard at last. Honestly! She made such a production out of it, you'd think it was something important, instead of ancient history. If I was still a little child, that would have been different, but at my age, when I already had a father I knew and loved!' Simon Maslin let out a hoot of pure joy. 'When I got to Heathcote Avenue he was all over me – *yuk*! Kept calling me "son", like they do in cowboy movies, and telling me all the great things I was going to do in physics with him to help me. When I said that what I wanted was to go into Holy Orders he just brushed it aside with a laugh, as if I'd said something I couldn't possibly mean seriously. I made us both some coffee – he didn't seem to have a clue how to do anything for himself; I suppose all those women hanging around must have spoilt him. We sat at the kitchen table drinking it. Then he began to talk about the baby Annie's going to have. On and on about how he – he never seemed to think it might be a girl – would be a physicist too, only this time he'd make sure the baby didn't get any silly ideas stuffed into his head the way Simon had stuffed them into me.

'I said it was time we got a move on, but he just sat there going on and on about what this new baby was going to be, until I began to feel quite sorry for the poor little thing, not even born and all those plans without him even having a say. I asked Tawno what he'd do if the baby turned out to be like Annie, a bit dim and no earthly good at science, just wanting to do the cooking, but he laughed and said "Ridiculous!" and went on some more. All the time I was sitting there thinking how lucky I was to be Christopher Maslin, not Christopher Smith, and feeling sorrier and sorrier for the unborn baby. I wished I could take him away the minute he was born, and bring him back to Feldon, so he could be brought up, like I was, by a father who only wanted him to be happy, not famous and all that.

'Then Tawno said, "You'll have to be good to the little fellow. After all, he'll be your half-brother." Looking very serious, he said, "I want you to make me a solemn promise you'll do everything in your power to help him in every possible way."

'That's what he said. Of course I promised. I liked the idea of a brother – I'd always wanted one, even though it wouldn't be the same, me grown up and him still a kid. Still, it would be nice for him, I thought, to have a big brother looking out for him. The trouble was, as Tawno went on and on, I saw that the best thing I could do to help my little brother would be to set him free from a father who didn't really give a fig for him as a person, a human being, but only as a potential Nobel Prize winner.'

Christopher Maslin paused for a moment of reflection. Then he looked directly into Jurnet's eyes, his own grown curiously opaque.

'To be honest, I don't really think I was *all* that lucky to have Simon Maslin as my father instead of Tawno Smith. I know I was lucky *in the circumstances*; but the circumstances should have been different. No, not the circumstances: Tawno. I felt more and more that my little brother had to be rescued while there was still time. Tawno had made me promise.'

The boy fell silent; recommenced his little jig on the spot where he stood, bobbing up and down.

'Can we go now? I'm beginning to feel chilly.'

Jurnet demanded: 'What happened?'

'People mustn't act God, you know,' was the answer. 'They mustn't think they can shape a human being's life for him in the way only God has a right to. It's the

279

worst kind of idolatry. Smashing idols isn't a sin. It's a Christian duty.'

'*What happened*?'

Christopher Maslin said unwillingly: 'There's a mallet Annie uses to make the meat tender – wood, with a knobbly bit of iron on one side. Tawno asked for a third cup of coffee. I could see he really wasn't all that keen on coming to Feldon. He'd just wanted some company. I got up and went behind him to get the coffee. That's what he thought, anyway. Actually, I picked up the mallet and hit him on the head with it.'

Simon Maslin put his hands over his face and wept.

'No need to carry on, Pa,' the boy said. 'I'm sure it didn't hurt him one bit. He was dead right away: I could tell. I shouldn't be surprised at the inquest they'll find he had a very thin skull. Perhaps that's what made him such a great physicist – his ideas could get out of his head without having to go through a lot of bone first.'

'But why the head?' Jurnet pleaded between clenched lips. 'Why in the name of heaven did you have to cut it off?'

'I had to be quite sure. For the baby's sake.'

'Sure in what way?'

'That he really was dead, not pretending. Gipsies are funny. They know things we don't.'

Christopher Maslin looked smug. 'It wasn't easy,' he confided, in the tone of one inviting praise for his perseverance against odds. 'But after all, Sir Thaddeus Brigg lost his head too, didn't he, so Tawno's in good company.'

'But why bring the head to Feldon? And why on the altar?'

'I don't see why not. John the Baptist's there to keep him company.' Brightly, with an explosive giggle: 'You know what they say, don't you? – two heads are better than one. Besides' – and now the handsome young face had become narrow and crafty – 'I thought my mother would appreciate a present from Cambridge.'

'Come along!' Jurnet commanded hoarsely. 'You as well' – turning towards the clergyman.

The detective spoke to empty air. The Revd Simon Maslin was already far down the sandy track.

Running.

Drained, aching from head to foot, Jurnet came home. Parked his car among the plastic bags, stubbed his toe on the O'Driscoll pram. Gratefully, floor by floor, he savoured the Nappi-San, the joss sticks, the slow-simmered underwear. If he never breathed fresh air again for a hundred years, it would be too soon.

He unlocked his front door, walked through to the living room, sat down on the armchair and eased off his shoes. '*Quang!* the armchair went, in its dear, familiar welcome.

He took a shower and still felt as stiff as a board. Naked, he looked into the kitchen and saw Tawno Smith's head on the draining board before he saw it was really a cauliflower he had bought he couldn't remember when, and left to grow a rather striking red mould. Striking and stinking.

He dropped the cauliflower into the bin, wondering what else he could do to make his pad the fun place it ought to be, him a dashing young dick with everything to play for.

The phone rang. Jurnet went through to the bedroom, sat down on the further side of the bed and watched the instrument on the bedside table the way a naturalist in a hide might watch some telephone-sized mammal to see what it would do next. He made himself as small and quiet as possible so as not to frighten it away.

The telephone still sported round its waist the bow tie he had hired from the dress agency long, long ago. It went on ringing: it seemed the only trick it knew.

Not one of nature's brainiest creations. Jurnet began to count. He counted up to twenty before he got up and changed round to the other side of the bed, where the bedside table was. Even then, he counted ten more before he picked up the receiver.